Everyman, I will go with thee,
and be thy guide

Elizabeth von Arnim

THE PASTOR'S WIFE

Edited by
DEBORAH SINGMASTER

EVERYMAN
J. M. DENT · LONDON
CHARLES E. TUTTLE
VERMONT

First published in Everyman in 1993
Reprinted 1996

Introduction, notes, bibliography, chronology
© J.M.Dent 1993

Made in Great Britain by
The Guernsey Press Co. Ltd., Guernsey, C.I.
J.M.Dent
Orion Publishing Group
Orion House
5 Upper St Martin's Lane,
London WC2H 9EA
and
Charles E. Tuttle Co. Inc.
28 South Main Street,
Rutland, Vermont
05701, USA

ISBN 0 460 87243 5

Everyman's Library
Reg. US Patent Office

CONTENTS

'The most remarkable of the Edwardian 'marriage problem' novels. *The Pastor's Wife* is a marvellous novel about isolation within marriage, and the almost inhuman durability of human feeling ... And this from the author of *Elizabeth and Her German Garden* and *Enchanted April*.'

London Review of Books

NOTE ON THE AUTHOR AND EDITOR

ELIZABETH VON ARNIM was born Mary Annette Beauchamp. She became Elizabeth, Countess Russell on her second marriage. She was born on 31 August 1866, in Sydney, Australia, the youngest of Henry and Louey Beauchamp's six children. In 1870 the Beauchamps travelled to England and May (this was her family nickname – 'Elizabeth' replaced it when she began writing) attended Queen's College School, Acton, and the Royal College of Music. In 1891 she married Count Henning August von Arnim-Schlagenthin. After living for five years in Berlin, the family moved to the von Arnim estate at Nassenheide in Pommerania, near the Baltic coast. It was here that Elizabeth began writing. Her bestselling *Elizabeth and her German Garden* was published in 1898. In 1899, von Arnim was arrested on a trumped up charge of embezzlement of which he was later acquitted. When he eventually lost all his money, through a combination of incompetence and misfortune, Elizabeth supported the family on earnings from her writing. In 1909 Elizabeth left Germany for England and placed her children in English schools. Von Arnim died in 1910 and by 1911 Elizabeth had embarked on an affair with H.G. Wells. In 1916 she married John Francis Stanley, Lord Russell, elder brother of Bertrand Russell, and a convicted bigamist. The marriage was a disaster and ended acrimoniously in 1919. Another lover was Alexander Stuart Frere-Reeves, thirty years younger than Elizabeth, later chairman of Heinemann. In 1929 Elizabeth moved to Mougins in the south of France and created another home, Les Mas des Roses. In 1939 she left Europe for America where three of her children were now living. A peripatetic existence ended with her death after a sudden illness at Charleston, South Carolina, on 9 February 1941. She wrote twenty-two books and one play.

DEBORAH SINGMASTER is a journalist on the staff of *The Architects' Journal*. She has published short stories and written plays and talks for BBC radio. Former careers have included film editing and working at the Royal Botanic Gardens in Kew. She has lived in Italy, America and China.

CHRONOLOGY OF VON ARNIM'S LIFE

Year	Age	Life
1866		Born Sydney, Australia
1870	4	Family sails to England
1890	24	Presented at Court
		Travels to Europe with parents. Meets Count von Arnim in Rome
1891	24	Marriage to von Arnim
		Birth of daughter Evi
1893	26	Birth of second daughter Beatrix
1897	30	Moves with family to Nassenheide and starts to write 'Elizabeth and Her German Garden'
1898	31	*Elizabeth and her German Garden*
1899	32	*The Solitary Summer*
		Birth of Felicitas
		Von Arnim arrested
1900	33	*The April Baby's Book of Tunes* illustrated by Kate Greenaway
1901	34	Von Arnim acquitted
		The Benefactress
1902	35	Birth of son, 'H.B.'
1904	37	*The Adventures of Elizabeth in Rügen*
1905	38	E.M. Foster comes as tutor at Nassenheide for three months
		Princess Priscilla's Fortnight
1907	40	*Fäulein Schmidt and Mr Anstruther*
		Hugh Walpole comes as tutor to Nassenheide

CHRONOLOGY OF HER TIMES

Year	Literary Context	Historical Events
1870–1		Prussia united under Bismarck Franco-Prussian War
1889	Edmund Gosse reviews Ibsen's plays	
1890	*A Doll's House* performed in London	
1894	Alfred Austin's *The Garden that I Love*	
1895	Oscar Wilde's *The Importance of Being Earnest* performed	
1901		Death of Queen Victoria
1903	*The Ambassadors* by Henry James *Man and Superman* by George Bernard Shaw	
1905	*Where Angels Fear to Tread* by E.M. Forster	

Year	Age	Life
1908	41	Elizabeth's first meeting with H.G. Wells
		Caravan tour in Kent. E.M. Forster joins the party
1909	42	*The Caravaners*
		Elizabeth leaves Germany and moves to England with children
1910	43	Nassenheide sold
		Play *Priscilla Runs Away* performed in London
		Count von Arnim dies in a sanatorium in Kissingen
		Start of liaison with H.G. Wells
1913	46	Building of Chalet Soleil in Montana completed
1914	47	Begins relationship with Francis, Lord Russell
		Elizabeth and two of her daughters flee from Switzerland with false passports
		The Pastor's Wife
1916	49	Marriage of Elizabeth and Francis, Lord Russell
		Felicitas dies of pneumonia near Bremen
1917	50	*Christine* under pseudonym 'Alice Cholmondeley', based on Felicitas's letters
		Elizabeth goes to stay with her daughter Liebet and her family in California
1919	52	Flees from Russell
		Christopher and Columbus
		Employs Alexander Stuart Frere-Reeves to catalogue her library in Switzerland
		Meets cousin the short story writer Katherine Mansfield and starts *Vera*
1920	53	*In the Mountains*
1921	54	Rents Castello in Rapallo for April
		Begins affair with Frere
		Vera
		Elizabeth's brother, Sir Sydney Beauchamp, run over by omnibus in the Mall, London
		Friendship develops with Katherine Mansfield and her husband Middleton Murry in Montana during Katherine's unsuccessful rest cure for tuberculosis

Year	Literary Context	Historical Events
1910	*The New Machiavelli* by H.G. Wells	
1913	*Sons and Lovers* by D.H. Lawrence	'Cat and Mouse Act' passed to strengthen government's hand against Suffragettes
1914		Beginning of First World War
1915	*Painted Roofs* Vol. 1 of Dorothy Richardson's *Pilgrimage* – first use of 'stream of consciousness'	
1918		Marie Stopes's *Married Love* spreads knowledge of birth control End of War Women gain limited suffrage
1920	*Women in Love* by D.H. Lawrence	

Year	Literary Context	Historical Events
1922	*The Garden Party and Other Stories* by Katherine Mansfield *Ulysses* by James Joyce *The Waste Land* by T.S. Eliot published in *Criterion*	
1923	Death of Katherine Mansfield	
1924	*A Passage to India* by E.M. Forster	
1925	*Mrs Dalloway* by Virginia Woolf	
1927	*To the Lighthouse* by Virginia Woolf	
1928	*The Intelligent Woman's Guide to Socialism* by G.B. Shaw	
1929	*A Room of One's Own* by Virginia Woolf	
1930	Death of D.H. Lawrence	
1933	*Flush* by Virginia Woolf	Hitler comes to power in Germany
1934	*A Handful of Dust* by Evelyn Waugh	
1939		Outbreak of Second World War
1941	Death of Virginia Woolf and publication of her last novel *Between the Acts* *Black Lamb and Grey Falcon* by Rebecca West	Pearl Harbour. America enters the War

INTRODUCTION

At the end of 1914, Elizabeth von Arnim wrote in her journal: 'So ends 1914 – it has been the happiest year of my life . . .' She had fallen passionately in love for the first time, she had recovered British citizenship after living in Germany for eighteen years, and her ninth novel, *The Pastor's Wife*, published in October, had been acclaimed by reviewers as her best work to date. Her euphoria was cut short by the continuing war, a disastrous second marriage and the death of her daughter, Felicitas, in 1916.

The Pastor's Wife was published, as were all Elizabeth's books but one, under the infuriating pseudonym, 'the author of *Elizabeth and her German Garden*'. Adopted initially to placate her husband (it was not the done thing for Junker wives to write books for money), it soon became essential, for Elizabeth had a habit of drawing on personal experience for the plots of her novels. Sometimes she deliberately embarked on schemes which she knew would produce material for a novel – organising a caravan excursion in Kent, or renting an Italian villa in Portofino; at other times the creative process would be used to exorcise painful episodes in her life, an outstanding example being *Vera*, published in 1921, and based on her unhappy marriage to Francis, Lord Russell, elder brother of Bertrand Russell. Though the pseudonym deceived no one in London society, least of all Russell, publication without it would have been impossible. 'Do not marry a novelist', was Bertrand Russell's advice to his children, after reading Elizabeth's savage portrayal of his brother as the bullying Everard Weymiss in *Vera*.

The Pastor's Wife owes much to Elizabeth's first marriage to Count Henning August von Arnim-Schlagenthin and may even have reached draft form before the whimsical bestseller about her German garden was conceived. Certain aspects of Elizabeth's courtship and that of her heroine, Ingeborg Bullivant, are almost identical to those of Elizabeth when she first met von Arnim in Rome; he was forty at the time and recently widowed, she was twenty-four. Elizabeth described von Arnim's proposal to her in *All the Dogs of My Life*, written near the end of her life:

> He followed me, panting a little, for, like other good Germans in those days who had ceased to be young, he wasn't thin, up the steps of the Duomo in Florence, to the top of which he was taking me in order to show me the view, he was addressing me thus: 'All girls like love. It is very agreeable. You will like it too. You shall marry me and see.' And having arrived at the top, he immediately and voluminously embraced me.
>
> I remember I struggled. Being embraced was entirely new to me, and I didn't at all like it.

Pastor Dremmel in the *The Pastor's Wife* also pants as he toils up the peak of the Rigi in Lucerne before proposing to Ingeborg. She is as unenthusiastic about her first embrace as Elizabeth was:

> 'Oh, but I can't – I won't – oh, stop – oh, stop – it's a mistake – ' she tried to get out in gasps.
>
> 'My little wife,' was all the notice Herr Dremmel took of that.

Part of Count von Arnim's income came from family estates. He was a keen experimental farmer and had a particular interest in breeding various types of potato. He also tried to develop a strain of lupins that could be converted into animal fodder. Similarly, Pastor Dremmel in the novel is obsessed with improving his annual rye crop. The topic of his first conversation with Ingeborg is – manure:

> 'It is,' he said solemnly, his eyes glistening with enthusiasm, 'the foundation of a nation's greatness.'
>
> 'I hadn't thought of it like that,' said Ingeborg.

Ingeborg's early married life at Kökensee, a village in the depths of East Prussia, is supremely happy until she has her first child and nearly dies from an infection which the incompetent midwife fails to notice. When her slow recovery is interrupted by a second pregnancy, Ingeborg realises that she is trapped in a cycle of childbearing from which there is no escape. Elizabeth had endured four pregnancies before producing the son that her husband demanded of her; her biographer Karen Usborne hints that she may have resorted to strategic infidelity to reduce the chances of producing a fifth daughter. After being denied chloroform for her first two confinements in Germany, she had her other three children in London where she was attended by her brother, Sir Sydney Beauchamp, gynaecologist to Queen Victoria. Elizabeth's clinical account of Ingeborg's pregnancy and childbirth was considered unusually outspoken at the time. 'She has abandoned her usual reticences, and makes no bones this time of calling a spade a spade, and, indeed, the whole Part 2 of the book might be labelled "Hints to a Wife" or "Mother, Nurse, and Baby", so full is it of obstetric details . . .' wrote a reviewer in the *Spectator*. It was a subject Elizabeth returned to in a later novel *Love* with devastating effect.

Elizabeth's critics have accused her of sentimentality, yet her attitude to sex, far from being sentimental, is not even romantic, and can best be summed up in the casual phrase 'one thing leads to another' used repeatedly in *Love*, a novel about a woman's marriage to a man young enough to be her son. (Once again Elizabeth was excavating a painful period in her past, her prolonged affair with a much younger man, Alexander Stuart Frere-Reeves.) Sex lurks palpably close to the surface of her three best novels – *The Pastor's Wife*, *Vera* and *Love*. Without ever straying beyond the bounds of propriety, she takes her couples – in effect – to the bedroom door and scrutinises them when they emerge the next morning. In the early and splendidly comic section of *The Pastor's Wife*, when Ingeborg returns home to break the news of her engagement to her family, we realise at once that her mother is wedded to the sofa in order to escape the attentions of her lawful wedded husband, the Bishop (a trick that Elizabeth's mother had also adopted):

'Herr who?' said Mrs Bullivant, a sharper note of life in her voice than there had been for years. 'Here's your father,' she added quickly, hastily composing herself into the lines of the unassailable invalid again as the door opened and the Bishop came in.

Between 1910 and 1911 Elizabeth had been having an affair with the writer H.G. Wells. After one of their first meetings, Wells wrote reassuringly to his wife about the bright little Countess von Arnim: 'She talks very well, she knows *The New Machiavelli* by heart, & I think she is a nice little friend to have ... her conversation is free but her morals are strict (sad experience has taught her that if she so much as *thinks* of anything she has a baby).' With Wells, Elizabeth became sufficiently abandoned to make love on Swiss mountain slopes and to help break more than one bed at wayside chalet inns; she had come a long way since that first embrace at the top of the Duomo, and she had at last learned how to avoid the babies. Information about birth control would not become generally available in Britain until the publication of *Married Love* by Marie Stopes in 1918.

At the same time as Elizabeth was waving Wells out of her life as a lover – they were to remain friends – she was writing him into *The Pastor's Wife* as the celebrated English artist who offers Ingeborg the companionship and intellectual stimulation that her husband denies her after the breakdown of their physical relationship. Ingram is a heady mix of egotistical genius and rake:

> The outer husk of Ingram at this time and for some years previously was a desire at all costs to dodge boredom, to get tight hold of anything that promised to excite him, squeeze it with diligence till the last drop of entertainment had been extracted, and then let it go again considerably crumpled.

Much of the dialogue in this section of the novel reads more like conversations that might have occurred between Elizabeth and Wells than between their fictional counterparts. ('"Gentility is the sole barrier, I expect really, between me and excess,"' says Ingeborg, speaking quite out of character, but offering a telling comment on Elizabeth.) Described as 'a long, thin-necked man with a short red beard', the Ingram who travels by train across Europe with Ingeborg, losing his temper with railway inspectors, railing at the weather and sulking in hotel rooms, rapidly assumes in the reader's mind, the squat, bull-necked contours of Wells who had been Elizabeth's travelling companion on a recent unsuccessful Italian holiday.

The Pastor's Wife is Elizabeth's most ambitious novel. It is also her richest because it incorporates not just one, but all her characteristic modes: satirist, nature lover, feminist. A favourite scheme was to have a charming heroine (often the only sympathetic character in the entire book) who is trapped and exploited by an authoritarian male; staunchly behind this figure of authority there is generally a phalanx of objectionable subservient female characters. To achieve happiness the heroine must break free from her subjugation and establish her independence. For Elizabeth, independence was synonymous with happiness. In *The Pastor's Wife* this scheme or pattern is used in triplicate.

Sunny submissive Ingeborg, a typical Elizabethan heroine whose one desire is to make people happy, is dominated by the three men in her life – her father, her husband and her would-be lover. The price of protest, as she learns to her cost, is banishment and, ultimately, destitution. But this feminist message is delivered with the most delicate irony – in her books, as in life, Elizabeth cooed, she never preached. She simply allows her characters to adjust the sexist noose about their own necks. Thus the Bishop reflects on 'the mechanical brainlessness that makes a woman [Ingeborg] so satisfactory as a secretary'; Dremmel, contemplating marriage, has no doubt 'that his wife would fall quite naturally into her place, which would, though honourable, be yet a little lower than the fertilizers'; and Ingram, as he schemes to seduce Ingeborg, silently marvels at 'the trouble one takes at the beginning over a woman'. They are tyrants all three and their tyranny is endorsed by the codes prevailing in their separate spheres of influence where women have neither freedom of expression or movement. ' "Why should I not go and come unquestioned? . . . *You* do," ' says Ingeborg to Dremmel. This is a theme that recurs throughout Elizabeth's work.

Elizabeth was described by the poet Alice Meynell as 'one of the three finest wits of her day'. It is a highly intelligent, often cruel wit, based on sharp observation and analysis of human behaviour, and it is seen at its most scintillating in the early section of *The Pastor's Wife* which is set in the Bishop of Redchester's palace (the echo of Barchester is deliberate, and Elizabeth emerges triumphant from the invited comparison with Trollope).

Elizabeth's plots are driven by her characters' psychological development rather than external events, to the extent that they sometimes lack any clearly defined corporeal presence. Their appearance is seldom described in any detail; the men are either thin or solid, the women frail or sturdy. Elizabeth seldom indulges in elaborate descriptions. Places are defined by the plants that grow in them, the play of light, and above all by smells (in Italy, Ingeborg identifies twelve different smells at the same time) rather than by architectural or geographical features. The first generation of 'Elizabeth' fans complained that they knew nothing of the house attached to the famous German garden. Readers of *The Pastor's Wife* learn equally little about the Dremmels' house and there is something surreal about the sun-baked East Prussian landscape through which Ingeborg wanders communing with nature and never ageing despite her six pregnancies.

As well as being the most consciously feminist of her novels, *The Pastor's Wife* is Elizabeth's valediction to Germany and the Germans. She had already ridiculed the archetypal German Junker officer in the character of Otto von Ottringel in *The Caravaners* (1909); in *The Pastor's Wife* she returns to the attack. Loathsome characters parade through Ingeborg's life at Kökensee – the slovenly midwife, Frau Dosch; the cold, snobbish baronness Glambeck; and Ingeborg's taciturn mother-in-law who dresses in black and wears her hair scraped back 'into the smallest of knobs'. Misunderstanding between Ingeborg and Frau Dremmel are the cause of much amusement while Ingeborg is still struggling to master the German language, but by the end of the book laughter has given way to a more sinister note as the old woman takes over the education of her grandchildren and instructs them daily never to forget that they are Germans. The only sympathetic character in Kökensee is the local doctor – a Jew.

Elizabeth has never recovered the popularity with later generations of readers that she enjoyed during her lifetime. The pseudonym may be partly to blame. Rebecca West (Elizabeth's successor in the affections of H.G. Wells) when reviewing *Vera* for the *New Statesman* summed up its legacy:

> One remembers with alarm the persistence with which she reminds us on her title pages of those not too creditable early successes which saw innumerable tiresome women all over England smirking coyly about their gardens as if they were having a remarkably satisfying affair with their delphiniums.

In the same review West praised Elizabeth's '. . . clear and brilliant head that enables her to write a peculiar kind of witty, well constructed fiction, a sort of sparkling Euclid which nobody can touch'. Euclid must have more than compensated for the jibe of 'humbug' with which the review opened.

Apart from an ingenious later novel, *Expiation* (1929), in which most of the action takes place within the space of two days, Elizabeth never experimented with the structure of her novels, although she was writing at a time when the form of the novel was being revolutionised by the work of Virginia Woolf, James Joyce, D.H. Lawrence and, until her early death, Katherine Mansfield. While Elizabeth's reputation declined, that of her cousin Katherine Mansfield soared. Yet to the critic Frank Swinnerton, writing in 1953, a comparison between the two writers seemed far from absurd.

> I should like to see a parallel drawn between Katherine Mansfield and her (in my opinion more talented and remarkable) cousin 'Elizabeth' the Countess von Arnim, later Countess Russell. When they were together Greek met Greek; and since pretence would have been useless on either side no rules restrained bitter retort. Katherine Mansfield was the only person whom Elizabeth feared. You would have said her fear must be retributory, since Elizabeth herself, who was small, drawling, protrusive-eyed, and relentless, frightened large numbers of people. She, too, in repose, was demure; but in reality she was a born and courageous adventurer, whose mind had greater range and strength than Katherine's and whose perception and speech could be so destructive that she could mock slower-witted persons into fury.

Elizabeth would have been the first to challenge Swinnerton's generous assessment of her literary merit. Towards the end of her life she referred in her journal to her 'chance little gift of writing, which keeps me', and there was never any doubt in her mind as to which Beauchamp was the finer writer. After Katherine's death in 1923, she wrote to her widower, John Middleton Murry: 'I admired her so – well, abjectly . . . I felt so gross when I was with her, such a clumsy thing, as if my hands were full of chilblains. And she pure lovely intelligence.' Yet there was deep respect on Katherine's side too; she felt proud of her cousin and in a letter to Elizabeth about *The Enchanted April* she compared her style to that of Mozart. There is nothing to suggest that the compliment was not sincere. Many readers – Elizabeth's biographer Karen Usborne is one – have succumbed to the spell of this particular book as to a haunting melody from a Mozart concert. When friends hinted that there was mutual influence at work, Katherine denied the charge but admitted: 'There is a kind of turn in our sentences which is alike but that is because we are worms of the same family.' Both worms had a tendency to gush.

In her journal Katherine Mansfield once described Elizabeth as looking 'fascinating in her black suit, something between a bishop and a fly'. The image was appropriate. Elizabeth had become associated in readers' minds with the 'twinkle of episcopal legs'. It is a characteristic she shares with a much later novelist, Barbara Pym. In a BBC radio talk called *Finding a Voice*, Barbara Pym said that as an undergraduate at Oxford she had particularly enjoyed the works of Elizabeth.

> Such novels as *The Enchanted April* and *The Pastor's Wife* were a revelation in their wit and delicate irony, and the dry, unsentimental treatment of the relationship between men and women which touched some echoing chord in me at the time ... these novels seemed ... perhaps even the kind of thing I might try to write myself.

Elizabeth's clerics and their womenfolk have much in common with characters that inhabit Barbara Pym's novels but the visceral relationship between Ingeborg and Pastor Dremmel in *The Pastor's Wife* would have been beyond her scope, as would the Prussian setting; she confined herself to English villages and institutions, whereas Elizabeth's outlook was thoroughly European. She lived much of her life outside England and the writers she most frequently turned to were not Jane Austen and George Eliot, but Thoreau, Goethe and Chateaubriand.

PARVA SED APTA are the words engraved on a commemorative plaque set above the spot where Elizabeth's ashes were scattered in Penn, Buckinghamshire: 'small but effective'. They are a modest but fair definition of her literary achievement; only in *The Pastor's Wife* did she attempt something on a grander scale.

DEBORAH SINGMASTER

ACKNOWLEDGEMENTS

The principal sources of information about Elizabeth von Arnim
are the autobiographical *All the Dogs of My Life* (1936, Heinemann), *Elizabeth of the German Garden* by Leslie de Charms,
Elizabeth's daughter (1958, Heinemann), and *Elizabeth: The
author of 'Elizabeth and Her German Garden'* by Karen Usborne
(1986, The Bodley Head). George Santayana, the poet and phil-
osopher, and a close friend of Francis Russell's, described Elizabeth's marriage to Russell in *My Host the World* (1953, Cresset
Press). Frank Swinnerton's comparison between Elizabeth and
Katherine Mansfield is in *Background with Chorus* (1956, Hutch-
inson). The fascinating relationship between Elizabeth and Katherine is covered in *The Letters* (1945, Constable), *The Journals of
Katherine Mansfield* edited by John Middleton Murry (1927,
Constable), and Antony Alper's *The Life of Katherine Mansfield*
(1980, Viking Press). *H.G. Wells in Love*, edited by G.P. Wells
(1984, Faber and Faber), and *The Life of H.G. Wells: The Time
Traveller* by Norman and Jeanne MacKenzie (revised edition
1987, Hogarth Press) are entertaining about Elizabeth's liaison
with Wells. The text of Barbara Pym's talk on BBC Radio 3 is
given in *Civil to Strangers and Other Writings*, edited by Hazel
Holt (1987, Macmillan). Lisa St Aubin de Terán's essay on *The
Pastor's Wife* originally appeared as an Afterword to the Virago
edition of the novel, published in 1987.

SUGGESTIONS FOR FURTHER READING

Other recommended books by Elizabeth von Arnim:

Vera
The Enchanted April
Love
Expiation
All the Dogs of My Life (autobiography)

Katherine Mansfield's short story *Bliss* is about sexual frustration and provides an interesting basis of comparison with Elizabeth's handling of the same theme in chapter 16 of *The Pastor's Wife*. The symbolic image of the pear tree is a further link between the two works.

Walden, or Life in the Woods by Henry Thoreau made a deep impression on Elizabeth and is the inspiration behind many of her novels.

A Literature of Their Own by Elaine Showalter (1978, Virago), outlines the struggle of women writers from George Eliot to Doris Lessing to acquire their own literary voice in a world traditionally dominated by male writers and critics.

Apart from the titles mentioned under 'Acknowledgements', there is a lively account of life at Nassenheide in the first volume of P.N. Furbank's *E.M. Forster, a Life* (1977, Secker & Warburg). Furbank believes that the character of Mrs Failing in Forster's *The Longest Journey* was modelled on Elizabeth but Forster denied this and said she was based on his uncle. The character of Mrs Harrowdean in *Mr Britling Sees it Through* by H.G. Wells is also based on Elizabeth, as is Rosemary Fell in Katherine Mansfield's short story *A Cup of Tea*.

PART 1

CHAPTER 1

On that April afternoon all the wallflowers of the world seemed to her released body to have been piled up at the top of Regent Street so that she should walk in fragrance.

She was in this exalted mood, the little mouse-coloured young lady slipping along southwards from Harley Street, because she had just had a tooth out. After weeks of miserable indifference she was quivering with responsiveness again, feeling the relish of life, the tang of it, the jollity of all this bustle and hurrying past of busy people. And the beauty of it, the *beauty* of it, she thought, fighting a tendency to loiter in the middle of the traffic to have a good look, – the beauty of the sky across the roofs of the houses, the delicacy of the mistiness that hung down there over the curve of the street, the loveliness of the lights beginning to shine in the shop windows. Surely the colour of London was an exquisite thing. It was like a pearl that late afternoon, something very gentle and pale, with faint blue shadows. And as for its smell, she doubted, indeed, whether heaven itself could smell better, certainly not so interesting. 'And anyhow,' she said to herself, lifting her head a moment in appreciation, 'it can't possibly smell more *alive*.'

She herself had certainly never been more alive. She felt electric. She would not have been surprised if sparks had come crackling out of the tips of her sober gloves. Not only was she suddenly and incredibly relieved from acute pain, but for the first time in her life of twenty-two years she was alone. This by itself, without the business of the tooth, was enough to make a dutiful, willing, and hardworked daughter tingle. She would have tingled if by some glorious chance a whole free day had come to her merely inside the grey walls of the garden at home; but to be free and idle in London, to have them all so far away, her family down there in the west, to have them so necessarily silent, so oddly vague already and pallid in the distance! Yet she had only left them that morning; it was only nine hours since her father, handsome as an archangel, silvery of head and gaitered of leg, had waved her off from the doorstep with offended resignation. 'And do not return, Ingeborg,' he had called into the fly where she sat holding her face and trying not to rock, 'till you are completely set right. Even a week. Even ten days. Have them all seen to.'

For the collapse of Ingeborg, daunted into just a silent feverish thing of pain, had convulsed the ordered life at home. Her family bore it for a week with perfect manners and hardly a look of reproach. Then they sent her to the Redchester dentist, a hitherto sufficient man, who tortured her with tentative stoppings and turned what had been dull and smooth into excitement and jerks. Then, unable to resist a feeling that self-control would have greatly helped, it began to find the etiquette of Christian behaviour, which insisted on its going on being silent while she more and more let herself go, irksome. The Bishop wanted things in vain. Three times he had to see himself off alone at the station and not be met when he came back. Buttons, because they were not tightened on in time, burst from his gaiters, and did it in remote places like railway carriages. Letters were unanswered, important ones. Engagements, vital ones, through lack of reminders went unkept. At last it became plain, when she seemed not even to wish to answer when spoken to or to move when called, that this apathy and creeping away to hide could not further be endured. Against all tradition, against every home principle, they let a young unmarried daughter loose. With offended reluctance they sent her to London to a celebrity in teeth – after all it was not as if she had been going just to enjoy herself – 'And your aunt will please forgive us,' said the Bishop, 'for taking her in this manner unawares.'

The aunt, a serious strong lady, was engaged for political meetings in the North, and had gone away to them that very morning, leaving a letter and her house at Ingeborg's disposal for so long as the dentist needed her. The dentist, being the best that money could buy, hardly needed her at all. He pounced unerringly and at once on the right tooth and pulled it out. There were no stoppings, no delays, no pain, and no aunt. Never was a life more beautifully cleared. Ingeborg went away down Harley Street free, and with ten pounds in her pocket. For the rest of this one day, for an hour or two to-morrow morning before setting out for Paddington and home, she could do exactly as she liked.

'Why, there's nothing to prevent me going *anywhere* this evening,' she thought, stopping dead as the full glory of the situation slowly dawned on her. 'Why, I could go out somewhere really grand to dinner, just as people do I expect in all the books I'm not let read, and then I could go to the play, – nobody could prevent me. Why, I could go to a music-hall if I chose, and *still* nobody could prevent me !'

Audacious imaginings that made her laugh – she had not laughed for weeks – darted in and out of her busy brain. She saw herself in her mouse-coloured dress reducing waiters in marble and gilt places to respect and slavery by showing them her ten pounds. She built up lurid fabrics of possible daring deeds, and smiled at the reflection of herself in shop windows as she passed, at the sobriety, the irreproachableness of the sheath containing these molten imaginings. Why, she might hire a car, – just telephone, and there you were with it round in five minutes, and go off in the twilight to Richmond Park or Windsor. She had never been to Richmond Park or Windsor; she had never been anywhere; but she was sure there would be bats and stars out there, and water, and the soft duskiness of trees and the smell of wet earth, and she could drive about them a little, slowly, so as to *feel* it all, and then come back and have supper somewhere, – have supper at the Ritz, she thought, of which she had read hastily out of the corner of an eye between two appearances of the Bishop, in the more interesting portions of the 'Times' – just saunter in, you know. Or she could have dinner first ; yes, dinner first, – dinner at Claridge's. No, not at Claridge's ; she had an aunt who stayed there, another one, her mother's sister, rich and powerful, and it was always best not to stir up rich and powerful aunts. Dinner at the Thackeray Hôtel, perhaps. That was where her father's relations stayed, fine-looking serious men who once were curates and, yet earlier, good and handsome babies. It was near the British Museum, she had heard. Its name and surroundings suggested magnificence of a nobler sort than the Ritz. Yes, she would dine at the Thackeray Hôtel and be splendid.

Here, coming to a window full of food, she became aware that, wonderfully, and for the first time for weeks, she was hungry ; so hungry that she didn't want dinner or supper or anything future, but something now. She went in ; and all her gilded visions of the

Ritz and the Thackeray Hôtel were swamped in one huge cup (she felt how legitimate and appropriate a drink it was for a bishop's daughter without a chaperon, and ordered the biggest size costing four-pence) of Aerated Bread Shop cocoa.

It was six o'clock when she emerged, amazingly nourished, from that strange place where long-backed elderly men with tired eyes were hurriedly eating poached eggs on chilly little clothless marble tables, and continued down Regent Street.

She now felt strangely settled in her mind. She no longer wanted to go to the Ritz. Indeed the notion of dining anywhere with the cocoa clothing her internally as with a garment – a thick winter garment, almost she thought like the closer kinds of fur – was revolting. She still felt enterprising, but a little clogged. She thought now more of things like fresh air and exercise. Not now for her the heat and glitter of a music-hall. There was a taste in that pure drink that was irreconcilable with music-halls, a satisfying property in its unadulteratedness, its careful cleanliness, that reminded her she was the daughter of a bishop. Walking away from the Aerated Bread Shop rather gravely, she remembered that she had a mother on a sofa; an only sister who was so beautiful that it was touching; and a class of boys, once unruly and now looking up to her, – in fact, that she had a position to keep up. She was still happy, but happy now in a thoroughly nice way; and she would probaby have gone back in this warmed and solaced condition to her aunt's house in Bedford Square and an evening with a book and an early bed if her eye had not been caught by a poster outside an office sort of place she was passing, a picture of water and mountains, with written on it in big letters : –

A WEEK IN LOVELY LUCERNE
SEVEN DAYS FOR SEVEN GUINEAS
THOSE WHO INTEND TO JOIN NEXT TRIP INQUIRE WITHIN.

Now Ingeborg's maternal grandmother had been a Swede, a creature of toughness and skill on skis, a young woman, when caught surprisingly by the washed-out English tourist Ingeborg's grandfather, drenched in frank reading and thinking and in the smell of the abounding forests and in wood strawberries and sour cream. She had lived, up to the day when for some quite undiscoverable reason she allowed herself to be married to the narrow stranger, in the middle of big beautiful things, – big stretches of water, big mountains, big winds, big lonelinesses; and

Ingeborg, who had never been out of England and had spent years in the soft and soppy west, seeing the picture of the great lake and the great sky in the window in Regent Street, felt a quick grip on her heart.

It was the fingers of her grandmother.

She stood staring at the picture, half-remembering, trying hard to remember quite, something beautiful and elusive and remote that once she had known – oh, that once she had known – but that she kept on somehow forgetting. The urgencies of daily life in episcopal surroundings, the breathless pursuit of her duties, the effort all day long to catch them up and be even with them, the Bishop's buttons, the Bishop's speeches, the Bishop's departures by trains, his all-pervadingness when at home, his all-engulfing mass of correspondence when away – 'She is my Right Hand,' he would say in stately praise – the Redchester tea-parties to which her mother couldn't go because of the sofa, the county garden-parties to which Judith had to be taken, the callers, the bazaars, the cathedral services, the hurry, the noise – life at home seemed the noisiest thing – these had smothered and hidden, beaten down, put out and silenced that highly important and unrecognised part of her, her little bit of lurking grandmother. Now, however, this tough but impulsive lady rose within her in all her might. Her granddaughter was in exactly the right state for being influenced. She was standing there staring, longing, seething with Scandinavia, and presently arguing.

Why shouldn't she? The Bishop, as she had remarked with wonder earlier in the afternoon, seemed to have faded quite pallid that long way off. And arrangements had been made. He had engaged an extra secretary; his chaplain had been warned; Judith was going perhaps to do something; her mother would stay safely on the sofa. They did not expect her back for at least a week, and not for as much longer as her tooth might ache. If her tooth were still in her mouth it *would* be aching. If the dentist had decided to stop it, it would have been a fortnight before such a dreadful ache as that could be suppressed, she was sure it would. And the ten pounds her father had given her for taxis and tips and other odds and ends, spread over a fortnight what would have been left of it anyhow? Besides, he had said – and indeed the Bishop, desirous of taking no jot from his generosity in the whole annoying business, had said it, and said it with the strong flavour of

Scripture which hung about even his mufti utterances – that she might keep any fragments of it that remained that nothing be lost.

'Your father is very good to you,' said her mother, in whose prostrate presence the gift had been made. – 'But bishops,' flashed across Ingeborg's undisciplined and jerky mind, 'have to be good' – (she caught the flash, however, and choked it out before it had got half-way) – 'you'll be able to get yourself a spring hat.'

'Yes, mother,' said Ingeborg, holding her face.

'And I should think a blouse as well,' said her mother thoughtfully.

'Yes mother.'

'My dear, remember I *require* Ingeborg here,' said the Bishop, uneasy at this vision of an indispensable daughter delayed by blouses. 'You will not, of course, forget that, Ingeborg.'

'No father.'

And here she was forgetting it. Here she was in front of a common poster forgetting it. What the Ritz and the Thackeray Hôtel with all their attractions had not been able to do, that crude picture did. She forgot the Bishop, – or rather he seemed at that distance such a little thing, such a little bit of a thing, a tiny little black figure with a dab of white on its top, compared to this vision of splendid earth and heaven, that she wilfully would not remember him. She forgot her accumulating work. She forgot that her movements had all first to be sanctioned. A whirl of Scandinavianism, of violent longing for freedom and adventure, seemed to catch her and lift her out of the street and fling her into a place of maps and time-tables and helpful young men framed in mahogany.

'When – when—' she stammered breathlessly, pointing to a duplicate of the same poster hanging inside, 'when does the next trip start ?'

'To-morrow madam,' said the young man her question had tumbled on.

A solemnity fell upon her. She felt it was Providence. She ceased to argue. She didn't even try to struggle. 'I'm going,' she announced.

And her ten pounds became two pounds thirteen, and she walked away conscious of nothing except that the very next day she would be off.

CHAPTER 2

She was collected by the official leader of this particular Dent's Excursion at Charing Cross the next morning and swept into a second-class carriage with nine other excursionists, and next door there were more – she counted eighteen of them at one time crowding round the leader asking him questions – and besides these there was a crowd of ordinary passengers bustling about with holiday expressions, and several runaway couples, and every single person seemed like herself eager to be off.

The runaway couples, from the ravaged expressions on their faces, were being torn by doubts, perhaps already by repentances; but Ingeborg, though she was deceiving her father who, being a bishop, should have been peculiarly inviolate, and her mother who, being sofa-ridden, should have appealed to her better nature, and her sister who, being exquisite, should have been guarded from any shadow that might dim her beauty, had none. She had been frightened that morning while she was packing and getting herself out of her aunt's house. The immense conviction of the servants that she was going home cowed her. And she had had to say little things, – Paddington, for instance, to the taxi driver when she knew she meant Charing Cross, and had blushed when she changed it through the window. But here she was, and there was a crowd of people doing exactly the same thing whose secure jollity, except in the case of those odd sad couples, was contagious, and she felt both safe and as though she were the most normal creature in the world.

'What *fun*,' she thought, her blood dancing as she watched the swarming, surging platform, 'what *fun*'.

Often had she been at the Redchester station in attendance on her departing father, but what a getting off was that compared with this hilarity. There was bustle, of course, because trains won't

wait and people won't get out of the way, but the Bishop's
bustlings, particularly when their end was confirmations, were
conducted with a kind of frozen offendedness; there was no life
in him, she thought, remembering them, he didn't let himself go.
On the other hand, she reflected, careful to be fair, you couldn't
snatch illicitly at things like confirmations in the way you could at
a Dent's Tour and devour them in secret with a fearful hidden joy.
She felt like a bulb must feel, she thought, at the supreme moment
when it has nosed its little spear successfully up through the mould
it has endured all the winter and gets it suddenly out into the light
and splendour of the world. The freedom of it! The joy of getting
clear.

The excursionists in the carriage struggled to reach the window
across her feet and say things to their friends outside. They all
talked at once, and the carriage was full of sound and gesticulations. The friends on the platform could not hear, but they
nodded and smiled sympathetically and shouted at intervals that
it was going to be a good crossing. Everybody was being seen off
except herself and the runaway couples; indeed, you could know
which those were by the gaps along the platform. She sat well
back in her place, anxious to make herself as convenient as
possible and to get her feet tucked out of the way, a typical
daughter of provincial England and a careful home and the more
expensive clergy, well-dressed, inconspicuous, and grey. Her soft
mouse-colour hat, as the fashion that spring still went on decreeing
in the west, came down well over her eyes and ears, and little
rings of cheerful hair of a Scandinavian colouring wantoned
beneath it. Her small face was swallowed up in the shadow of the
hat; you saw a liberal mouth with happy corners, and the nostrils
of a selective nose, and there was an impression of freckles, and of
a very fair sunny sort of skin.

The square German gentleman opposite her, knowing nobody
in London and therefore being, but for a different and honourable
reason, in her position of not having any one to see him off, filled
up the time by staring. Entirely unconscious that it might be
embarrassing he sat and stared. With the utmost singleness of
mind he wished to see the rest of her, when he would be able to
determine whether she were pretty or not.

Ingeborg, absorbed by the wild excitement on the platform, had
not noticed him; but immediately the train started and the other
passengers had sorted themselves into their seats and were begin-

ning the furtive watchfulness of one another that was presently to resolve itself into acquaintanceship, she knew there was something large and steady opposite that was concentrated upon herself.

She looked up quickly to see what it was, and for a moment her polite intelligent eyes returned his stare. He decided that she had missed being pretty, and with a faint regret wondered what God was about.

'Fattened up – yes, possibly,' he thought. 'Fattened up – yes, perhaps.'

And he went on staring because she happened to be exactly opposite, and there was nothing else except tunnels to look at.

The other excursionists were all in pairs; they thought Ingeborg was too, and put her down at first as the German gentleman's wife because he did not speak to her. There were two couples of young women, one of ladies of a riper age, and one of earnest young men who were mentioning Balzac to each other almost before they had got to New Cross. Indeed, a surprising atmosphere of culture pervaded the compartment. Ingeborg was astonished. Except the riper ladies, who persisted in talking about Shoolbred, they were all presently saying educated things. Balzac, Blake, Bernard Shaw and Mrs Florence Barclay were bandied backwards and forwards across the carriage as lightly and familiarly as though they had been balls. In the far corner Browning was being compared with Tennyson; in the middle, Dickens with Thackeray. The two elder ladies, who kept to Shoolbred, formed a sort of dam between these educated overflowings and the silent backwater in which Ingeborg and the German gentleman sat becalmed. Presently, owing to a politeness that could not allow even an outlying portion of any one else's clothing or belongings to be brushed against without 'Excuse me' having been said and 'Don't mention it' having been answered, acquaintanceships were made; chocolates were offered; they introduced each other to each other; for a brief space the young men's caps were hardly on their heads, and the air was murmurous with gratified noises. But the two riper ladies, passionately preoccupied by Shoolbred, continued to dam up Ingeborg and her opposite neighbour into a stagnant and unfruitful isolation.

She tried to peep round the lady next to her, who jutted out like a mountain with mighty boulders on it, so as to see the three people hidden in the valley beyond. Glimpses of their knees revealed that they were just like the ones on the seat opposite.

They were neat knees, a little threadbare; not with the delicate threadbareness of her own home in the palace at Redchester where splendours of carved stone and black oak and ancient glass were kept from flaunting their pricelessness too obviously in the faces of the local supporters of Disestablishment by a Christian leanness in the matter of carpets, but knees that were inexpensive because they had to be. Who were these girls and young men, and the two abundant ladies, and the man with the vast thick head and unalterable stare? All people who did things, she was certain. Not just anything, like herself, but regular things that began and stopped at fixed times, that were paid for. That was why they were able to do frankly and honourably what she was snatching at furtively in a corner. For a brief astonishing instant she was aware she liked the corner way *best*. Staggered at this, for she could in no way reconcile it with the Bishop, the cathedral, the home, nor with any of her thoughts down there while enfolded in these three absorbing influences, she tried to follow her father's oft-repeated advice and look into herself. But it did not help much. She saw, indeed, that she was doing an outrageous thing, but then she was very happy; happier than she had ever been in Redchester, plied with legitimate episcopal joys. There was a keenness about this joy, the salt freshness of something jolly and indefensible done in secret. She did look at penitence sideways for an instant, but almost at once decided that it was a thing that comes afterwards. First you do your thing. You must of course do your thing, or there couldn't be any penitence.

She sat up very straight, her face lit with these thoughts that both amused and frightened her, her lips slightly parted, her eyes radiant, ready for anything life had to offer.

'A little fattened up,' thought the German gentleman; 'a *little* even would probably suffice.'

There was to be a night in Paris – no time to see it, but you can't have everything, and Paris is Paris – and next morning into the train again, and down, down, all down the slope of the map of France to Bâle, the Gate of Beauty, surely of heavenly beauty, and then you got there, and there were five whole days of wonder, and then . . .

Her thoughts hesitated. Why then, she supposed, making an effort, you began to come back. And *then* . . .

But here she thought it wisest not to go on thinking.

'Excuse me, but do you mind having that window up?' asked the lady on her right.

'Oh no,' said Ingeborg, darting at the strap with the readiness to help and obey she had been so carefully practised in.

It was stiff, and she fumbled at it, wondering a little why the man opposite just watched.

When she had got it up he undid the woollen scarf round his neck and unbuttoned the top button of his overcoat.

'At last,' he said in a voice of relief, heaving an enormous sigh. He looked at her and smiled.

Instantly she smiled back. Any shreds of self-consciousness she may have had clinging to her in her earlier days had been finally scraped off when Judith, that amazing piece of loveliness, came out.

'Were you cold?' she asked, with the friendly interest of a boy.

'Naturally. When windows are open one is always cold.'

'Oh?' said Ingeborg, who had never thought of that.

She perceived from his speech that he was a foreigner. From the turned-down collar and white tie beneath his opened scarf she also was made aware that he was a minister of religion. 'How they pursue me,' she thought. Even here, even in a railway carriage reserved for Dent's excursionists only, one of them had filtered through. She also saw that he was of a drab complexion, and that his hair, drab too and close-cropped and thick, seemed to be made of beaver.

'But that's what windows are *for*,' she said, after reflecting on it.

'No.'

The two large ladies let Shoolbred pause while they looked at each other.

They considered Ingeborg's behaviour forward. She ought not to have spoken first. Impossible on a Dent's tour not to make friends – indeed the social side of these excursions is the most important – but there are rules. The other end of the carriage had observed the rules. The two ladies hoped they had not joined anything not quite high-toned. The other end had carried out the rules with rigid *savoir-vivre*; had accidentally touched and trodden on; had apologised; had had its apologies accepted; had introduced and been introduced; and so had cleared the way to chocolates.

'No?' repeated Ingeborg inquiringly.

'The aperture was there first,' said the German gentleman.

'Of course,' said Ingeborg, seeing he waited for her to admit it.

'And in the fulness of the ages came man, and mechanically shut it.'

'Yes,' said Ingeborg. 'But—'

'Consequently, the function of windows is to shut apertures.'

'Yes. But—'

'And not to open that which, without them, was open already.'

'Yes. But—'

'It would be illogical,' said the German gentleman patiently, 'to contend that their function is to open that which, without them, was open already.'

Reassured by the word illogical, which was a nice word, well known to and quite within the spirit of a Dent's tour, the two ladies went on with Schoolbred where they had left him off.

'The first day I was in England I went about logically, and shut each single window in my boarding house. I then discovered that this embittered the atmosphere around me.'

'It would thicken it,' nodded Ingeborg, interested.

'It did. And my calling after all being that of peace, and my visit so short that whatever happened could be endured, I relinquished logic and purchased in its place a woollen scarf. This one. Then I gave myself up unrestrictedly to their air.'

'And did you like it?'

'It made me recollect with pleasure that I was soon going home. In East Prussia there are, on the one hand, drawbacks; but, on the other, are double windows, stoves, and a just proportion of feathers for each man's bed. Till the draughts and blankets of the boarding-house braced me to enduring instead of enjoying I had thought my holiday too short, and when I remembered my life and work at home – my official life and work – it had been appearing to me puny.'

'Puny?' said Ingeborg, her eyes on his white tie.

'Puny. The draughts and blankets of the boarding-house cured me. I am returning gladly. My life there, I say to myself, may be puny but it is warm. So,' he added, smiling, 'a man learns content.'

'Taught by draughts and blankets?'

'Taught by going away.'

'Oh?' said Ingeborg. Had Providence then only led her to that poster in order that she should learn content? Were Dent's Tours really run, educationally, by Providence?

'But—' she began, and then stopped.

'It is necessary to go away in order to come back,' said the German gentleman, again with patience.

'Yes. Of course. But—'

'The chief use of a holiday is to make one hungry to have finished with it.'

'Oh *no*,' she protested, the joy of holiday in her voice.

'Ah. You are at the beginning.'

'The very beginning.'

'Yet at the end you, too, will return home reconciled.'

She looked at him and shook her head.

'I don't think reconciled is quite the—' She paused, thinking.'To what?' she went on. 'To puniness too?'

The two ladies faltered in their conversation, and glanced at Ingeborg; and then at each other.

'Perhaps not to puniness. You are not a pastor.'

There was a distinct holding of the breath of the two ladies. The German gentleman's slow speech fell very clearly on their sudden silence.

'No,' said Ingeborg. 'But what has that—'

'I am. And it is a puny life.'

Ingeborg felt a slight curdling. She thought of her father, – also, if you come to that, a pastor. She was sure there was nothing in anything he ever did that would strike him as puny. His life was magnificent and important, filled to bursting point with a splendid usefulness and with a tendency to fill the lives of every one who came within his reach to their several bursting points too. But he, of course, was a prince of the Church. Still, he had gone through the Church's stages, beginning humbly ; yet she doubted whether at any moment of his career he had looked at it and thought it puny. And was it not indeed the highest career of all ? However breathless and hurried it made one's female relations in its upper reaches, and drudging in its lower, the very highest ?

But though she was curdled she was interested.

'It might not be amiss,' continued the pastor, looking out of the window at some well-farmed land they were passing, 'if it were not for the Sundays.'

Again she was curdled.

'But—'

'They spoil it.'

She was silent; and the silence of the two ladies appeared to acquire a frost.

'It is the fatal habit of Sundays,' he went on, following the disappearing land with his eyes, 'to recur.'

He paused, as if waiting for her to agree.

She had to, because it was a truth one could not get away from. 'Yes,' she said, reluctantly. 'Of course. It's their nature.' Then a wave of memories suddenly broke over her, and she added warmly, 'Oh *don't* they !'

The frost of the ladies seemed to settle down. It grew heavy.

'They interrupt one's work,' he said.

'But they *are* your work,' she said, puzzled.

'No.'

She stared. 'But,' she began, 'a pastor—'

'A pastor is also a man.'

'Yes,' said Ingeborg, 'but—'

'You have no doubt observed that he is, invariably, also a man.'

'Yes,' said Ingeborg, 'but—'

'And a man of intelligence – I am a man of intelligence – cannot fill up his life with the meagre materials offered by the practice of the tenets of the Lutheran Church.'

'Oh – the *Lutheran* Church,' said Ingeborg, catching at a straw.

'Any Church.'

She was silent. She felt how immensely her father would not have liked it. She felt it was wicked to sit there and listen. She also felt, strange and dreadful to observe, refreshed.

'Then,' she began, knitting her brows, for really this at its best was bad taste, and bad taste, she had always been taught, was the very worst – oh, but how nice it was, a little bit of it, after the swamps of good taste one waded about in in Cathedral cities ! She knitted her brows, aghast at her thoughts. 'Then what,' she asked, '*do* you fill your life up with ?'

'Manure,' said the German gentleman.

The ladies leapt in their places.

'Ma—' began Ingeborg; then stopped.

'I am engaged in endeavouring to teach the peasants of my parish how best to farm their poor pieces of land.'

'Oh really,' said Ingeborg, politely.

'I do it by example. They do not attend to words. I have bought a few acres and experiment before their eyes. Our soil is the worst in Germany. It is inconceivably thankless. And the peasants resemble it.'

'Oh really,' said Ingeborg.

'The result of the combination is poverty.'

'So then, I suppose,' said Ingeborg, with memories of the Bishop's methods, 'you preach patience.'

'Patience ! I preach manure.'

Again at the dreadful word the ladies leapt.

'It is,' he said solemnly, his eyes glistening with enthusiasm, 'the foundation of a nation's greatness.'

'I hadn't thought of it like that,' said Ingeborg, seeing that he waited.

'But on what then does a State depend in the last resort ?'

She was afraid to say, for there seemed to be so many possible answers.

'Naturally on its agriculture,' said the pastor, with the slight irritation of one obliged to linger over the obvious.

'Of course,' said the pliable Ingeborg, trained in acquiescence.

'And on what does agriculture depend in the last resort ?'

Brilliantly she hazarded 'Manure.'

For the third times the ladies leapt, and the one next to her drew away her dress.

He showed his appreciation of her intelligence by nodding slowly.

'A nation must be fed,' he said, 'and empty fields will feed no one.'

'Of course not,' said Ingeborg.

'So that it is the chief element in all progress ; for the root of progress flourishes only in a filled stomach.'

The ladies began to fan themselves violently, nervously, one with *The Daily Mirror* the other with *Answers*.

'Of course,' said Ingeborg.

'First,' said the German gentleman, 'you fill your stomach—'

The lady next to Ingeborg made a sudden lunge across her at the strap.

'Excuse me, but do you mind putting that window *down* ?' she said in a sort of burst.

The German gentleman, stemmed in his speech, used the interval while Ingeborg opened the window in buttoning up his overcoat again with care and patience and readjusting his muffler.

When he had attended to these things he resumed his enthusiasm; he seemed to switch it on again.

'The infinite combinations of it!' he exclaimed. 'It's infinite varieties! Kali, Kainit, Chilisaltpetre, Superphosphates' – he rolled out the words as though they were on the verse of a psalm. 'When I shut the door on myself in the little laboratory I have constructed I shut in with me all life, all science, every possibility. I analyse, I synthesize, I separate, reduce, combine. I touch the stars. I stir the depths. The daily world is forgotten. I forget, indeed, everything, except my research. And invariably at the most profound, the most exalted moments some one knocks and tells me it is Sunday again, and will I come out and preach.'

He looked at her indignantly, demanding sympathy. 'Preach!' he repeated.

'Then why,' she asked, with the coverage of curiosity, 'are you a pastor?'

'Because my father made me one.'

'But why are you still one?'

'Because a man must live.'

'He oughtn't to want to,' said Ingeborg with a faint flush, for she had been carefully trained to shyness when it came to pronouncing opinions, – the Bishop called it being womanly – 'he oughtn't to want to at the cost of his convictions.'

'Nevertheless,' said the pastor, 'he does.'

'Yes,' said Ingeborg, obliged to admit it; even at Redchester cases were not unknown. 'He does,' she said nodding. 'Of course he does.' And unable not to be at least as honest as the pastor she added: 'And so does a woman.'

'Naturally,' said the pastor.

She looked at him a moment, and then said impulsively, pulling herself a little forward towards him by the window strap –

'*This* woman does. She's doing it now.'

The two ladies exchanged glances and fluttered their fans faster.

'Which woman?' inquired the pastor, whose mastery of English though ripe was not nimble.

'This one,' said Ingeborg, pointing at herself. 'Me. I'm living at this very moment – I'm whirling along in this train – I'm running away for this holiday *entirely* at the cost of my convictions.'

CHAPTER 3

After this it was not to be expected that Dent's Tour should look favourably on either Ingeborg or the German gentleman. Running away? And something happened at Dover that clinched it in its coldness.

The train had slowed down, and the excursionists had become busy and were all standing up expectant and swaying with their bags and umbrellas ready in their hands, except Ingeborg and the pastor. The train stopped, and still the two at the door did not move. They were so much interested in what they were saying that they went on sitting there, barbarously corking up the congested queue inside the carriage while streams of properly liberated passengers poured past the window on their way to the best places on the boat.

The queue heaved and waited, holding on to its good manners till the last possible moment, quite anxious, with the exception of the two ladies who were driven to the very verge of naturalness by the things they had had to listen to, lest it should be forced to show what it was feeling (for what one is feeling, Dent's Excursionists had surprisingly discovered, is always somehow something rude), and seconds passed and still it was kept there heaving.

Then the pastor, gazing with a large unhurried interest at the people pushing by the window, people disfigured by haste and the greed for the best places on the boat, said in a voice of mild but penetrating complaint – it almost seemed as if in that congested moment he saw only leisure for musing aloud, – 'But why does the good God make so many ugly old women?'

It was when he said this that the mountainous lady at the head of the queue flung behaviour to the winds and let herself go uncontrolledly. '*Will* you allow me to pass?' she cried. Nor did she give him another instant's grace, but pressed between his and Ingeborg's knees, followed torrentially by the released remainder.

'To keep us all waiting there just while he blasphemed !' she panted on the platform to her friend.

And during the rest of the time the party was together it retired, led by these two ladies, into an icy exclusiveness, outside which and left together all day long Ingeborg and the pastor could not but make friends.

They did. They talked and they walked, they climbed and they sight-saw. They did everything Dent had arranged, going with him but not of him, always as it were bringing up his rear. Equally careful, being equally poor, they avoided the extras which seemed to lurk beckoning at every corner of the day. Their frugality was flagrant, and shocked the other excursionists even more than the dreadful things they said. 'Such bad *taste*,' the Tour declared when, on the third day, after having provoked criticism by their negative attitude towards afternoon tea and the purchase of picture postcards, they would not lighten its several burdens by taking their share of an unincluded outing in flys along the lake. Even Mr Ascough, Dent's distracted representative, thought them undesirable, and especially could make nothing of Ingeborg, except that somehow she was not Dent's sort. And the German gentleman, though in appearance a more familiar type, became whenever he opened his mouth grossly unfamiliar. 'Foul-mouthed' was the expression the largest lady had used, bearing down on Mr Ascough at Dover to complain, adding that as she had done all her travelling for years with and through Dent's she felt justified in demanding that this man's mouth should be immediately cleansed.

'I'm not a toothbrush, Mrs Bawn,' replied the distracted Mr Ascough, engaged at that moment in struggling for air and light in the middle of his clinging flock.

'Then I shall write to Mr Dent himself,' said Mrs Bawn indignantly.

And Mr Ascough, intimidated, fought himself free and followed her down the platform, inquiring dreadfully – really he seemed to be a person of little refinement – whether, then, the German gentleman's conversation had been obscene.

'I can get rid of him if it's been obscene, you know,' said Mr Ascough. 'Was it ?'

So that Mrs Bawn, incensed and baffled, was obliged for the

dignity of her womanhood to say she was glad to have to inform him she did not know what that word meant.

But the pastor – his name was Dremmel, he told Ingeborg: Robert Dremmel – took everything that happened with simplicity. They might shut him out, and he would never notice it; they might turn their backs, and he would never know. Nothing that Dent's tour could do in the way of ostracizing would have been able to pierce through to his consciousness. Having decided that the women of it were plain and the men uninteresting he thought of them no more. With his customary single-mindedness he concentrated his attention at first only on Switzerland, which was what he was paying to see, and he found it pleasant that the young lady in grey should so naturally join him in this concentration. Just for a few hours at the very beginning he had thought her naturalness, her ready friendliness, a little unwomanly. She was, he thought, a little too productive of an impression that she was a kind of boy. She had no selfconsciousness, which he had been taught by his mother to confound with modesty, and no desire whatever apparently to please the opposite sex. She went to sleep, for instance, towards the end of the long journey right in front of him, letting her mouth open if it wanted to, and not bothering at all that he should probably be looking at it.

Herr Dremmel, who besides his agricultural researches prided himself on a liberal if intermittent interest in womanly charm, regretted these short-comings, but only for a few hours at the very beginning. By the end of the first day in Lucerne he was finding it pleasant to pair off with her, womanly or unwomanly. He liked to talk to her. He discovered he could talk to her as he had been unable to talk to the few East Prussian young ladies he had met, in spite of the stiff intensity of their desire to please him. He searched about for a reason, and concluded that it was because she was interested. Whatever subject he discoursed upon she came, so it seemed, running to meet him. She listened intelligently, and with a pliability – he did not then know about the Bishop's training – rarely to be found in combination with intelligence. Intelligent persons are very apt, he remembered, to argue and object. This young lady was intelligent without argument, a most comfortable compound, and before a definite opinion had a graceful knack of doubling up. And if her doublings up were at all, as they sometimes were, delayed while she put in 'But—' he only needed repeat with patience to bring out an admirable submissive sunniness. He could not of course know of her severe training in sunniness.

By the end of the second day he had told her more about his life and his home and his work and his ambitions than he had ever told anybody, and she had told him, only he was unable to find that so interesting, about her life and her home and her work. She had no ambitions, she explained, which he said was well in a woman. He was hardly aware of the Bishop, so lightly did she skim over him.

By the end of the third day he had observed what had, curiously, escaped him before, that she was pretty. Not of course in the abundant East Prussian way, the way of generous curves and of what he now began to think were after all superfluities, but with delicacy and restraint. He no longer considered she would be better fattened up. And he was noticing her clothes, and after a painstaking comparing of them with those of the other ladies applying to them the adjective elegant.

By the end of the fourth he admitted to himself that, very probably, he was soon going to be in love.

By the end of the fifth he knew without a doubt that the thing had happened; the, to him incontrovertible, proof being that on this day Switzerland sank into being just her background.

Even the Rigi, he observed with interest, was nothing to him. He walked up it, he who never walked up anything, because she wanted to. He toiled up panting, and forgot how warmly he was dissolving inside his black clothes in the pleasure of watching her on ahead glancing in and out of the sunshine that fell clear and white on her as she fluttered above him among the pine trunks. And when he got to the top, instead of looking at the view he sat down on the nearest seat and became absorbed in the way the burning afternoon light seemed to get caught in her hair as she stood on the edge of the plateau, and made it look the colour of flames.

This was very interesting. He had never yet within his recollection preferred hair to views. A curious result, he reflected, of his harmless holiday enterprise.

He had not intended to marry. He was thirty-five, and dedicated to his work. He felt it was a noble work, this patient proving to ignorance and prejudice of what could be done with barrenness if only you mixed it with brains. He was fairly comfortable in his housekeeping, having found a woman who was a widow and had therefore learned the great lesson that only widows ever really know, that a man must be let alone. He was poor, and what he could spare by rigid economies went into the few acres of sand that were to be the Light he had to offer to lighten the Gentiles. Every man, he thought, should offer some light to the abounding Gentiles before he died, some light which, however small, might be kept so clear that they could not choose but see it. A wife, he had felt when considering the question from time to time, which was each year in the early spring, would come between him and his light. She would be a shadow; and a voluminous, all-enveloping shadow. His church and the business of preaching in it were already sufficiently interrupting, but they were weekly. A wife would be every day. He could lock her out of the laboratory, he would reflect, and perhaps also out of the sitting-room ... When he became aware that he was earnestly considering what other rooms he could lock her out of and discovered that he would want to lock her out of nearly all he, as a wise and honest man, decided he had best leave the much-curved virgins of the neighbourhood alone.

The question occupied him regularly every year in the first warm days of spring. For the rest of the year he mostly forgot it, absorbed in his work. And here he was on the top of the Rigi, a cool place, almost wintry, with it suddenly become so living that compared to it his fertilizers seemed ridiculous.

He examined this change of attitude with care. He was proud of the way he had fallen in love; he, a poor man, doing it without any knowledge of whether the young lady had enough or indeed any money. He sat there and took pleasure in this proof that though he was thirty-five he could yet be reckless. He was greatly pleased at finding himself so much attracted that if it should turn out that she was penniless he would still manage to marry her, and would make it possible by a series of masterly financial skirmishings, the chief of which would be the dismissal of the widow and the replacing of her dinginess, her arrested effect of having been nipped in the bud although there was no bud, by this incorporate sunshine. The young lady's tact, of which he had seen several instances, would cause her to confine her sunshine to appropriate moments. She would not overflow it into his working hours. Besides, marriage was a great readjuster of values. After it, he had not a doubt, his wife would fall quite naturally into her place, which would, though honourable, be yet a little lower than the fertilizers. If it were not so, if marriage did not readjust the upset incidental to its preliminaries, what a disastrous thing falling in love would be. No serious man would be able to let himself do it. But how interesting it was the way Nature, that old Hostility, that Ancient Enemy to man's thought, did somehow manage to trip him up sooner or later; and how still more interesting the ingenuity with which man, aware of this trick and determined to avoid the disturbance of a duration of affection, had invented marriage.

He gazed very benevolently at the little figure on the edge of the view. Why not marry her now, and frugally convert the tail-end of Dent's Excursion into a honeymoon?

With the large simplicity and obliviousness to banns and licences of a man of scientific preoccupations he saw no reason against this course. It was obvious. It was desirable. It would not only save her going back to England first, it would save the extra journey there for him. They would go straight home to East Prussia together at the end of the week; and as for doing it without her family's knowledge, if she could run away from them as she had told him she had done just for the sake of a jaunt, how much more readily, with what increase of swiftness indeed, would she run for the sake of a husband?

'Tell me, Little One,' he said when she rejoined him, 'will you marry me?'

CHAPTER 4

Ingeborg was astonished.

She stared at him speechless. The gulf between even the warmest friendliness and marriage! She had, she knew, been daily increasing in warm friendliness towards him, characteristically expecting nothing back. That he too should grow warm had not remotely occurred to her. Nobody had ever grown warm to her in that way. There had always been Judith, that miracle of beauty, to blot her into plainness. It is true the senior curate of the Redchester parish church had said to her once in his exhausted Oxford voice, 'You know, I don't mind about faces — will you marry me?' and she had refused so gingerly, with such fear of hurting his feelings, that for a week he had supposed he was engaged; but one would not call that warmth. As the sun puts out the light of a candle so did the radiance of Judith extinguish Ingeborg. They were so oddly alike; and Ingeborg was the pale, diminished shadow. Judith was Ingeborg grown tall, grown exquisite, Ingeborg wrought wonderfully in ivory and gold. No man could possibly fall in love with Ingeborg while there before his very eyes was apparently exactly the same girl, only translated into loveliness.

From the first it had been the most natural thing in the world to Ingeborg to be plain and passed over. Judith was always beside her. Whenever there was a pause in her work for her father it was filled by the chaperoning of Judith. She accepted the situation with complete philosophy, for nothing was quite so evident as Judith's beauty; and she used, in corners at parties, to keep herself awake by saying over bits of Psalms, on which, not being allowed to read novels, her literary enthusiasms were concentrated.

It was, then, really a very astonishing thing to a person practised in this healthy and useful humility to have some one asking her to marry him. That it should be Herr Dremmel seemed to her even more astonishing. He didn't look like somebody one married. He didn't even look like somebody who wanted to marry one. He sat there, his hands folded on the knob of his stick, gazing at her with an entirely placid benevolence and asked her the surprising question as though it were a way of making conversation. It is true he had not called her Little One before, but that, she felt as she stood before him considering this thing that had happened to her, was pretty rather than impassioned.

Here was an awkward and odd result of her holiday enterprise.

'It's – very unexpected,' she said, lamely.

'Yes,' he agreed. 'It is unexpected. It has greatly surprised me.'

'I'm very sorry,' she said.

'About what are you sorry, Little One?'

'I can't accept your – your offer.'

'What! There is some one else?'

'Not *that* sort of some one. But there's my father.'

He made a great sweep with his arm. 'Fathers,' he said; and pushed the whole breed out of sight.

'He's very important.'

'Important! Little One, when will you marry me?'

'I can't leave him.'

He became patient. 'It has been laid down that a woman shall leave father and mother and any other related obstacle she may have the misfortune to be hampered with, and cleave only to her husband.'

'That was about a man cleaving to his wife. There wasn't anything said about a woman. Besides—' She stopped. She couldn't tell him that she didn't want to cleave.

He gazed at her a moment in silence. He had not contemplated a necessity for persuasion.

'This,' he then said with severity, 'is prevarication.'

She sat down on the grass and clasped her hands round her knees and looked up at him. She had taken off her hat when first she got to the top to fan herself, and had not put it on again. As she sat there with her back to the glow of the sky, the wind softly lifted the rings of her hair and the sun shone through them wonderfully. They seemed to flicker gently to and fro, little tongues of fire.

'Why,' said Herr Dremmel, suddenly leaning forward and staring, 'you are like a spirit.'

This pleased her. For a moment her eyes danced.

'Like a spirit,' he repeated. 'And here am I talking heavily to you, as though you were an ordinary woman. Little One, how does one trap a spirit into marrying? Tell me. For very earnestly do I desire to be shown the way.'

'One doesn't,' said Ingeborg.

'Ah, do not be difficult. You have been so easy, of such a comfortable response in all things up to now.'

'But this—' began Ingeborg.

'Yes. This, I well know—'

He was more stirred than he had thought possible. He was becoming almost eager.

'But,' asked Ingeborg, exploring this new interesting situation, 'why do you want to?'

'Want to marry you?'

'Yes.'

'Because,' said Herr Dremmel, immensely prompt, 'I have had the extreme good fortune to fall in love with you.'

Again she looked pleased.

'And I do not ask you,' he went on, 'to love me, or whether you do love me. It would be presumption on my part, and not, if you did, very modest on yours. That is the difference between a man and a woman. He loves before marriage, and she does not love till after.'

'Oh?' said Ingeborg, interested. 'And what does he—'

'The woman,' continued Herr Dremmel, 'feels affection and esteem before marriage, and the man feels affection and esteem after.'

'Oh,' said Ingeborg, reflecting. She began to tear up tufts of grass. 'It seems – chilly,' she said.

'Chilly?' he echoed.

He let his stick drop, and got up and came and sat down, or rather let himself down carefully, on the grass beside her.

'Chilly? Do you not know that a decent chill is a great preservative? Hot things decay. Frozen things do not live. A just measure of chill preserves the life of the affections. It is, by a very proper dispensation of Nature, provided before marriage by the woman, and afterwards by the man. The balance is, in this way, nicely held, and peace and harmony, which flourish best at a low temperature, prevail.'

She looked at him and laughed. There was no one in Redchester, and Redchester was all she knew of life, in the least like Herr

Dremmel. She stretched herself in the roomy difference, happy, free, at her ease.

'But I cannot believe,' burst out Herr Dremmel with a passionate vigour that astonished him more than anything in his whole life as he seized the hand that kept on tearing up grass, 'I cannot believe that you will not marry me. I cannot believe that you will refuse a good and loving husband, that you will prefer to remain with your father and solidify into yet one more frostbitten virgin.'

'Into a what ?' repeated Ingeborg, struck by this image of herself in the future.

She began to laugh, then stopped. She stared at him, her grey eyes very wide open. She forgot Herr Dremmel, and that he was still clutching her hand and all the grass in it, while her mind flashed over the years that had gone and the years that were to come. They would be alike. They had not been able to frostbite her yet because she had been too young; but they would get her presently. Their daily repeated busy emptiness, their rush of barren duties, their meagre moments of what when she was younger used to be happiness but had lately only been relief, those rare moments when her father praised her, would settle down presently and freeze her dead.

Her face grew solemn. 'It's true,' she said slowly. 'I shall be a frostbitten virgin. I'm doomed. My father won't ever let me marry.'

'You infinitely childish one !' he cried, becoming angry. 'When it is well known that all fathers wish to get rid of all daughters.'

'You don't understand. It's different. My father – why,' she broke out, 'I used to dose myself secretly with cod liver oil so as to keep up to his level. He's wonderful. When he praised me I usedn't to sleep. And if he scolded me it seemed to send me lame.'

Herr Dremmel sawed her hand up and down in his irritation.

'What is this irrelevant talk ?' he said. 'I offer you marriage, and you respond with information about cod liver oil. I do not believe the father obstacle. I do not recognise my honest little friend of these last days. It is waste of time, not being open. Would you, then, if it were not for your father marry me ?'

'But,' Ingeborg flashed round at him, swept off her feet as she so often was by an impulse of utter truth, 'it's *because* of him that I *would*.'

And the instant she had said it she was shocked.

She stared at Herr Dremmel wide-eyed with contrition. The

disloyalty of it. The ugliness of telling a stranger – and a stranger with hair like fur – anything at all about those closely related persons she had been taught to describe to herself as her dear ones.

'Oh,' she cried, dragging her hand away, 'let my hand go – let my hand *go*.'

She tried to get on to her feet, but with an energy he did not know he possessed he pulled her down again. He did not recognise any of the things he was feeling and doing. The Dremmel of his real nature, of those calm depths where lay happy fields of future fertilizers, gazed at this inflamed conduct going on at the top in astonishment.

'No,' he said, with immense determination, 'you will sit here and explain about your father.'

'It's a dreadful thing,' replied Ingeborg, suddenly discovering that of all things she did not like being clutched, and looking straight into his eyes, her head a little thrown back, 'that one can't leave one's home even for a week without getting into a scrape.'

'A scrape ! You call it a scrape when a good man—'

'Here's a person who goes away for a little change – privately. And before she knows where she is she's being held down on the top of the Rigi and ordered by a strange man—'

'By her future husband !' cried Herr Dremmel, who was finding the making of offers more difficult than he had supposed.

' – by a strange man to explain her father. As though anybody could ever explain their father. As though anybody could ever explain *anything*.'

'God in Heaven,' cried Herr Dremmel, 'do not explain him then. Just marry me.'

And at this moment the snake-like procession of the rest of Dent's Tour, headed by Mr Ascough, watch in hand, emerged from the hôtel where it had been having tea on to the plateau, wiping its mouths in readiness for the sunset.

With the jerk of a thing that has been stung it swerved aside as it was about almost to tread on the two on the grass.

Ingeborg sat very stiff and straight and pretended to be staring intently at the view, forgetting that it was behind her. She flushed when she found there was no time to move far enough from Herr Dremmel for a gap to be visible between them.

'Look at those two now,' whispered the young lady last in the procession to the young man brushing bread and butter out of his tie who walked beside her.

He looked, and seemed inclined to linger.

'She's very *pretty*, isn't she?' he said.

'Oh, do you think so?' said his companion. 'I never think anybody's pretty who isn't – you know what I mean – really *nice*, you know – lady-like—'

And she hurried him on, because, she said, if he didn't hurry he'd miss the sunset.

CHAPTER 5

Ingeborg spent most of the night on a hard chair at her bedroom window earnestly endeavouring to think.

It was very unfortunate, but she found an immense difficulty at all times in thinking. She could keep her father's affairs in the neatest order, but not her own thoughts. There were so many of them, and they all seemed to jump about inside her and want to get thought first. They would not go into ordered rows. They had no patience. Often she had suspected they were not thoughts at all but just feelings, and that depressed her, for it made her drop, she feared, to the level of the insect world and enter the category of things that were not going to be able to get to heaven; and to a bishop's daughter this was disquieting. Most of her thoughts she was immediately sorry for, they were so unlike anything she could, with propriety, say out loud at home. To Herr Dremmel she had been able to say them all as far as speech, a limping vehicle, could be made to go, and this was another of his refreshing qualities. She did not of course know of that absorbed man's habit of listening to her with only one ear – a benevolent ear, but only one – while with the other, turned inwards, he listened to the working out in his mind of problems in Chilisaltpetre and superphosphates.

She sat staring out of the window at the stars and chimney-pots, her hands held tightly in her lap, and told herself that the moment had come for clear, consecutive thought, – *consecutive* thought, she repeated severely, aware already of the interlaced dancing going on in her brain. What was she going to do about Herr Dremmel? About going home? About – oh, about anything?

They had come down the Rigi soberly and in the train. Nobody, as usual, spoke to them, and for the first time in their friendship neither had they spoken to each other. They had had a speechless dinner. He had looked preoccupied. And when directly after it she said good night, he had drawn her out into the passage and solemnly adjured her, while the hall porter pretended he was out of ear-shot, to have done with prevarications. What he would suggest, he said, was a comfortable betrothal next day; it was too late for one that night, he said, pulling out his watch, but next day; and as she retreated sideways step by step up the stairs, silent through an inability immediately to find an answer that seemed tactful enough, he had eyed her very severely and inquired of her with a raised voice what, then, the ado was all about. She had turned at that, giving up the search for tact, and had run up the remaining stairs rather breathlessly, feeling that Herr Dremmel on marriage had an engulfing quality; and he, after a moment's perplexity on the mat at the bottom, had gone to the reading-room a baffled man.

Now she sat at the window considering.

Her journey home was only two days off, and the thought of what would be said to her when she got there and of what her answers would be like, ran down the back of her neck and spine as though some one were drawing a light, ice-cold finger over the shrinking skin. She had been persuading herself that her little holiday was harmless and natural; and now this business with Herr Dremmel would, she felt, do away with all that, and justify a wrath in her father that she might else for her private solace and encouragement have looked upon as unreasonable. It is a peculiarity of parents, reflected Ingeborg, that they are always being justified. However small and innocent what you are doing may be, if they disapprove something turns up to cause them to have been altogether right. She remembered little things, small occasions of her younger days ... This was a big occasion, and what had turned up on it was Herr Dremmel. It was a pity – oh, it was a pity she hadn't considered before she left London so impulsively whether when she got back to Redchester she was going to be untruthful or not. She had considered nothing, except the acuteness of the joy of running away. Now she was faced by the really awful question of lying or not lying. It was ugly to lie at all. It was dreadful to lie to one's father. But to lie to a Bishop raised the operation from just a private sin which God would deal with kindly on being asked, to a crime you were punished for if it was a cathedral you did it to, a real crime, the crime of sacrilege. Impossible to profane a sacred and consecrated object like a Bishop. Doubly and trebly impossible if you were that object's own daughter. Her tightly folded hands went cold as she realised she was undoubtedly going to be truthful. She was every bit as valiant as her Swedish grandmother had been, that grandmother who was aware of the dangers of the things she did with her mountains and her gusty lakes and defied them, but her grandmother knew no fear and Ingeborg knew it very well. Hers was the real courage found only in the entirely terrified, who, terrified, yet see the thing, whatever it is, doggedly through. She was faint, yet pursuing.

She saw much terror in her immediate future. She dreaded having to be courageous. She felt she was too small really for the bravely truthful answering of her magnificent father's questions. He would have the catechism and the confirmation service on his side, as well as the laws of right behaviour and filial love. It didn't seem fair. One couldn't argue with a parent, one couldn't answer back; while as for a Bishop, one couldn't do anything at all with him except hastily agree. There was just a possibility – but how remote – that her father would be too busy to ask questions; she sighed as she reflected how little she could count on that, and how the most superficial inquiry about her aunt or the dentist would bring out the whole story.

And here was Herr Dremmel who thought nothing at all of him, even in regard to an enormous undertaking like his daughter's marriage. There was something sublime in such detachment. She felt the largeness of the freedom of it blowing in her face like a brisk invigorating wind. There seemed to be no hedges round Herr Dremmel. He was as untied-up a person as she had ever met. He cared nothing for other people's opinion, that chief enslavement of her home, and he was an orphan. Sad to be an orphan, thought Ingeborg sighing. Sad, of course, not to have any dear ones. But it did seem to be a condition that avoided the dilemma whose horns were concealment by means of untruths and the screwing up of oneself to that clammily cold and forlorn condition, having courage.

Of course, Herr Dremmel didn't know her father. He hadn't faced that impressive personality. Would he be quite so detached and easily indifferent if he had? She thought with a shiver of what such a meeting, supposing, just for the sake of supposing, that she allowed herself to become engaged, would be like. Would Herr Dremmel in that setting of carefully subdued splendour, of wainscoting and oriels, seem to her as free and delightful as he seemed on a tour of frugal backgrounds? Would she, in the presence of the Bishop's horrified disapproval, be able to see him as she had been seeing him now?

She had not explored very far into her own resources yet, but she had begun lately to perceive that she was pliable. She bent easily, she felt, and deplored having to feel, in the direction desired by the persons she was with and who laid hold of her with authority. It is true she sprang back again, as she had discovered so surprisingly in London, the instant the hold was relaxed, but it seemed that she sprang only to do, as she now with a headshake admitted, difficulty-bringing things. And her training in acquiescence and distrust of herself was very complete, and back in her home would she not at once bend into the old curve again? Was it possible, would it ever be possible, in her father's presence to disassociate herself from his points of view? What his view of Herr Dremmel would be she very exactly knew. Did she *want* to disassociate herself from it?

She pushed back her chair, and began to walk quickly up and down the narrow little room. If she didn't disassociate herself it meant marriage; and marriage in stark defiance of the whole of her world. Redchester would be appalled. The diocese would grieve for its Bishop. The county would discuss her antagonistically at a hundred tea-tables. Well; and while they were doing it, where would she be? Her blood began suddenly to dance. She was seized, as she had been in London, by that overwhelming desire to shake off old things and set her face towards the utterly new. While all these people were nodding and whispering in their stuffy stale world she would be safe in East Prussia, a place that seemed infinitely remote, a place Herr Dremmel had described to her as full of forests and water and immense stretches of waving rye. The lakes were fringed with rushes; the forests came down to their edges; his own garden ended in a little path through a lilac hedge that took you down between the rye to the rushes and the water and the first great pines. Oh, she knew it as though she had seen it, she had lured him on so often to describing it to her. He thought nothing of it; talked, indeed, of it with disgust as a God-forsaken place. Well, it was these God-forsaken places that her body and spirit cried out for. Space, freedom, quiet; the wind ruffling the rye; the water splashing softly against the side of the punt (there was a punt, she had extracted); the larks singing up in the sunlight; the shining clouds passing slowly across the blue.

She wanted to be alone with these things after the years of deafening hurry at Redchester with a longing that was like homesickness. She *remembered* somehow that once she used to be with them – long ago, far away . . . And there used to be little things when you lay face downwards on the grass, little lovely things that smelt beautiful – wild-strawberry leaves, and a tiny aromatic plant with a white flower like a star that you rubbed between your fingers . . .

She stood still a moment, frowning, trying to remember more; it wasn't in England . . . But even as she puzzled the vision slipped away from her and was lost.

She wanted to read, and walk, and think. She was hungry to read at last what she chose, and walk at last where she chose, and think at last exactly what she chose. Was the *Christian Year* enough for one in the way of poetry? And all those mild novels her mother read, sandwiched between the biographies of more bishops and little books of comfort with crosses on them that asked rude questions as to whether you had been greedy or dainty or had used words with a double meaning during the day – were they enough for a soul that had, quite alone, with no father giving directions, presently to face its God?

Her family held strongly that for daughters to read in the daytime was to be idle. Well if it was, thought Ingeborg lifting her head, that head that drooped so apologetically at home, with the defiance that distance encourages, then being idle was a blessed thing and the sooner one got away to where one could be it uninterruptedly the better. In that parsonage away in East Prussia, for instance, one would be able to read and read . . . Her Dremmel had explained a hundred times about his laboratory, and he himself locked into it and only asking to be left locked. Surely that was an admirable quality in a husband, that he kept himself locked up? And the parsonage was on the edge of the village, and the little garden at the back had nothing between it and the sunset and all God's other dear arrangements except a solitary and long-unused windmill . . .

It was about one o'clock in the morning that her courage, however, altogether ebbed at the prospect of going home. What would it be like, taking up her filialities again, and all of them henceforth so terribly tarnished? She would be a returning prodigal for whom no calf was killed, but who instead of the succulences of a more liberal age would be offered an awful opportunity of explaining her conduct to a father who would interrupt her the instant she began and do the explaining himself.

How was she going to face it, all alone?

If only she could have been in love with Herr Dremmel! With what courage she would have faced her family then, if she had been in love with him and come to them her hand in his. If only he looked more like the lovers you see in pictures, like the one in Leighton's 'Wedded,' for instance – a very beautiful picture, Ingeborg thought, but not like any of the wedded in Redchester – so that if she couldn't be in love she could at least persuade herself she was. If only he had proper hair instead of just beaver. She liked him so much. She had even at particular moments of his conversation gone so far as to delight in him. But – marriage?

What was marriage? Why did they never talk about it at home? In the Bishop's Palace it might, for all the mentioning it got, be one of the seven deadly sins. You talked there of the married, and sometimes, but with reserve, of getting married, but marriage itself and what it was and meant was never discussed. She had received the impression, owing to these silences, that though it was God's ordinance, as her father in his official capacity at weddings reiterated, it was a reluctant ordinance, established apparently because there seemed no other way of getting round what appeared to be a difficulty. What was the difficulty? She had never in her busy life thought about it. Marriage had not concerned her. It would not be nice, she had felt, unconsciously adopting the opinion of her environment, for a girl who was not going to marry to get thinking of it. And it really had not interested her. She had quite naturally turned her eyes away.

But now this question of facing her father, this need of being backed up, this longing to get away from things, forced her to look. Besides, she would have to give Herr Dremmel some sort of answer in the morning, and the facing of Herr Dremmel required courage too – of a different kind, but certainly courage. She was so reluctant to hurt or disappoint. It had seemed all her life the most beautiful of pleasures to give people what they wanted, to get them to smile, to see them look content. But suppose Herr Dremmel, before he could be got to smile and look content, wanted to clutch her again as he had clutched her on the top of the Rigi? She had very profoundly disliked it. She had been able to resent it there and get loose, but if she were married and he clutched could she still resent? She greatly feared not. She greatly

suspected, now she came to a calm consideration of it, that that
was what was the matter with marriage: it was a series of
clutchings. Her father had no doubt realised this as she was
realising it now, and very properly didn't like it. You couldn't
expect him to. That was why he wouldn't talk about it. In this she
was entirely at one with him. But perhaps Herr Dremmel didn't
like it either. Wasn't she rather jumping at conclusions in imagining that he did? Hadn't he after all clutched rather in anger up
there than in anything else? And what about his earnest wish, so
often explained, to be left all day locked up in his laboratory?
And what about his praise, that very afternoon, of chill in human
relationships?

At that moment her eye was arrested by something white
appearing slowly and with difficulty beneath her door. She sat up
very straight and stared at it, watching its efforts to get over and
past the edge of her mat. For an instant she wondered whether it
were not a kind of insect ghost; then she saw, as more of it
appeared, that it was a letter.

She held her breath while it struggled in. Nobody had ever
pushed a letter under her door before. She grew happy instantly.
What *fun*. Her heart beat quite fast with excitement while she
waited to hear footsteps going away before getting up to fetch it.
Herr Dremmel, however, must have been in his goloshes, objects
from which he was seldom separated, for she heard nothing; and
after a few seconds of breathless listening she got up with immense
caution and went on tiptoe to the letter and picked it up.

'Why,' she thought, pausing for a moment with a sort of
solemnity before opening it, 'I suppose this is my first love-letter.'

There was nothing on the envelope and no signature, and this
was what it said –

'LITTLE ONE,
    *I wish to tell you that before going to my room to-night I
instructed the hall porter to order a betrothal cake, properly
iced and with what is customary in the matter of silver leaves,
to be in the small salon adjoining the smoking-room to-morrow
morning at nine o'clock. Since no man can be betrothed alone,
it will be necessary that you should be there.'*

CHAPTER 6

It was a perturbed betrothal, there were so many people at it.

Seven ladies besides Ingeborg appeared in the small *salon* adjoining the smoking-room next morning at nine o'clock. What Herr Dremmel had done, being ignorant which was Ingeborg's room and after laborious thought deciding that to demand her number of the hall-porter later than dusk might very conceivably cast a slur on her reputation, young ladies being, as he well knew, of all living creatures the most easily slurred, was to write as many copies of the letter as there were doors on her landing and thrust them industriously one by one beneath each door, strong in the knowledge that she would in this manner inevitably get one of them.

He was greatly pleased with this plan. It seemed of a beautiful simplicity and effectiveness. 'Being unaware of the context,' he reasoned, 'no lady except the right one will be able to guess what the letter can possibly refer to. She will therefore throw it aside as an obvious mistake and think no more about it.'

But the ladies did think. And none of the inhabitants of the third floor, except Mr Ascough who never thought anything about anything, having discovered that if once you begin to think there is no end to it, and a dried and brittle little man lately pensioned off by the firm he had been clerk to and taking his first trip on the continent in a condition of profound uninterestedness, threw it aside. These two did; but the seven ladies not only did not throw it aside they read it many times, and instead of thinking no more about it thought of nothing else. Even Mrs Bawn, who had been a widow for six months and was heartily tired of it, was pleased. She liked, particularly, being addressed as Little One. There was a blindness about this that suggested genuine feeling. She had not been so much pleased since her dear Bawn, now half a year in glory, had told her one day, before their marriage, that he did not care what anybody said he maintained that she was handsome.

They all thought the letter very virile, and that nothing could be more gentlemanly than its restraint. Four of them expected a different male member of the party to be waiting in the small *salon*, the remaining three expected Mr Ascough. Mr Ascough had a caressing way with pats of butter and the closing of the doors of filled flys that had before now led him, on these tours, into misapprehensions. He was long since married, but had omitted to mention it. The ladies, therefore, when they arrived in the small *salon* at nine o'clock did not find Mr Ascough nor any of the other four friends they expected. They found, surprisingly, each other; and, standing thick and black near a decorated table at the window and scowling in a fresh astonishment every time the door opened and another lady came in, that very undesirable fellow-tourist, the German gentleman.

Each one immediately knew it was Ingeborg who had been written to, and that the letter had gone astray. Each one also thought she knew that Ingeborg had not got the letter and would not come. But each one, except Mrs Bawn, was helped to cover up her shock by being sure the others did not know of it; and the custom of life lying heavy on them they were able, after one little start on first seeing Herr Dremmel, to drift into the corners of the room and pretend that what they had come for was books. Except Mrs Bawn. Mrs Bawn saw, stared, turned on her heel, and went out again volcanically; and the corridor shook to her departing footsteps and to the angry unintentional rhymes she was making aloud with words like hoax and jokes.

With astonishment and disgust Herr Dremmel saw the seven ladies accumulate. It was most unfortunate that on that morning of all mornings the small *salon*, so invariably empty, should be visited. His inexperienced mind did not connect their appearance with his letters; it never occurred to him that his reasoning as to what they would do on receiving them could possibly be wrong. Nor did he, as he watched the door open and shut seven times and seven times admit the wrong woman, guess that their presence, if Ingeborg came, would immensely help his betrothal.

The ladies, fingering dusty Tauchnitzes and magazines and eyeing the table in the window with heads as much averted as could be combined with the seeing of it, gradually found the shock they had had being soothed by the interest they felt in what Herr

Dremmel would do when he realised that that unladylike Miss
Bullivant, all unaware of what was waiting for her, was not
coming. Now that they were there they might as well stay and see
the end of it. It was really very interesting in its way; so German;
so unlike, thank goodness, what English people ever did. Would
he stand there all day, they wondered, with that really most
improperly suggestive cake, so very like a christening cake? One
or two of them sat down squarely on the sofas behind months-old
magazines round whose edges they peeped, making it clear to the
unhappy man that they, at least, intended to stay there; and they
all coughed a little every now and then in the way a waiting
congregation coughs in church.

Then the door was pushed open with the jerk of somebody who
is either in a hurry or has come to a sudden determination, and
who should appear but that Miss Bullivant.

A thrill ran through the seven ladies, and they instantly became
behind their magazines stiff with excitement. Chance; what a
chance; she had chanced to look in; it was like a play; dear me,
thought each of the seven.

And Ingeborg, who believed as lately as the last moment on the
doormat outside that she had only come in order to tell Herr
Dremmel she was not coming, when she saw the cake, very white
and bridal, on a white cloth with white flowers in pots round it,
and on either side of it a bottle with a white ribbon about its neck,
and on the other for the sake of symmetry two glasses was
staggered. How could she, who so much loved to please, to make
happy, cruelly hurt him, spoil his little feast, wipe out the glow,
the immense relief that beamed from his face when he saw her?

She turned round quickly, realising the presence of the seven
ladies. Amazed she stared at them, mechanically counting them.
How could she make him ridiculous, humiliate him, before all
those women?

Hesitating, torn, poised on the tip of flight, she stood there. Her
hand was on the door to open it again and run; but Herr
Dremmel's simplicity came to his help more effectually than the
cunningest plans. He forgot the ladies, and stepping forward took
her hand in his and quite simply kissed her forehead, sealing her
then and there, with the perfect frankness of his countrymen when
engaged in legitimate courtship, as his betrothed. He then slipped
a ring he wore on his little finger on to her thumb, that being the
only bit of her hand he could find that it would stay on and he

being free from prejudices in the matter of fingers, and the thing –
at least so he supposed – was done.

Ingeborg in her bewilderment let these things happen to her.
Her thoughts as she stood being betrothed were jerking themselves
into a perfect tangle of knots. She was astonished at the tricks life
stoops to. A cake and the eyes of seven women. Her whole future
being decided by a cake and the eyes of seven women. Oh no, it
couldn't be. It was only that she couldn't stop now. Impossible,
utterly, to stop now. She had never dreamed she wouldn't find
him alone. These women were all witnesses. He had kissed her
before them all. His methods were really overwhelming. Suppose
her father could see her. But the kiss had been administered very
ceremoniously; it had been quite cooling; such a one as even a
bishop might feel justified in applying to the brow of a sick person
or a young child. Later, at a more convenient time, when the
pathetic cake was out of sight, when these women were out of
ear-shot, she would tell him she hadn't meant . . .

Amazingly she found herself advancing towards the cake with
Herr Dremmel and standing in front of it with him hand in hand.
Oh, the *mischief* people got into who came up to London to
dentists! She now saw what provincial dentists were for: they
kept you in pain, and pain kept you out of mischief. For the first
time she understood what her spirit had till then refused to accept,
the teaching so popular with the Bishop that pain was a necessary
part of the scheme of things. Of course. You were safe so long as
you were in pain. In that condition the very nearest you could get
to the most seductive temptation was to glance at it palely, with a
sick distaste. And you stayed at home, and were grateful for
kindnesses. It was only when you hadn't anything the matter with
you that you ran away from your family and went to Lucerne and
took up with a strange man positively to the extent of letting him
promise to marry you.

Somebody coughed so close behind her that it made her jump.
She turned round nervously, Herr Dremmel still holding her hand,
and beheld the seven ladies flocked about her for all the world like
seven bridesmaids.

They had hastily consulted together in whispers while she was
being led away to the cake as to whether they ought not to
congratulate her. Their hearts were touched by the respectful
ceremony with which Herr Dremmel had conducted his betrothal.
It had had the solemn finality of a marriage, and what woman can

look on at a marriage unmoved? They had agreed in whispers that this was one of those moments in which one lets bygones be bygones. The two at the altar – they meant at the cake – had no doubt said many terrible and vulgar things and had behaved in a way no lady and gentleman would, – the girl, for instance, openly admitting she had run away from home; but what they were doing now at least was beyond reproach, and, by uniting, two blacks were after all, in spite of what people said about its not being possible, going to make one white. At any rate it was charitable to hope so.

So they cleared their throats and wished her joy.

'Thank you,' said Ingeborg a little faintly, looking from one to the other, 'it's so kind of you – but—'

They then shook hands with Herr Dremmel and said they were sure they wished him joy too, and he thanked them with propriety and bows.

'Such a thing has never happened on a Dent's Tour before – oh no, never before at all I'm sure,' said the most elderly lady nervously, with a number of nods.

'There isn't time enough, that's what I sometimes think,' said the young lady who had hurried her companion away to the sunset the evening before. 'What's a week?' And she stared at the cake and frowned.

'Dent's had a funeral once,' said a square small lady who kept her hands plunged in the pockets of a grey jersey.

'Now Miss Jewks, really—' protested the elderly lady. 'One doesn't mention—'

'Well, it wasn't their fault, Miss Andrews. They didn't *want* to have it, I'm sure. It was a gentleman from Gipsy Hill—'

'What a beautiful – er – cake,' hastily interrupted the elderly lady.

'Funny thing, I sometimes think,' continued Miss Jewks, 'to go for a holiday and die instead.'

'Those silver leaves—' said the elderly lady, raising her voice, 'I call them dainty.'

'It's like a wedding-cake, isn't it?' said the young lady of the sunset, peering close at it with a face of gloom.

'Will you not, Ingeborg,' said Herr Dremmel, calling her for the first time by her name, 'cut the cake? And perhaps these ladies will do us the honour of tasting it.'

She did not recognise him in this persistent ceremoniousness.

Every trace of his usual lax behaviour was gone, his ease and familiarity of speech, and he was as stiff and correct and grave as if he were laying a foundation stone or opening a museum. They were the manners, though she did not know it, which all Germans are trained to produce on public occasions.

'Oh, thank you—'

'Oh, you're really very kind—'

'Oh, thank you very much I'm sure—'

There was a murmur of awkward and reluctant thanks. The seven ladies were not at all certain that their cordiality ought to stretch as far as cake. They had been moved by an impulse that did honour to their womanliness to offer congratulations, but they did not for all that forget the dreadful things the couple had constantly been heard talking about and the many clear proofs it had provided that it was what Dent's Tours were accustomed to describe as no class; and though they all liked cake, and were getting steadily hungrier as the Dent week drew to its close, they were doubtful as to the social wisdom of eating it. It would be very unpleasant if these people, encouraged, were later on to presume; if they were to try to use the eaten cake as a weapon for forcing their way into English society. If, in a word, when the Tour got back to England, they were to want to call.

So they took the cake reluctantly that Ingeborg, in a sort of dream, cut and offered them; and with even more reluctance they sipped the wine in which the German gentleman requested them to drink the newly-betrothed couple's health.

'But—' said Ingeborg, trying to rouse herself even at this eleventh hour.

'True. There are not enough glasses. I will ring for more,' was the way Herr Dremmel finished her sentence for her.

The immense official promptness of him! She felt numbed.

And when the glasses were brought there was another ceremony, – a clinking of Herr Dremmel's glass with each glass in turn, his heels together as in the days of his soldiering, his body stiff and his face a miracle of solemnity; and before drinking he made a speech, the Asti held high in front of him, in which he thanked the ladies for their good wishes on behalf of his betrothed, Miss Ingeborg Bullivant, whose virtues he dwelt upon singly and at length in resounding periods, before proceeding to assure those present of his firm resolve to prove, by the devotion of the rest of his life, the extremity of his gratitude for the striking proof she had given before them all of her confidence in him; and every sentence seemed to set another and a heavier seal on her as a creature undoubtedly bound to marry him.

Dimly she began to realise something of the steely grip of a German engagement. She wondered whether there were any more room left on her forehead for further seals. She felt that it must be covered with great red things, scrawled over with the inscription:

DREMMEL'S

Well, she was after all not a parcel to be picked up and carried away by the first person who found her lying about, and the minute she was alone with him she would, she *must*, tell him that what she had really come down for, though appearances were certainly by this time rather against her, was to refuse him. She would be as gentle as possible, but she would be plain and firm. The minute these women left them alone she would tell him.

With a start she saw that the women were leaving them alone, and that the minute had come. She wanted them not to go; she wanted to keep them there at any cost. She even made a step after them as the last one, nodding to the end, went out and shut the door, but Herr Dremmel still had hold of her hand.

When the door had finally shut she turned to him quickly. Her head was thrown back, her eyes were full of a screwed-up courage.

'But you know—' she began, determined to clear things up, however much it might hurt them both.

And again he promptly finished her sentence for her, this time by enfolding her in his arms and kissing her with a largeness and abundance which no bishop, her mind flashed as her body stood stiff with surprise and horror, could possibly approve.

She felt engulfed.

She felt she must be disappearing altogether.

He seemed infinitely capacious and soft.

'Oh, but I can't – I won't – oh, stop – oh, stop – it's a mistake—' she tried to get out in gasps.

'My little wife,' was all the notice Herr Dremmel took of that.

CHAPTER 7

It was raining at Redchester when Ingeborg got out at the station a week and a day after she left it, – the soft persistent fine rain, hardly more than a mist, peculiar to that much-soaked corner of England. The lawns in the gardens she passed as her fly crawled up the hill were incredibly green, the leaves of the lilac bushes glistened with wet, each tulip was a cup of water, the roads were chocolate, and a thick grey blanket of cloud hung warm over the town, tucking it in all round and keeping out any draught that might bite and sting the inhabitants, she thought, into real living.

The porter told her it was fine growing weather, and she wondered stupidly why, after the years she had had of the sort of thing, she had not grown, then, more thoroughly herself. A retired colonel she knew – she knew all the retired colonels – waved his umbrella and shouted a genial inquiry after her toothache, and she looked at him with a dead, ungrateful eye. A passing postman touched his cap, and she turned the other way. The same sensible female figures she had seen all her life draped in the same sensible mackintoshes bowed and smiled, and she pretended she hadn't seen them. Everybody, in fact, behaved as though she were still good which was distressing, embarrassing, and productive of an overwhelming desire to shut her eyes and hide.

There were the shops, with the things in the windows unchanged since she left nine days ago, the same ancient novelties nobody ever bought, the same flies creeping over the same buns. There was the bookseller her *Christian Year* had come from, his windows full of more of them, endless supplies for endless dieted daughters, vegetarians in literature she called them to herself, forcibly vegetabled vegetarians ; and there was the silversmith who provided the Bishop with the crosses after a good Florentine fifteenth-century pattern he presented to those of his confirmation candidates who were the daughters in the diocese of the great. The Duke's daughter had one. The Lord-Lieutenant's daughter had one. On this principle Ingeborg herself had been given one, and wore it continually night and day, as her father expected, under her dress, where it bruised her. It was pleasant to her father to be able to recollect, in the stress and dust of much in his work that was unrefreshing, how there was a yearly increasing though severely sifted number of gentle virgin blouses belonging to the best families beneath which lay and rhythmically heaved this silver reminder of the wearer's Bishop and of her God.

'Father,' Ingeborg said, after she had worn hers for a week, 'may I take my cross off at night ?'

'Why, Ingeborg ?' he had inquired; adding quietly, 'Did our Saviour ?'

'No; but – you see when one turns round in one's sleep it sticks into one.'

'Sticks, Ingeborg ?' the Bishop said gently, raising his eyebrows at such an expression applied to such an object.

'Yes, and I'm getting awfully bruised.' She was still in the schoolroom, and still saying awfully.

'By His stripes we are healed,' said the Bishop, shutting up the conversation as one shuts up a book.

In spite of the wet warmth she shivered as the silversmith's window reminded her of this. It had happened years ago, but even farther back, as far back as she could remember, every time she had asked leave of her father to do anything it had been refused; and refused with bits of Bible, which was so peculiarly silencing.

And now here she was about to face him covered with the leaves she had not asked for at all but had so tremendously taken, and going to ask the most tremendous one of all, the leave to marry Herr Dremmel.

For that was how the last two days of her Dent's Tour had been spent, in being openly engaged to Herr Dremmel. She had found her attempts to explain that she was not so really availed nothing against his conviction that she was. And public opinion, the public opinion of the whole Tour, also never doubted but that she was, – had not seven of its most reliable members actually seen her in the act of becoming it ? In fact it not only did not doubt it, it was sternly determined that she should be engaged whether she liked it or not. It was the least, the Tour felt, that she could do. So that there was nothing for it now but to face the Bishop.

She felt cold. No amount of the familiar moist stuffiness could warm her. Vainly she tried to sit up, to be proud and brave, to recapture something at least of the courage that had seemed so easy just at the end in Switzerland with Herr Dremmel to laugh at her doubts. Her head would droop, and her hands and feet were like stones.

It was the place, the place, she thought, the hypnotic effect of it, of her old environment. The whole of Redchester was heavy with recollections of past obediences. Not once had she ever in Redchester even dreamt of rebellion. She had questioned latterly, in the remoter and less filial corners of her heart, but she had never so much as thought of rebellion. And the moment she got away out of sight and hearing of home, things she knew here were wicked had appeared to be quite good and extremely natural. How strange that was. And how strange that now she was back everything was beginning to seem wicked again. What was a poor wretch to do, she asked herself with sudden passion, confronted by these shuffling standards that behaved as if they were dancing a quadrille? This was the place in which for years her conscience had been cockered to size and delicacy; and though it had become temporarily tough in Herr Dremmel's company she felt it relapsing with every turn of the wheels more and more into its ancient softness.

Yet she undoubtedly, conscience-stricken and frightened or not, had to tell her father what she had done. She had got to be brave, and if needs be she had got to defy. She was bound to Herr Dremmel. He had only gone home to set his house in order, and then, he announced, she meanwhile having prepared the Bishop, he was coming to Redchester to marry her. Prepared the Bishop! She shivered. Herr Dremmel had tried to marry her in Lucerne; but the Swiss, it seemed, would not be hurried, so that here she was, and within the next few hours she was going to have to prepare the Bishop.

She shut her eyes and thought of Herr Dremmel; — of Robert, as she was learning to call him. With all her heart she liked him. And he had been so kind when he found she really disliked being engulfed in embraces, and had restricted his exhibitions of affection to the kissing of her hand, telling her he could very well wait till later on, sure that she would after marriage warm, as he had explained to her on the Rigi all women did, to a just appreciation of the value of the caresses of an honest man. He had also

produced a number of German love-names from some hitherto
fallow corner of his mind, and garnished his conversation with
them in a way that made her who, nourished as she had been on
the noble language of the Bible and the Prayer-book, was instantly
responsive to the charm of words, laugh and glow with pleasure.
She was his Little Heart, his Little Tiny treasure, his Little Sugar
Lamb, – a dozen little sweet diminished German things translated
straight away just as they were into English. The freshness of it!
The freshness of being admired and petted after the economies in
these directions practised in her home. And his ring at that very
moment dangled beneath her dress on the same chain as her
father's cross. Yes, she was bound to him. Duty, she perceived,
could be a very blessed thing sometimes if it protected one from
some other duty. It was Herr Dremmel now who had become her
Duty.

She put up her hand to get courage by feeling the ring, for her
spirit was fainting within her, – she had just caught sight of the
cathedral. The ring had been slung on the chain alongside the
confirmation cross because it was impossible to wear it on her
thumb; and out there in Switzerland, where one was simple, it
had seemed a most natural and obvious place to put it. Yet now,
as the fly rattled over the cobbles of the Close and the familiar
cathedral rose before her like a menace, she hung her head and
greatly doubted but what the juxtaposition was wicked.

Nobody was on the doorstep when she arrived beneath the
great cedar that spread its shade, an intensified bit of dripping
gloom where all was gloom and dripping, across from the lawn to
the Palace's entrance except the butler, whose black clothes struck
her instantly as very neat and smooth, and his underling, a youth
kept carefully a little on the side of a suitable episcopal shabbiness.
She had telegraphed her train from Paddington, but that, of
course, was no reason why any one should be on the doorstep. It
was she whose business lay with doorsteps when people arrived
or left, she was the one who welcomed and who sped, and, since
she could not welcome herself, there was nobody there to do it.

She stole a nervous look at Wilson as he helped her out, but his
face was a blank. The boy on her other side had an expression,
she thought, as though under happier conditions he might have let
himself go in a smirk, and she turned her eyes away with a little
sick feeling. Did they know already, all of them, that she had left

her aunt's a week ago? But, indeed, that seemed a small thing now compared with the things she had done since.

'I'm a dead girl,' thought Ingeborg, as she passed beneath her parents' porch.

The servants brought in her luggage, off which in her newness at deceit she had not thought to scrape the continental labels, and she crossed the hall, treading on the dim splashes of lovely blurred colour that fell from the vast stained glass windows on to the stone flags of its floor. It was the noblest hall, as bare of stuffs and carpets as the cathedral itself, and she looked more than insignificant going across it to the carved oak door that opened into the wide panelled passage leading to the drawing-room, a little figure braced to a miserable courage, the smallest thing to be going to defy powers of which this magnificence was only one of the expressions.

Her mother was as usual on her sofa near a fire whose heat, that warm day, was mitigated by the windows being wide open. Beside her was her own particular table with the usual flowers, needlework, devotional books, and biographies of good men. It was difficult to believe her mother had got off that sofa nine times to go to bed, had dressed and undressed and had meals – thirty-six of them, counted Ingeborg mechanically, while she looked about for the Bishop, if you excluded the before breakfast tea, forty-five if you didn't – since she saw her last, so immovable did she appear, so exactly in the same position and composed into the same lines as she had been nine days before. The room was full of the singing of thrushes, quite deafeningly full, as she opened the door, for the windows gave straight into the green and soppy garden and it was a day of many worms. Judith was making tea as far away from the fire as she could get, and there was no sign of the Bishop.

'Is that you, Ingeborg?' said her mother, turning her face, grown pale with years of being shut up, to the door.

Ingeborg's mother had found the sofa as other people find salvation. She was not ill. She had simply discovered in it a refuge and a very present help in all the troubles and turmoil of life, and in especial a shield and buckler when it came to dealing with the Bishop. It is not easy for the married, she had found when first casting about for one, to hit on a refuge from each other that shall be honourable to both. In a moment of insight she perceived the sofa. Here was a blameless object that would separate her entirely from duties and responsibilities of every sort. It was respectable; it was unassailably effective; it was not included in the Commandments. All she had to do was to cling to it, and nobody could make her do or be anything. She accordingly got on to it and had stayed there ever since, mysteriously frail, an object of solicitude and sympathy, a being before whose helplessness the most aggressive or aggrieved husband must needs be helpless too. And she had gradually acquired the sofa look, and was now very definitely a slightly plaintive but persistently patient Christian lady.

'Is that you, Ingeborg?' she said, turning her head.

'Yes mother,' said Ingeborg, hesitating in spite of herself on the threshold.

She looked round anxiously, but the Bishop was not lurking anywhere in the big room.

'Come in, dear, and shut the door. You see the windows are open.'

Judith glanced up at her a moment from her tea-making and did not move. Even in the midst of her terrors Ingeborg was astonished, after not having seen it for a while, at her loveliness. She seemed to have taken the sodden greys of the afternoon, the dulness and the gathering dusk, and made out of their gloom the one perfect background for her beauty.

'We thought you would have written,' said Mrs Bullivant, putting her cheek in a position convenient for the kiss that was to be applied to it.

'I – I telegraphed,' said Ingeborg, applying the kiss.

'Yes, dear, but only about your train.'

'I – thought that was enough.'

'But, Ingeborg dear, such a great occasion. One of *the* great occasions of life. We did expect a little notice, didn't we, Judith?'

'Notice?' said Ingeborg faintly.

'Your father was wounded, dear. He thought it showed so little real love for your parents and your sister.'

'But—' said Ingeborg, looking from one to the other.

'We wrote to you at once – directly we knew. Didn't we, Judith?'

'Of course,' said Judith.

Ingeborg stood flushing and turning pale. Had one of the Dent's Tour people somehow found out where she lived and written about her engagement and the impossible had happened and they weren't going to mind? Was it possible? Did they know? And were taking it like this? If only she had called at her aunt's house on the way to Paddington and got the letters – what miserable hours of terror she would have been spared!

'But—' she began. Then the immense relief of it suddenly flooded her whole being with a delicious warm softness. They did know. Somehow. And a miracle had happened. Oh, how *kind* God was!

She dropped on her knees by the sofa and began to kiss her mother's hand, which surprised Mrs Bullivant; and indeed it is a foreign trick, picked up mostly by those who go abroad. 'Mother,' she said, 'are you really pleased about it? You don't mind then?'

'Mind?' said Mrs Bullivant.

'Oh, how glad, how glad I am. And father? What does he say? Does he – does *he* mind?'

'Mind?' repeated Mrs Bullivant.

'Father is very pleased, I think,' said Judith, with what in one less lovely would have been a slight pursing of the lips. And she twisted a remarkable diamond ring she was wearing straight.

'Father is – pleased?' echoed Ingeborg, quite awestruck by the amount and quality of these reliefs.

'I must say I think it is really *good* of your dear father to be pleased, when he loses—' began Mrs Bullivant.

'Oh, yes, yes,' interrupted the overcome Ingeborg, 'it's a wonder – a wonder of God.'

'Ingeborg dear,' her mother gently rebuked, for this was excess; and Judith looked still more what would have been a little pursed in any other woman.

'When he loses,' then resumed Mrs Bullivant with the plaintive determination of one who considers it the least she may expect as a sofa-ridden mother to be allowed to finish her sentences, 'so much.'

'Yes, yes,' assented Ingeborg eagerly, whose appreciation of her parents' attitude was so warm that she almost felt she must stay and bask in its urbanity for ever and not go away after all to the bleak distance of East Prussia.

'Your father loses not *only* a daughter,' continued Mrs Bullivant, 'but £500 a year of his income.'

'Would one call it his income?' inquired Judith, politely but yet, if one could suspect a being with an angel's face of such a thing, with some slight annoyance. 'I thought our grandmother—'

'Judith dear, the £500 a year your grandmother left to each of you was only to be yours when you married,' explained Mrs Bullivant, also with some slight annoyance beneath her patience. 'Till you married it was to be mine – your father's, I mean, of course. And if you never did marry it would have been mine – I mean his – always.'

Ingeborg had heard of her Swedish grandmother's will, but had long ago forgotten it, marriage being remote and money never of any interest to her who had no occasions for spending. Now her heart bounded with yet more thankfulness. What a comfort it would be to Robert. How it would help him in his research. Extraordinary that she should have forgotten it. When he told her of his stipend of five thousand marks – £250 it was in English money, he explained, and there was the house and land free – most of which went in his experiments, but what was left being ample, he said, for the living purposes of reasonable beings if they approached it in a proper spirit, it all depending, he said, on whether they approached it in a proper spirit, 'And after all,' he had added triumphantly, throwing out his chest just as she was about to inquire what the proper spirit was, 'no man can call me *thin*—' – to think she had forgotten the substantial help she was going to be able to bring him !

The full splendour of her father's generosity in being pleased at her engagement was now revealed to her. The relief of it. The glad, warm relief. So must one feel who is born again, all new, all clean from old mistakes and fears. She felt lifted up, extraordinarily happy, extraordinarily good, more in harmony with Providence and the Bible than she had been since childhood. She would have been willing, and indeed found it perfectly natural, to kneel down with her mother and Judith then and there and say prayers together out loud. She would have been willing on the crest of her wave of gratefulness quite readily to give up Herr Dremmel in return for the family's immense kindness in not asking her to give him up. She had felt nothing like this exaltation before in her life, this complete being in harmony with the infinite, this confidence in the inherent goodness of things, except on the afternoon her tooth was pulled out.

'Oh,' she exclaimed, laying her cheek on her mother's hand, 'oh I do *hope* you'll like Robert !'

'Robert ?' said Mrs Bullivant ; and at the tea-table there was a sudden silence among the cups, as though they were holding their breath.

'His name's Robert,' said Ingeborg, still with her cheek on her mother's hand, her eyes shut, her face a vision of snuggest, safest contentment.

'What Robert, Ingeborg?' inquired Mrs Bullivant, shifting her position to stare down more conveniently at her daughter.

'Herr Dremmel. It's his Christian name. He's got to *have* one, you know,' said Ingeborg, still with her eyes shut in the blissfulness of perfect confidence.

'Herr who?' said Mrs Bullivant, a sharper note of life in her voice than there had been for years. 'Here's your father,' she added quickly, hastily composing herself into the lines of the unassailable invalid again as the door opened and the Bishop came in.

Ingeborg jumped up. 'Oh father,' she cried, running to him with the entire want of shyness one may conceive in the newly-washed and forgiven soul when it first arrives in heaven and meets its Maker and knows there are going to be no more misunderstandings for ever, 'how *good* you've been!'

And she kissed him so fervently in a room gone so silent that the kiss sounded quite loud.

The Bishop was nettled.

Was he then at any time not good? His daughter's excessive gratitude, really almost noisy gratitude, for what after all had been inevitable, the permission to go up to London and place herself in the hands of a dentist, suggested that humaneness on his part came to her as a surprise. He did feel he had been good to let her go, but he also felt he would have been not good if he had not let her go. Certainly Redchester opinion would have condemned him as cruel even if he himself, who knew all the circumstances, was not able to think so. What had really been cruel was the terrible muddle his papers and letters had got into owing to her prolonged absence. Grave dislocations had taken place in the joints of his engagements, several with far-reaching results; and all because, he could not help feeling, Ingeborg, in spite of precept and example, did not in her earlier years use her toothbrush with regularity and conscientiousness. Manifestly she did not, or how could she have needed nine enormous days to be set in repair? He himself, who regarded his body as a holy temple, which was the one solution of the body question that at all approached satisfactoriness, and had accordingly brushed his teeth from the point of

view of their being pillars of a sacred edifice after every meal for
forty years, had never had a toothache in his life.

'Let us hope now, Ingeborg,' he said, reflecting on the instance
she had provided of the modern inversion of the Mosaic law
which visited the sins of the fathers on the children, the original
arrangement, the Bishop felt, being considerably healthier, and
gently putting her away in order to go over to the tea-table where
he stood holding out his hand for the cup Judith hastened to place
in it, 'let us now hope, now you have had your lesson, that in
future you will remember cleanliness is next to godliness.'

And this seemed to Ingeborg an answer so surprising that she
could only stare at him with her mouth fallen a little open, there
where he had left her in the middle of the carpet.

But the Bishop had not done. He went on to say another thing
that surprised her still more; nay, smote her cold, shook her to
her foundations. He said, after a pause during which the silence in
the room was remarkable, his back turned to her while at the tea-
table he carefully selected the particular piece of bread and butter
he intended to eat, 'And pray, Ingeborg, why did you not write
the moment you heard from us, and congratulate your sister on
her engagement ?'

CHAPTER 8

Ingeborg was dumb.

Her father's question was like a blow, shocking her back to consciousness. The warm dream that all was well, that she was understood, that there was love and kindliness for her at home after all and welcome and encouragement, the warm feeling of stretching herself in her family's kind lap, confident that it would hold her up and not spill her out on to the floor, was gone in a flash. She was hit awake, hit out of her brief delicious sleep. Her family had not got a lap, but it had an entirely unprepared mind, and into that unprepared mind she had tumbled the name of Dremmel.

'Judith — engaged?' she stammered faintly, on the Bishop's wheeling round, cup in hand, to examine into the cause of her prolonged silence.

'Your incredulity is not very flattering to your sister,' he said; and Judith's eyelashes as she concentrated her gaze on the teapot were alone sufficiently lovely, the curved, dusky-golden soft things, to make incredulity simply silly.

Mrs Bullivant avoided all speech and clung to her sofa.

'It's — so sudden,' faltered Ingeborg.

'Much may happen in a week,' said the Bishop.

'Yes,' murmured Ingeborg, who knew that terribly too.

'We never can tell what a day may bring forth,' said the Bishop; and Ingeborg, deeply convinced, drooped her head acquiescent.

'No man,' began the Bishop, habit being strong within him, 'knoweth the hour when the bride-groom—' But he stopped, recollecting that Ingeborg was not engaged and therefore could not with propriety be talked to of bridegrooms. Instead he inquired again why she had not written; and eyeing her searchingly asked himself if it were possible that a child of his could be base enough to envy.

'I – didn't get the letters,' said Ingeborg, her head drooping.

'You did not? That is very strange. Your mother wrote at once. Let me see. It was on Friday it happened. It *was* Friday, was it not, Judith? You ought to know' – Judith blushed obediently – 'and to-day is Tuesday. Ample time. Ample time. My dear,' he said, turning to his wife who at once twitched into a condition of yet further relaxed defencelessness, 'do you think it possible your letter was not posted?'

'Quite, Herbert,' murmured Mrs Bullivant, closing her eyes and endeavouring to imagine herself unconscious.

'Ah. Then that's it. That's it. Wilson is growing careless. This last week there have been repeated negligences. You will make inquiries, Ingeborg, and tell him what I have said.'

'Yes father.'

'And you will discharge him if he goes on like this.'

'Yes father.'

'Unfaithful servant. Unfaithful servant. He that is unfaithful in a few things – '

The Bishop, frowning at it, took a second piece of bread and butter, and went over to the hearth-rug, where he stood from force of habit, in spite of the warmth of the day, drinking his tea, and becoming vaguely and increasingly irritated by the action of the fire behind him.

'Then,' he said, looking at Ingeborg, 'you know nothing about it?'

She shook her head. She was the oddest figure in the middle of the splendid old room, travel-stained, untidy, her face white with fatigue, her hat crooked.

Judith glanced at her every now and then, but it was impossible at any time to tell what the delicate white rose at the tea-table was thinking; so impossible that the young men who clustered round her like bees when they first saw her gave it up and went on presently to more communicative flowers. The local Duchess had hoped her first-born would marry her, – a creature so lovely, so entirely respectable with that nice Bishop for a father, and so happily adapted in the perfection of her proportions for the successful production of further dukes; and she pointed out various aspects of the girl's exquisiteness to her son, and told him he would have the most beautiful wife in England. But the young man, after a reproachful look at his mother for supposing he could have missed noticing even the humblest approach to a pretty woman let alone Judith Bullivant, said he didn't want to marry a picture but something that was alive and, anyhow, something that talked.

'She's right enough, of course,' he remarked, 'and I like looking at her. I'd be blind if I didn't. But Lord, dull? The girl hasn't got a word to say for herself. I never met any woman who looked so ripping and then somehow wasn't. She won't talk. She won't *talk*,' he almost wailed. 'She ain't got the remotest resemblance to anything approaching *kick* in her.'

'You might end by being thankful for that,' said his mother.

He would not, however, be persuaded, and went his way and married, as the Duchess had feared, a young lady from the halls, – a young lady nimble not only of toes but of wits, nimble, that is to say, as he proudly pointed out to his mother, at both ends, with whom he lived in great contentment, for she amused him, which is much.

'I have not observed you offer any congratulations, Ingeborg,' said the Bishop, becoming more and more displeased by her strange behaviour, and not at all liking her crumpled and forlorn appearance. He again thought of envy, but that alone could not crumple clothes. 'And yet your sister,' he said, getting a little further away from the fire which had begun to scorch him unpleasantly, 'is to be the wife of the Master.'

'The Master?' repeated Ingeborg, stupidly. For a moment her tormented brain supposed Judith must be going to be a nun.

'There is only one Master,' said the Bishop, in his stateliest manner. 'Everybody knows that. The Master of Ananias.'

Ingeborg knew this was a great thing. The Master of Ananias, the most celebrated of Oxford colleges, was in every way, except perhaps that of age, desirable; but what was age when it came to all the other desirabilities? Her father had rebuked her once for speaking of him as old Dr Abbot, and had informed her the Master was only sixty, and that everybody was sixty, – that is, said the Bishop, everybody of any sense. He was not a widower, he was pleasant to look at in a shaven iron-grey way, he was brilliantly erudite, and extremely well off apart from his handsome salary, one of the handsomest salaries in the gift of the Crown. Several years before, when Judith was still invisible in a pinafore, he had stayed at the Palace – it was then Ingeborg spoke of him as old – and had been treated by her father with every attention and respect. He had on that occasion seemed glad to go. Now it appeared he had been again, and must have fallen immediately and overwhelmingly in love with Judith for his short visit to bridge the distance between a first acquaintance and an engagement. Who, however, knew better than herself how quickly such distances can be bridged?

She wanted to go and kiss Judith and say sweet things to her, but her feet seemed unable to move. She wanted to congratulate everybody with all her heart if only they would be kind and congratulate her a little too. For Judith had heard what she said before her father came in, and her mother had heard it, and the room was heavy with the uttered name of Dremmel.

She looked round at them, – her father waiting for her to show at least ordinary decency and feeling, Judith so safe in the family's approval, so entirely clear from hidden things, her mother lying with closed eyes and expressionless face, and she suddenly felt intolerably alone.

'Oh, oh—' she cried, holding out her hands, 'doesn't anybody love me?'

This was worse than her toothache.

Her family had endured much during those days, but at least there was a reason then for the odder parts of her behaviour. Now they were called upon to endure the distressing spectacle of a hitherto reserved relative letting herself go to unbridledness. Ingeborg was going to make a scene; and a scene was a thing that had never yet, anyhow not during the entire Bullivant period, been made in that house.

Mrs Bullivant shut her eyes tighter and tried to think she was not there at all.

Judith turned red and again became absorbed in the teapot.

The Bishop, after the first cold shock natural to a person called upon to contemplate nakedness where up to then there had been clothes, put down his cup on the nearest table and, with an exaggerated calm, stared.

They all felt intensely uncomfortable; as uncomfortable as though she had begun, in the middle of the drawing-room, to remove her garments one by one and cast them from her.

'This is very sad, Ingeborg,' said the Bishop.

'Isn't it – oh *isn't* it—,' was her unexpected answer, tears in her eyes. She was so tired, so frightened. She had been travelling hard since the morning of the day before. She had had nothing to eat for a time that seemed infinite. And yet this was the moment, just because she had betrayed herself to her mother and Judith, in which she was going to have to tell her father what she had done.

'It is the most distressing example,' said the Bishop, 'I have ever seen of that basest of sins, envy.'

'Envy?' said Ingeborg. 'Oh no – that's not what it is. Oh if it were only that! And I do congratulate Judith. Judith, I do, I do, my dear. But – father, I've been doing it too.'

It was out now, and she looked at him with miserable eyes, prepared for the worst.

'Doing what, Ingeborg?'

'I'm engaged too.'

'Engaged? My dear Ingeborg.'

The Bishop was alarmed for her sanity. She really looked very strange. Had they been giving her too much gas?

His tone became careful and humouring. 'How can you,' he said quietly, 'have become engaged in these few days?'

'Much may happen in a week,' said Ingeborg. It jumped out. She did try not to say it. She was unnerved. And always when she was unnerved she said the first thing that came into her head, and always it was either unfortunate or devastating.

The Bishop became encased in ice. This was not hysteria, it was something immeasurably worse.

'Be so good as to explain,' he said sharply, and waves of icy air seemed to issue from where he stood and heave through the room.

'I'm engaged to – to somebody called Dremmel,' said Ingeborg.

'I do not know the name. Do you, Marion?'

'No, oh no,' breathed Mrs Bullivant, her eyes shut.

'Robert Dremmel,' said Ingeborg.

'Who are the Dremmels, Ingeborg?'

'There aren't any.'

'There aren't any?'

'I – never *heard* of any,' she said, twisting her fingers together. 'We usedn't to talk about – about things like *more* Dremmels.'

'What is this man?'

'A clergyman.'

'Oh. Where is he living?'

'In East Prussia.'

'In where, Ingeborg?'

'East Prussia. It – it's a place abroad.'

'Thank you. I am aware of that. My education reaches as far as and includes East Prussia.'

Mrs Bullivant began to cry. Not loud, but tears that stole quietly down her face from beneath her closed eyelids. She did not do anything to them, but lay with her hands clasped on her breast and let them steal. What was the use of being a Christian if one were exposed to these scenes?

'Pray why is he in East Prussia?' asked the Bishop.

'He belongs there.'

Again the room seemed for an instant to hold its breath.

'Am I to understand that he is a German?'

'Please father.'

'A German pastor?'

'Yes father.'

'Not by any chance attached in some ecclesiastical capacity to the Kaiser?'

'No father.

There was a pause.

'Your aunt – what did she say to this?'

'She didn't say anything. She wasn't there.'

'I beg your pardon?'

'I haven't been at my aunt's.'

'Judith, my dear, will you kindly leave the room?'

Judith got up and went. While she was crossing to the door and until she had shut it behind her there was silence.

'Now,' said the Bishop, Judith being safely out of harm's way, 'you will have the goodness to explain exactly what you have been doing.'

'I think I wish to go to bed,' murmured Mrs Bullivant, without changing her attitude or opening her eyes. 'Will some one please ring for Richards to come and take me to bed.'

But neither the Bishop nor Ingeborg heeded her.

'I didn't *mean* to do anything, father—' began Ingeborg. Then she broke off and said, 'I – can explain better if I sit down—' and dropped into the chair nearest to her, for her knees felt very odd.

She saw her father now only through a mist. She was going to have to oppose him for the first time in her life, and her nature was one which acquiesced and did not oppose. In her wretchedness a doubt stole across her mind as to whether Herr Dremmel was worth this; was anything, in fact, worth fighting about? And with one's father. And against one's whole bringing-up. Was she going to be strong enough? Was it a thing one ought to be strong about? Would not true strength rather lie in a calm continuation of life at home? What, when one came to think of it, was East Prussia really to her, and those rye-fields and all that water? She wished she had had at least a piece of bread and butter. She thought perhaps bread and butter would have helped her not to doubt. She looked round vaguely so as not to have to meet her father's eye for a moment, and her glance fell on the tea-table.

'I think,' she said faintly, getting up again, 'I'll have some tea.'

To the Bishop this seemed outrageous.

He watched her in a condition of icy indignation such as he had not yet in his life experienced. His daughter. His daughter for whom he had done so much. The daughter he had trained for years, sparing no pains, to be a helpful efficient Christian woman. The daughter he had honoured with his trust, letting her share in the most private portions of his daily business. Not a letter had he received that she had not seen and been allowed to answer. Not a step in any direction had he taken without permitting her to make the necessary arrangements. Seldom, he supposed bitterly, had a child received so much of a father's confidence. His daughter. That crumpled and disreputable – yes, now he knew what was the matter with her appearance – disreputable-looking figure cynically pouring itself out tea while he, her father whom she had been deceiving, was left to wait for her explanations until such time as she should have sated her appetite. Positively she had succeeded, he said to himself, bitterly enraged that he should be forced to be bitterly enraged, in making him feel less like a bishop should feel than he had done since he was a boy.

'It's because I've had nothing to eat since Paris,' Ingeborg explained apologetically, holding the teapot in both hands because one by itself shook too much, and feeling too that the moment was not exactly one for tea.

The Bishop started. 'Since where?' he said.

'Paris,' said Ingeborg; adding tremulously, having quite lost her nerve and only desiring to fill up the silence, 'it – it's a place abroad.'

Mrs Bullivant murmured a more definitely earnest request that Richards might be rung for to take her to bed.

'Ingeborg,' said the Bishop in a voice she did not know. 'Paris?'

'Yes, father – last night.'

'Ingeborg, come here.'

He was pointing to a chair a yard or two from the hearthrug on which he stood, and his voice was very strange.

She put down the cup with a shaking hand and went to him. Her heart was in her mouth.

'What have you been doing?' he said.

'I told you father. I'm engaged to Herr—'

'How did you get to Paris?'

'By train.'

'Will you answer me? What were you doing in Paris?'

'Having dinner.'

She was terrified. Her father was talking quite loud. She had never in her life seen him like this. She answered his questions quickly, her heart leaping as he rapped them out, but her answers seemed to make him still angrier. If only he would let her explain, hear her out; but he hurled questions at her, giving her no time at all.

'Father,' she said hurriedly, seeing that after that last answer of hers he did for a moment say nothing, but stood looking at her very extraordinarily, 'please let me tell you how it all happened. It won't take a minute – it won't really. And then, you see, you'll *know*. I didn't mean to do anything, I really didn't; but the dentist pulled my tooth out so quickly, that very first day, and so instead of coming home I went to Lucerne—'

'To— ?'

'Yes,' she nodded, in a frenzy of haste to get it all said, 'to Lucerne – I couldn't tell you why, but I did – I seemed pushed there, and after a while I got engaged, and I didn't in the least mean to do that either, really I didn't – but somehow—' Was there any use trying to tell him about the white and silver cake and the seven witnesses and the undoubting kind Herr Dremmel and all the endless small links in the chain? Would he ever, ever understand? – 'somehow I *did*. You see,' she added helplessly, looking up at him with eyes full of an appeal for comprehension, for mercy, 'one thing leads to another.' And as he still said nothing she added, even more helplessly, 'Herr Dremmel sat opposite me in the train.'

'You picked him up casually, like any servant girl, in a train?'

'He was one of the party. He was there from the beginning. Oh yes, I forgot to tell you – it was one of Dent's Tours.'

'You went on a Dent's Tour?'

'Yes, and he was one of it too, and we all, of course, always went about together, rather like a school, two and two – I suppose because of the pavement,' she said, now saying in her terror anything that came into her head, 'and as he was the other one of my two – the half of the couple I was the other one of, you know, father – we – we got engaged.'

'Do you take me for a fool ?' was the Bishop's comment.

Ingeborg's heart stood still. How could her father even *think*—'

'Oh father,' was all she could say to that; and she hung her head in the entire hopelessness, the uselessness of trying to tell him anything.

She knew she had been saying it ridiculously, tumbling out a confusion of what must sound sad nonsense, but could he not see she was panic-stricken ? Could he not be patient, and help her to make her clean breast ?

'I'm stupid,' she said, looking up at him through tears, and suddenly dropping into a kind of nakedness of speech, a speech entirely simple and entirely true, 'stupid with fright.'

'Do you suggest I terrorize you ?' inquired the incensed Bishop.

'Yes,' she said.

This was terrible. And it was peculiarly terrible because it made the Bishop actually wish he were not a gentleman. Then, indeed, it would be an easy matter to deal with that small defying creature in the chair. When it comes to women the quickest method is, after all, to be by profession a navvy . . .

He shuddered, and hastily drew his thoughts back from his abyss. To what dread depths of naturalness was she not by her conduct dragging him ?

'Father,' said Ingeborg, who had now got down to the very bottom of the very worst, a place where once one has reached it an awful sincerity takes possession of one's tongue, 'do you see this ? Look at them.'

And she held up her hands and showed him, while she herself watched them as though they were somebody else's, how they were shaking.

'Isn't that being afraid ? Look at them. It's fear. It's fear of you. It's you making them do that. And think of it – I'm twenty-two. A woman. Oh, I – I'm *ashamed*—'

But whether it was a proper shame for what she had done or a shocking shame for her compunctions in sinning, the Bishop was not permitted that afternoon to discover; because when she had got as far as that she was interrupted by being obliged to faint.

There was a moment's confusion while she tumbled out of the chair and lay, a creased, strange object, on the floor, owing to Mrs Bullivant's having produced an exclamation; and this to the Bishop, after years of not having heard her more than murmur, was almost as disconcerting as if, flinging self-restraint to the winds, she had suddenly produced fresh offspring. He quickly, however, recovered the necessary presence of mind and the bell was rung for Richards; who, when she came, knelt down and undid Ingeborg's travel-worn blouse, and something on a long chain fell out jingling.

It was her father's cross and Herr Dremmel's ring metallically hitting each other.

The Bishop left the room without a word.

CHAPTER 9

A pall descended on the Palace and enveloped it blackly for four awful days, during which Mrs Bullivant and her daughters and the chaplain and the secretary and all the servants did not so much live as feel their way about with a careful solicitude for inconspicuousness.

This pall was the pall of the Bishop's wrath; and there was so much of it that it actually reached over into the dwellings of the Dean and Chapter and blackened those white spots, and it got into the hither-to calm home of the Mayor, who had the misfortune to have business with the Bishop the very day after Ingeborg's return, and an edge of it — but quite enough to choke an old man — even invaded the cathedral, where it extinguished the head verger, a sunny octogenarian privileged to have his little joke with the Bishop, and who had it unfortunately as usual, and was instantly muffled in murkiness and never joked again.

That the Bishop should have allowed his private angers to overflow beyond his garden walls, he who had never been anything in public but a pattern in his personal beauty, his lofty calm, and his biblically flavoured eloquence of what the perfect bishop should be, shows the extreme disturbance of his mind. But it was not that he allowed it: it was that he could not help it. He had, thanks to his daughter, lost his self-control, and for that alone, without anything else she had done, he felt he could never forgive her.

Self-control gone, and with it self-respect. He ached, he positively ached during those first four black days in which his natural man was uppermost, a creature he had forgotten so long was it since he had heard of him, thoroughly to shake his daughter. And the terribleness of that in a bishop. The terribleness of being aware that his hands were twitching to shake, — hands which he acutely knew should be laid on no one except in blessing, consecrated hands, divinely appointed to bless and then dismiss in peace. That small unimportant thing, that small weak thing, the thing he had generously endowed with the great gift of life and along with that gift the chance it would never have had except for him of re-entering eternal blessedness, the thing he had fed and clothed, that had eaten out of his hand and been all bright tameness, – to bring disgrace on him! Disgrace outside before the world, and inside before his abased and humiliated self. And she had brought it not only on a father, but on the best known bishop on the bench; the best known also and most frequently mentioned, he had some-times surmised with a kind of high humility, in the – how could one put it with sufficient reverence? – holy gossip of the angels. For in his highest moods he had humbly dared to believe he was not altogether untalked about in heaven. And here at the moment of much thankfulness and legitimate pride when his other daugh-ter was so beautifully betrothed came this one, and with impish sacrilegiousness dragged him, her father, into the dust of base and furious instincts, the awful dust in which those sad animal men sit who wish to and do beat their women-folk.

He could not bring himself to speak to her. He would not allow her near him. Whatever her repentance might be it could never wipe out the memory of these hours of being forced by her to recognise what, after all the years of careful climbing upwards to goodness, he was still really like inside. Terrible to be stirred not only to unchristianity but to vulgarity. Terrible to be made to wish not only that you were not a Christian but not a gentleman. He, a prince of the Church, was desiring to be a navvy for a space during which he could be unconditionally active. He, a prince of the Church, was rent and distorted by feelings that would have disgraced a curate. He could never forgive her.

But the darkest hours pass, and just as the concerned diocese was beginning to fear appendicitis for him, unable in any other way to account for the way he remained invisible, he emerged from his first indignation into a chillier region in which, still much locked in his chamber, he sought an outlet in prayer.

A bishop, and indeed any truly good and public man, is restricted in his outlets. He can with propriety have only two, – prayer and his wife; and in this case the wife was unavailable because of her sofa. For the first time the Bishop definitely resented the sofa. He told himself that the wife of a prelate, however ailing

– and he believed with a man's simplicity on such points that she did ail – had no business to be inaccessible to real conversation. With no one else on earth except his wife can a prelate or any other truly good and public man have real conversation without losing dignity, or, if the conversation should become very real, without losing office. That is why most prelates are married. The best men wish to be real at times.

When Ingeborg stripped off her deferences, and, after having most scandalously run away and most scandalously entangled herself with an alien clerical rogue, had the face to hold up her hands at him and accuse him, accuse *him*, her father, of being the cause of their shaking, the Bishop had been as much horrified as if his own garden path on which he had trodden pleasantly for years had rent itself asunder at his feet and gaped at him. He had made the path; he had paid to have it tidied and adorned; and he required of it in return that it should keep quiet and be useful. To have it convulsed into an earthquake and its usefulness interrupted must be somebody's fault, and his instinct very properly was to go to his wife and tell her it was hers.

But there was the sofa.

He desired to converse with his wife. He had an intolerable desire for even as few as five minutes' real conversation with her. He wanted to talk about the manner in which Ingeborg must have been brought up, about the amount of punishment she had received in childhood; he wished to be informed as to the exact nature of the participation her mother had taken in her moral education; he wished to discuss the responsibility of mothers, and to explain his views on the consequences of maternal neglect; and he wanted, too, to draw his wife's attention to the fact she easily apparently overlooked, that he had bestowed a name grown celebrated on her, and a roof that through his gifts and God's mercy was not an ordinary but a palace roof, and that in return the least he might expect . . . In short, he wanted to talk.

But when driven by his urgencies he went to her room to break down the barricade of the sofa, he found not only Richards hovering there tactfully, but the doctor; for Mrs Bullivant had foreseen her husband's probable desire for conversation, and the doctor, a well-trained man, was in the act of prescribing complete silence.

It was then that, thwarted and debarred from the outlet a man prefers, he sought his other outlet, and laid all these distressful matters in prayer at the feet of heaven. On his knees in his chamber he earnestly begged forgiveness for his descent to naturalness, and a restoration of his self-respect. Without his self-respect what would become of him? He had lived with it so intimately and long. Fervently he desired the molten moments in which his hands had twitched wiped out and forgotten. He asked for help to conduct himself henceforth with calm. He implored to be given patience. He implored to be given self-control. And presently, after two days of his spare moments spent in this manner, he was sitting up on a chair and telling himself that the main objection to praying, if one might say so with all due reverence, is that it is one-sided. It is a monologue, said the Bishop – also with all due reverence – and in troubles of the kind he was in one needs to be sure one is being attended to. He did not think he could possibly be being attended to, because, pray as he might, withdraw and wrestle as he might, he continued to want to shake his daughter.

For there was the constant irritation going on of the affairs of the diocese getting into a more hopeless disorder. All that time she was away guiltily gadding, and now all this time she was not away but unavailable till she should have utterly repented, his letters were piling themselves up into confused heaps, and his engagements were a wilderness in which he wandered alone in the dark. The chaplain and the typist did what they could, but they had not been with him so long as his daughter and were not possessed of the mechanical brainlessness that makes a woman so satisfactory as a secretary. His daughter, not having what might be called actual brains, was not troubled by thought. The distress of possible alternatives did not disturb her. She did not, therefore, disturb him by suggesting them. She was mechanically meticulous. She respected detail. She remembered. She knew not only what had to be done, which was easy, but what had to be done exactly first. And both the chaplain and the typist were men with ideas, and instead of assisting him along one straight and narrow path which is the only way of really getting anywhere, including, remembered the Bishop, to heaven, they were constantly looking to the right and the left, doubting, weighing, hesitating. The chaplain had as many eyes for a question as a fly, and saw it from as many angles. Fairness, desirability, the probable views of the other side, their equal rightness, these things faltered interminably round each letter to be answered, were hesitated over interminably in the mellow intonations of that large-minded, well-educated young man's voice, and he was echoed and supported by the typist, who was also from Oxford, and had been given this chance of nearness to the most distinguished of bishops at such a youthful age that the undergraduate milk had not yet dried on the corners of his eloquent and hesitating mouth, and gave a peculiarly sickly flavour, thought the irritated Bishop, to whatever came out of it.

The Bishop felt that if this went on much longer the work of the diocese would come to a standstill. In ten days the Easter recess would be over, and he was due in the House of Lords, where he had been put down for a speech on the Home Rule Bill from the point of view of simple faith, and how was he to leave things in this muddle at home, and how was he to have the peace of mind, the empty clarity, appropriate to a proper approach of the measure if his inward eye went roving away to Redchester all the time and to the increasing confusion on his study table ?

The trail of Ingeborg was over all his day. When, warm and ruffled from prayer, he plunged down into his work again, he could not do a thing without being reminded she was not there. He was forced to think of her every moment of his time. It was ignoble, but without her he was like an actor who has learned not his part but to lean on the prompter, and who finds himself on the stage with the promptor gone dead in his box. She was dead to him, dead in obstinate sin ; and dignity demanded she should continue dead until she came of her own accord and told him she had done with that terrible affair of the East Prussian pastor. He did not know whether he would then forgive her – he would probably defer forgiveness as a disciplinary measure, after having implored heaven's guidance – but he would allow a certain amount of resurrection, sufficient to enable her to sit up at her desk every day and disentangle the confusion her wickedness alone had caused. In the evenings she would, he thought, at any rate for a time, be best put back to her grave.

At this point he began to be able to say 'Poor girl,' and to feel that he pitied her.

But it was not till the end of the week, as Sunday drew near, that his prayers did after all begin to be answered, and he regained enough control of his words if not of his thoughts to be able to reappear among his family and show nothing less becoming than reserve. He even succeeded, though without speaking to her, in kissing Ingeborg's forehead night and morning and making the sign of the Cross over her when she went to bed as he had done from her earliest years. She seemed smaller than ever, hardly there at all, and made him think of an empty dress walking about with a head on it. Contemplating her when she was not looking his desire to shake her became finally quenched by the perception that really there would be nothing to shake. It would be like shaking out mere clothes, garments with the body gone out of them; there would be dust, but little satisfaction. She had evidently been feeling, he was slightly soothed to observe, for not only was her dress empty but her face seemed diminished, and she certainly was remarkably pale. She struck him as very unattractive, entirely designed by Providence for a happy home life. And to think that this nothing, this amazing littleness – well, well; poor girl.

On the Sunday afternoon he determined to help her by getting into touch with her from the pulpit. On that day he several times assured himself before preaching that his only feeling in the sad affair was one of concern for her and grief. The pulpit, he knew from experience, was a calm and comfort-bringing place when he was in it; it was, indeed, his way with a pulpit that had brought the Bishop to the pinnacle of the Church on which he found himself. He was at his best in it, knowing it for a blessed spot, free from controversy, pure from contradiction, a place where personal emotions could find no footing owing to the wise custom that prevented congregations from answering back. Put into common terms, the terms of his undergraduate days, he could let himself rip in the pulpit; and the Bishop was in a ripped condition altogether at his greatest.

He spoke that Sunday specially to Ingeborg, and he told himself that what had come straight from his heart must needs go straight to hers. The Bible was very plain. It did not mince matters as to the dangers she was running. The punishment for her class of sin right through it was various and severe. Not that the ravens of another age and the eagles of a different climate, – he had taken as his text that passage, or rather portion of a passage – he described it as remarkable – in the Proverbs: 'The ravens of the valley shall pick it out and the young eagles shall eat it' – were likely ever miraculously to appear in Redchester, though even on that point the Bishop held that nothing was certain; but there were, he explained, spiritual ravens and eagles provided by an all-merciful Providence for latter-day requirements whose work was even more thorough and destructive. He earnestly implored those

members of his flock who knew themselves guilty of the particular
sin the passage referred to, to seek forgiveness of their parents
before Heaven interfered. He pointed out that what is most
needed, if people are to live with any zest and fine result at all, is
encouragement, and what encouragement could equal full and
free forgiveness ? The Bible, he said, understood this very well,
and the Prodigal Son's father never hesitated in his encouragement.
It seemed difficult to suppose one could equal the lavishness of the
best robe, the ring, the shoes, and the fatted calf, yet he felt certain
– he *knew* there were fathers at that very moment, there in that
town, nay in that cathedral, ready with all and more than that.
Who would wish to punish his dear child, the soul given into his
hands to be whitened for heaven ? One knew from one's own
experience – all who had once been children must know – how
sorry one was for having done wrong, how *bleeding* one felt about
it ; and just then, just at that moment of sorrow, of heart's blood,
was not what one needed so that one might get on one's feet again
quickly and do better than ever, not punishment but forgiveness ?
A frequent and free forgiveness, said the Bishop, and his voice was
beautiful as he said it, was one of the chief necessities of life. What
poor children want, poor frail children, so infinitely apt to fall, so
infinitely clumsy at getting up, is a continual wiping out and never
thinking again of the yesterdays, a daily presentation by authority
to yesterday's stumblers of that most bracing object, the cleaned
and empty slate. Why, it was as necessary, he declared, his fine
face aglow, if one was to work well and add one's cheerful
contribution to the world's happiness, as a nourishing and sufficient breakfast – the congregation thrilled at this homely touch –
and to numb a human being's powers of cheerful contribution by
punishment was *waste*. How cruel, then, to force a father by one's
stubbornness to punish ; how cruel and how sinful to hinder him,
by not seeking out at once what he so freely offered, to hinder
him from bringing forth his best robe, his ring, his fatted calf.
What a heavy responsibility towards their fathers did children
bear, said the Bishop, who had ceased himself being anybody's
child many years before. This, he said, is a sermon to children ; to
erring children ; to those sad children who have gone astray. We
are all children here he explained, and if life has been with us so
long that we can no longer find any one we may still with any
certainty call father, we are yet to the end Children of the
Kingdom. But, he continued, though every single soul in this

cathedral is necessarily some one's child, not every single soul in it is inevitably some one's father, and he would say a few words to the fathers and remind them of the infinite effect of love. To punish your child is to make its repentance go sour within it. Do not punish it. Love it. Love it continuously, generously, if needs be obstinately; smite its hardness, as once a rock was smitten, with the rod of generosity. Give it a chance of gushing forth into living repentance. Generosity begets generosity. Love begets love. Show your love. Show your generosity. Forgive freely, magnificently. Oh my brothers, oh my children, my little sorry children, what could not one, what would not one do in return for love?

The Bishop's face was lifted up as he finished to the light of the west window. His voice was charged with feeling. He had forgotten the ravens and eagles of the beginning, for he never allowed his beginnings to disturb his endings, well knowing his congregation forgot them too. He was an artist at reaching into the hearts of the uneducated. Everything helped him, – his beauty, his voice, and the manifest way in which his own words moved him.

And the typist, as he walked back to the Palace with the chaplain across the daisies of the Close, was unable to agree with the chaplain that a course at Oxford even now in close reasoning might help the Bishop. The typist thought it would spoil him; and offered to lay the chaplain twenty to one that Redchester that afternoon would be full of erring children upsetting their fathers' Sunday by wanting to be forgiven.

It was; and Ingeborg was one of them.

CHAPTER 10

She waylaid him after tea on the stairs.

'Father,' she said timidly, as he was passing on in silence.

'Well, Ingeborg?' said the Bishop, pausing and gravely attentive.

'I – want to tell you how sorry I am.'

'Yes, Ingeborg?'

'So sorry, so ashamed that I – I went away like that on that tour. It was very wrong of me. And I went with your money. Oh, it was ugly. I – hope you'll forgive me, father?'

'Freely, Ingeborg. It would be sad indeed if I lagged behind our Great Exemplar in the matter of forgiveness.'

'Then – I may come back to work?'

'When you tell me you have broken off your clandestine engagement.'

'But father—'

'There are no buts, Ingeborg.'

'But you said in your sermon—'

The Bishop passed on.

In her eagerness Ingeborg put her hand detainingly on his sleeve, a familiarity hitherto unheard of in that ordered and temperate household.

'But your sermon – you said in your sermon, father – why, how can free forgiveness have conditions? They didn't do it that way in the Bible' – (this to him who was by the very nature of his high office a specialist in forgiveness; poor girl, poor girl) – 'You said yourself about the Prodigal Son – his father forgave *everything*, and perhaps he'd done worse things even than going to Lucerne—'

'We are not told, Ingeborg, of any clandestine engagement,' said the Bishop, pursuing his way hampered, but, as he was glad to remember afterwards, calm.

'But you know about it – how can it be clandestine when you know about it?'

'Once more, Ingeborg, there are no buts.'

'But why shouldn't I marry a good man?'

She was actually following him up quite a number of the stairs, still with her hand on his arm, and her face, so unattractive in its unwomanly eagerness, quite close to his.

'Why should I have to be forgiven for wanting to marry a good man? Everybody marries good men. Mother did, and you never told her she wasn't to. Oh, oh—' she went on, as his dressing-room door was quietly closed upon her, 'that isn't free forgiveness at all – it isn't what you *said* – it isn't what you *said* – it's *conditions*' . . .

And her voice from the door-mat became quite a cry, regardless of possible listening Wilsons.

How glad he was that he had been able to put her aside quietly and get himself, still controlled, into his dressing-room. How strange and new were these reckless outbreaks of unreserve. And her reasoning, how wholly deplorable. She wished, unhappy girl, to enjoy the advantages and privileges of the forgiven state while continuing in the sin that had procured the forgiveness. She wished, he reflected, though in educated language, to eat her cake and have it too. Yet was it not clear that a free forgiveness could only be bestowed on an unlimited penitence? There could be no reservations of particular branches of sin. All must be lopped. And the East Prussian pastor was a branch that must be lopped with the cleanest final cut before real submission could be said to have set in.

But the Bishop in his dressing-room, though he retained his apparent calm, was sore within him. His sermon had failed. The girl must be a stone. It wasn't, he thought profoundly worried, as if he hadn't given her nearly a week for undisturbed thought and hadn't approached her that day with all the helpfulness in his power from the pulpit. Both these things he had done; and she was no nearer recovery than before. Was training them nothing? Was environment nothing? Was blood nothing? Was the blood of bishops, that blood which of all bloods must surely be most potent in preventing its inheritors in all their doings, nothing?

On the following afternoon there was a party at the Palace, arranged by Mrs Bullivant in the confident days before she knew what Ingeborg was really like. It was a congratulatory party for

Judith, and all Redchester and all the county had been invited. Nothing could stop this party but a death in the household, – any death, even Richards' might do, but nothing short of death, thought the afflicted lady, wondering how she was to get through the afternoon; and as she crept on to her sofa at a quarter to four to be put by Richards into the final folds and knew that as four struck a great surge of friends would pour in over her and that for three hours she would have to be bright and happy about Judith, and sympathetically explanatory about Ingeborg – who looked altogether too odd to be explained only by a long past dentist – she felt so very low that she was unable to stop herself from thinking it was a pity people didn't die a little oftener. Especially maids. Especially maids who were being so clumsy with the cushions . . .

And the Master of Ananias had been there since before luncheon, and how exhausting that was. She had had to do most of the entertaining of him, the Bishop being unavoidably absent from the meal, and Ingeborg, who did the conversation in that family, not being able to now because she was in disgrace, and Judith, dear child, never saying much at any time. And the Master had been very exuberant; and his vitality, delightful of course but just a little overwhelming at his age, had reminded her that she needed care. How difficult it had been to get him out into the garden, to somewhere where she wasn't. She hadn't got him there till half-past two, by which time he had been vital without stopping since twelve, and even then she had had to invent a pear-tree in full blossom that she wasn't at all sure about, and tell him she had heard it was a wonderful sight and ought not to be missed. But how difficult it had been. Judith had not seemed to want to show him the pear-tree, and he would not go and look at it unless she went too. Judith had gone at last, but with an expression on her face as though she thought she was going to have to bear things, and no girl should show a thought like that before marriage. And then there had been an immense number of small matters to see to because of the party, matters Ingeborg had always seen to but couldn't now because she was in disgrace, and how difficult all that was. Still, Mrs Bullivant felt deeply if vaguely that nobody temporarily evil should be allowed to minister to anybody permanently good. Such persons, she felt, should be put aside into a place made roomy for repentance by the clearing out of all claims. During the whole of the week since her daughter's return she had

not let her even pour out tea, either when the riven family was by
itself or when congratulatory callers came. 'Poor Ingeborg isn't
very well,' she had murmured, quenching the inquisitiveness
natural to callers. She had made up her mind that first evening,
when the full horror of what her daughter had done became clear
to her, that she would ask nothing of her, not even tea.

But it did make difficulties. She felt entirely low, quite damp
with the exertion of meeting them, when she crept into position
on the sofa at a quarter to four and waited with closed eyes for
the next wave of life that would wash over her. And it all
happened as she had feared, – she was perpetually having to
explain Ingeborg. Guest after guest came up with the expressions
of rejoicing proper to guests invited to rejoice over Judith, and the
smiling laudations of what was indeed a vision of beauty each
ended with a question about Ingeborg. What had she been doing ?
– (the awful innocence of the question –) ; how perfectly miserably
seedy she looked; poor little Ingeborg; was it really just that
tiresome tooth ?

Mrs Bullivant, as she murmured what she could in reply to this
ceaseless flow of sympathy from the retired officers and their
wives and daughters, and the cathedral dignitaries and their wives
and daughters, and the wives and daughters of the county who
came without their men because their men wouldn't come, felt
vaguely but deeply that it was somehow wrong that Ingeborg
should both sin and be sympathised with. She had no right, her
injured mother felt, to look so small and stricken. Her family had
quite properly removed her outside the pale of their affection till
she should announce her broken-off engagement to that dreadful
German and ask to be forgiven for ever having been engaged at
all, but she ought not to look like somebody who is outside a pale.
She seemed positively to be advertising the pale. It was bad taste.
It was really the worst of taste when you were the sinner to look
like the sinned against; to look ill-used; to droop openly. Yet
never could a girl who had done such horrible, such detestably
deceitful and vulgar things, have been treated so gently by her
family. It had been, Mrs Bullivant felt, the only good thing in a
wretched affair, the perfect breeding with which the Bullivants
had met the situation. Not one of them had even remotely alluded
to the scene she had made the first afternoon. No one had
questioned her, no one had troubled her in any way. She had been
left quite free, and no one had exacted the smallest sacrifice of her

time to any of their needs. Her father had given her a complete holiday, not allowing her at all in his study, and whenever she had attempted to do anything for her mother or in the house Richards had been rung for. Judith, dear child, seemed instinctively to do the right thing, and without a word from her mother avoided Ingeborg; she was so delicate about it, so fine in her feeling that here was something not quite nice, that she turned red each time Ingeborg during the first day or two tried to talk to her, and quietly went into another room. All the last part of the week Ingeborg had spent in the garden, quite free, quite undisturbed, not a claim on her. And yet here she was, standing about at the party or sitting alone in foolish corners, thin, and pale, and unsmiling, like a reproach.

Through a gap in the crowd Mrs Bullivant presently saw her being talked to by one who had once been a general but now in retirement wreaked his disciplines on bees. She just had time to notice how her daughter started and flushed when this man suddenly addressed her – such bad manners to start and flush – before the crowd closed again. She shut her eyes for a moment and felt very helpless. Who knew to what lengths Ingeborg's bad manners might not go, and what she might not be saying to the man?

What the general was telling her, with the hearty kindliness fathers of other daughters use to daughters of other fathers – will use, indeed, commented the Bishop observing the incident from afar and allowing himself the solace of an instant's bitterness, to any created female thing if only she will oblige them by not being their own – was that he couldn't have her looking like this.

'Oh, like what?' asked Ingeborg quickly, starting and flushing; for her week as an outcast had lowered her vitality to such an extent that she was morbidly afraid her face might somehow have become a sort of awful crystal in which everybody would be able to see the Rigi, and herself being proposed to on its top.

'Shocking white about the gills,' said the hearty man standing over her, cup in hand and see-sawing on his toes and heels because his boots creaked and it gave him a vague pleasure to make them go on doing it. 'You must come round and have a good game of tennis with Dorothy some afternoon. You've been shut up working too hard at that letter-writing business, that's what you've been doing, young lady.'

'I wish I had – oh, I wish I had,' said Ingeborg, pressing her hands together and looking up at this stray bit of kindliness with a quick gratefulness.

'We always think of you as sitting there writing, writing,' the hearty man went on, more intent on what he was saying than on what she was saying. 'Father's right hand, mother's indispensable, you know. I tell Dorothy—'

Ingeborg twisted on her chair. 'Oh,' she said, 'don't tell Dorothy – don't tell her—'

'Tell her what? You don't know what I was going to say.'

'Yes I do – about that's how daughters ought to be – like *me*. And Dorothy's so good and dear, and wouldn't ever in this world have gone off to—'

She stopped, but only just in time, and looked at him frightened.

She had all but said it. The general, however, was staring at her with kindly incomprehension. Her head drooped a little, and she gazed vaguely at his toes as they rhythmically touched and were lifted up from the carpet. 'Nobody knows what anybody else is really like inside,' she finished forlornly.

'You come up and have some tennis,' he said, patting her on the shoulder. And later on to the Bishop he remarked, in his hearty desire to have everything trim and in its proper place, the young in the fresh air, older persons at desks in studies, white faces reserved for invalids, roses blooming in the cheeks of girls, that he mustn't overwork that little daughter of his.

'Overwork!' exclaimed the Bishop, full of bitter memories of an empty week.

'Turn her out a bit into the sun, Bully my boy,' said the general whose fag the Bishop had been at Eton.

'Into the sun!' exclaimed the Bishop, having for six mortal days observed her from windows horribly idling in it.

'If you keep 'em shut up you can't expect girls any more than you can expect a decent bee to provide you with honey.'

'Honey!' exclaimed the Bishop.

That Duchess who had wanted her eldest son to marry Judith, tapped Ingeborg on the arm with her umbrella as she passed her followed by her daughter and said 'Little pale child, little pale child,' and shook her head at her and frowned and smiled, and whispered to Pamela that it looked very like jealousy; and Pamela said Nonsense to that, and tried to linger and talk to Ingeborg, but her mother, filled with the passion for refreshment that seizes all persons who go to parties, dragged her along with her to where it could be found, and on the way she was seen by the Bishop, who at once left the old lady who was talking to him to enfold Lady Pamela in his care and compass her about with a cloud of little attentions, – chairs, ices, fruit; for not only had he confirmed her but he felt a peculiar interest in her particular kind of clean-limbed intelligent beauty. Of all the confirmation crosses he had given away he liked best to think of Lady Pamela's. Certainly in that soft cradle, beneath the muslin and lace of propriety, he could be sure it would not jangle against an illicit and alien ring.

'You still wear it?' he said, his beautiful voice, lowered to suit the subject, charged with feeling as with his own hands he brought her tea; and he felt a little checked, a little disappointed, when she said, smiling at him, her grey eyes level with his so well grown was she, 'Wear what?'

And another thing this young woman did that afternoon that checked and disappointed him, – she showed a disposition to take care of him; and no bishop of sixty, or indeed any other honest man of sixty likes that. 'She thinks me *old*,' he thought with acute and pained surprise as she charmingly made him sit down lest he might be tired standing, and charmingly shut a window behind them lest he should be in a draught, and charmingly later on when he took her down the garden to show her the pear-tree turned her pretty head and asked him over her shoulder whether she were walking too fast. 'She thinks me *old*,' he thought; and it was an amazement to him, for only last year he was still fifty-nine, still in the fifties, and the fifties, once one was used to them, were nothing at all.

He became very grave with Lady Pamela. He felt that the showing of the pear-tree had lost a good deal of its savour. He felt it still more when, turning the bend in the path that led to the secluded corner that made the pear-tree popular as a resort, he perceived Ingeborg sitting beneath it.

She was alone.

'Why is she always by herself?' asked Lady Pamela, who was, the Bishop could not help thinking, being rather steadily tactless.

He made no answer. He was too seriously nettled. Apart from everything else, to have one's daughter cropping up . . .

'Ingeborg!' called Lady Pamela, waving her sunshade to attract her attention as they walked on towards her, for Ingeborg, under the tree, was sitting with her chin on her hand looking at nothing and once more advertising by her attitude, Mrs Bullivant would have considered, that she was outside the pale.

'I think,' said the Bishop pausing, 'we ought perhaps to go back.'

'Ought we ? Oh why ? It's lovely here. Ingeborg !'

'I think,' said the Bishop, now altogether annoyed at this persistent determination to include his daughter – as though one could ever satisfactorily include daughters – in what might have been a poetic conversation between beauty and youth on the one side and prestige and more than common gifts on the other, beauty, too, if you come to that, and as great in its male ripe way as hers in its girlishness – 'I think that I at any rate must go back. My wife—'

'Ingeborg ! Wake up ! What are you dreaming about ?'

Postively Lady Pamela was not listening to him.

He turned on his heel and left her to go on waving her sunshade at his daughter if that was what she liked, and went back towards the house reflecting that women really are quite sadly deficient in imagination and that it is a great pity. Even this one, this well-bred, well-taught bright being, was so unimaginative that she actually saw no reason why a man's grown-up daughter . . . Really a deficiency of imagination amounted to stupidity. He hardly liked to have to admit that Lady Pamela was stupid, but anyhow women ought not to have the vote.

He went away back into the main garden along the path by the great herbaceous border then in a special splendour of tulips and all the clean magnificence of May, thinking with his eyes on the ground how different things would have been if when he was a curate he had been sane enough not to marry. The clearness now in his life if only he had not done that ! Nobody sofa-ridden in it, no grown-up thwarting daughters, and himself vigorous, distinguished, entirely desirable as a husband, choosing with the mellow, yet not too mellow, wisdom of middle life exactly who was best fitted to share the advantages he had to offer. Even Lady Pamela would not then have been able to think of him as old. It was his family that dated him : his grey-haired wife, his grown-up daughters. The folly of curates ! The black incurable folly of curates. And he forgot for a gloomy instant what he as a rule with a sigh acknowledged, that it had all been Providence, even then restlessly at work guiding him, and that Mrs Bullivant and the girls merely constituted one of its many inscrutable ends.

The baser portion of the Bishop's brain was about to substitute another word for guiding when he was saved – providentially, the nobler portion of his brain instantly pointed out – by encountering the Duchess.

She was coming slowly along examining the plants in the border with the interest of a garden-lover, and pointing out by means of her umbrella the various successes to a man the Bishop took to be one of her party. He was a big man in ill-fitting shiny black with something of the air of one of the less reputable Cabinet Ministers and was, in fact, Herr Dremmel; but no one except Herr Dremmel knew it. He had arrived that afternoon, a man animated by a single purpose, which was to marry Ingeborg as soon as possible and get back quickly to his work; and he had come straight from the station to the Palace and walked in unquestioned with all the others, and after a period of peering about in the drawing-room for Ingeborg had drifted out into the garden, where he had at once stumbled upon the Duchess, who was being embittered by a prebendary of servile habits who insisted on agreeing with her as to the Latin name of a patch of Prophet-flower when she knew all the time she was wrong.

'You tell me,' she said, turning on Herr Dremmel who was peering at them.

'What shall I tell you, madam?' he inquired, politely sweeping off his felt hat and bowing beautifully.

'This. What is its name? I've forgotten.'

Herr Dremmel, who took a large interest in botany, immediately told her.

'Of course,' said the Duchess. 'I knew it was Arnebia even when I said it was something else. It's a borage.'

'*Arnebia echinoides*, madam,' said Herr Dremmel peering closer. 'A native of Armenia.'

'Of course they'll conquer us,' remarked the Duchess to the prebendary.

'Oh, of course,' he agreed, though he did not take her meaning, for he had been a prebendary some time and was a little slow, intellectually, at getting under way.

Then the Duchess dropped him and turned entirely to Herr Dremmel, who though he had never seen a herbaceous border in his life by sheer reasoning was able to tell her very intimately what the Bishop, who he supposed did the digging, had been doing to it the previous autumn, and the exact amount and nature of the fertilizers he had put in.

She was suggesting he should come back with her that afternoon to Coops and stay there indefinitely, so profound and attractive did his knowledge seem of what her own garden and her farm needed in the way of a treatment he alluded to as cross-dressing, when he interrupted her – a thing that had never happened to her before while inviting somebody to Coops – to inquire why there were so very many people in the drawing-room and on the lawn.

The Duchess stared. 'It's a party,' she said. 'To celebrate the betrothal. Don't you know ?'

'I am gratified,' said Herr Dremmel, 'to find the parents so evidently pleased. It adds a grace to what was already full of charm. But would it not have been more complete if they had invited me ?'

'I quite agree with you,' said the Duchess. 'Much more complete. Well, anyhow here you are. So you think my soil wants nitrogen ?'

'Certainly, madam. In the form of rape cape and ammonia salts – but combined with organic manure. Aritifical manure alone will not, in hot weather – who is that ?' he broke off, pointing with his umbrella to the Bishop advancing along the path, his eyes on the ground, sardonically mediating.

'What ?' said the Duchess, intent on the notes she was making of his recommendations in her notebook.

'That,' said Herr Dremmel.

The Duchess looked up. 'Why, the Bishop of course. Go on about the hot weather.'

'Her father,' said Herr Dremmel ; and he advanced, hat in hand, and the other held out in friendliest greeting, to meet him.

The Duchess went after him. 'Bishop,' she said, 'this is a man who knows all the things worth knowing.' And the Bishop, taking this to be her introduction of a friend, cordially returned Herr Dremmel's handshake.

He was never cordial again.

'Sir,' said Herr Dremmel, 'I am greatly pleased to make your acquaintance. My name is Dremmel. Robert Dremmel.

The Bishop had just enough self-control not to snatch his hand away, but to let Herr Dremmel continue to hold and press it. His mind began to leap about. How to get the Duchess away ; how to get Herr Dremmel turned, noiselessly, out of the house ; how to

prevent Ingeborg's coming at any moment along the path behind
them with Lady Pamela.

'We have every reason, sir,' said Herr Dremmel, holding the
Bishop's hand in a firm pressure, 'to congratulate each other, I
you, on the possession of such a daughter, you me—'

'Isn't she a lovely girl,' said the Duchess, for whom only Judith
existed in that family. 'Would rape cake and the other thing help
my flowers at all, or is it only for the mangels?'

'Mangels!' thought the Bishop, 'Rape cake!' And swiftly
glanced behind him down the path.

'Sir,' said Herr Dremmel, desiring to be very pleasant to the
Bishop and slightly waving the Duchess aside, 'permit me also to
congratulate you—'

'*Have* you had any tea?' inquired the Bishop desperately of the
Duchess, turning to her and getting his hand away.

'Thank you, yes. Well, Mr Dremmel? Don't interrupt him,
Bishop, he's *most* interesting.'

'—on the results,' continued Herr Dremmel to the Bishop, 'of
your autumnal activities. This blaze of flowers is sufficient witness
to the devotion, the assiduity—'

'You don't suppose he did it himself, do you?' said the Duchess.

'And your costume, sir,' said Herr Drummel, concentrated on
the Bishop and earnestly desiring to please, 'suggests a quite
particular and familiar interest in what this lady rightly calls the
things really worth knowing.'

'But he can't help wearing that,' said the Duchess.

Again Herr Dremmel, and with some impatience, waved her
aside.

'It is a costume most appropriate in a garden,' he continued.
'Even the gaiters are horticultural, and the apron is pleasantly
reminiscent of the innocence of our first parents. So Adam might
have dressed—'

'Oh, but you *must* come to Coops!' cried the Duchess. 'Bishop,
he's to come back with me.'

'Sir,' said Herr Dremmel with something of severity, for he was
beginning to consider the Duchess forward, 'is this lady Mrs
Bishop?'

'Oh, oh,' screamed the Duchess, while Herr Dremmel watched
her disapprovingly and the Bishop struggled not to seize him by
the throat.

'My dear Bishop,' said the Duchess wiping her eyes, 'I never had such a compliment paid me. The best looking Bishop on the bench—'

'*Do* come indoors,' he implored. 'I can't really let you stand about like this—'

'Thank you, I'm not in the least tired. Go on, Mr Dremmel.'

'Sir, can I see you alone ?' said Herr Dremmel, now without any doubt as to the Duchess's forwardness. 'On such an occasion as this, before we begin together openly to rejoice it seems fitting we should first by ourselves, unless this lady is your daughter's mother—'

'Oh, oh !' again screamed the Duchess.

The Bishop turned on him in a kind of blaze, quite uncontrollable. 'Yes sir, you can,' he said. 'Come into my study—'

'What ? Are you going to take him away from me ?' cried the Duchess.

'My dear Duchess, if he has business with me—' said the Bishop. 'I'll take you indoors first,' he said, offering her his arm. 'This gentleman' – he glared at him sideways, and Herr Dremmel, all unused as he was to noticing hostility, yet was a little surprised at the expression on his face – 'will wait here. No, no, he won't, he'll come too' – for approaching round the bushes behind which grew the pear-tree the Bishop had caught sights of skirts. 'Come on, sir—'

'But—' said the Duchess, as the Bishop drew her hand hastily through his arm and began to walk her off more quickly than she had been walked off for years.

'Come on, sir—' the Bishop flung back, almost hissed back, at Herr Dremmel.

'One moment,' said Herr Dremmel holding up his hand, his gaze fixed on what was emerging from the bushes.

'Come *on*, sir !' cried the Bishop, 'I can only see you alone if you come at once—'

But Herr Dremmel did not heed him. He was watching the bushes.

'Will you come ?' said the Bishop, pausing and stamping his foot, while he held the Duchess tight in the grip of his arm.

'Why,' said Herr Drummel without heeding him, 'why – yes – why it *is* – why, here at last appears the Little Sugar Lamb !'

'The little *what* ?' said the Duchess, resolutely pulling out her hand from the Bishop's arm and putting up her eyeglass. 'Heavens above us, he can't mean Pamela ?'

But nobody answered her; and indeed it was not necessary, for Herr Dremmel, gone down the path with a swiftness amazing in one of his appearance, was already, in the sight of all Redchester and most of the county, enfolding Ingeborg in his arms.

'Of course,' was the Duchess's comment to the Bishop as she watched the scene with her eyeglass up and the placidity of relief, 'of course they will conquer us.'

CHAPTER 11

And so it came to pass that Herr Dremmel, armed only with simplicity, set aside the resistances of princes, potentates and powers, and was married to Ingeborg by her father the Bishop in his own cathedral. And it was done as quickly as the law allowed, not only because Herr Dremmel was determined it should be, but because the enduring of his daily arrival for courting purposes from Coops, where he was staying, became rapidly impossible for the Bishop. Also there was the Master of Ananias, spurred to a frenzy of activity by Herr Dremmel's success in getting things hurried on, insisting that he had been engaged long enough and demanding to be married on the same day.

In the end he was, and Ingeborg's wedding, being Judith's as well, was unavoidably splendid. All along the line the Bishop's hand was forced. The very wedding-dress had to be as beautiful for the one as for the other of his daughters; and, absurdly and wickedly, he was obliged to spend as much on her trousseau who was going into pauperdom and obscurity for the rest of her days as on hers who would no doubt be soon, though of course only in God's good time, the most magnificent of widows. He never afterwards was able to feel quite the same to the Duchess. Without knowing anything of the circumstances, of the secret disgrace of the affair, of the blank undesirability in any case of such a son-in-law, of the extraordinary inconvenience and pecuniary loss of Ingeborg's marrying at all, she had taken up Herr Dremmel to an extent that was positively near making her ridiculous, supposing that, humanly speaking, were possible, and had rammed him down the county's throat till at last it believed that of the two husbands Ingeborg had secured the better. And this gossip filtered through into the Palace, and Judith, who never did speak, spoke less than ever, but edging away more and more decidedly from the blandishments of the Master, who had not been invited to Coops, spent most of her time in her own room engaged in not looking at her trousseau; and the Palace became such an uncomfortable place what with one thing and another, and the strain of remaining calm and becoming in conduct to the ducally protected Herr Dremmel was so great, that at last the Bishop was as eager as any one to get the wedding over and feverishly furthered any scheme that would, by hastening it, deliver him.

To Ingeborg he never spoke, but turned away with the same cold horror that came over the rest of the family when from windows he or it beheld her being courted with what seemed a terrible German thoroughness in places like the middle of the lawn. He could no longer walk round his own garden without meeting an interlaced couple; and though he suggested to Herr Dremmel with what he felt was really admirable self-restraint that these public endearments might give rise to comment, Herr Dremmel merely replied that as Ingeborg was his *Braut* it ought to give rise to much more comment, even to justifiable complaints, if his manner to her were less warm.

'In England we do not—' began the Bishop; but broke off for fear of losing his self-restraint. And Herr Dremmel and Ingeborg continuing to perambulate the garden slowly, with a frequent readjusting of their steps to each other's – for it is a difficult method, the interlaced one, of getting along a path – the Bishop and Mrs Bullivant retreated for refreshment and comfort to the delicacy of Judith, to her lovely withdrawals. That the Master should blandish was natural, because a man is natural; but they knew that a woman, if she is to approach any ideal of true womanhood, cannot be too carefully unnatural, and should she be persuaded or betrayed into some expression of affection for her lover, some answering caress, at least she must not like it. And there was Ingeborg progressing round the garden as described, or in the middle of the lawn openly having her hand held, and looking pleased.

It was rank.

Ingeborg, in fact, was pleased. She was more, she was extremely happy. Here she was suddenly no longer a disgraced and boycotted and wicked girl, but that strangely encouraging object, that odd restorer of faith in oneself, a Little Sugar Lamb. The *cosiness* of being a Sugar Lamb! She had been so very miserable. She had dragged through such cold, anæmic days. She had had such a horrible holiday, forced upon her on the very scene of her activities, and had had it brought home to her so freezingly, so blightingly, that she had done too dreadful a thing to be allowed apparently ever again to associate with the decent. And Robert – she quickly began calling him that to herself under the influence of her family's methods of reclaiming her – had not written a single letter.

'But he came,' said Herr Dremmel, for whose enlightenment she was picturing the week she had had.

And her father would not speak to her at all, would not look at her.

'Old sheep,' said Herr Dremmel good-naturedly.

And Judith had seemed entirely horrified, and used to blush if she tried to speak to her.

'Foolish turkey,' said Herr Dremmel placidly.

But now somehow it did seem as if she needn't have been quite so miserable, and might have had more faith.

'What ought the little one to have had more of?' asked Herr Dremmel; for his thoughts had not much time to spare, and he profitably employed them while she talked in working out the probable results of, say, the treatment of three acres of sugar-beet with sulphate of potash, sulphate of ammonia, and nitrate of soda respectively, all of them receiving 400 lbs of basic slag as well, – would not sulphate of ammonia be more effective as a nitrogenous manure than nitrate of soda in the case of sugar-beets, whose roots grew smaller and nearer the surface than mangels? 'This is what little women should constantly have more of,' he said, breaking away from sugar-beets to a zestful embracing; for on this occasion they were under the pear-tree, a place she seldom went to because she had not yet acquired, in spite of his assurances that she undoubtedly would, any real enthusiasm for embracings, keeping by preference to the only immune place in the garden, which was the middle of the lawn.

'I wonder,' she thought while it was being done, 'if this will really grow on me . . .'

And, while it was still being done, 'Mother must have been kissed too, and she's still alive . . .'

And presently, while it was still being done, 'But mother isn't *much* alive – there's the sofa – perhaps that's why . . .'

Well, he loved her; somehow; she did not now care how. Whether it was a spiritual affection or one that would go on requiring at frequent intervals to enfold her capaciously did not matter any more, for it was a warm thing, a warm human thing, he was offering her, and she had been half-dead with cold. What did it matter if she herself was not in love? It was the dream of a schoolgirl to want to be in love. Life was not like that. Life was a thing full of friendliness and happy affection; and love, anyhow on the woman's side, was not a bit necessary. The Bishop would have been surprised if he had known how nearly she approached his ideal of womanhood. She was going to be so good, she said to herself and to Herr Dremmel too, her heart full of gratitude and glad relief, – oh, so good! She was never going to be dejected or beaten out of hope and courage again. She would work over there, work hard at all sorts of happy things in the parish, and among the poor and sick, and she would help Robert in his work if he would let her, and if he wouldn't then she'd help him when he had done, – help him to play and rest. They would laugh together and talk together and walk together, and he would explain his experiments to her and teach her to understand. And the first thing she would do would be to learn German very thoroughly, so as to be able to write all his letters for him, and even his sermons if needs be, and save his precious time.

'Those,' said Herr Dremmel, who in the lush meadows of dalliance had forgotten that what had first attracted him to her had been a certain bright baldness of brain, 'would be pretty little nonsense sermons the small snail would produce.'

'You'll see,' said Ingeborg confidently; and she suddenly flung out her arms and turned her face up to the sun and the blue through the little leaves and all the light and promise of the world, and stretched herself in an immense contentment. 'Oh,' she sighed, 'isn't it all *good* – isn't it all *good*—'

'It is,' agreed Herr Dremmel. 'But it is nothing to how good it will be presently, when we are surrounded by our dear children.'

'Children?' said Ingeborg.

She dropped her arms and looked at him. She had not thought of children.

'Then, indeed, my little wife will not wish to write letters or compose sermons.'

'Why?' said Ingeborg.

'Because you will be a happy mother.'

'But don't happy mothers—'

'You will be entirely engaged in adoring your children. Nothing else in the world will interest you.'

Ingeborg stood looking at him with a surprised face. 'Oh?' she said. 'Shall I?' Then she added, 'But I've never *had* any children.'

'It was not to be expected,' said Herr Dremmel.

'Then how do you know nothing else in the world will interest me?'

'Foolish little one,' he said, taking her in his arms, his eyes moist with tenderness, for he knew that here against his breast he held in her slender youth the mother of all the Dremmels and the knowledge profoundly moved him. 'Foolish little one, is not throughout all nature every mother solely preoccupied by interest in her young?'

'Is she?' said Ingeborg doubtfully, quite a number of remembered family snapshots dancing before her eyes. Still, she was very willing to believe.

She looked at him a moment thinking. 'But—' she said, gently pushing herself a little way from him, both hands on his chest.

'But what then, small snail?'

'Wouldn't they be German children?'

'Undoubtedly,' said Herr Dremmel proudly.

'All of them?'

'All of them?' he echoed.

'It wouldn't be like Roman Catholics and Protestants marrying, and half the children be German and half English?'

'Certainly not,' said Herr Dremmel emphatically.

'But Robert—'

'Continue, little hare.'

'What are German children *like*?'

It was now Herr Dremmel's turn to say confidently, 'You'll see.'

A week later they were married; and the Bishop, inscrutably watching Ingeborg from the doorstep as she was being tucked in by deft hands into the rugs of the car that was to take her to the station, observing how cushions were put in the right places at her back, how a footstool was carefully inserted under her feet, how her least movement was interpreted and instantly attended to, made his farewell remark to his daughter – the last remark, as it happened, that he ever did make to her.

'You will miss Wilson,' he said; and re-entered the Palace a slightly comforted man.

She never saw him again.

PART 2

CHAPTER 12

On her honeymoon, which was only as long as it took to get from Redchester to Kökensee, except for a day in Holland where a brief and infinitely respectful visit, or rather waiting on, was made to the eminent De Vries, Ingeborg said to herself at frequent intervals as she had said to herself under the pear-tree in what now seemed a remote past, 'Perhaps this will grow on me.' But even before they reached Kökensee on the fourth day after their marriage she was deciding, though a little reluctantly for she had always heard them praised, that probably she had no gift for honeymoons.

Robert, luckily, was apparently liking his and was quite happy and placid and slept sonorously in the trains. The meals were invariably cheerful. From Bromberg on he woke up and became attentive to the country they were passing through; and once in his own part of the world he expanded into much talk, pointing out and explaining the distinctive features of the methods employed on the different farms along the line.

Ingeborg drank it in eagerly. She was zealous to learn; resolute to be a helpmeet. Had he not delivered her from the immense suffocation of Redchester? She was obsequious with gratitude. It was a country of an exhilarating spaciousness; no hedges, no shutting off of one field from another, no shutting off, indeed, of the sky itself or of the blue delicious distance by little interfering hills like those they had round Redchester. It was all one great sweep, one great roll of earth up to heaven and of heaven down to earth, fresh and free and with a quality in the air of clear bright hardness she thought adorable after the wadded effect of the climate at home. And once, when the train pulled up in the open, she could hear from far away up in the blue the cry of a hawk.

From Allenstein they went on by a light railway with toy

carriages and a tiny engine through an infinity of rye-fields and seemingly uninhabited country to the nearest station to Kökensee, a place called Meuk, of some pretension to being a little town, with an enormous church rising out of its middle and containing, among other objects of interests, explained Herr Dremmel, his mother.

'Oh?' said Ingeborg, surprised. 'Have you got one?' For he somehow produced a completely motherless impression.

'Invariably, my treasure,' said Herr Dremmel with patience, 'do people have mothers.'

'Yes,' she said, reaching down his hat for him and putting it carefully on his head, 'but then they say so.'

'Perhaps. Sooner or later. I well remember, however, informing you that my father was dead. From that it was possible to reason that my mother was not. She is a simple woman. No longer young. We will visit her on our way through the town.'

Outside the station a high vehicle drawn by two long-tailed horses, one of which reached a head and neck further than the other, so that when you looked at them sideways and could not see that they both began at the same place it seemed to be perpetually winning a race, was in readiness to take them to Kökensee.

'This,' said Herr Dremmel, introducing it with a wave of the hand, 'is my carriage. And this,' he continued, similarly introducing the driver, 'is my faithful servant Johann. He has been with me now nearly a year.'

Ingeborg shook Johann's hand, when he had carefully clambered down over the sacks of kainit that filled the front part of the carriage, very politely. 'Do they all stay as long as that?' she murmured to Herr Dremmel.

'All? There is but my widow, and she is adjusting her feathers for flight. She will wing her way to some other bachelor nest as soon as my little one has been inducted.'

'But does she like that?' asked Ingeborg. For she had acquired a habit, due to much repetition of the Litany, of regarding widows as brittle, needing special care. There was an instant's vision before her eyes of this one flapping blackly athwart the fields of East Prussia, turned out, desolate and oppressed, and with perhaps some cackling trail of curses stridulously marking her course.

'No doubt she will feel it. She too has been very faithful. She has been with me now nearly eight months. But if it were less she would still feel it. Widows,' he continued abstractedly, peering among the sacks of kainit in search of some Chilisaltpetre that was not there, 'are in a constant condition of feeling.'

Johann explained – he was a shabby man, grown grey and frayed, Ingeborg supposed, in service – that the precious stuff did not seem to have caught its train, and Herr Dremmel went off to make anxious inquiries of the stationmaster while Ingeborg stood smiling with an excessive friendliness at Johann to make up for her want of words, and wondering how her luggage would get on to a carriage already so much occupied by sacks.

In the end most of it did not and was left at the station till some future vague time, and clutching her dressing-bag with one hand and the iron rail of the carriage with the other she was rattled away over the enormous cobbles of Meuk with a great cracking of Johann's whip and barking of dogs and kickings of the horses, whose tails were long and kept on getting over the reins. The planks of the carriage's bottom heaved and yawned beneath her feet. The horses shied in and out of the gutters. Her hat wanted to blow off, and she did not dare let either of her hands go free to hold it. She bent her head to try to keep it on. Her skin pricked and tingled from the shaking. She had an impression of red houses flush with the street, railless dwellings giving straight on to it; of a small shop or two; of people stopping to stare; of straw and paper and dust dancing together in the wind.

Herr Dremmel chose these flustered moments to expand conversationally, and raising his voice above the tumult explained in shouts that the three sacks in front were not so much sacks as mysterious stomachs filled with the future. She strained to catch what he said, but only heard a word now and then when she bumped against him – 'divine maws – richly furnished banquet – potential energy—' She found it difficult to answer with any sort of connected intelligence, more especially because he kept on breaking off to lean forward and hit the horse-flies that alighted on the back of Johann's neck. When he did this Johann started and the horses kicked.

'Faithful servant' – he shouted in her ear – 'nearly a year – must not be stung—'

It was a disorganized and breathless Ingeborg trying to rub things out of her eyes who found herself finally in the passage of the elder Frau Dremmel's house.

The door stood ajar, and her husband pushed it open and called loudly on his mother to appear. 'She lurks, she lurks,' he said, impatiently looking at his watch ; and redoubled his cries.

'Does she expect us ?' asked Ingeborg at last, who was trying to pin up her loosened hair.

'She is a simple woman,' he said, 'consequently she never expects anything.' And he pulled open a door out of which came nothing but darkness and a great cold smell.

'That is not my mother,' he said, shutting it again.

'Does she know we're coming home to-day ?' asked Ingeborg, a doubt beginning to take hold of her.

'She is a simple woman. Consequently she never knows anything. Mother ! Mother !'

'Does she know you're married ?' asked Ingeborg, the doubt growing bigger.

'She is a simple woman. Consequently—' He broke off and stared down at her, reflecting. 'Is it possible that I forgot to tell her ?' he said.

It evidently was possible, for at that moment Frau Dremmel came slowly up some steps at the end of the passage from a lower region, and perceiving her son and a strange young woman stood still and said nothing whatever.

'Mother, this is my wife,' said Herr Dremmel, taking Ingeborg's hand and leading her to the motionless figure.

'*Ach*,' said Frau Dremmel, without moving.

'Kiss her, little one,' directed Herr Dremmel.

'Yes, yes,' said Ingeborg, blushing a vivid red and going a convulsive step nearer.

Frau Dremmel was regarding her with sombre, unblinking eyes, eyes that had the blankness of pebbles. From her waist downwards she wore a big dark-blue apron. She was entirely undecorated. Her black dress ended at the neck abruptly in its own binding and a hook and eye. Her hair was drawn back into the smallest of knobs. Ingeborg felt suddenly that she herself was a thing of fallals, – a showy thing, bedizened with a white collar and a hat she had till then considered neat, but that she now knew for a monstrous piece of frippery crushed on to insufficiently pinned-up hair.

'You are married to her ?' asked the elder Frau Dremmel, turning her pebble eyes slowly from one to the other.

'Undoubtedly,' said Herr Dremmel ; and to Ingeborg, in English, 'Kiss her, little one, and we will go on home.'

He himself put his arm round his mother's shoulder and gave her a hasty kiss.

'My wife is English,' he said. 'She does not yet either speak or understand our tongue. Kiss her, mother, and we will go on home.'

But it did not seem possible to get the two women to kiss. Ingeborg went another shy step nearer. Frau Dremmel remained immobile.

'This,' said Frau Dremmel, moving her slow eyes over Ingeborg and then fixing them on her son, 'is a pastor's wife?'

'Undoubtedly. I regret I omitted to tell you, mother, but one does occasionally omit.' And, in English to Ingeborg, 'She is a simple woman. Consequently—'

'But I heard,' said Frau Dremmel. 'Through your housekeeper. And others. Thus I heard. Of my only son's marriage. I a widow.'

Ingeborg, not understanding, stood smiling nervously. She thought on such an occasion somebody ought to smile, but she did not like doing it. The immobility of Frau Dremmel, who moved nothing but her eyes, the dark bare passage, the rush of cold smell that had escaped out of the one door in it, the bleak air of poverty about her mother-in-law – poverty in some strange way regarding itself as virtuous for no reason except that it was poor – did not make her smiling easy. But she was a bride; just coming home; just being introduced to her husband's people. Somebody, she felt, on such an occasion must smile, and, trained as she had been by her father to do the things no one else wanted to do, she provided all the smiling for the home-coming entirely herself.

'Please Robert tell your mother how sorry I am I can't talk,' she said. 'Do tell her I wish I weren't so dumb.'

'How much has she?' Frau Dremmel was asking across this speech.

'Enough, enough,' said her son, putting on his hat and making movements of departure.

'Ah. I am not to know. More secrets. It is all to go in further unchristian tampering with God's harvests.'

Herr Dremmel bestowed a second abstracted kiss somewhere on his mother's head. He had not listened to anything she said for a quarter of a century.

'Nothing for the mother,' she went on. 'No, no. The mother is only a widow. She is of no account. Yet your sainted father—'

'Farewell, and God be with you,' said Herr Dremmel, departing down the passage and forgetting in his hurry to get his bride home as quickly as possible to take her with him.

For a moment she was left alone confronting her new relation. She made a great plunge into filialness and, swiftly blushing, picked up her mother-in-law's passive hand.

She had meant to kiss it, but looking into her eyes she found kissing finally impossible. She shyly murmured an English leave-taking and got herself, infinitely awkwardly, out of the house.

'One has to have them,' was Herr Dremmel's only comment.

Kökensee lay three miles along the high road between Meuk and Wiesenhausen, and they could see the spire of its little church over the fields on the left the whole way. The road, made with as few curves as possible, undulated gently up and down between rye-fields. It was carefully planted on each side with mountain ashes, on that day in full flower, and was white and hard as though there had been no rain for a long while. The wind blew gaily over the rye; the sky was flecked with small white clouds. Ingeborg could see for miles. And there were dark lines of forest, and flashes of yellow where the broom grew, and shining bits of water, and larks quivering out joy, and everywhere on the higher places busy windmills, and the whole world seemed to laugh and flutter and sing.

'It's beautiful – oh beautiful !' she said.

'Beautiful ? I tell you what is beautiful, little one – the fat red soil of your girlhood's home. The fat red soil and the steady drip, drip of the heavens.'

And he bent forward and inquired of Johann when it had rained last, and became very gloomy on hearing that it was three weeks ago, and said things to himself in German. They seemed to be unpastoral things, for Ingeborg saw Johann's ears lifted up by what was evidently, in the front of his face, being a grin.

A weather-beaten sign-post with one bent arm pointed crookedly down a field-track at right angles to the road, and with a lurch and a heave they tilted round the corner. There was an immediate ceasing of sound. She could now hear all sorts of little birds singing besides larks, – chaffinches, tits, yellow-hammers, blackcaps. The carriage ploughed along slowly through the deep sand between rye that grew more reluctantly every yard. The horses were completely sobered and covered with sweat. Before them on an upward slope was Kökensee, one long straggling street of low cottages lying up against the sunset, its church behind it, and near the church two linden trees which were the trees, she knew for she had often made him tell her, in front of her home.

Ingeborg felt a quick tug at her heart. Here was the place containing all her future. There was nothing left to her to feel, she supposed, that she would not feel here. The years lay spread out before her, spacious untouched canvases on which she was presently going to paint the picture of her life. It was to be a very beautiful picture, she said to herself with an extraordinary feeling of proud confidence; not beautiful because of any gifts or skill of hers, for never was woman more giftless, but because of all the untiring little touches, the ceaseless care for detail, the patient painting out of mistakes; and every touch and every detail was going to be aglow with the bright colours of happiness. Exulting bits out of the Prayer-book, the book she knew altogether best, sang in her ears – *Lift up your hearts . . . We lift them up unto the Lord our God. . . .* Oh the beautiful words the beautiful world, the wonder and the radiance of life !

'When the Devil,' said Herr Dremmel, who had been scanning the crops on either side of the track with deepening depression, 'took our Saviour up on to a high place to tempt him with the offer of the kingdoms of earth, he was careful to hide Kökensee by keeping his tail spread out over it, it was so ugly and so undesirable.'

'Oh – the Devil,' said Ingeborg, shrugging her shoulder in a splendid contempt, her face still shining with what she had been thinking.

She turned to him and laughed. 'You can't expect *devils* to know what's what,' she said, slipping her hand through his arm and throwing up her head in a kind of proud glee.

He smiled down at her. 'Little treasure,' he said, for a moment becoming conscious that this was a very bright thing he had got and was bringing home with him.

The carriage was hauled up through an opening between two cottages out of the sand on to the stones of the village street by a supreme last effort of the horses, and was dragged in great bumps across various defects through an open gate on the opposite side. There was a yard with sheds, a plough, a manure heap, some geese, some hens, a pig, the two linden trees, and in between the linden trees behind wire netting a one-storied house like a vener-able bungalow, which Herr Dremmel, on their drawing up in front of it, introduced to her.

'My house,' he said, with a wave of the hand.

CHAPTER 13

There followed a time of surprising happiness for Ingeborg. It was the happiness of the child escaped from its lessons and picnicking gloriously in freedom and unrebukedness. The widow it is true slightly smudged the brightness of the beginning by, as it were, dying hard. Her body clung to life, – the life she had known, she lamented, for eight long months. She was the last, she explained, of the Herr Pastor's widows, who reached back in a rusty row to the days when he first came elastic with youth to cure the souls of Kökensee, and as she had stayed the longest it was clear she must be the best. She remained at the parsonage, dingily persistent, for several days on the pretext of initiating Ingeborg into the ways of the house; and each time Herr Dremmel, who seemed a little shy of embarking on controversy with her, mentioned trains, she burst in his presence into prayer and implored aloud on his behalf that he might never know what it was to be a widow. She did ultimately, however, become dislodged, and once she was gone there was nothing but contentment.

Ingeborg was young enough to think the almost servantless housekeeping a thing of charm and humour. Herr Dremmel was of the easiest unconcern as to what or when or if he ate. It was early summer, and there was only delight in getting up at dawn and pottering about the brick-floored kitchen before the daily servant came – a girl known to Kökensee as Müller's Ilse – and heating water, and making coffee, and preparing a very clean little breakfast-table somewhere in the garden, and decorating it with freshly-picked flowers, and putting the butter on young leaves, and arranging the jar of honey so that a shaft of sunlight between the branches shone straight through it turning it into a miracle of golden light. It was the sort of breakfast-table one reads about in story books; and on its fragility Herr Dremmel would presently descend like some great geological catastrophe, and the whole in a few convulsed moments would be just crumbs and coffee stains. Then he would put on leggings and go off with Johann to his experimental fields, and she would give herself up eagerly to the duties of the day.

She could not talk at first to Ilse, a square girl with surprisingly thick legs, because though she went about always with a German grammer in one hand she found that what she had learned was never what she wanted to say. Ilse, whose skirt was short, did not wear stockings, and when Ingeborg by pointing and producing a pair had conveyed to her that it would be well if she did, Ilse raised her voice and said that she had no money to get a husband with but at least, and *Gott sei Dank*, she had these two fine legs, and if the Frau Pastor demanded that she should by hiding them give up her chances, then the Frau Pastor had best seek some girl on whom they grew crooked or lean, and who for those reasons would only be too glad to cover them up. Ingeborg, not understanding a word but apprehending a great objection, smiled benevolently and put the stockings away, and Ilse's legs went on being bare. They worked together in great harmony, for there could be no argument. Cut off from conversation, they sang; and Ingeborg sang hymns because her memory was packed with them, and Ilse sang long loud ballads, going through them slowly verse by verse in a sort of steady howl. The very geese paused on their way to the pond to listen anxiously.

Dinner, which Ingeborg found convenient to prepare entirely in one pot, simmered placidly on the stove from twelve o'clock onwards. Anybody who was hungry went and ate it. You threw in potatoes and rice and bits of meat and carrots and cabbages and fat and salt, and there you were. What are these mysterious difficulties of housekeeping, she asked herself, that people shake their heads over? Her dinners were wholesome always, delicious if one were hungry, and quite amazingly hot. They stayed hot as persistently as poultices. And once when Ilse had the misfortune to be stung by a wasp on one of her admirable legs, Ingeborg, with immense presence of mind, seized the dinner and emptying it into a fair linen cloth bound it over the swollen place; so that when Herr Dremmel arrived, as it happened hungrily that day, about two o'clock and asked for his dinner, he was told it was on Ilse's leg and had to eat sandwiches. He could not but admire the resourcefulness of Ingeborg; but it was not until he had eaten several sandwiches that he was able still to say, as he patted her shoulder, 'Little Treasure.'

It was the busiest, happiest time. Every minute of the day was full. It was life at first hand, not drained dry of its elemental excellences by being squeezed first through the medium of servants. To have a little kitchen all to yourself, to be really mistress of every corner of your house, to watch the career of your food from its very beginning, to run out into the garden and pull up anything you happened to want, to stand at the back door with your skirt full of grain and call your own chickens round you and feed them, to go yourself and look for eggs, to fill the funny little dark rooms with flowers and measure the stone-floored passage for a drugget you would presently order in the only carpet shop you had faith in, which was the one in Redchester, – what pleasures did the world contain that could possibly come up to these? Things were a little untidy, but what did that matter? It was possible to become the slave of things; possible to miss life in preparation for living.

And the weather was so beautiful, – at least, Ingeborg thought it was. There was the hottest sun, and the coolest wind, and bright, clear-skied starry nights. It is true Robert, when he scanned the naked heavens the last thing at night and peered at the thermometer outside his window the first thing in the morning, said it was the Devil's own weather, and that if there was not soon some rain all his fertilizers, all his activities, all his expenditure would be wasted; but though this would throw a shadow for a moment across her joy in each new wonderful morning she found it impossible not to rejoice in the light. Out in the garden, for instance, down there beyond the lime trees at the end, where you could stand in the gap in the lilac hedge and look straight out across the rye-fields, the immense unending rye-fields, dipping and rising, delicate grey, delicate green, shining in sunlight, dark beneath a cloud, restlessly waving, on and on, till over away at the end of things they got to the sky and were only stopped by brushing up against it, – out there with one's hand shading one's eyes from the too great brightness, who could find fault with anything, who could do anything but look and see that it was all very good? Oh, but it *was* good. It made one want to sing the Te Deum, or the Magnificat, or still better that hymn of exultation, *We praise Thee, we bless Thee, we worship Thee, we glorify Thee, we give thanks to Thee for Thy great glory. . . .*

Whenever there was a spare half-hour, such as between where
dinner ended and tea began, she would run out to the lime-trees,
and pacing up and down that leafy place with the gooseberry
bushes and vegetables and straggling accidental flowers of the
garden lying hotly in the sun between her and the back of the
house, she learned German words by heart. She learned them
aloud from her grammar, saying them over and over again glibly,
mechanically, while her thoughts danced about the future, from
the immediate future of what she would do to-morrow, the future
of an afternoon in the punt among the reeds and perhaps paddling
along to where the forest began, to the more responsible vaguer
future of further down the months, when, armed with German,
she would begin among the poor and go out into the parish and
make friends with the peasants and be a real pastor's wife.
Particularly she wished to get nearer her mother-in-law. It seemed
to her to be her first duty to get near her. Ceaselessly she trotted
up and down repeating the German for giants, umbrellas, keys,
spectacles, wax, fingers, thunder, beards, princes, boats and
shoulders. Ceaselessly her lips moved, while her eyes followed the
movements of the birds darting in and out of the lilac hedge and
hopping among the crumbs where breakfast had been; and
through her giants, umbrellas, keys, spectacles and wax she
managed not to miss a word the yellow-hammers were chirping to
each other in cheerful strophe and antistrophe: *A little bit of
bread and no che-e-e-e-ese — a little bit of bread and no che-e-e-
e-e-ese.*

At four she would go in and make some coffee by the simple
method of uniting the coffee to hot water and leaving them to
settle down together on the mat outside the laboratory's locked
door. Herr Dremmel did not wish to be disturbed once he was in
there, and she would steal down the passage on tip-toe, biting her
under-lip in the intentness of her care that no rattling of the things
on the tray should reach his ears.

When he was in the house all singing ceased. She arranged that
Ilse should do her outdoor duties then, — clean out the hen-house,
milk the cow whether it wanted to be milked or not, and minister
to the pig. Johann was away all day at the experiment ground,
and Ilse waded about the farmyard mess with her bare legs
thoroughly enjoying herself, for no one ever scolded her whatever
she did, and the yard was separated from the village street only by
a low fence, and the early manhood of Kökensee, as it passed,

could pause and lean on this and learn from her manner of solacing the pig the comfortableness of the solacements awaiting her husband.

At seven Ilse went home, and Ingeborg prepared a supper so much like breakfast that nobody could have told it was evening and not morning except that the ray of sunshine fell through the honey from the west instead of the east, and there was cheese. At this meal Herr Dremmel, full of his fertilizers, was mostly in a profound abstraction. He drank the coffee with which he was becoming saturated and ate great slices of bread and cheese in an impenetrable silence. Ingeborg sat throwing crumbs to the birds and watching the sky at the edge of the world grow first a mighty red, then fade, then light up into clear green; and long after the shadows beneath the lime-trees were black and the stars and the bats were out and the frogs down in the reeds of the lake and the occasional creaking of the village pump were all that one could hear outside the immense stillness, they would go on sitting there, Herr Dremmel silently smoking, Ingeborg silently making plans.

Sometimes she would get up and cross over to him and bend her face down close to his and try in the dark to explore his eyes with hers. 'The *noise* you make!' she would say, brushing a kiss, so much used does marriage make one to what once has seemed impossible, across the top of his hair; and he would wake up and smile and pat her shoulder and tell her she was a good little wife.

Then she felt proud. It was just what she wanted to be, – a good little wife. She wanted to give satisfaction, to be as helpful to him as she had been to her father in the days before her disgrace; and more helpful, for he was so much kinder, he was so dear. For this extraordinary happiness, for this delicious safety from disapproval, for these free, fearless, wonderful days, she would give in return all she had, all she was, all she could teach herself and train herself to be.

Nearly always Herr Dremmel went back to his laboratory about ten and worked till after midnight; and she would lie awake in the funny bare bedroom across the passage as long as she could so as not to miss too much of life by being asleep, smelling with the delight delicate sweet smells gave her the various fragrances of the resting garden. And the stars blinked in through the open window, and she could see the faint whiteness of a bush of guelder roses against the curtain of the brooding night. When Herr Dremmel came in he shut the window.

On Sundays there was a service at two o'clock once a fortnight. On the alternating Sundays Herr Dremmel was driven by Johann to another village three miles distant which was part of his scattered parish, and here he preached the sermon he had preached to Kökensee the Sunday before. He practised a rigorous economy in sermons; and it had this advantage that an enthusiast – only there was no enthusiast – by waiting a week and walking three miles, most of which was deep sand, might hear again anything that had struck him the previous week. By waiting a year, indeed, the same enthusiast, supposing him there, could hear everything again, for Herr Dremmel's sermons numbered twenty-six and were planned to begin on January 1st with the Circumcision, and leaping along through the fortnights of the year ended handsomely and irregularly with an extra one at Christmas. However inattentive a member of the congregation might be, as the years passed over him he knew the sermons. They were sermons weighty, according to the season, either with practical advice or with wrathful expositions of duty. There was one every year when the threshing time was at hand on the text Micah iv. 13 *Arise and thresh*, explaining with patient exactitude the newest methods of doing it. There was the annual Harvest Thanksgiving sermon on Matthew xiii, part of verse 26, *Tares*, after yet another year of the congregation's obstinate indifference to chemical manure. There was the sermon on Jeremiah ix. 22, *Is there no physician there?* preached yearly on one of the later Sundays in Trinity when the cold, continuous rains of autumn were finding out the weak spots in the parish's grandparents, and the peasants, having observed that once one called in a doctor the sick person got better and one had to pay the doctor into the bargain, evaded calling him in if they possibly could, inquiring of each other gloomily how one was to live if death were put a stop to. And there was the Advent sermon when the annual slaughter of pigs grew near, on Isaiah lxv, part of the 4th verse, *Swine's flesh*.

This sermon filled the church. In spite of the poor opinion of pigs in both the Old and New Testaments, where, Herr Dremmel found on searching for a text, they were hardly mentioned except as convenient receptacles for devils, in his parishioners' lives they provided the nearest, indeed the only, approach to the finer emotions, to gratitude, love, wonder. The peasant, watching this pink chalice of his future joys, this mysterious moving crucible into which whatever dreary dregs and leavings he threw, uttermost dregs of uttermost dregs that even his lean dog would not touch, they still by Christmas emerged as sausages, could not but feel at least some affection, at least some little touch of awe. While his relations were ill and having to have either a doctor or a funeral and sometimes, rousing him to fury, both, or if not ill were well and requiring food and clothing, his pig walked about pink and naked, giving no trouble, needing no money spent on it, placidly transmuting into the fat of future feastings that which without it would have become, in heaps, a source of flies and corruption. Herr Dremmel on pigs was full of intimacy and local warmth. He was more – he was magnificent. It was the sermon in the year which never failed to fill every seat, and it was the one day on which Kökensee felt its pastor thoroughly understood it.

Ingeborg went diligently to church whenever there was church to go to. She explained to Herr Dremmel that she held it to be her duty as the pastor's wife to set an example in this matter, and he pinched her ear and replied that it might possibly be good for her German. He seemed to think nothing of her duty as a pastor's wife; and when she suggested that perhaps she ought to begin and go the rounds of the cottages and not wait for greater stores of language, he only remarked that little women's duty is to make their husbands happy.

'But don't I?' she asked confidently, seizing his coat in both her hands.

'Of course. See how sleek I become.'

'And I can do something besides that.'

'Nothing so good. Nothing half so good.'

'But Robert, one thing doesn't exclude—'

Herr Dremmel had already however ceased to listen. His thoughts had slid off again. She seemed to sit in his mind on the top of a slope up which he occasionally clambered and caressed her. Eagerly on these visits she would buttonhole him with talk and ask him questions so that he might linger, but even while she buttonholed his gaze would become abstracted and off he slid, leaving her peering after him over the edge filled with a mixture of affection, respect for his work, pride in him, and amusement.

You might as well try, she thought, to buttonhole water; and she would laugh and go back to whatever she was doing with a blithe feeling that it was very ideal, this perfect independence of one another, this spaciousness of freedom to do exactly what each one liked. The immense tracts of time she had! How splendid this leisure was after the close detail of every hour at home in her father's study. When she had got over the first difficulties of German and need no longer devote most of her day to it she would get books from England and read and read; all the ones she had wanted to read but had not been allowed to. Oh the magnificence of marriage, thought Ingeborg, beating her hands together, the splendour of its liberations ! She would go off in the morning with the punt full of books, and spend long glorious days away in the forest lying on the green springy carpet of whortleberries, reading. She would most diligently work at furnishing her empty mind. She would sternly endeavour to train it not to jump.

All the books she possessed she had brought with her and spread over the living-room: the wedding-presents which had enriched her with Hardy and Meredith and Kipling and Tennyson and Ruskin, and her own books she had had as a girl. These were three, the Christian Year, given to her on her confirmation by her father, Longfellow's Poems, given her on her eighteenth birthday by her mother, and Dumas' *Tulipe Noire*, given her as a prize for French because Judith did not know any, one summer when a French governess was introduced (thoughtlessly, the Bishop said afterwards) into the Palace. This lady had been removed from the Palace again a little later with care, every corner of her room being scrupulously disinfected by the searching of Richards who found, however, nothing except one book in a yellow paper cover called *Bibi et Lulu: Mœurs du Montparnasse*; and even this was not in her room at all, but in Judith's, beneath some stockings.

Herr Dremmel took up one of the wedding volumes when first he saw them in the sitting-room and turned its pages. It was *The Shaving of Shagpat*. 'Tut, tut,' he said presently, putting it down.

'Why, Robert ?' asked Ingeborg, eager to hear what he thought. But he patted her abstractedly, already slid off again down into regions of reality, the regions in which his brain incessantly worked out possible chemical combinations and forgot with a completeness that sometimes even surprised himself that he had a wife. Invariably, however, he found it pleasant on re-emerging to remember her.

She asked to be shown his experimental fields, and he took her with him very amiably one hot morning, promising to explain them to her ; but instantly on reaching them he became absorbed, and after she had spent an hour sitting on a stone at the edge of a strip of lupins beneath a haggard little fir tree which gave the solitary bit of shade in that burning desert watching him going up and down the different strips examining apparently every single plant with Johann, she began to think she had better go home and look after the dinner, and waving a good-bye to him, which he did not see, she went.

A day or two later she asked whether it would not be good and pleasant that his mother should come over to tea with them soon.

He replied amiably that it would be neither good nor pleasant.

She asked whether it might not be a duty of theirs to invite her.

He replied, after consideration. 'Perhaps.'

She asked whether he did not love his mother.

He replied unhesitatingly, 'No.'

She then went and sat on his knee and caught hold of his ears and pulled his head up so that he should look at her.

'But Robert—' she said.

'Well, little sheep?'

Since their marriage he had instinctively left off calling her a lamb. The universe, which for a time she had managed to reduce into just a setting for one little female thing, had arranged itself into its proper lines again; the lamb had become a sheep, – a little one, but yet no longer and never again a lamb. He was glad he had been able to be so thoroughly in love. He was glad he had so promptly applied the remedy of marriage. His affection for his wife was quite satisfactory: it was calm, it was deep, it interfered with nothing. She held the honourable position he had always, even at his most enamoured moments, known she would ultimately fill, the position next best in his life after the fertilizers. His house, so long murky with widows, was now a bright place because of her. Approaching poetry, he likened her to a little flitting busy bird in spring. Always he was pleased when she came and perched on his knee.

'Well, little sheep?' he said, smiling at her as she looked very close into his eyes.

Her face, seen so near, was charming in its delicate detail, in its young perfection of texture and colouring. Scrutinizing her eyes he was glad to notice once again how intelligent they were. Presently there would be sturdy boys tumbling about the garden with eyes like that, grey and honest and intelligent. His boys. Carrying on, far more efficiently, the work he had begun.

'Well, little sheep?' he said, suddenly moved.

'*Oughtn't* one to love one's mother?' she asked.

'Perhaps. But one does not. Do you?'

'Oh poor mother—' said Ingeborg quickly.

Her mother, far away, was already becoming a rather sad and a quite tender memory. All those days and years on a sofa, and all the days and years still to come ... Now she knew better, now that she was married herself, what it must have been like to be married to the Bishop, to have twenty years of unadulterated Bishop. She no longer wondered at the sofa. She was full of understanding and pity.

'One does, no doubt, at the beginning,' said Herr Dremmel.

'And then leaves off? Is that all children are born for, that they may leave off loving us?'

He became cautious. He talked of the general and the individual. Of many mothers and some mothers. Of the mothers of the present generation – he called them the *Gewesene* – and the mothers of the generation to be born – he called them the *Werdende*. And presently, as she sat rather enigmatically silent on his knee, he developed affection for his mother, explaining that no doubt it had always been there, but like many other good things when life was busy and a man had little time to go back and stir them had lain dormant, and he now thought, indeed he recognised, that it would be excellent to urge her to come over soon and spend an afternoon, – or still better a morning.

'But you're not here in the morning,' said Ingeborg.

'Ah – that is true. I am present, however, at dinner.'

'But nobody ever knows when.'

'I might, perhaps, arrive early.'

In this way the elder Frau Dremmel, who had her pride to consider as the widow of her neglectful son's traditionally appreciative father, and who would consequently never have taken what she called in her broodings the first step, did, about seven weeks after the marriage, cross the threshold of her daughter-in-law's home.

CHAPTER 14

The visit was arranged to begin the following Friday at four, for Ingeborg thought the afternoon feeling was altogether more favourable to warmth than anything you were likely to get before midday, and Johann drove in to Meuk to fetch Frau Dremmel in time for that hour.

There was to be tea out in the garden the first thing, because tea lubricates the charities, and then, with the aid of a dictionary, conversation. Ingeborg had had time to think out her mother-in-law, and was firm in her resolve that no artificial barrier such as language should stand in the way of the building up of affection. If necessary she might even weave the German for giants, umbrellas, keys and spectacles into a sentence as a conversational opening, and try her mother-in-law with that; and if Frau Dremmel showed the least responsiveness to either of these subjects she might go on to wax, fingers, thunder and beards, and end with princes, boats and shoulders. That would be three sentences. She could not help thinking they would be pregnant with conversational possibilities. There would be three replies; and Frau Dremmel, being in her own language, would of course enlarge. Then Ingeborg would open her dictionary and look up the words salient in the enlargement, and when she had found them smile back, brightly comprehending and appreciative.

This, including have tea, would take, she supposed, about fifty minutes.

Then they would walk a little up and down in the shade, pointing out the rye-field to each other, and that would be another ten minutes perhaps.

Then at five, she supposed, Frau Dremmel would ask for and obtain the carriage and go away again. Ingeborg made up her mind to kiss her at the end when the visit had reached the doorstep stage. It would not be difficult, she thought. The door-step she well knew, was a place of enthusiasms.

She and Ilse were immensely active the whole morning preparing, both of them imbued with much the same spirit with which as children they prepared parties for their dolls. But this was a live doll who was coming, and they were making real cakes which she would actually eat. The cakes were of a variety of shapes, or rather contortions, the coffee was of a festival potency, sandwiches meant to be delicate and slender were cut, but under the very knife grew bulky – it must be the strong German air, Ingeborg thought watching them, perplexed by this conduct – and there were the first gooseberries.

When the table was set out under the lime-trees and finished off with a jug of roses she gazed at her work in admiration. And the further she got away from it the more delightful it looked. Nearer it was still attractive, but more with the delusive attractiveness of tables at a school treat. Perhaps there was too much food, she thought; perhaps it was the immense girth of the sandwiches. But down from the end of the path it looked so charming that she wished she could paint it in water-colours, – the great trees, the tempered sunlight, the glimpse of the old church at one end, the glimpse of the embosomed lake at the other, and in the middle, set out so neatly, with such a grace of spotlessness, the table of her first tea-party.

Frau Dremmel arrived in a black bonnet with a mauve flower in its front to mark that ten years had been at work upon the mitigation of her grief. Her son came out of his laboratory when he heard the crashes of the carriage among the stones and holes of the village street, and he was ready at the door to help her down. He was altogether silent, for he had been torn from the middle of counting and weighing the grains in samples of differently treated rye, and would have to begin the last saucerful all over again. Beside this gravity Ingeborg, in a white frock and wearing the buckled shoes of youth, with the sun shining on her freckled fairness and bare neck and her mouth framed into welcoming smiles, looked like a child. She certainly did not look like anybody's wife; and the last thing in the world that she at all resembled was the wife of a German pastor.

Again Frau Dremmel, as she had done that day at Meuk, turned her eyes slowly all over her while she was receiving her son's abstracted kiss; but she said nothing except, to her son, *Guten*

Tag, and passively submitted to Ingeborg's shaking both her hands, which were clothed in the black cotton of decent widowhood.

'Do say something, Robert,' murmured Ingeborg. 'Say how glad I am. Say all the things I'd say if I could say things.'

Herr Dremmel gazed at his wife a moment collecting his thoughts.

'Why should one say anything?' he said. 'She is a simple woman. No longer young. My wife,' he said to his mother, 'desires me to welcome you on her behalf.'

'*Achf*,' said Frau Dremmel.

Ingeborg began to usher her along the passage towards the back door and the garden. Frau Dremmel however, turned aside half way down it into the living-room.

'Oh, not in there,' cried Ingeborg. 'We're going to have tea in the garden. Robert, please tell her—'

But looking round for help she found Robert had gone, and there was the sound of a key being turned in a lock.

Frau Dremmel continued to enter the living-room. Before she could be stopped she had arranged herself firmly on its sofa.

'But tea,' said Ingeborg, following her and gesticulating, 'tea, you know. Out there – in the garden—'

She pointed to the door, and she pointed to the window. Frau Dremmel slowly took off her gloves and rolled them together, and undid her bonnet strings and looked at the door and at the window and back again at her daughter-in-law, but did not move. Then Ingeborg, making a great effort at gay cordiality and determined that when words failed affectionate actions should fill up the gaps, bent over the figure on the sofa and took its arm. 'Won't you come?' she said; adding a sentence she had taken special pains to get by heart, '*liebe Schwiegermutter?*' And smilingly, but yet when it came to touching her, rather gingerly, and certainly with her heart in her mouth, she gently pulled at her sleeve.

Frau Dremmel stared up at her without moving.

'*Liebe Schwiegermutter* – tea – garden – better,' said Ingeborg, still smiling but now quite hot. She could not remember a single German word except *liebe Schwiegermutter*.

Frau Dremmel, urged and encouraged, was finally got out of the house and into the garden and along between the gooseberry bushes to where the tea-table stood and an armchair for her with a cushion on it. She went with plain reluctance. She did not cease to stare at her daughter-in-law. Especially her gaze lingered on her feet. Becoming aware of this Ingeborg tried to hide them, but you cannot hide feet that are being walked on, and when she sat down to pour out the coffee she found her short skirt was incapable of hiding anything lower than above her ankles.

She grew nervous. She spilt the milk and dropped a spoon. Beside the rigid figure in the armchair she seemed and felt terribly fluid and uncontrolled. The cheek that was turned to her mother-in-law flushed hotly. She acutely knew her mother-in-law was observing this, and that made it hotter. If only, thought Ingeborg, she would look at something else or say something. Over the rim of her cup, however, Frau Dremmel's eyes moved up and down and round and through the strange creature her son had married. The rest of her was almost wholly motionless. Ingeborg had nervously swallowed three cups of the black stuff before Frau Dremmel was half through one. At last a German word flashed into her mind and she flung herself on it. '*Schön – wunderschön*,' she cried, waving her hands comprehensively all over the scenery.

For an instant Frau Dremmel removed her eyes from her daughter-in-law's warm and quivering body to follow her gesture, but seeing nothing soon got them back again. She made no comment on the scenery. Her face remained wholly impassive; and Ingeborg realised that the rye-field would be no use as a means of entertainment.

She could not again say *schön*, and the meal went on in silence. Frau Dremmel's method of eating it was to begin a piece of each of the cakes and immediately leave it off. This afflicted Ingeborg, who had supposed them to be very lovely cakes. Frau Dremmel's place at the table – she had pulled her chair close up to it – was asterisked with begun and abandoned cakes. On the other hand she ate many of the sandwiches, and they drew forth the only word she said to Ingeborg during the whole of tea. '*Fleisch*,' said Frau Dremmel, removing her eyes for one moment from Ingeborg to the sandwiches that were being offered her, and with a dingy, investigating forefinger lifting up that portion of each sandwich which may be described as its lid.

'*Ja, ja*,' said Ingeborg responsively, delighted at this flicker of life.

It was, however, the only one. After it silence complete and impenetrable settled down on Frau Dremmel. She did not even

speak to her son when half an hour later he came out in search of
the coffee he had failed to find on his door-mat. Her manners
prevented her, in his house on this first visit after his marriage,
from uttering the unmanageable truths that come so naturally
from the mouths of neglected mothers; and except for those she
had nothing to say to him. Herr Dremmel expected nothing. His
deeply engaged thoughts left no room in him for anything but a
primitive simplicity. He was hungry, and he ate; thirsty, and he
drank. The silent figure at the table, of whose presence every nerve
in Ingeborg's body was conscious, produced no impression on him
whatever.

'Robert – do tell your mother how I really *do* want to talk to
her if only I could,' said Ingeborg, pressing her hands together in
her lap and tying and untying her handkerchief into knots. There
were little beads on her upper lip. The rings of hair on her temples
were quite damp.

He glanced at his mother, drawn up and taut in her chair, and
immediately she turned her eyes on to him and stared back at him
steadily.

'Little one,' he said, 'I have told you she is a simple woman, not
used to or capable of wielding the weapons of social arts. Be
simple too, and all will be well.'

'But I *am* being simple,' protested Ingeborg. 'I'm dumb; I'm
blank; what can I be simpler than that?'

'Then all is well. Give me coffee.'

He ate and drank in silence, and got up to go away again.

Frau Dremmel looked at him and said something.

'Is it the carriage?' asked Ingeborg.

'She wants to go indoors,' said Herr Dremmel.

'Indoors?'

'She says she does not like mosquitoes.'

He went away into the house. There was nothing for it but to
follow. As they reached the back door the church clock struck
five, but Ingeborg, glancing at her mother-in-law's impassive face,
saw this sound meant nothing to her. She followed her into the
living-room and watched her helplessly as she arranged herself
once more on the sofa.

When the clock struck half-past five she was still on it. She
seemed to be waiting. For what was she waiting? Ingeborg asked
herself, whose handkerchief was now rubbed into a hard ball
between her nervous hands. Impossible either to move her or

communicate with her. Rigidly she sat, her eyes examining the room and each object in it but yet not for an instant missing the least of her daughter-in-law's movements. Ingeborg seized her dictionary and grammar and made a final effort to build a bridge out of them across which their souls might even now go out to meet each other, but Frau Dremmel did not seem to understand the nature of her efforts, and only stared with a deepened blankness when Ingeborg read her out a sentence from the grammar that dealt with weather they were not that day having.

What was she waiting for? Seven o'clock struck, and still she waited. The clock in the room ticked through the minutes, and every half hour they could hear the church clock striking. Ingeborg brought her a footstool; brought her a cushion; brought her, in extremity, a glass of water; began to sew at a torn duster; left off sewing at it; fluttered nervously among the pages of her grammar; pored in her dictionary; and always Frau Dremmel watched her. She found herself struggling against a tendency to think of her mother-in-law as It. At seven she heard Ilse go home singing, — happy Ilse, able to go away. Soon afterwards she finally faltered into immobility, giving up, sitting now quite still herself in her chair, the flush faded from her cheek, pale and crumpled. It was her and Robert's supper-time. Soon it would be their bed-time. Quite soon it would be to-morrow. And then it would be next week. And then there would be winter coming on ... Was this visit never to end?

At eight it at last became plain to her that what Frau Dremmel was waiting for must be supper. This was terrible, for there was none. At least, there was only that repetition of tea and breakfast that made her and Robert's lives so wholesome. She had calculated the visit on the basis of tea only, and had prepared only and elaborately for that. For half an hour she sat on and hoped she was mistaken. She did not know that in East Prussia if you are invited to tea you also stay to supper. But at half-past eight she realised that there was nothing for it but to go and fetch it in.

When the ruins of the same meal that had been offered her once already were produced a second time and set out clumsily on the unaccustomed living-room table among the pushed-aside Merediths and Kiplings, the bones of this skeleton being, slowly put together under her very eyes, and Ingeborg at last be ceasing to go in and out fetching things and sinking into a chair indicated that that was all, Frau Dremmel, after waiting a little longer, opened her mouth and startled her daughter-in-law by speech.

'*Bratkartoffel*,' said Frau Dremmel.

Ingeborg sat up quickly. After the hours of silence it was uncanny.

'*Bratkartoffel*,' said Frau Dremmel.

'Did you – did you speak?' said Ingeborg, staring at her.

'*Bratkartoffel*,' said Frau Dremmel a third time.

Ingeborg jumped up and ran across the passage to the laboratory door.

'Robert – Robert,' she cried, twisting the handle, 'come – come quickly – your mother – she's talking, she's saying things – ' There was the same excitement and wonder in her voice as there is in that of a parent whose baby has suddenly and for the first time said Papa.

Herr Dremmel came out at once. From the sound of her he felt something must have happened.

She seized him and pulled him into the living-room. 'Now – listen,' she said, holding him there facing the sofa.

Herr Dremmel looked perplexed. 'What is it, little one?' he asked.

'Listen – she'll say it again soon,' said Ingeborg eagerly.

'What is it, mother?' he asked in German.

Frau Dremmel, without moving her head, ran her eyes over the tables.

'Are there not even – not even—' she began, but stopped. She was evidently combating an emotion.

'Thunder of heaven,' said Herr Dremmel, looking from one woman to the other, 'what is it?'

But Frau Dremmel was not able, after the hours of waiting for a supper that seemed to her in every detail a studied insult on her daughter-in-law's part, to bear harshness from her son. Drawing out her handkerchief that had no end and that reached to her eyes while yet remaining in her pocket, she began to cry.

Ingeborg was appalled. She ran to her, and, kneeling down begged her in English to tell her what was the matter. She called her *liebe Schwiegermutter* over and over again. She stroked her sleeve, she patted her, she even laid her head on her lap.

But Frau Dremmel for the first time did not notice her. She was saying detached things into her handkerchief, and they were all for her son.

'A widow,' wept Frau Dremmel. 'A widow for ten years. When I think of your dear father. How much he thought of me. My first visit. My visit on your marriage. Treated as though I were anybody. Forced to drink coffee out of doors. Like a homeless animal. No sofa. No real table. Flocks of mosquitoes. No supper. No supper at all. Nothing prepared for me. For the mother. For your sainted father's wife. His cherished wife long before you were thought of. If it had not been for me you would not have been here at all. Nor she. And I am to go home unfed. Uncared for. Not even the least one has a right to expect given one. Not even what the poorest peasant has each night. Not even' – again she said the magic word – '*Bratkartoffel*—'

'There, there,' said Ingeborg soothingly, stroking her anxiously, – 'there, there. Robert, what *is Bratkartoffel?*'

'But never mind. Never mind,' said Frau Dremmel, wiping her eyes only to weep afresh, – 'soon I shall be with him. With him again. With your dear father. And this – this is nothing, all nothing. It is only the will of God.'

'There, there,' said Ingeborg, anxiously stroking her.

CHAPTER 15

It was not until some days later that she discovered the reason for her mother-in-law's tears.

She could get no information from Herr Dremmel. His thoughts were not to be pinned a minute to such a subject. He swept her questionings away with the wave of the arm of one who sweeps his surroundings clear of rubbish, and the most that could be extracted from him was a general observation as to the small amount of good to be obtained from proximities. But Ingeborg one afternoon, walking longer than usual, facing the hot sun and the flies and sand of the road beyond the village to see where it led to instead of, as she generally did, exploring footpaths in the forest, came after much heat and exertion to a thicket of trees that were not firs or pines but green cool things, oaks, and acacias and silver birches, and going through them along a grass-grown road fanning herself with her hat as she walked in the pleasant shade, found herself stopped by a white gate, a notice telling her she was not to advance further, and a garden. Beyond the flower beds and long untidy grass of this garden she saw a big steep-roofed house built high on a terrace. On the terrace a dog was lying panting, with its tongue out. Nothing else alive was in sight, and there were no sounds except the rustling of the leaves over her head and such faint chirping as birds make in July.

'Who lives in that big white house away over there?' she asked Herr Dremmel when next she saw him, which was not till that evening at supper; and she nodded her head, her hands being full of the coffee pot, in the direction of the north.

Herr Dremmel was ruffled. He had been plunged in parish affairs since breakfast, for it was the day appointed by him and recurring once a fortnight into which by skilful organising he packed them all. The world in consequence on every second

Tuesday appeared to him a place of folly. People were born and lived embedded in ancient folly. The folly of their parents, already stale when they got it, was handed down to them intact, not shot at all, thought Herr Dremmel on these alternate Tuesdays, with the smallest ray of perception of different and better things. The school children were still learning about Bismarck's birthday, the schoolmaster was still laboriously computing attendances and endeavouring to obey the difficult law which commanded him to cane the absent, the elders of the church were still refusing to repair the steeple in time, the confirmation class was still meeting explanations and exhortations with thick inattention, the ecclesiastical authorities were still demanding detailed reports of progress when there was not and could not be progress, couples were still forgetting marriage until the last hurried moment and then demanding it with insistent cries, infants were still being hastily christened before the same neglects that killed those other infants who else might have been their proud and happy grandparents carried them off, and peasants were still slinking away at the bare mention of intelligence and manure.

He was exceedingly ruffled; for while he had been wrestling with these various acquiescences and evasions his real work was lying neglected out there in the sun, in there in the laboratory, and a whole day of twelve precious hours was gone for ever; and when Ingeborg said, 'Who lives in that big white house?' Herr Dremmel, with his wasted day behind him, and the continued brassiness of the heavens above him, and the persistence in that place of trees of mosquitoes, stared at her a moment and then said, bringing his hands down violently on the table, 'Hell and Devils.'

'Who?' said Ingeborg.

'We must call on them at once.'

'What?'

'My patron. He will be incensed that I have not presented you sooner. I forgot him. That will be another day lost. These claims, these social claims—'

He got up and took some agitated steps about the table.

'No sooner,' he said, frowning angrily at the path, 'has one settled one thing than there appears another. To-day, all day the poor. To-morrow, all day the rich—'

'Do we call continuously all day?'

'—both equally obstinate, both equally encased from head to

foot in the impenetrable thick armour of intellectual sloth. How,' he inquired, turning to her with all the indignant wrath of the thwarted worker, 'is a man to work if he lives in a constant social whirl?'

Ingeborg sat regarding him with astonishment. 'He can't,' she said. 'But – do we whirl, Robert? Would one call what we do here whirling?'

'What? When my work has been neglected all day to-day on behalf of the poor and will be neglected all day to-morrow on behalf of the rich?'

'But why will it take us all day?'

'A man must prepare. He cannot call as he is. He must,' said Herr Dremmel with irritable gloom, 'wash.' And he added with still greater irritation and gloom, 'There has to be a clean shirt.'

'But—' began Ingeborg.

He waved her into silence. 'I do not like,' he said, with a magnificent sweep of his arm, 'clean shirts.'

She stared at him with the parted lips of interest.

'I am not at home in them. I am not myself in a clean shirt for at least the first two hours.'

'Don't let's call,' said Ingeborg. 'We're so happy as we are.'

'Nay,' said Herr Dremmel, immediately brought to reason by his wife's support of his unreason, 'but we must call. There are duties no decent man neglects. And I am a decent man. I will send a messenger to inquire if our visit to-morrow will be acceptable. I will put on my shirt early in order to get used to it. And I will endeavour, by a persistent amiability so long as the visit lasts, to induce my patron to forget that I forgot him.'

Herr Dremmel had for some time past been practising forgetting his patron. He had found this course, after divers heated differences of opinion, simplest and most convenient. The patron, Baron Glambeck of Glambeck, was a serious real Christian who believed that the poor should, like some vast pudding that will not otherwise turn out well, be constantly stirred up, and he was unable to approve of a pastor who except in church and on every alternate Tuesday forbore to stir. It was for this forbearance, however, that Herr Dremmel was popular in the parish. Before his time there had been a constant dribble of pastor all over it, making it never a moment safe from intrusion. Herr Pastor Dremmel might be fiery in the pulpit, but he was quite quiet out of it; he was like a good watchdog, savage in its kennel and indifferent when loose. Kökensee had as one man refused to support the patron when he had wished some time before to bring about Herr Dremmel's removal. Its pastor did not go from house to house giving advice. Its pastor was invisible and absorbed. These were great things in a clergyman, and should not lightly be let go. Nothing could be done in the face of the parish's opposition, and Kökensee kept its pastor; but Baron Glambeck ceased to patronise Divine Service in Kökensee, and until Herr Dremmel brought Ingeborg to make his wedding call he had had no word with him for three years.

The Dremmels had announced themselves for four o'clock, and when they drove up to the house along the shady grass road and through the white gate they were met on the steps of the terrace by a servant who, if he had been in Redchester, would have been Wilson. On the top of the steps stood Baron Glambeck, tightly buttoned-up in black, formal, grave. Further back, beneath the glass roof of the terrace, stood his wife, tightly buttoned-up in black, formal, grave. They were both, if Ingeborg had known it, extremely correct according to the standards of their part of the country. They were unadorned, smoothed out, black, she abundant in her smoothneess, he spare in his; and they greeted Ingeborg with exactly the cordiality suitable to the reception of one's pastor's new wife, who ought to have been brought to call long ago but was not in any way responsible for those bygones which studded their memory so disagreeably in connection with her husband, a cordiality with the chill on. Dignity and coats of arms pervaded the place. Monograms with coronets were embroidered and painted on everything one sat on or touched. The antlers of deer shot by the Baron, with the dates and places of their shooting affixed to each, bristled thickly on the walls. They saw no servant who was not a man.

'Please take your hat off,' said the Baroness in English, carefully keeping her voice slightly on the side of coldness.

Ingeborg was very nearly frightened.

She would have been quite frightened if she had been less well trained by the Bishop in unimportance. She had, however, owing to this training, left off being shy years before. She had so small an opinion of herself that there was no room in her at all for self-consciousness; and she arrived at the Glambecks' in her usual condition of excessive naturalness, ready to talk, ready to be pleased and interested.

But it was conveyed to her instantly on seeing the Baroness —
there was an astonishment in the way she looked at her — that her
clothes were not right. And just the request or suggestion or
demand — she did not know which of these it really was — that she
should take off her hat, made her realise she was on new ground,
in places where the webs of strange customs were thick about her
feet.

She was, for a moment, very nearly frightened.

'You will be more comfortable,' said the Baroness, 'without
your hat.'

She took it off obediently, glancing beneath her eyelashes, as
she drew out the pins, at the Baroness's smooth black head and
unwrinkled black body, perceiving with the clearness of a revelation that that was how she ought to look herself. Skimpier, of
course, for the years had not yet had their will with her, but she
ought to be a version of the effect done in lean. She resolved, in
her thirst after fulfilled duty, to get a black dress and practise.

She thought it wisest not to think what her hair must be looking
like when her hat was off, for she had not expected to be hatless;
and well did she know it by nature for a straggler, a thing inclined
to wander from the grasp of hairpins and go off on its own
account into wantonings and rings which were all the more
conspicuous because of their lurid approach in colouring to the
beards of her ancestors, — sun-kissed Scandinavians who walked
the earth in their strength hung, according to the way the light
took them, with beards that were either the colour of flames, or
of apricots, or of honey. Well, if they *would* make her take her
hat off . . .

By the time she was on the sofa she was presently put on in the
inner hall she had caught up with her usual condition of naturalness again, and sat on it interested and forgetful of self. The
Baroness's eyes wandered over her, and they wandered over her
with much the same quality in their look that had been in her
mother-in-law's. And always when they got to her feet they
lingered. Her skirt again reached only to her ankles. All her
outdoor skirts did that. 'But I can't help *having* feet,' thought
Ingeborg, noticing this. They were small by nature, and the artful
shoes of the London shoemaker who had shared in providing her
and Judith's trousseau made them seem still smaller. She did not
try to hide them as she had tried when Frau Dremmel stared. It

was Frau Dremmel's heavy silence that had unnerved her. These people talked; and the Baroness's English was reassuringly good.

Nobody, the Baroness was thinking, and also simultaneously the Baron, who was fit to be a pastor's wife had feet like that – little, incapable feet. Nobody, indeed, who was a really nice woman had them. One left off having them when one was a child and never had them again. The errands of domesticity on which one ran, the perpetual up and down of stairs, the hours standing on the cold stone floor of servants' quarters seeing that one was not cheated, the innumerable honourable activities that beautified and dignified womanhood, necessitated large loose shoes. A true wife's feet should have room to spread and flatten. Feet were one of those numerous portions of the body that had been devised by an all-wise Creator for use and not show.

As for the rest of the Frau Pastor's appearance there were, it is true, some young ladies in the country who dressed rather like that in the summer, but they were ladies in the Glambeck set, ladies of family or married into family. That the person who had married one's pastor, a man whose father had been of such obscure beginnings, and indeed continuations, that even his having been dead ten years hardly made him respectable, should dress in this manner was a catastrophe. Already they had suffered too much from the conduct of their loose-talking, unchristian pastor; and now, instead of bringing a neat woman in black to be presented to them, a neat woman with a gold chain, perhaps, round her high black collar, it being a state occasion and she, after all, newly married – but only a very light chain, and inherited not bought – and a dress so sufficient that it reached beyond and enveloped anything she might possess in the way of wrist or ankle or throat, here was the most unsuitable wife he could have chosen, – short, of course, of marrying among Jews. While as for her hair, when it came to her hair their thoughts ceased to formulate. That small and flattened and disordered head, like a boy's head run wild, like something on fire, which emerged when she took off her hat . . .

Coffee was served on the big table in front of the sofa. The Baroness sat beside Ingeborg, and the Baron and Herr Dremmel drew up chairs opposite. The coffee was good, and there was one excellent cake. No gooseberries, no flowers, no unwieldy sandwiches; just plainness and excellence.

The two men talked to each other, not to the women, the Baron

stiffly and on his guard, Herr Dremmel taking immense pains to
be amiable and not offend. Between them hung the memories of
altercations. Between them also hung the knowledge of the three
years during which the Baron and his wife, as a result of the last
and hottest difference of opinion, had attended Divine Service in a
church that did not belong to them. They had altogether cut
Kökensee. For three years their private gallery in the church in
which their ancestors had once a fortnight feared God had been a
place where mice enjoyed themselves. Its chairs were covered with
dust; its hymn-books, growing brown, still lay open at the place
the Glambecks had praised God out of last. Such a withdrawal of
approval would have made any other pastor's life a thing of chill
and bleakness; Herr Dremmel hardly observed it. He had no
vanities. He was pleased that the rival pastor should be gratified.
He cared nothing for comment, and had no eye for shrugs and
smiles. His eyes, his thoughts, were wanted for his work; and he
found it a relief, a release from at least one interruption, when his
patron took to leaving him frigidly alone.

Indeed, when he drove up to the Glambecks' house and
remembered he had not had to go there for three peaceful years
he felt really grateful, and he showed his gratitude by performing
immense feats of social pleasantness during the visit. He agreed
gigantically with everything the Baron said. Whatever subject was
touched upon – very cautiously, for the Baron mistrusted all
subjects with Herr Dremmel – he instantly dragged if off the
dangerous shoals of the immediate and close up to a cosmic height
and distance, a height and distance so enormous that even what
the Kaiser said last became a negligible tinkling and Conscience
and Dogma quavered off into silence; and he explained to the
Baron, who guardedly said 'Perhaps,' that though people's opinions might and did vary seen near, if one spread them out wide
enough, pushed them back far enough, took them up high enough,
bored them down deep enough, got them away from detail and
loose from foregrounds, one would come at last to the great
Mother Opinion of them all, in whose huge lap men curled
themselves up contentedly like the happy identities they indeed
were and went, after kissing each other, in placidest agreement to
sleep.

'Perhaps,' said the Baron.

Personalities, immediate interests, duties, daily life, were
swamped in the vast seas in which, with politeness but determina-

tion, Herr Dremmel took the Baron swimming. One only needed,
he repeated, warm with the wish to keep in roomy regions, to
trace back any two opinions, however bitterly different they now
were, far enough to get at last to the point where they sweetly
kissed.

'Perhaps,' said the Baron.

'One only needed—' went on Herr Dremmel, making all-
embracing movements with his arms.

But the Baron cleared his throat and began to enumerate
contrary facts.

Herr Dremmel agreed at once that he was right just there, and
pushed the point of kissing back a little further.

The Baron went after him with more facts.

Herr Dremmel again agreed, and went back further. In this way
they came at last to the Garden of Eden, beyond which the Baron
refused to budge, alleging that further back than that no Christian
could go; and even in that he repudiated the kiss. He was
convinced, though he concealed it, that at no period of human
thought could his and Herr Dremmel's opinions, for example,
have kissed.

But it was an amiable view, and Herr Dremmel was extremely
polite and was bent evidently on peace, and the Baron, recognising
this, became less distrustful. He even contributed a thought of his
own at last, after having been negatively occupied in dissecting
Herr Dremmel's, and said that in his opinion it was details that
made life difficult.

The Baroness, who loved him and overheard him, was anxious
he should have more coffee with plenty of milk in it after this.

'Men,' she explained to Ingeborg in careful English as she
poured it out, 'need much nourishment because of all this head-
work.'

'I suppose they do,' said Ingeborg.

'When I was first married I remember it was my chief pride and
joy that at last I had some one of my very own to nourish.'

'Oh?' said Ingeborg.

'It is an instinct,' said the Baroness, who had the air of
adminstering a lesson, 'in a true woman. She wishes to nourish.
And naturally the joy of nourishing two is double the joy of
nourishing one.'

'I suppose it is,' said Ingeborg, who did not quite follow.

'When my first-born—'

'Oh yes,' said Ingeborg, glad to understand.

'When my first-born was laid in my arms I cannot express, Frau Pastor, what happiness I had in being given yet another human being to nourish.'

'I suppose it was delightful,' said Ingeborg, politely sympathetic.

The Baroness's eyes dropped a moment inquiringly from Ingeborg's face to her body.

'For six years,' she went on, after a pause, 'I had fresh reason for happiness regularly at Christmas.'

'I suppose you have the loveliest Christmases here,' said Ingeborg. 'Like the ones in books. With trees.'

'Trees? Naturally we have trees. But I had babies as well. Every Christmas for six years regularly my Christmas present to my dear husband was able to be a baby.'

'What?' said Ingeborg, opening her eyes. 'A fresh one?'

'Naturally it was fresh. One does not have the same baby twice.'

'No of course not. But – how did you hide it till Christmas day?'

'It could not, naturally,' said the Baroness stiffly, 'be as much a surprise as a present that was not a baby would have been, but it was for all practical purposes hidden till Christmas. On that day it was born.'

'Oh, but I think that was very wonderful,' said Ingeborg, genuinely pleased by such neatness. She leaned forward in her enthusiasm and clasped her hands about her knees.

'Yes,' said the Baroness, relaxing a little before this flattering appreciation. 'Yes. It was. Some people would call it chance. But we, as Christians, knew it was heaven.'

'But how *punctual*,' said Ingeborg admiringly, 'how *tidy*.'

'Yes. Yes,' mused the Baroness, relaxing still more in the warm moisture of remembrance, 'they were happy times. Happy, happy times. One's little ones coming and going—'

'Oh? did they go as well as come?' asked Ingeborg, lowering her voice to condolence.

'About one's knees, I mean, and the house.'

'Oh, yes,' said Ingeborg, relieved.

'Every year the Christmas candles shining down on an addition to our treasures. Every year the gifts of past Christmases gathered about the tree again, bigger and stronger instead of being lost or broken as they would have been if they had been any other kind of gift.'

'But what happened when there weren't any more to give ?'

'Then I gave my husband cigar-cases.'

'Oh.'

'After all, most women have to do that all their lives. I did not grumble. When heaven ceased to provide me with a present for him, I knew how to bow my head and went and bought one. There are excellent cigar-cases at Wertheim's in Königsberg if you wish to give one to Herr Pastor next Christmas. They do not come unsewn at the corners by July or August in the way those one buys in other shops do. Ah, yes. Happy years. Happy, happy years. First the six years of great joy collecting my family, and then the years of happiness bringing it up. Of course you are fond of children ?'

'I've never had any.'

'Naturally you have not,' said the Baroness, stiffening again.

'So I don't know,' said Ingeborg.

'But every true woman loves little children,' said the Baroness.

'But they must be *there*,' said Ingeborg.

'One has God-implanted instincts,' said the Baroness.

'But one must *see* something to practise them on,' said Ingeborg.

'A true woman is all love,' said the Baroness, in a voice that sounded very like scolding.

'I suppose she is,' said Ingeborg, who felt that she never could have met one. She had a vision of something altogether soft and squelchy and humid and at the same time wonderful. 'Are any of your children at home ?' she asked, thinking she would like to test her instincts on the younger Glambecks.

'They are grown up and gone. Out into the world. Some far away in other countries. Ah, yes. One is lonely—' The Baroness became loftily plaintive. 'It is the lot of parents. Lonely, lonely. I had five daughters. It was a great relief to get them all married. There was naturally the danger where there were so many of some of them staying with us always.'

'But then you wouldn't have been lonely,' said Ingeborg.

'But then, Frau Pastor, they would not have been married.'

'No. And then,' said Ingeborg, interested, 'you wouldn't have been able to *feel* lonely.'

The Baroness gazed at her.

'These things are *nice*, you know,' said Ingeborg, leaning forward again in her interest. 'One does *like* it somehow – being sad, you know, and thinking how lonely one is. Of course it's much more delicious to be happy, but not being happy has its jollinesses. There's a perfume . . .' She sought about in her mind – 'It's like a wet day. It looks gloomy and miserable compared to what yesterday was like, but there *is* an enjoyment. And things—' she hesitated, groping – 'things seem to grow. Different ones. Yet they're beautiful too . . .'

But the Baroness, who did not follow and did not want to, for it was not her business to listen to her pastor's wife, drooped an inquiring eye again over Ingeborg's body and cut her tendency to talk more than was becoming in her position short by remarking that she was still very thin.

When they had sat there till the coffee was cold Ingeborg, in a pause of the talk, got up to go.

The three others stared at her without moving. Even her own Robert stared uncomprehending. It seemed a lame thing to have to explain that she was now going home, but that was what she did at last murmur down to the motionless and surprised Baroness.

'Are you not feeling well?' inquired the Baroness.

'What is it, Ingeborg?' asked Herr Dremmel.

The Baron went over to a window and opened it. 'A little faint, no doubt,' he said; adding something about young wives.

The Baroness asked her if she would like to lie down.

Herr Dremmel became alert and interested. 'What is it, little one?' he asked again, getting up.

'I think it would be good if the Frau Pastor rested a little before supper,' said the Baroness, getting up too.

'Certainly,' said Herr Dremmel, quite eagerly, and with a funny expression on his face.

Ingeborg gazed from one to the other.

'But Robert,' she said, wondering why he looked like that, 'oughtn't we to go home?'

'Dear Frau Pastor,' said the Baroness quite warmly, 'you will feel better presently. Believe me. There is an hour still before supper. Come with me, and you shall lie down and rest.'

'But Robert—' said Ingeborg, astonished.

She was, however, taken away – it seemed a sort of sweeping of her away – through glass doors, down a carpetless varnished passage into a spare bedroom, and commanded to put herself on the high white bed with her head a little lower than her feet.

'But,' she said, 'why?'

'You will be better by supper-time. Oh, I know all these things,' said the Baroness, who was opening windows and had grown suddenly friendly. 'Do you feel sick?'

'Sick?'

She wondered whether the amount of cake she had eaten had appeared excessive. She had had two pieces. Perhaps there was a rigid local custom prescribing only one. She felt again that she was in a net of customs, with nobody to explain. The Baroness seemed quite disappointed when she assured her she did not feel sick at all. Ought guests to feel sick? Was it a subtle way of drawing attention to the irresistibleness of the host's food? It then occurred to her that it might very possibly be the custom in these country places to put callers to bed for an hour in the middle of their call, and that her omission to put her mother-in-law there was one of the causes of her tears. Next to going home as quickly as one did in England she felt going to bed was altogether the best thing.

This thought, that it must be the custom, made her instantly pliable. With every gesture of politeness she hastened to clamber up on to the billows of feathers and white quilt. There was a smell of naphthalin as she sank downwards, a smell of careful warfare carried on incessantly with moth.

The Baroness came away from letting in floods of air, and looked at her. 'I am sure' she said, 'you do feel sick.'

'I think I do – a little,' said Ingeborg, anxious to give every satisfaction.

It was evidently the right thing to say, for her hostess's face lit up. She went out of the room quickly and came back with some Eau de Cologne and a fan.

Ingeborg watched her with bright alert eyes over the edge of a billow of feathers while she fetched a litle table and brought it to the bed and arranged these things on it.

How odd it was, she thought, greatly interested. Was the Baron simultaneously putting Robert to bed in some other room? She felt she had grown suddenly popular, that she was doing all the right things at last. Contrasted with its loftiness during the first part of the call the Baroness's manner was quite human and warm. She put the table close to her side, and told her the best thing she could do, quite the best thing, would be to try and sleep a little; if she wanted anything she was to ring, and the maid Tina would appear.

'Ah, yes,' she said in conclusion, standing for a moment looking down at her and heaving a great sigh that seemed to Ingeborg somehow to be pleasurable, 'ah, yes. When one has said A, dear Frau Pastor, one must say B. Ah, yes.'

And she went out again on tip-toe, softly closing the door and leaving Ingeborg in a state of extreme and active interest and interrogation. 'When one has said A one must say B . . .' Why must one? And what was B? What, indeed, if you came to that, was A?

She listened a moment, raised on her elbow, her bright head more ruffled than ever after its descent into the billows, then she slid down onto the slippery floor and ran across in her stockings to one of the big open windows.

It looked on to a tangle of garden, a sort of wilderness of lilac bushes and syringa and neglected roses and rough grass and hemlock at the back of the house. There was nobody anywhere to be seen, and she got up on to the sill and sat there in great enjoyment swinging her feet, for it all smelt very sweet at the end of the long hot day, till she thought the hour, the blessed hour, must be nearly over. Then she stole back and rearranged herself carefully on the bed.

'But this is *the* way of paying calls,' she thought, pulling the quilt up tidily under her chin and waiting for what would be done to her next.

CHAPTER 16

They did not get away till nine o'clock.

There was supper at seven, an elaborate meal, and they sat over it an hour and a half. Then came more coffee, served on the terrace by servants in white cotton gloves, and half an hour later, just before they left, tea and sandwiches and cakes and fruit and beer.

Ingeborg was now quite clear about the reason for her mother-in-law's tears. She saw very vividly how dreadful her behaviour must have seemed. That groaning supper-table, that piling up as the end of the visit drew near of more food and more and more, and the refreshment of bed in the middle . . .

'I shall invite her all over again,' she said suddenly, determined to make amends.

When she said this the carriage had finally detached them from sight and sound of the now quite cordial Glambecks, and was heaving through the sand of the dark wooded road beyond their gate.

'Whom will the little one invite?' asked Herr Dremmel, bending down. He had got his arm round her, and at the bigger joltings tightened his hold and lifted her a little. His voice was tender, and when he bent down there was an enveloping smell of cigars and wine, mixed with the india-rubber of his mackintosh.

Ingeborg knew that for some reason she could not discover she had made herself popular. There was the distinct consciousness of having suddenly, half way through the visit, become a success. And she was still going on being a success, she felt. But why? Robert was extraordinarily attentive. Too attentive, really, for oh, what a wonderful night of stars and warm scents it was, once they were in the open, – what a night, what a marvel of a night! And when he bent over her it was blotted out. Dear Robert. She did love him. But away there on that low meadow, far away over there where a white mist lay on the swampy places and the leaves of the flags that grew along the ditch stood up like silver spears in the moonlight, one could imagine the damp cool fragrance rising up as one's feet stirred the grass, the perfect solitariness and the perfect silence. Except for the bittern. There was a bittern, she had discovered, in those swamps. If she were over there now, lying quiet quite on the higher ground by the ditch, quite quiet and alone, she would hear him presently, solemnly booming.

'Whom will the little one invite?' asked Herr Dremmel, bending down across the whole of the Milky Way and every single one of all the multitude of scents the night was softly throwing against her face.

He kissed her very kindly and at unusual length. It lasted so long that she missed the smell of an entire clover field.

'Your mother,' said Ingeborg, when she again emerged.

'Heavens and earth,' said Herr Dremmel.

'I know now what I did – or rather didn't do. I know now why she kept on saying *Bratkartoffel*. Oh Robert, she must have been *hurt*. She must have thought I didn't care a bit. And I did so want her to be happy. Why didn't you tell me?'

'Tell you what, little sheep?'

'About there having to be supper, and about her having to go to bed.'

'To bed?'

'Did the Baron put you?'

'Put me?'

'To bed?'

Herr Dremmel bent down again and looked a little anxiously at as much of her face as he could see in the moonlight. It seemed normal; not in the least flushed or feverish. He touched her cheek with his finger. It was cool.

'Little one,' he said, 'what is this talk of beds?'

'Only that it would save rather a lot of awful things happening if you would just give me an *idea* beforehand of what is expected. It wouldn't take a minute. I wouldn't disturb you at your work for anything, but at some odd time – breakfast, for instance, or while you're shaving – if you'd *say* about beds and things like that. One couldn't guess it, you know. In Redchester one didn't do it, you see. And it's such a really beautiful arrangement. Oh' –

she suddenly flung her arms around him and held him tight – 'I *am* glad I married one of you !'

'One of me ?'

Herr Dremmel again peered anxiously at her face.

'One of you wonderful people – you magnificent, spacious people. In Redchester we got rid of difficulties by running away. You face them and overcome them. There isn't much doubt, is there, which is the finer ?'

He transferred his cigar to the hand that was round her shoulder and spread his right one largely over her forehead. It was quite cool.

'Who,' went on Ingeborg enthusiastically, jerking her head away from his hand, 'would have a custom that makes calls last five hours without rebelling ? You are too splendidly disciplined to rebel. You don't. You just set about finding some way of making the calls endurable, and you hit on the *nicest* way. I loved that hour in bed. If only I'd known that the other day when your mother came ! The relief of it . . .'

'But my mother—' began Herr Dremmel in a puzzled voice. Then he added with a touch of severity, 'Your remarks, my treasure, are not in your usual taste. You forget my mother is a widow.'

'Oh ? Don't widows ?'

'Do not widows what ?'

'Go to bed ?'

'Now kindly tell me,' he said, with an impatience he concealed beneath calm, for he had heard that a husband who wishes to become successfully a father has to accommodate himself to many moods, 'what it is you are really talking about.'

'Why, about your not explaining things to me in time.'

'What things ?'

'About your mother having to go to bed.'

'Why should my mother have to go to bed ?'

'Oh Robert, – because it's the custom.'

'It is not. Why do you suppose it is the custom ?'

'What ? When I've just been put there ? And you saw me go ?'

'Ingeborg—'

'Oh don't call me Ingeborg—'

'Ingeborg, this is levity. I am prepared for much accommodating of myself to whims in regard to food and kindred matters, but am I to endure levity for nine months ?'

She stared at him.

'You went to bed because you were ill,' he said.

'I wasn't,' she said, indignantly. Did he, too, think she did not know how to control herself in the presence of cake?

'What? You were not?'

There was a note of such sharp disappointment in his voice that in her turn she peered at his face.

'Now kindly tell me, Robert,' she said, giving his sleeve a slight pull, 'what it is you are *really* talking about.'

'You did not feel faint? You feel quite well? You do not feel ill after all?'

Again the note of astonished disappointment.

'But why should I feel ill?'

'Then why did you ask to be taken home almost before we had arrived?'

For the first time she heard anger in his voice, anger and a great aggrievedness.

'Almost before we'd arrived? We'd been there hours. You hadn't *told* me a call meant supper.'

'Almighty Heaven,' he cried, 'am I to dwell on every detail of life? Am I personally to conduct you over each of the inches of your steps? Do you regard me as an elementary school? Can you not imagine? Can you not calculate probabilities? Can you not construct some searchlight of inference of your own, and illuminate with it the outline of at least the next few hours?'

She gazed at him a moment in astonishment.

'*Well*,' she said.

If her father had asked her only one of these questions in that sort of voice she would have been without an answer, beaten down and crushed. But Robert had not had the steady continuous frightening of her from babyhood. He could not hold over her, like an awful rod, that she owed her very existence to him. He could not claim perpetual gratitude for this remote tremendous gift, bestowed on her in the days of her unconsciousness. He was a kindly stranger appointed by the Church to walk hand in hand with her along the path of grown-up life. He had admired her, and kissed her, and quite often during their engagement had abased himself at her feet. Also she had seen him at moments such as shaving.

'I believe,' she said after another astonished pause, 'that you're scolding me. And you're scolding me because you're angry with me, and you're angry with me – Robert, is it possible you're angry with me because I'm *not* ill ?'

He threw away his cigar and seized her in his arms and began to whisper voluminously into her ear.

'What ?' she kept on saying. 'What ? You're tickling me – what ? I can't hear—'

But she did in the end hear, and drew herself a little back from him to look at him with a new interest. It seemed the oddest thing that he, so busy, so nearly always somewhere else in thought, so deeply and frequently absent from the surface of life, so entirely occupied by his work that often he could hardly remember he had a wife, should want to have yet another object of the kind added unto him, a child; and that she who lived altogether on the surface, who knew, as it were, the very taste of each of the day's minutes and possessed them all, who never lost consciousness of the present and never for an instant let go of her awareness of the visible and the now, should be without any such desire.

'But,' she said, 'we're so happy. We're so happy as we are.'

'It is nothing compared to what we would be.'

'But I haven't even begun to get used to *this* happiness yet – to the one I've got.'

'You will infinitely prefer the one that is yet to come.'

'But Robert – don't rush me along. Don't let us rush past what we've got. Let us love all this thoroughly first—'

He looked at her very gravely. 'We have now been married two months,' he said. 'I become anxious. To-night – I cannot tell you how glad I was. And then – it was nothing after all.'

She gazed at him with a feeling of a new incumbency. He had said the last words in a voice she did not know, with a catch in it.

'Robert—' she said quickly, putting out her hand and touching his with a little soft stroking movement.

She wished above all things to make him perfectly happy. Always she had loved making people happy. And she was so grateful to him, so grateful for the freedom she had got through him, that just her gratitude even if she had not loved him would have made her try to do and be everything he wished. But she did love him. She certainly loved him. And here was something he seemed to want beyond everything, and that she alone could provide him with.

He turned his head away; and as he did this did she see

something actually glistening in his eyes, glistening like something wet?

In an instant she had put her arms round him. 'Of course I do – of course I want one,' she said, rubbing her cheek up and down his mackintosh, 'some – heaps – of course we'll have them – everybody has them – of course I'll soon begin – don't mind my not having been ill to-night – I'm so sorry – I *will* be ill – dear Robert – I didn't know I had to be ill – but I will be soon – I'm sure I will be – I – I feel quite like *soon* being ill now—'

He patted her face, his face still turned away. 'Good little wife,' he said; 'good little wife.'

She felt nearer to him than she had ever felt, so close in understanding and sympathy. She had seen tears, a man's tears. Of what tremendous depths of feeling were they not the signal? The sentence, *A strong man's tears*, floated up from somewhere and hung about her mind. She pressed him to her in a passion of desire to make him altogether happy, to protect him from feeling too much. She held him like that, her cheek against his arm, rubbing it up and down every now and then to show how well she understood, till they got home. When he lifted her down from the carriage at their door she slipped her hand round the back of his neck and kept it there a moment with the tenderest lingering touch.

'Dear Robert,' she whispered, her lips on his ear while he lifted her down; and implicit in the words was the mother-assurance, the yearning mother-promise, 'Oh little thing, little man thing, I'll take *care* of you.'

She hung about the parlour and the passage while he went, as he said, for a moment into his laboratory for a final look round, waiting for him in a strangely warmed exalted state, entirely at one with him, suddenly very intimate, sure that after letting her see things so sacred as tears he would only want to spend the rest of the evening with her, being comforted and reassured, held close to her heart, talking sweetly with her in the quiet dark garden.

But there were six saucerfuls of differently treated last year's rye ready on the laboratory table for counting and weighing. Herr Dremmel beheld them, and forgot the world. He began to count and weigh. He continued to count and weigh. He ended by counting and weighing them all; and it was dawn before, satisfied and consoled for his lost afternoon, it occurred to him that perhaps it might be bedtime.

CHAPTER 17

The winter came before Ingeborg, after many false alarms due to her extreme eagerness to give Robert the happiness he wanted, was able to assure him with certainty that he would presently become a father. 'And I,' she said, looking at him with a kind of surprised awe now that it had really come upon her, 'I suppose I will be a mother.'

Herr Dremmel remarked with dryness that he supposed in that case she would, and refused to become enthusiastic until there was more certainty.

He had been disappointed during the summer so often. It had so often been only gooseberries; it had so often been only the beginning of a chill due to her fondness for the leaking punt and for haunting in inadequate shoes the froggier portions of the edge of the lake. Her zeal to meet his wishes made her pounce upon the slightest little feeling of not being well and run triumphantly to his laboratory, daring its locked door, defying its sacredness, to tell him the great news. She would stand there radiantly saying things that sounded like paraphrases of the Scripture, and almost the first German she really learned and used was the German so familiar in every household for being of Good Hope, for being in Blessed Circumstance.

For some time Herr Dremmel greeted these tidings with emotion and excitement; but as the summer went on, and pears and plums became plentiful both in their unripe and over-ripe state, and the sun was hot, and the time of melons was at hand, he began to cut her announcements short by inquiring what she had been eating. So incredulous had he become that she fainted twice in December before he was convinced. Then, indeed, for nearly a whole day his joy was touching. One cannot however keep up such joy, and Ingeborg found that things after this brief upheaval of emotion settled back again into how they were before, except that she felt extraordinarily and persistently ill.

Well, she had had the most wonderful summer; she had got that anyhow tucked away up the sleeve of her memory, and could bring it out and look at it when the days were wet and she felt cold and sick. The summer that year in East Prussia had been a long drought, a long bath of sunshine, and Ingeborg lived out in it in an ecstasy of freedom. Her body, light and perfectly balanced, did wonders of exploration in the mighty forests that began at the north of the Kökensee lake and went on without stopping to the sea. She would get Robert's dinner ready for him early, and then put some bread and butter and a cucumber into a knapsack with her German grammar, and paddle the punt down the lake, tie it up where the trees began, and start. Nothing seemed to tire her. She would walk for miles along the endless forest tracks, just as much suited to her environment, just as harmonious and as much a creature of air and sunshine as the white butterflies that fluttered among the enormous pine trunks. Every now and then, for sheer delight in these things, she would throw herself down on the springy delicious carpet of whortleberries and lie still watching the blue-green tops of the pine-trees delicately swaying backwards and forwards far away over her head against the serene northern sky. They made a gently sighing noise in the wind. It was the only sound, except the occasional cry of a woodpecker or the cry, immensely distant, of a hawk.

Nobody but herself seemed to use the forests. It was the rarest thing that she met a woodman, or children picking whortleberries. When she did she was much stared at. The forests were quite out of the beat of tourists or foreigners, and the indigenous ladies were too properly occupied by indoor duties to wander, even if they liked forests, away from their home anchorage; and for those whose business sent them into these lonely places to come across somebody belonging to the class that can have dinner every day regularly in a house if it likes and to the sex that ought to be there cooking it, was an amazement.

The young lady, however, seemed so happy that they all smiled at her when she looked at them. They supposed she must be some one grown white in a town, and come to stay the summer weeks with one of the Crown foresters. That would explain her detachment from duty, her knapsack, and the colour of her skin. Anyhow, just her passing made their dull day interesting; and they would watch her glinting in and out of the trees till at last, hardly distinguishable from one of the white butterflies, the distance took her.

When she was quite hot she would sit down in a carefully chosen spot where, if possible, a deciduous tree, a maple or a bird cherry, splashed its vivid green exquisitely against the peculiar misty bloom of pink and grey that hung about the pine trunks, a tree that looked quite little down among these giants, hardly as if it reached to their knees, and yet when she stood under it was almost as big as the lime-trees in the Kökensee garden. She did not sit in its shade; she went some distance away where she could look at it quivering in the light, and leaning her back against a pine-tree she would eat her bread and cucumber and feel utterly filled with the love and glory of God.

Impossible to reason about this feeling. It was there. It seemed in that summer to go with her wherever she went and whatever she did. She walked in blessing. It was in the light, she thought, looking round her, the wonderful light, the soft radiance of the forest; it was in the air, warm and fresh, scented and pungent; it was in the feel of the pine needles and the dry crisp last year's cones she crushed as she went along; it was in the cushions of moss so green and cool that she stopped to pat them, or in the hot lichen that came off in flakes when her feet brushed a root; it was in being young and healthy and having had one's dinner and sitting quiet and getting rested and knowing the hours ahead were roomy; it was in all these things, everywhere and in everything. She would pick up her German grammar in a quick desire to do something in return, something that gave her real trouble – shall one not say somehow Thank you? – and she engulfed huge tracts of it on these expeditions, learning pages of it by heart and repeating them aloud to the pine-trees and the wood-peckers.

When the sun began to go down she set out for home, sometimes losing her way for quite a long while, and then she would hurry because of Robert's supper, and then she would get very hot; and the combined heat and hurry and cucumber, to which presently was added fatigue, would end in one of those triumphal appearances later on in his laboratory to which he was growing so much accustomed.

In January, when she was just a sick thing, she thought of these days as something too beautiful to have really happened.

There was from the first no shyness about her on the subject of babies. She had not considered it during her life at home, for babies were never mentioned at the Palace – of course, she thought, remembering this omission, because there were none, and it would be as meaningless to talk about babies when there were none as it would be in Kökensee to talk about bishops when there were none. She arrived, therefore, at Kökensee with her mind a blank from prejudice, and finding the atmosphere thick with babies immediately with her usual uninquiring pliability adopted the prevailing attitude and was not shy either.

The neighbourhood did not wait till they were born to talk about its own children. It did not think of its children as unmentionable until they had been baptised into decency by birth. They were important things, the most important of all in the life of the women, and it was natural to discuss them thoroughly. The childless woman was a pitied creature. The woman who had most children was proudest. She might be poor and tormented by them, but it was something she possessed more of than her neighbours. Ilse had early inquired which room would be the nursery. That obvious pattern of respectability, Baroness Glambeck, talked of births with a detail and interest only second to that with which she talked of deaths. It seemed to her a most proper topic of conversation with any young married woman; and on her returning the Dremmel call a fortnight after it had been made she was quite taken aback and annoyed to find it had become irrelevant owing to Ingeborg's being perfectly well.

Indeed, this failure of Ingeborg's entirely spoilt the visit. The Baroness, who had arrived friendly, withdrew into frost with the manner of one who felt she had been thawed on the last occasion on false pretences. Impossible to meet one's pastor's wife – and such an odd-looking and free-mannered one, too – with any familiarity except on the Christian footing of impending birth or death. A pastor's wife belonged to the class one is only really pleasant with in suffering or guilt. Offended, yet forced to continue the call, the Baroneess confined such conversation as she made to questions that had a flavour of hostility: where was it possible to get such shoes, and did the Frau Pastor think toes so narrow good for the circulation and the housework?

Ingeborg could not believe this was the motherly lady who had fussed round her bed that day at Glambeck. She felt set away at a great distance from her, on the other side of a gulf. For the first time it was borne in upon her that her marriage made a difference to her socially, that here in Germany the gulf was a wide one. She was a pastor's wife; and when asked about her family, which happened early and searchingly in the call, could only give an impression of more pastors.

'Ah, that is the same as what we call superintendent,' said the Baroness, nodding several times slowly on learning that Ingeborg's father was a bishop; and after a series of questions as to the Frau Pastor's sister's marriage nodded her head slowly several times again, and informed Ingeborg that what her sister had married was a schoolmaster. 'Like Herr Schultz,' said the Baroness, – Herr Schultz being the village schoolmaster.

There was a photograph of Judith on the table that caught and kept the Baroness's eye and also, in an even greater but more careful degree, the Baron's. It was Judith dressed in evening beauty, bare-necked, perfect.

Ingeborg took it up with a natural pride in having such a lovely thing for her very own sister and handed it to the Baroness.

'Here she is,' said Ingeborg, full of natural pride.

The Baroness stared in real consternation.

'What?' she said. 'This is a schoolmaster's wife? This is our pastor's sister-in-law? I had thought—'

She broke off, and with a grim gesture put the photograph on the table again and said she could not stay to supper.

Since then there had been no intercourse with Glambeck, and the Baroness did not know of the satisfactory turn things had taken at the parsonage till on Christmas Eve, from her gallery in church to which she and the Baron had decided to return on the greater festivals as a mark of their awareness that Herr Dremmel desired to make amends, she beheld during the drawn-out verses of the chorale Ingeborg drop sideways on the seat in her pew below and remain motionless and bunched up, her hymn-book pushed crooked on the desk in front of her, and her attitude one of complete indifference to appearances.

The Baroness did not nudge the Baron because in her position one does not nudge, but her instinct was all for nudging.

Herr Dremmel could not see what had happened, custom concealing him during the singing in a wooden box at the foot of the pulpit where he was busy imagining agricultural experiments. Till he came out the singing went on; and suppose, thought the Baroness, he were to forget to come out? Once he had forgotten, she had heard, and had stayed in his box, having very unfortunately been visited there by a revelation concerning potash that caught him up into oblivion for the best part of an hour, during which the chorale was gone through with an increasing faintness fifteen times. She knew about the hour, but did not know it was potash. Suppose he once again fell into a meditation? There was no verger, beadle, pew-opener or official person of any sort to take action. The congregation would do nothing that was outside the customary and the prescribed. There was no female relative such as the Frau Pastor would have had staying with her over Christmas if she had been what she ought to have been, and what every other pastor's wife so felicitously was, a German. And for her herself to descend and help in the eyes of all Kökensee would have been too great a condescension, besides involving her in difficulties with the wife of the forester, and the wife of the Glambeck schoolmaster who was also the postman, both of whom were of the same social standing as the younger Frau Dremmel and would jealously resent the least mark of what they would interpret as special favour.

Herr Dremmel, however, came out punctually and went up into the pulpit and opened his well-worn manuscript and read out the well-known text, and the congregation sat as nearly thrilled as it could be waiting for the moment when his eye would fall on to his own pew and what was in it. Would he interrupt the service to go down and carry his wife out? Would the congregation have to wait till he came back again, or would it be allowed to disperse to its Christmas trees and rejoicings?

Herr Dremmel read on and on, expounding the innocent Christmas story, describing its white accessories of flocks and angels and virgins and stars with the thunderous vehemence near scolding that had become a habit with him when he preached. His text was *Peace on earth, goodwill among men*, and from custom he hit his desk with his clenched fist while he read it out and hurled it at his congregation as if it were a threat.

He did not look in his wife's direction. He was not thinking of her at all. He wondered a little at the stillness and attention of his listeners. Nobody coughed. Nobody shuffled. The school children hung over the edge of the organ loft, motionless and intent. Baron Glambeck remained awake.

At the end of the service Herr Dremmel had to stay according to custom in his wooden box till everyone had gone, and it was not till he came out of that to go through the church to its only door that he perceived Ingeborg. For a moment he thought she was waiting for him in an attitude of inappropriately childish laxity, and he was about to rebuke her when it flashed upon him that she had fainted, that it was the second time in ten days, and that he was indeed and without any doubt at last the happiest of men.

In spite of the bitter wind that was raking the churchyard every person who had been inside the church was waiting outside to see the pastor come out. The Glambecks and elders of the church would have waited in any case on Christmas Eve to wish him the compliments of the season and receive his in return, but on this occasion they waited with pleasure as well as patience, and the rest of the congregation waited too.

They were rewarded by seeing him presently appear in the doorway in his gown and bands carrying the bundle that was the still unconscious Frau Pastor as if she were a baby, his face illuminated with joy and pride. It was as entertaining as a funeral. Double congratulations were poured upon him, double and treble handshakes of the hand he protruded for the purpose from beneath Ingeborg's relaxed body, and his spectacles as he responded were misty, to the immense gratification of the crowd, with happy tears.

This was the first popular thing Ingeborg had done since her arrival. She could not if she had planned it out with all her care and wits have achieved anything more dramatically ingratiating. The day was the most appropriate day in the whole year. It had been well worth waiting, thought her overjoyed Robert, in order to receive such a Christmans gift. The Baroness, who with the Baron was most cordial, felt flattered, as if – only of course less perfectly, for she herself had produced her children in actual time for the tree – her example had been taken to heart and followed. The village was deeply gratified to see an unconscious Frau Pastor carried through its midst, and her limp body had all the prestige of a corpse. Everybody was moved and pleased; and when Ingeborg, after much persuasion, woke up to the world again on the sofa of the parsonage parlour it was to live through the happiest day she had yet had in her life, the day of Robert's greatest joy in her and devotion and care and pride and petting.

Once more and for this day she outstripped the fertilizers in interest, and the laboratory was a place forgotten. She was pampered. She lay on the sofa, feeling quite well again, but staying obediently on it because he told her to and she loved him to care, watching him with happy eyes as he tremendously hovered. He finished the arranging of the tree for her and fixed the candles on it, interrupting himself every now and then to come and kiss her hands and pat her. Beams seemed to proceed from him and penetrate into the remotest corners. In a land where all homes were glowing that Christmas night this little home glowed the brightest. The candles of the tree shone down on Ingeborg curled up in the sofa corner, talking and laughing gaily, but with an infinitely proud and solemn gladness in her heart that at last he believed, that at last she was fairly started on the road of the Higher Duty, that at last she was going to be able to do something back, something in return for all this happiness that had come to her through and because of him.

Ilse was called in, and came very rosy and shining from careful washing to be given her presents. There were surprises for Ingeborg – she had to shut her eyes while they were arranged – that touched and astonished her, so totally blind had Robert seemed to be for weeks past to anything outside his work, – a pot of hyacinths twisted about with pink crinkly paper and satin bows that he must have got with immense difficulty and elaborate precautions to prevent her seeing it, a volume of Heine's poetry, a pair of fur gloves, a silver curb bracelet, and a smiling pig of marzipan with a label round its neck, *Ich bringe Glück*. She, not realising what a German Christmas meant, had only a cigar-case for him; and when, her lap full of his presents and her wrist decorated with the bracelet in which he showed an honest pride, carefully explaining the trick of its fastening and assuring her it was real silver and that little women, he well knew, liked being hung with these barbaric splendours, she put her arm round his neck and apologised for her dreadful ignorance of custom and want of imagination and solitary, unsurprising, miserable cigar-case – when she did this, with her cheek laid on his furry head, he drew her very close to him and blessed her, blessed her his little wife and that greatest of gifts that she was bringing him.

Both of them had wet eyes when this blessing, solemnly administered and received, was over. It was done in the presence of Ilse, who looked on benevolently and at the end came and shook their hands and joined to her thanks for what she had been given her congratulations on the happy event of the coming summer.

'July,' said Ilse, after a moment's reflection. 'We must furnish that room,' she added.

Ingeborg felt as though her very bones were soft with love.

CHAPTER 18

But these high moments of swimming in warm emotion do not last, she found; they are not final, they are not, as she had fondly believed, a state of understanding and cloudless love at last attained to and rested in radiantly. She discovered that the littlest thing puts an end to them, just such a little thing as its being bedtime, for instance, is enough, and the mood does not return, and not only does it not return but it seems forgotten.

She became aware of this next morning at breakfast, and it caused at first an immense surprise. She had got the coffee ready with the glow of the evening before still warming her rosily, she was still altogether thinking *dear* Robert, and wondering, her head on one side as he cut the bread – Ilse was a little cross after the marzipan – and a smile on her lips, at the happiness the world contains; and when he came in she ran to him, shiningly ready to take up the mood at the exact point where bedtime had broken it off the night before.

But Herr Dremmel had travelled a thousand miles in thought since then. He hardly saw her. He kissed her mechanically and sat down to eat. To him she was as everyday and usual again as the bread and coffee of his breakfast. She was his wife who was going presently to be a mother. It was normal, ordinary and satisfactory; and the matter being settled and the proper first joy and sentiment felt, he could go on with more concentration than ever with his work, for there would not now be the perturbing moments so frequent in the last six months when his wife's condition, or rather negation of condition, had thrust itself with the annoyance of an irrepressible weed up among his thinking. The matter was settled; and he put it aside as every worker must put the extraneous aside. Just on this morning he was profoundly concerned with the function of potash in the formation of carbohydrates. He had sat

up late – long after Ingeborg, feeling as if she were dissolved in
stars and happily certain that Robert felt just as liquidly starry,
had gone to bed – considering potash. He wanted more starch in
his grain, more woody-fibre in his straw. She was not across the
passage into their bedroom before his mind had sprung back to
potash. More starch in his grain, more woody-fibre in his straw,
less fungoid disease on his mangels . . .

At breakfast his thoughts were so sticky with that glucose and
cane sugar of digestible carbohydrates that he could not even get
them free for his newspaper, but sat quite silently munching bread
and butter, his eyes on his plate.

'Well, Robert?' said Ingeborg, smiling at him round the coffee
pot, a smile in which lurked the joyful importance of the evening
before.

'Well, little one?' he said absently, not looking at her.

'Well, Robert?' she said again, challengingly.

'What is it, little one?' he asked, looking up with the slight
irritation of the interrupted.

'What? You're not pleased any more?' she asked, pretending
indignation.

'Pleased about what?'

She stared at him at this without pretending anything.

'About what?' she repeated, her lips dropping apart.

He had forgotten.

She thought this really very extraordinary. She poured herself
out a cup of coffee slowly, thinking. He had forgotten. The thing
he had said so often that he wanted most was a thing he could
forget, once he had the certain promise of it, in a night. The
candles on the Christmas tree in the corner were not more burned
out and finished than his tender intensity of feeling of the evening
before.

Well, that was Robert. That was the way, of course, of clever
men. But – the tears? He had felt enough for tears. It was without
a doubt true that he had felt tremendously. How wonderful then,
she thought, slowly dropping sugar into her cup, for even the
memory of it to be wiped out!

Well, that too was Robert. He did not cling as she did to
moments, but passed on intelligently; and she was merely stupid
to suppose anyone with his brains would linger, would loiter
about with her indefinitely, gloating over their happiness.

She left her coffee and got up and went over to him and kissed

him. 'Dear Robert,' she murmured, accommodating herself to
him, proud even, now, that he could be so deeply pre-occupied
with profound thoughts as to forget an event so really great: for
after all, a child to be born, a new life to be launched, was not
that something really great? Yet his thoughts, her husband's
thoughts, were greater.

'Dear Robert,' she murmured; and kissed him proudly.

But the winter, in spite of these convictions of happiness and of
having every reason for pride, was a time that she dragged through
with difficulty. She who had never thought of her body, who had
found in it the perfect instrument for carrying out her will, was
forced to think of it almost continuously. It mastered her. She had
endlessly to humour it before she could use it even a little. She
seemed for ever to be having to take it to a sofa and lay it down
flat and not make it do anything. She seemed for ever to be trying
to persuade it that it did not mind the smell of the pig, or the smell
that came across from Glambeck when the wind was that way of
potato spirits being made in the distillery there. When these smells
got through the window chinks she would shut her eyes and think
hard of the scent of roses and pinks, and of that lovely orange
scent of the orange-coloured lupin she had seen grown everywhere
in the summer; but sooner or later her efforts however valiant
ended in the creeping coldness, the icy perspiration, of sick
faintness.

As the months went on her body became fastidious even about
daily inevitable smells such as the roasting of coffee and the frying
of potatoes, which was extremely awkward when one had to see
to these things oneself; and it often happened that Ilse, coming
out of the scullery or in from the yard fresh and energetic with
health, would find her mistress dropped on a chair with her head
on the kitchen table in quite an absurd condition considering that
everybody assured her it was not an illness at all of feeling as
though it were one.

Ilse would look at her with a kind of amused sympathy. 'The
Frau Pastor will be worse before she is better,' she would say
cheerfully; and if things were very bad and Ingeborg, white and
damp, clung to her in a silent struggle to feel not white and damp,
she used the formula first heard on the lips of Baroness Glambeck
and nodded encouragingly, though not without a certain air of
something that was a little like pleasure, and said, '*Ja, ja* those
who have said A must also say B.'

When Ingeborg's spirit was at its lowest in these unequal combats she would droop her head and shut her eyes and feel she hated – oh, she faintly, coldly, sicklily hated – B.

The fun of housekeeping, of doing everything yourself, wore extremely thin during the next few months. She no longer jumped out of bed eager to get to her duties again and bless the beginning of each new day by a charming and cheerful breakfast table for her man. She felt heavy; reluctant to face the business of dressing; sure that no sooner would she be on her feet than she would feel ill again. She talked of getting another servant, a cook; and Herr Dremmel, who left these arrangements entirely to her, agreed at once. But when it came to taking the necessary steps, to advertising or journeying in to Königsberg to an agency, she flagged and did nothing. It was all so difficult. She might faint on the way. She might be sick. And she could not ask Robert to help her because she did not know what problem nearing a triumphant solution she might not disastrously interrupt.

It seemed to her monstrous to take a man off his thinking, to tear its threads, perhaps to spoil for good that particular line of thought, with demands that he should write advertisements for a cook or go with her in search of one. And as no cook was to be found locally, every wife and mother except ladies like Baroness Glambeck carrying out these higher domestic rites herself, she did nothing. She resigned herself to a fate that was, after all, everybody else's in Kökensee. It was easier to be resigned than to be energetic. Her will grew very flabby. Once she said prayers about cooking, and asked that she might never see or smell it again; but she broke off on realising suddenly and chillily that only death could get her out of the kitchen.

Herr Dremmel was, as he had always been, good and kind to her. He saw nothing, as indeed there was nothing, but the normal and the satisfactory in anything she felt, yet he did what he could, whenever he remembered to, to cheer and encourage. When, coming out of his laboratory to meals, he found her not at the table but on the sofa, her face turned to the wall and buried in an orange so that the dinner smell might be in some small measure dissembled and cloaked, he often patted her before beginning to eat and said, 'Poor little woman.' One cannot, however, go on saying poor little woman continuously for nine months, and of necessity there were gaps in these sympathies; but at least twice he put off his return to work for a few minutes in order to hearten her by painting the great happiness that was in store for her at the end of these tiresome months, the marvellous moment not equalled, he was informed, by any other moment in a human being's life, when the young mother first beheld her offspring.

'I see my little wife so proud, so happy,' he would say ; and each time the picture dimmed his eyes and brought him over to her to stroke her hair.

Then she would forget how sick she felt, and smile and be ashamed that she had minded anything. The highest good, – what would not one practise in the way of being sick to attain the highest good ?

'And he'll be full of brains like yours,' she would say, pulling down his hand from her hair and kissing it and looking up at him smiling.

'And I shall have to double the size of my heart,' Herr Dremmel would say, 'to take in two loves.'

Then Ingeborg would laugh for joy, and for quite a long while manage very nearly to glory in feeling sick.

About March, when the snow that had been heaped on either side of the path to the gate all the winter began to dwindle dirtily, and at midday the eaves dripped melting icicles, and the sun had warmth in it, and great winds set the world creaking, things got better. She no longer felt the grip of faintness on her heart. She left off looking quite so plain and sharp-nosed. An increasing dignity attended her steps, which every week were slower and heavier. After months of not being able to look at food she grew surprisingly hungry, she became suddenly voracious, and ate and ate.

Ilse's amused interest continued. Her mother had had fourteen children and was still regularly having more, and Ilse was well acquainted with the stages. The Frau Pastor, it is true, took the stages more seriously, with more difficulty, with a greater stress on them than Ilse's mother or other Kökensee women, but roughly it was always the same story. 'It will be easier next time,' prophesied Ilse inspiritingly ; though the thought of a next time before she had finished this one depressed rather than inspirited Ingeborg.

She had written home to Redchester to tell her great news, and received a letter from Mrs Bullivant in return in which there was an extremity of absence of enthusiasm. Indeed, the coming baby was only alluded to sideways as it were, indirectly, and if written

words could whisper, in a whisper. '*Your father is overworked*,'
the letter went on, getting away as quickly as possible from
matters of such doubtful decency as an unborn German, '*he has
too much to do. Delicate as I am, I would gladly help him with
his correspondence if I could, but I fear the strain would be too
much. He sadly needs a complete rest and change. Alas, short-
handed as he is and obliged now as we are to retrench, there is no
prospect of one.*'

Whereupon Ingeborg impulsively wrote suggesting in loving
and enthusiastic terms a visit to Kökensee as the most complete
change she could think of, and also as the most economical.

The answer to this when it did come was an extraordinarily
dignified No.

In April Baroness Glambeck drove over one fine afternoon and
questioned her as to her preparations, and was astonished to find
there were none.

'But my dear Frau Pastor!' she cried, holding up both her
yellow kid hands.

'What ought there to be?' asked Ingeborg, who had been too
busy wrestling with her daily tasks in her heavily handicapped
state to think of further labours.

'But naturally a layette. Swaddling clothes, pilchers, shirts,
flannels. Your mother – what is your mother about not to tell
you?'

'Mother is very delicate,' said Ingeborg, flushing a little.

'And a swaddle table you must have—'

'A swaddle table?'

'Naturally. To swaddle the child on. And a cradle. And a
perambulator. And many things for yourself – necessary, indispensable things.'

'What things?' asked Ingeborg faintly.

She had little spirit. She was more tired every day. Just the
difficulty of keeping even with her housekeeping, of keeping
herself tidy in dresses that seemed to shrink smaller each time she
put them on, took up what strength she had. There was none left
over. 'What things?' she asked; and her hands, lying listlessly on
her lap, were flaccid and damp.

Then the Baroness poured forth an endless and bewildering list
with all the gusto and interest of health and leisure. When her
English gave out she went on in German. Her list began with a

swaddle table, which seemed a very important item, and ended with a midwife.

'Have you spoken with her?' she asked.

'No,' said Ingeborg. 'I didn't know – where is she?'

'In our village. Frau Dosch. It is lucky for you she is not further away. Sometimes there is none for miles. She is a very good sort of person. A little old now, but at least she *has* been very good. You ought to see her at once and arrange.'

'Oh?' said Ingeborg, who felt as if the one blessednesss in life would be to creep away somewhere and never arrange anything about anything for ever.

But it did after this become clear to her that certain preparations would undoubtedly have to be made, and she braced herself to driving into Meuk with Ilse and going by train to Königsberg for a day's shopping.

With sandwiches in her pocket and doubt in her heart she went off to shop for the first time in German. Ilse, full of importance, and dressed astonishingly in stockings and new spring garments, sat by her side with an eye to right and left in search of some one to witness her splendour. Herr Dremmel had laid many and strict injunctions on her to take care of her mistress, and in between these wandering glances she did her best by loud inquiries as to Frau Pastor's sensations. Frau Pastor's sensations were those of a perilously jolted woman. She held tight to the hand rail on one side while the Meuk cobbles lasted and to Ilse's arm on the other, and was thankful when the station was reached and she somehow, with a shameful clumsiness, got down out of the high carriage. Incredible to remember that last time she had been at that station she had jumped up into the same carriage as lightly as a bird. She felt humiliated, ashamed of her awkward distorted body. She drew the foolish little cloak and scarf she had put on anxiously about her. People stared. She seemed to be the only woman going to have a child; all the others were free, unhampered, vigorous persons like Ilse. It was as though she had suddenly grown old, this slowness, this fear of not being able to get out of the way of trucks and porters in time . . .

In Königsberg the noise in the streets where the shops were was deafening. All the drays of all the world seemed to be spending that day driving furiously over the stones and tram-lines filled with cases of empty beer bottles or empty milk cans or long, shivering, screaming iron laths, while endless processions of electric-trams rang their bells at them.

Ingeborg clung to Ilse's arm bewildered. After Kökensee alone in its fields, after the dignified tranquillities of Redchester, the noise hammered on her head like showers of blows. There were not many people about, but those there were stared to the extent of stopping dead in front of the two women in order not to miss anything. It was at Ingeborg they stared. Ilse was a familiar figure, just a sunburnt country girl with oiled hair, in her Sunday clothes; but Ingeborg was a foreigner, an astonishment. Men and women stopped, children loitered, half-grown youths whistled and called out comments that her slow German could not follow. She flushed and turned pale, and held on tighter to Ilse. She supposed she must be looking more grotesque even than she had feared. She put it all down to her condition, not knowing on this her first walk in a German provincial town that it was her being a stranger, dressed a little differently, doing her hair a little differently, that caused the interest. She walked as quickly as she could to get away from these people into a shop, little beads of effort round her mouth, looking straight before her, fighting down a dreadful desire to cry; and it was with thankfulness that she sank on to a chair in the quiet mid-day emptiness of Berding and Kühn's drapery and linen establishment.

The young lady behind the counter stared too, but then there was only one of her. She very politely called Ingeborg *gnädiges Fräulein* and inquired whether her child was a boy or a girl.

'Lord God,' cried Ilse, 'how should we know?'

But Ingeborg, with dignity and decision, said it was a boy.

'Then,' said the young lady, 'you require blue ribbons.'

'Do I?' said Ingeborg, very willing to believe her.

The young lady sorted out small garments from green calico boxes labelled *For Firsts*. There were little jackets, little shirts, little caps, everything one could need for the upper portion of a baby.

'*So*', said the young lady, pushing a pile of these articles across the counter to Ingeborg.

'God, God,' cried Ilse in an ecstasy at such tininess, thrusting her red thumb through one of the diminutive sleeves and holding it up to show how tightly it fitted.

'*Nicht wahr?*' agreed the young lady, though without excitement.

'But,' said Ingeborg, laboriously searching out her words, 'the baby doesn't leave off there, at its middle. It'll go on. It'll be a whole baby. It'll have legs and things. What does one put on the rest of it?'

The young lady looked at Ilse for enlightenment.

'It'll *have* a rest, Ilse,' said Ingeborg, also appealing to her. 'These things are just clothes for cherubs.'

'*Ach so*,' said the young lady, visited by a glimmer of understanding: and turning round she dexterously whipped down more green boxes, and taking off the lids brought out squares of different materials, linen, flannel, and a soft white spongy stuff.

'Swaddle,' she said, holding them up.

'Swaddle?' said Ingeborg.

'Swaddle,' confirmed Ilse.

And as Ingeborg only stared, the young lady gradually plumbing her ignorance produced a small mattress in a white and frilly linen bag, and diving down beneath the counter, brought up a dusty doll which she deftly rolled up to the armpits in the squares, inserted it into the bag with its head out, and tied it firmly with tapes. '*So*,' she said, giving this neat object a resounding slap: and picking it up she pretended to rock it fondly in her arms. 'Behold the First Born,' she said.

After that Ingeborg put herself entirely into these experienced hands. She bought all she was told to. She even bought the doll to practise on, – 'It will not do *everything* of course,' explained the young lady. The one thing she would not buy was a sewing machine to make her own swaddle with, as Ilse economically counselled. The young lady was against this purchase, which could only be made in another shop; she said true ladies always preferred Berding and Kühn to do such work for them. Ilse said true mothers always did it for themselves, and it was one of the chief joys of this blessed time, Ilse said, seeing the house grow fuller and fuller of swaddle.

At this the young lady pursed her lips and shrugged her shoulders and assumed an air of waiting indifference.

Ilse, resenting her attitude, inquired of her heatedly what, that, she knew of *Müttergluck*.

The young lady, for some reason, was offended at this, though nothing was more certain than that knowledge of *Müttergluck* would have meant instant dismissal from Berding and Kühn's. It became a wrangle across the counter, and was only ended by Ingeborg's altogether siding with the young lady and the interests of Berding and Kühn, and ordering, as the Baroness had directed, ten dozen each of the ready-made squares.

'I'd die if I had to hem ten dozen of anything,' she explained apologetically to Ilse.

And it was very bitter to Ilse, who meant well, to see the young lady look at her with a meditative comprehensiveness down her nose; it left no honourable course open to her but to sulk, and in her heart she would rather not have sulked on this exciting and unusual excursion. She was forced to, however, by her own public opinion, and she did it vigorously, thoroughly, blackly, all the rest of the day, all the way home; and neither cakes nor chocolate nor ices earnestly and successively applied to her by Ingeborg at the pastrycook's were allowed to lighten the gloom.

'But I suppose,' Ingeborg said to herself as she crept into her bed that night in the spiritless mood called philosophical, for Ilse was her stay and refuge and to have her not speaking to her, to feel she had hurt her, was a grievous thing, a thing when one is weary very like the last straw, – 'I suppose it's all really only a part of B. Oh, oh,' she added with a sudden flare of rebellion that died out immediately in shame of it, 'I don't think I *like* B – I don't think I *like* B . . .'

CHAPTER 19

There was nevertheless an absorption and an excitement about this new strange business that did not for a moment allow her to be dull. She might feel ill, wretched, exhausted, but she was always interested. A tremendous event was ahead of her, and all her days were working up to it. She lived in preparation. Each one of her sensations was a preparation, an advance. There was a necessity for it; something was being made, was growing, had to be completed; life was full of meaning, and of plain meaning; she understood and saw reasons everywhere for what happened to her. Things had to be so if one wanted the supreme crown, and her part of the work was really very easy, it was just to be patient. She was often depressed, but only because the months seemed so endless and she was so tired of her discomfort, – never because she was afraid. She had no fears, for she had no experience. She contemplated the final part of the adventure, the part Ilse alluded to cheerfully as her Difficult Hour, with the perfect tranquillity of ignorance. On the whole she was very free from the moods Herr Dremmel had braced himself to bear, and continued right through not to be exacting. She had no examples of more fussed over and tended women before her eyes to upset her contentment, and saw for herself how the village women in like condition worked on at their wash-tubs and in the fields up to the end. Besides, she had been trained in a healthy self-effacement.

She only cried once, but then it was February and enough to make anybody cry, with the sleet stinging the windows and the wind howling round the dark little house. She put it down to February, a month she had never thought anything of, and hid from herself as she hurriedly wiped away her tears – where did they all come from ? – that she was disgracefully crying because she had been alone so long, and Ilse had gone out somewhere without asking, and Robert hadn't spoken to her for days, and there was nobody to bring in the lamp if she didn't fetch it herself, and she couldn't fetch it because she felt so funny and might drop it, and what she wanted most in the world was a mother. Not a mother somewhere else, away in Redchester, but a real soft warm mother sitting beside her in that room, with her (the mother's) arm under her (Ingeborg's) head, and her (Ingeborg's) face against her (the mother's) bosom. A mother with feathers all over her like a kind hen would be very ideal, but short of that there was a soft black dress she remembered her mother used to wear with amiable old lace on it that wouldn't scratch, and the comfort it would be, the *comfort*, if for half an hour she might put her cheek against this and keep it there and say nothing.

And she cried more and more, and told herself more and more eagerly, with a kind of rage, that February was no sort of month at all.

When Herr Dremmel came out of his laboratory to ask why his lamp had not been brought, and found no light anywhere and no Ilse when he shouted, he was vexed; but when he had fetched a lamp himself and put it on the table where it shone on to Ingeborg's swollen and blinking eyes, he was still more vexed.

'This is foolish,' he said, staring down at her a moment. 'You will only harm my child.'

She did not cry again.

Towards the end of the time she left off feeling giddy and faint, and though her nights were either sleepless or full of peculiarly horrible dreams, her days became placid with a heavy placidity and absence of misgivings that was almost bovine. The spring had dried up the roads, but she did not for all that take her clumsy ridiculous body – it was holy and consecrated, she knew, but she could see for herself that it was also shamefully ridiculous – for walks that obliged her to pass through the village, but spent hours in the budding garden up and down on one of the two available paths, the one at the end on the edge of the rye-fields which were now the vividest green, or the one on the east side of the house beneath Robert's laboratory windows where the lilacs grew.

His table was at right angles to the end window, and she often stood on the path watching him, his head bent over his work in an absorption that went on hour after hour. He kept the windows shut because the spring disturbed him. It had a way of coming in irrepressibly and wantoning among his papers, or throwing a handful of lilac blossoms into his rye samples, or sending an officious bee to lumber round him.

Ingeborg walked up and down, up and down on this path every day, taking the exercise Baroness Glambeck had recommended, and for three weeks just this path was the most beautiful thing in the world, for it was planted on either side with ancient lilac bushes and they were a revelation to her when they came out after the spare and frugal lilacs in the gardens at home. Above their swaying scented loveliness of light and colour and shape she could see Robert's tow-coloured head inside the window bending over his table every time she came to the end of her tramp and turned round again. It was the best part of the whole nine months, these three weeks of lilacs and fine weather on that scented path, with Robert busy and content where she could see him. She loved being able to see him; it was a companionable thing.

By June everything was ready. The nursery was furnished, the cradle trimmed, a pale blue perambulator blocked the passage, neat stacks of little clothes filled the cupboards, and Frau Dosch, a hoary person of unseemly conversation, interviewed and told to be on the alert. The idea of arranging for a doctor to be on the alert too would not of itself have entered Ingeborg's head, and nobody put it there. Such a being was indeed mentioned once by Baroness Glambeck, whose interest, increasing with the months, brought her over several times, but only vaguely as some one who had to be sent for when the midwife judged the patient to have reached the stage described by the Baroness as in extremity. Then, apparently, the law obliged the midwife to send for a doctor.

'There is much difference, however,' said the Baroness, 'between thinking one is in extremity and really being in it,' and the patient was apt to be biassed on these occasions, she explained, and inclined rashly to jump to conclusions. Therefore wisdom dictated the leaving of such a decision to the midwife.

'Yes,' said Ingeborg placidly.

'Of course,' said the Baroness, 'all this is different from other illnesses, because it is not one.'

'Yes,' said Ingeborg, placidly.

'And when I speak of the patient I do not mean the patient, because without an illness there cannot be a patient.'

'No,' said Ingeborg, placidly.

'Nor without a patient can there be an illness.'

'No,' said Ingeborg, placidly.

She was leaning back in a low chair watching the sun shining on the tops of the lime-trees over her head, for it was the end of June and they were in the garden. It all seemed very satisfactory. Nobody was ill, nobody was going to be ill. There would be rather a troublesome moment that would be met and got over with patience and Frau Dosch, but no illness, just nature having its way, and then, — it really seemed altogether too wonderful that then, quite soon now, perhaps in a week or two, any day really, there would be a baby. And she was going to love it with this passion of love that only mothers know, and it was going to fill her life most beautifully to the brim, and it would make her so happy that she would never want anything but just it.

That is what they had told her. On her own account she had added to this that the baby would be every bit as clever as Robert but with more leisure; that it would have his brains but not his laboratory; that it wouldn't be able, it wouldn't want, to get out of its perambulator and go and lock itself up away from her and weigh rye grains; and that it wouldn't mind, in fact it would prefer, being fetched out of its thoughts to come and be kissed.

For ages, for years, it was going to be her dear and close companion, her fellow-paddler in the lake, her fellow-wanderer in God's woods. Her eyes were soft with joy at the thought of how soon now she was going to be able to tuck this precious being under her arm and take it with her lightly and easily into the garden, restored to her own slim nimbleness again, and point out the exceeding beauty of the world to its new, astonished eyes. She would show it the rye-fields, and the great heaped-up sky. She would make it acquainted with the frogs, and introduce it to the bittern. She would draw its attention to the delight of lying face downwards on hot grass where tufts of thyme grew and watching the busy life among the blades and roots. She would insist on its observing the storks standing in their nest on the stable roof and how the light lay along their white wings, and how the red of their legs was like the red of the pollard willows in March. And at night, if it were so ill-advised as not to sleep, she would pick it up and take it to the window and impress its soft mind all over with shining little stars. Wonderful to think that before the orange-coloured lupins, those August glories, had done flowering, she would be out among them again, only with her son this time, her flesh of her flesh and blood of her blood, her Robertlet.

Baroness Glambeck watched her face curiously as she lay

looking up at the sunny tree-tops with the amused smile of these thoughts on it. It was clear the Frau Pastor had forgotten her presence; and even her being so near her Difficult Hour did not explain or excuse a social lapse. Indeed, the Frau Pastor received her visits with an absence of excitement and of realisation of the honour being done her that was almost beyond the limits of the forgivable. Always she behaved as though she were an equal, and a particularly equal equal. Much, however, could be excused in a person who was not only English – a nation the Baroness had heard described as rude – but so near her first confinement. When this was over there would be a severe readjustment of relation-ships, but meanwhile one could not really be angry with her; just her amazing and terrible ignorance of the simplest facts connected with child-bearing made it impossible to be angry with her. She reminded the Baroness of a sheep going tranquilly to the slaughter, quite pleased with the promenade, quite without a thought of what lay at the end of it. Did English mothers then all keep their daughters in such darkness on the one great subject for a woman?

For some subtle reason the expression of extreme placidness on Ingeborg's face as she lay silently watching the tree-tops and planning what she would do with her baby annoyed the Baroness.

'It will hurt, you know,' she said.

Ingeborg brought her gaze slowly down to earth again, and looked at her a moment.

'What?' she said.

'It will hurt,' repeated the Baroness.

'Oh yes,' said Ingeborg. 'I know. But it's all natural.'

'Certainly it is natural. Nevertheless—'

The Baroness stopped grimly, screwed up her mouth, and shook her head three times with an awful suggestiveness.

Ingeborg looked at her, and then suddenly some words out of her cathedral-going days at Redchester flashed into her mind. She had totally forgotten them, and now her memory began jerking them together. They came, she knew, in the Prayer-book some-where; was it in the Litany? No; but anyhow they were in that truthful book, the Book of Common Prayer, and they were – yes, that was it: *The great danger of child-birth.* Yes; and again: *The great pain and peril of child-birth.*

A quick flush came into her face, and for the first time a look of fear into her eyes. She sat up, leaning on both her hands, and stared at the Baroness.

'Is it so very dreadful ?' she asked.

The Baroness merely shook her head.

'It can't be *very*,' said Ingeborg, watching the Baroness's expression in search of agreement, 'or there wouldn't be any mothers left.'

The Baroness went on screwing up her mouth and shaking her head.

'It must be *bearable*,' said Ingeborg again, anxiously.

The Baroness would not commit herself.

'They'd die, you see, if it wasn't – the mothers all would. But there seem' – her voice trembled a little in her desire for the Baroness's agreement – 'there seem to be lots of mothers still about.'

She paused, but the Baroness continued not to commit herself.

'I can bear anything,' said Ingeborg, with a great show of pride and a voice that trembled, 'if it's – if it's reasonable.'

'It is not reasonable,' said the Baroness. 'It is the Will of God.'

'Oh that's the same thing, the same thing,' said Ingeborg, throwing herself back on her cushions and nervously pulling some white pinks she had been smelling to pieces.

She was ashamed of her terror. But her body, her distorted body, – she had only to look at it to see that some very appalling convulsion would be required before it could become what it used to be nine months ago. How blind she had been not to realise this before.

All that evening she was restless and nervous, struggling with this new feeling of fear. She could not keep still, but walked about the sitting-room while Robert ate his supper at the table, pressing her cold hands together, trying to reason herself into tranquillity again. Then sometimes it was so unbearable that one could not bear it and died ? What a way to die ! What a *way* . . .

She stood still a moment watching Robert's quiet black back as he bent over his supper. Then she went over to him impulsively and rubbed both her hands quickly through his hair, which had not been cut for some time, making it stand up on ends.

'There,' she said. 'Now you look *really* sweet.' And she bent and kissed him, lingeringly, on the back of his neck. He was near her, he was alive, she could hold on to him for a little before she went alone into whatever it was of icy and awful and unknown that waited for her.

'Good little wife,' he said, still going on eating, but putting his left arm round her while his right continued to do what was necessary with the supper, and not looking up.

His affection at this time had watered down into a mild theory. She was not a wife to him, though he called her so, she was a *werdende Mutter*. This, Herr Dremmel told himself when he too felt bored by the length of the months, is a most honourable, creditable, and respectable condition; but no man can feel warm towards a condition. His little sheep had disappeared into the immensities of the *werdende Mutter*. He would be glad when she was restored to him.

The next day she got a letter from Mrs Bullivant, dated from the Master's House, Ananias College, Oxford.

'*It may interest you to hear,*' wrote Mrs Bullivant, '*that your sister has a little daughter. The child was born at daybreak this morning. I am worn out with watching. It is a very fine little girl, and both mother and child are doing well. I am not doing well at all. We had that excellent Dr Williamson I am thankful to say, or I don't know what would have happened. Of course our darling Judith was mercifully spared knowing anything about it, for she was kept well under chloroform, but I knew and I feel very upset. I only wish I too could have been chloroformed during those anxious hours. As it is I am suffering much from shock, and will be a long while before I recover. Dr Williamson says that on these occasions he always pities most the mothers of the mothers. Your father—*'

But here Ingeborg let the letter drop to the floor and sat thinking.

When Robert came in to dinner late that day, hot and pleased from his fields which were doing particularly well after the warm rains of several admirably-timed thunderstorms, she gave him his food and waited till he had eaten it and begun to smoke, and then asked him if she were going to have chloroform.

'Chloroform?' he repeated, gazing at her while he fetched back his thoughts from their pleasurable lingering among his fields. 'What for?'

'So that I don't know about anything. Mother writes Judith had some. She's got a little girl.'

Herr Dremmel took his cigar out of his mouth and stared at her. She was leaning both elbows on the table at her end and, with her chin on her hands, was looking at him with very bright eyes.

'But this is cowardice,' he said.

'I'd *like* some chloroform,' said Ingeborg.

'It is against nature,' said Herr Dremmel.

'I'd *like* some chloroform,' said Ingeborg.

'You have before you,' said Herr Dremmel, endeavouring to be patient, 'an entirely natural process, as natural as going to sleep at night and waking up next morning.'

'It may be as natural,' said Ingeborg, 'but I don't believe it's as nice. I'd *like* some chloroform.'

'What! Not nice? When it is going to introduce you to the supreme—'

'Yes, I know. But I – I have a feeling it's going to introduce me rather roughly. I'd *like* some chloroform.'

'God,' said Herr Dremmel solemnly, 'has arranged these introductions Himself, and it is not for us to criticise.'

'That's the first time,' said Ingeborg, 'that you've talked like a bishop. You might be a bishop.'

'When it comes to the highest things,' said Herr Dremmel severely, 'and this is the holiest, most exalted act a human being can perpetrate, all men are equally believers.'

'I expect they are,' said Ingeborg. 'But the others – the ones who're not men – they'd *like* some chloroform.'

'No healthy, normally-built woman needs it,' said Herr Dremmel, greatly irritated by this persistence. 'No doctor would give it. Besides, there will not be a doctor, and the midwife may not administer it. Why I do not recognise my little wife, my little intelligent wife who must know that nothing is being required of her but that which is done by other women every day.'

'I don't see what being intelligent has to do with this,' said Ingeborg, 'and I'd *like* some chloroform.'

Herr Dremmel looked at her bright eyes and flushed cheeks in astonishment. Up to now she had rejoiced in her condition whenever he mentioned it, and indeed he could see no reason for any other attitude; she had apparently felt very little that was not pleasant during the whole time, known none of those distresses he had heard that women sometimes endure, been healthily free from complications. There had been moods, it is true, and he had occasionally found her lounging on sofas, but then women easily become lazy at these times. It had all been normal and would no doubt continue normal. What, then, was this shrinking at the eleventh hour, this inability to be as ordinarily courageous as every peasant woman in the place? It was a most unfortunate, unpleasant whim, the most unfortunate she could have had. He had been prepared for whims, but had always supposed they would be tinned pineapples. Of course he was not going to humour her. Too much was at stake. He had heard anæsthetics were harmful on these occasions, harmful and entirely unnecessary. The best thing by far for the child was the absence of everything except nature. Nature in this matter should be given a free hand. She was not always wise, he knew from his experience with his fields, but in this department he was informed she should be left completely to herself. If his wife was so soft as not to be able to bear a little pain what sort of sons was she likely to give him? A breed of shrinkers; a breed of white-skinned hiders. Why, he had not asked for gas even when he had three teeth out at one sitting two years before – it was the dentist who had insisted he should have it – and that was only teeth, objects of no value afterwards. But to have one's son handicapped at the very beginning because his mother was not unselfish enough to endure a little for his sake . . .

Ingeborg got up and came and put her arms round his neck and whispered. 'I'm – frightened,' she breathed. 'Robert, I'm – frightened.'

Then he took her on his knee, or rather tried to, but finding it no longer possible went with his arms about her to the sofa, and made her sit down beside him while he reasoned with her.

He reasoned for at least twenty minutes, taking great pains and being patient. He told her she was not really frightened, but that her physical condition caused her to fancy she thought she was.

Ingeborg was interested by this, and readily admitted that it was possible.

He told her about the simple courage of the other women in Kökensee, and Ingeborg agreed, for she had seen it herself.

He told her how God had arranged she should bring forth in sorrow, but she fidgeted and began again to talk of bishops.

He told her it would only be a few hours' suffering, perhaps less, and that in return there was a lifetime's joy for them in their child.

She listened attentively to this, was quite quiet for a few minutes, then slid her hand into his.

He told her she might, by letting herself go to fear, hurt her child, and would she not in that case find difficulty afterwards in forgiving herself?

She sat up straight at this, and began to look determined and brave.

Finally he told her that anæsthetics, while they might numb her for a time only to add to her subsequent discomforts, would be harmful for the child, would prolong its birth, and might even send it suffocated into the world.

This completed her cure. An enormous courage took the place of her misgivings. She rose up from the sofa so superfluously brave, so glowing with enterprise, that she wanted to begin at once that she might show how much she could cheerfully endure. 'As though,' she said, lifting her chin, 'I couldn't stand what other women stand — as though I wouldn't stand *anything* sooner than hurt my baby!' And she flung back her head in the proudest defiance of whatever might be ahead of her.

Her baby; her husband; her happy home; to suffer for these would be beautiful if it were not such a little thing, almost too little to offer up at their dear altar. She would have been transfigured by her shining thoughts if anything could have transfigured her, but no thoughts however bright could pierce through that sad body. Her outlines were not the outlines for heroic attitudes. She not only had a double chin, she seemed to be doubled all over. She looked the queerest figure, heavy, middle-aged, uncouth, ugly, standing there passionately expressing her readiness to begin; and Herr Dremmel unconsciously seeing this, and bored by having had to explain the obvious at such length and spend a valuable half-hour bringing a woman to reason — why could they never go to it by themselves? — wasted no more words having got her there, but brushed a hasty kiss across her hair and went away looking at his watch.

And next day, just as she was putting the potatoes into that dinner-pot that so much simplified her cooking, she uttered a small exclamation and turned quickly to Ilse with a look of startled questioning.

'*Geht's los*?' asked Ilse, pausing in the wiping dry of a wooden ladle.

'I — don't know,' said Ingeborg, gasping a little. 'No,' she added after a minute, during which they stood staring at each other, 'it wasn't anything.'

And she went on with the potatoes.

But when presently there was another little fluttering exclamation Ilse, with great decision, laid down her gloomy drying-cloth and sought out Johann, Herr Dremmel not having come in, and bade him harness the horses and fetch Frau Dosch.

'The first thing,' said Frau Dosch arriving two hours later, surprisingly brisk and business-like considering her age and the heat, 'the first thing is to plait your hair in two plaits.'

And still later, when Ingeborg had left off pretending or trying to be anything at all, when courage and unselfishness and stoicism and a desire to please Robert – who was Robert? – were like toys for drawing-room games, shoved aside in these grips with death, when she was battered into being nothing but a writhing animal, nothing but a squirming thing without a soul, without a reason, without anything but a terrible, awful body, Frau Dosch nodded her head philosophically while she ate and drank from the trays Ilse kept on bringing her, and said at regular intervals, '*Ja, ja – was sein muss sein muss.*'

Such were the consolations of Frau Dosch.

CHAPTER 20

These things began on Tuesday at midday; and on Wednesday night, so late that bats and moths were busy in the garden and often in the room, Frau Dosch, grown very wispy about the hair and abandoned in the dress, dabbed a bundle of swaddle with a small red face emerging from it down on to the bed beside Ingeborg and said, tired but triumphant, 'There.'

The great moment had come: the supreme moment of a woman's life. Herr Dremmel was present, dishevelled and moist-eyed, Ilse was present, glowing and hot. It was a boy, a magnificent boy Frau Dosch pronounced, and the three stood watching for the first ray of *Mutterglück*, the first illumination that was to light the face on the pillow.

'There,' said Frau Dosch; but Ingeborg did not open her eyes.

She was lying sideways, a huddled, crumpled figure, one arm hanging over the edge of the bed, her eyes shut, her mouth open, her hair, matted and moist and dark, drooping over her white indifferent face.

'There,' said Frau Dosch again, picking up the bundle and laying it slantwise on Ingeborg's breast and addressing her very loudly. 'Frau Pastor – rouse yourself – behold your son – a splendid boy – almost a man already.'

She took Ingeborg's arm and laid it round the bundle.

It slid off and hung over the edge of the bed as before.

'Tut, tut,' said Frau Dosch becoming scandalised; and stooping down she shouted into Ingeborg's ear, 'Frau Pastor – wake up – look at your son – a magnificent fellow – with a chest, I tell you – oh, but he will break the hearts of the maidens he will—'

Still the blankest indifference on the face on the pillow.

Herr Dremmel knelt down so as to be on a level with it, and took the limp damp hand hanging down in his and patted it.

'Little wife,' he said in German, 'it is all over. Open your eyes and rejoice with me in our new happiness. You have given me a son.'

'*Ja eben*,' said Frau Dosch emphatically.

'You have filled my cup with joy.'

'*Ja eben*,' said Frau Dosch still louder.

'Open your eyes, and welcome him to his mother's heart.'

'*Ja eben*,' said Frau Dosch indignantly.

Then Ingeborg did slowly open her eyes – it seemed as if she could hardly lift their heavy lids – and looked at Robert as though she were looking at him from an immense distance. Her mouth remained open; her face was vacant.

Frau Dosch seized the bundle, and with clucking sounds jerked it up and down between the faces of the parents so that its mother's eyes must needs fall upon it. Its red contents began to cry.

'Ah – there now – now we shall see,' exclaimed Frau Dosch, who had been secretly perturbed by the newborn's absence of comment while it was being washed and swaddled.

'The first cry of our son,' said Herr Dremmel, kissing Ingeborg's hand with deep emotion.

'*Now* we will try,' said Frau Dosch, once more laying the baby on Ingeborg's chest and folding her arm round it. This time she took the precaution to hold the mother's arm firmly in position herself. 'Oh the splendid fellow!' she exclaimed. 'Frau Pastor, what do you say to your eldest son?'

But Frau Pastor said nothing. Her eyelids drooped over her eyes again, and shut the world and all its vigours out. The sound of these people round her bed came to her from far away. There was a singing in her ears, a black remoteness in her soul. Somewhere from behind the vast sea of nothingness in which she seemed to sink, through the constant singing in her ears came little faint voices with words. She wanted to listen, she wanted to listen, why would these people interrupt her – the same words over and over again, faintly throbbing in a rhythm like the rhythm of the wheels of the train that had brought her through the night long ago across Europe to her German home, only very distant, tiny, muffled – 'From battle and murder' – yes, she had caught that – 'from all women labouring with child' – yes – 'from all sick persons' – yes – 'and young children' – yes, go on – 'Good Lord deliver us' – oh, yes – please . . . Good Lord deliver us – please – please – deliver us . . .

'Perhaps a little brandy?' suggested Herr Dremmel, puzzled.

'Brandy! If her own son cannot cheer her— Does the Herr Pastor then not know that one gives nothing at first to a lady lying-in but water-soup?'

Herr Dremmel, feeling ignorant, let go the idea of brandy. 'Her hand is rather cold,' he said, almost apologetically for who knew but what it was cold because it ought to be?

Frau Dosch expressed the opinion that it was not, and that if it were it was not so cold as her heart. 'See here,' she said, 'see this beautiful boy addressing his mother in the only language he knows, and she not even looking at him. Come, my little fellow – come, then – we are not wanted – come with Aunt Dosch – the old Aunt Dosch—'

And she took the baby off Ingeborg's passive chest, and after a few turns with it up and down the room slapping the underside of its swaddle in a way experience had taught choked out crying, put it in the pale blue cradle that stood ready on two chairs.

'Well, well,' said Herr Dremmel getting up, for his knees were hurting him, and looking at his watch, 'it is bedtime for all of us. It is past midnight. To-morrow, after a sleep, my wife will be herself again.'

He went towards the door, followed by Ilse with one of the two lamps that were adding to the stifling heat in the room, then paused and looked back.

Ingeborg was lying as before.

'You are sure only water-soup?' he said, hesitating. 'Is that – will that by the time it reaches my son nourish him?'

For all answer Frau Dosch advanced heavily and shut the door.

She was tired to death. She was not, at that hour of the night, going to defend her methods to a husband. She locked the door and began pulling off her dress. She could hardly stand. It had been one of those perfectly normal births that yet are endless and half kill an honest midwife who is not as young as she used to be. Before dropping on to the bed provided for her she took a final look at the object in the cradle, which was noiselessly sleeping, and then at the other object on the bed, which was lying as before. Well, if the Frau Pastor preferred behaving like a log instead of a proud mother – Frau Dosch shrugged her shoulder, put on a coloured dimity jacket over her petticoat, kicked off her slippers, and went, stockinged and hairpinned, to bed and to instant sleep.

But the life in the parsonage puzzled Herr Dremmel during the next few weeks. He had expected the simple joys of realised family happiness to succeed the act of birth. It was a reasonable expectation. It occurred in other houses. He had been patient for nine months, supported during their interminableness by the thought that what he bore would be amply made up to him at the end of them by a delighted young wife restored to him in her slenderness and health, running singing about the house with a healthy son in her arms. The son was there and seemed satisfactory, but where was the healthy young wife ? And as for running about the house, when the fifth day came, the day on which the other women in the parish got up and began to be brisk again, Ingeborg made no sign of even being aware it was expected of her. She looked at him vaguely when he suggested it, with the same vagueness and want of interest in anything with which she lay for hours staring out of the window, her mouth always a little open, her position always the same, unless Ilse came and changed it for her.

Frau Dosch had left the morning after the birth according to the custom of midwives, returning on each of the three following mornings to wash the mother and child, and after that Ilse had taken over these duties, and as far as he could see performed them with zeal and vigour. Everything was done that could be done ; why then did Ingeborg remain apathetic and uninterested in bed, and not take the trouble even to shut her mouth ?

He was puzzled and disappointed. The days passed, and nothing was changed. He could not but view these manifestations of want of backbone with uneasiness, occurring as they did in the mother of his children. The least thing that was demanded of her in the way of exertion made her break out into a perspiration. She had not yet, so far as he knew, voluntarily put her arms once round her son, – Ilse had to hold them round him. She had not even said anything about him. He might have been a girl for any pride she showed. And that holiest function of a mother, the nursing of her child, instead of being a recurring joy was a recurring and apparently increasing difficulty. Whenever his son wished to be fed and was taken to his mother for the purpose, instead of welcoming him eagerly she flushed and shrank and shut her eyes, and while the meal lasted came out in a profuse perspiration, lying with her head turned away and both hands clutching the sheet as if she were enduring something.

'Ingeborg,' he had said to her the first time he witnessed this peculiar behaviour, 'what is it ?'

'Hurts,' she breathed – so indistinctly that he had had to bend down to hear her.

He had pointed out to her that this must be fancy, for it was not only the greatest privilege of a mother to nurse her child but it was an estabished fact that it gave her the deepest, the holiest satisfaction. In all pictures where there is a mother, he had reminded her, she is invariably either nursing or has just been doing so, and on her face is the satisfied serenity that attends the fulfilment of natural functions.

She had not answered, and her face remained turned away and flushed, with beads rolling down it. Ilse held the baby, he observed; there was a most regrettable want of hold in his wife.

And she appeared to have odd fancies. She imagined, for instance, that the pieces of buttered bread Ilse put on a plate and laid beside her on her bed at tea-time were stuck to the plate. He had found her struggling one afternoon and becoming hot endeavouring to lift one of these pieces up off the plate. He had asked her, Ilse not being in the room, what she was doing. As usual she had whispered – it was another of her fancies that she had lost her voice – and when he bent down he found that she was whispering the word *stuck*.

He had taken up the piece to show her she was mistaken, and had shaken the plate and made all the pieces on it spring about, and she had watched him and then begun over again to behave as if she could not lift one.

Then she dropped her hands down on to the sheet and looked up at him and began to whisper something else. '*Heavy*,' she whispered, but not, he was glad to say, without at least some sort of a slight smile indicating her awareness that she was conducting herself childishly, and Ilse, coming in, had taken the bread and fed her as if it were she who were the baby and not his son.

Herr Dremmel therefore, was both puzzled and worried. He was still more puzzled and worried when, on the very day week after the birth, Ilse came to him and said that Frau Pastor was shaking her bed about and that she feared if she did not soon stop the bed, which was enfeebled as Herr Pastor knew by having two mended legs among its four, might break. She had reminded Frau Pastor of this, but she did not seem to care and continued to shake it.

'The good bed,' said Ilse, 'the excellent bed. The best we have in the house. Would Herr Pastor step across?'

Herr Pastor stepped across, and found Ingeborg shivering with such astonishing energy that the bed did, as Ilse had described, rattle threateningly.

In reply to his questions Ilse told him, for Ingeborg was too busy shaking to explain, that nothing had happened except that Frau Pastor said she was thirsty and would like a glass of cold water, and she had fetched it fresh from the pump and Frau Pastor had asked to be held up to drink it and had drunk it all at one draught and immediately fallen back and begun this shaking.

'Ingeborg, what is this?' said Herr Dremmel with a show of severity, for he had heard severity acted as a sedative on those who, for instance, shake.

When, however, Ingeborg, instead of replying like a reasonable being, continued to shake and seem unaware of his presence, and when on touching her he found that in spite of the shivering she was extremely hot, he sent Johann for Frau Dosch, who on seeing her could only suggest that Johann should drive on into Meuk and bring out the doctor.

And so it was that Ingeborg, coming suddenly out of a thin, high confusion in which she seemed to have been hurrying since the world began, found it was night, for lamps were alight, and people – many people – were round her bed, and one was a man she did not know with a short black beard. But she did know him. It was the doctor. It flashed across her instantly. Then she had really got to being in extremity. That woman had said so, that big woman who used to come and see her in the garden long ago. And Ilse – that was Ilse at the foot of the bed crying. When one was in extremity Ilses did cry. She found herself stroking the doctor's beard and begging him not to let go of her. She was reminded that it was unusual to stroke the doctor's beard by his drawing back, but she thought it silly not to let one's beard be stroked if somebody wanted to. She heard herself saying, 'Don't let go of me – please – don't let go of me – please' – but it seemed that he could not hold her, for she was caught away almost immediately again into that thin, hot, hurrying confusion, high up in the treble, high up at the very top, where all the violins were insisting together over and over again on one thin, quivering, anxious note . . .

'It is impossible,' said the doctor, a Jew from Königsberg, lately married and set up at Meuk, looking at Frau Dosch, 'that this should have happened.'

And he proceeded to explain to Herr Dremmel that if his wife's skin had not been so thin and if its thinness had been observed in time all would have been well. It was impossible to credit a human being, otherwise perfectly normal, with so thin a skin, he said, but yet, forced by the facts, one had to. The child, hungry and hard of gum, had bitten the Frau Pastor at its first meal —

'No,' said Frau Dosch, 'for I was there.'

The doctor shrugged his shoulder. It was impossible, he said, not to have seen the bite at once, nevertheless — he looked at Frau Dosch, who shut her mouth in a grim line of defensiveness — the impossible had happened. Dirt had entered. There was now an abscess. He might have to operate. In any case the child in future would have to seek its nourishment in tins.

'What?' exclaimed Herr Dremmel.

'Tins,' said the doctor.

'Tins? For my son? When there are cows in the world? Cows, which at least more closely resemble mothers than tins?'

'Tins,' repeated the doctor firmly. 'Herr Pastor, cows have moods just as frequently as women. They are fed unwisely, and behold immediately a mood. Not having the gift of tongues they cannot convey their mood by speech, and baffled at one end they fall back upon the other, and express their malignancies in milk.'

Herr Dremmel was silent. The complications and difficulties of family life were being lit up into a picture at which he could only gaze in dismay. On the bed Ingeborg was ceaselessly turning her head from one side to the other and rubbing her hands weakly up and down, up and down over the sheet. While he talked the doctor was watching her. Frau Dosch stood looking on with a locked-up mouth. Ilse wept. The baby whimpered.

The doctor said he would send some tins of patent food out by Johann on his return journey; if there should be much delay and the baby was noisy, said the doctor, a little water—

'Water! My son fed on water?' exclaimed Herr Dremmel. 'Heavens above us, what diet is this for a good German? Tins and water in the place of blood and iron?'

The doctor shrugged his shoulder, and gently putting down Ingeborg's hand which he had been holding for a moment to see if he could quiet it, prepared to go away, saying he would also send out a nurse.

'Ah,' said Herr Dremmel, greatly relieved, 'you know of a thoroughly healthy wet one?'

'Completely dry. For Frau Pastor. Impossible to leave her unnursed. There will be bandages. There must be punctuality and care' – he looked at Frau Dosch – 'cleanliness, efficiency' – at each word he looked at Frau Dosch. 'I will come out to-morrow. Perfectly normal, perfectly normal,' he said, as he got into the carriage while Herr Dremmel stood ruefully on the doorstep, 'but, as I say, a thin skin.'

The illness went its perfectly normal course. A nurse came out from the principal Königsberg hospital and the disordered house at once became perfectly normal too. Ilse returned to her kitchen, the baby was appeased by its scientific diet, Ingeborg's bed grew smooth and spotless, her room was quiet, nobody knocked any more against the foot of the bed in passing or shook the floor and herself by heavy treading; she was no longer tended with the same vigour that made the kitchen floor spotless and the pig happy; bandages, unguents and disinfectants stood neatly in rows, clean white cloths covered the tables, the windows were wide open day and night, and lamps left off burning exactly where they shone into her eyes. Everything was normal, including the behaviour of the abscess, which went its calm way, unhurried and undisturbed by anything the doctor tried to do to it, ripening, reaching its perfection, declining, in an order and obedience to causation that was beautiful for those capable of appreciating it. Everything was normal except the inside of Ingeborg's mind.

There, in a black recess, crouched fear. She suspected life. She had lost, on that awful night and day and night again of birth, confidence in it. She knew it now. It was all death. Death and cruelty. Death and nameless horror. Death pretending, death waiting, waiting to be cruel again, to get her again, and get her altogether next time. What was this talk of life? It was only just death. The others didn't know. She knew. She had seen it and been with it. She had been down into the valley of the shadow of it uncomforted. Her eyes had been wide open while she went. Each step of the way was cut into her memory. They had let her miss nothing. She knew. Out there in the garden the rustling leaves looked gay, and the sun looked cheerful, and the flowers she had so confidently loved looked beautiful and kind. They were death dressed up. Oh, she was not to be taken in any more. She knew the very sound of him. Often, while she was in that fever, she had heard him coming across the yard, up the steps, along the passage, pausing just outside the door, going back each time, but only for a little while. He would come again. The horror of it. The horror of living with that waiting. The horror of knowing that love ended in this, that new life was only more death. Fearfully she lay staring at the realities that she alone in that house could see. And she could hear her heart beating – if only she needn't have to hear her heart beating – it beat in little irregular beats, little flutters, and then a pause – and then a sudden *ping* – oh, the weak, weak helplessness – nothing to hold on to anywhere in all the world – even the bed hadn't an underneath – she was always dropping downwards, downwards, through it, away . . .

Sometimes the nurse came and stood beside her, and with a big wholesome hand smoothed back the hair from her absorbed and frowning forehead. 'What are you thinking about?' she would ask, bending down and smiling.

But Ingeborg never told.

To Herr Dremmel the nurse counselled patience.

He said he had been having it for ten months.

'You must have some more,' said the nurse, 'and it will come right.'

And so it gradually did. Slowly Ingeborg began to creep up the curve of life again. It was a long and hesitating creeping, but there did come a time when there were definite and widening gaps in her vision of the realities. The first day she had meat for dinner she lost sight of them for several hours. The next day she had meat she shut her mouth. The day after, a feeling of shame for her black thoughts crept into her mind and stayed there. The day after that, when she not only had meat but began a new tonic, she asked for Robertlet and put her arms round him all by herself.

Then the nurse slipped out and called Herr Dremmel; and he, hurrying in and finding her propped on pillows, holding his baby and smiling down at him just as he had pictured she would, went down once more on his knees beside the bed and took the whole group, mother, baby, and pillows, into his arms, and quite frankly and openly cried for joy.

'Little sheep . . . little sheep, . . .' he kept on saying. And Ingeborg, having reached that point in convalescence where one never misses a chance of crying, at once cried too; and Robertlet beginning to cry the nurse, who laughed, broke up the group.

After that things grew better every day. Ingeborg visibly improved; every hour almost it was possible to see some new step made back to her original self. She clung to the nurse, who stayed on long after the carrying into the next room stage had been passed and who did not leave her till she was walking about quite gaily in the garden and beginning to do the things with Robertlet that she had planned she would. She seemed, after the long months of ugliness, to be prettier than before. She was so glad, so grateful, to be back again, and her gladness lit her up. It was so wonderful to be back in the bright world of free movement, to be presently going to punt, and presently be off for a day in the forests, to be able to arrange, to be in clear possession of her time and her body. The deliciousness of health, the happiness of being just normal made her radiant.

The September that year was one of ripe days and glowing calms. Neither Herr Dremmel nor Ingeborg had ever been quite so happy. He loved her as warmly as before their marriage. He found himself noticing things like the fine texture of her skin, and observing how pretty the back of her neck was and the way her hair behaved just at that point. She was the brightest adornment and finish to a man's house, he said to himself, independently busy with her baby and her house keeping, not worrying him, not having to be thought about in his laboratory when he wished to work, absorbed in womanly interests, cheerful, affectionate, careful of her child. It was delightful to have her sit on his knee again, delightful to hear her talk the sweet and sometimes even amusing nonsense with which her head seemed full, delightful to see her sudden solemnity when there was anything to be done for the personal comfort of Robertlet.

'Aren't we *happy*,' said Ingeborg one evening when they were strolling after supper along the path through the rye-field, all the old fearlessness and confidence in life surging in her again. 'Did you ever *know* anything like it?'

'It is you, my little sun among sheep,' said Herr Dremmel, standing still to kiss her as energetically as though he had been beneath the pear-tree in the Bishop's garden, 'it is all you.'

'And presently,' she said, 'I'm going to do such things – Robert, such things. First I'm going to be a proper pastor's wife at last and turn to in the village thoroughly. And besides that I'm going to—'

She stopped and flung out her hands with a familiar gesture.

'Well, little hare?'

'Oh, I don't know – but it's fun being alive, isn't it? I feel as if I'd only got to stretch up my hands to all those stars and catch as many of them as I want to.'

And hardly had the nurse left and the household had returned to its normal arrangements, and the parlour was no longer disfigured by Herr Dremmel's temporary bed, and life was clear again, and all one had to do was to go ahead praising the dear God who had made it so spacious and so kind, than she began to have her second child.

PART 3

CHAPTER 21

There was a little bay about five minutes' paddle down the lake round a corner made by the jutting out of reeds. You took your punt round the end of an arm of reeds, and you found a small beach of fine shells, an oak tree with half-bared roots overhanging one side of it, and a fringe of coarse grass along the top. On this you sat and listened to the faint wash of the water at your feet and watched the sun flashing off the wings of innumerable gulls. You couldn't see Kökensee and Kökensee couldn't see you, and you clasped your hands round your knees and thought. Behind you were the rye-fields. Opposite you was the forest. It was a place of gentleness, of fair afternoon light, of bland colours, – silvers, and blues, and the pale gold that reeds take on in October.

Ingeborg did not bring Robertlet to this place. She decided, after four months' close association with him had cleared her mind of misconceptions, that he was too young. She would not admit, with all her dreams about what she was going to do with him still vivid in her memory, that she preferred to be alone. She would not admit that she did anything but love him ardently. He was so good. He never cried. Nor did he ever do what she supposed must be the converse of crying, crow. He neither cried nor crowed. He neither complained nor applauded. He ate with appetite and he slept with punctuality. He grew big and round while you looked at him. Who would not esteem him? She did esteem him, – more highly perhaps than she had ever esteemed anybody; but the ardent love she had been told a mother felt for her first-born was a thing about which she had to keep on saying to herself, 'Of course.'

He was a grave baby; and she did her best by cheery gesticulations and encouraging, humorous sounds, to accustom him to mirth, but her efforts were fruitless. Then one day as she was bending over him trying to extract a smile by an elaborate tickling of his naked ribs she caught his eye, and instantly she jerked back and stared down at him in dismay, for she had had the sudden horrid conviction that what she was tickling was her mother-in-law.

That was the first time she noticed it, but the resemblance was unmistakable, was, when you had once seen it, overwhelming. There was no trace, now that she tremblingly examined him, of either Robert or herself; and as for her own family, what had become of all that very real beauty, the beauty of the Bishop, the dazzlingness of Judith, and the sweet regularities of her mother?

Robertlet was as much like Frau Dremmel as he might have been if Frau Dremmel had herself produced him in some miraculous manner entirely unassisted. The resemblance was flagrant. It grew with every bottle. He had the same steady eyes. He had the same prolonged silences. His nose was a copy. His head, hairless, was more like Frau Dremmel's, thought Ingeborg, than Frau Dremmel's could ever have possibly been, and if ever his hair grew, she said to herself gazing at him wide-eyed, it would undoubtedly do it from the beginning in a knob. Gradually as the days passed and the likeness appeared more and more she came, when she tubbed him and powdered his many creases, to have a sensation of infinite indiscretion; and she announced to Herr Dremmel, who did not understand, that Robertlet's first word would certainly be *Bratkartoffel*.

'Why?' asked Herr Dremmel, from the other side of a wall of thinking.

'You'll see if it isn't,' nodded Ingeborg, with a perturbed face.

But Robertlet's first word, and for a long time his only one, was *Nein*. His next, which did not join it till some months later, was *Adieu*, which is the German for good-bye and which he said whenever anybody arrived.

'He isn't very *hospitable*,' thought Ingeborg; and remembered with a chill that not once since her marriage had her mother-in-law invited her to her house in Meuk. But she made excuses for him immediately. 'Everybody,' she said to herself, 'feels a little stiff at first.' . . .

To this beautiful corner of the lake, for it was very beautiful those delicate autumn afternoons, she went during Robertlet's dinner sleep to do what she called think things out; and she sat on the little shells with her hands round her knees, staring across the quiet water at the line of pale reeds along the other shore, doing it. Presently however she perceived that her thinking was more a general discomfort of the mind punctuated irregularly by flashes than anything that could honestly be called clear. Things would not be thought out, — at least they would not be thought out by her; and she was feeling sick again; and how, she asked herself, can people who are busy being sick be anything *but* sick? Besides, things wouldn't bear thinking out. Her eyes grew bright with fear when one of those flashes lit up what was once more ahead of her. It was like a scarlet spear of terror suddenly leaping at her heart . . .

No, thought Ingeborg, turning quickly away all cold and trembling, better not think; better just sit in the sun and wonder what Robertlet would look like later on if he persisted in being exactly like Frau Dremmel and yet in due season had to go into trousers, and what would happen if the next one were like Frau Dremmel too, and whether she would presently be teaching a row of little mothers-in-law its infant hymns. The thought of Frau Dremmel become plural, diminished into socks and pinafores, standing neatly at her knee being taught to lisp in numbers, seized her with laughter. She laughed and laughed; and only stopped when she discovered that what she was really doing was crying.

'Perhaps it's talking I want more than thinking,' she said to Herr Dremmel at last, returning from one of these barren expeditions in search of understanding.

She said it a little timidly, for she was already less to him than she had been in that brief interval of health, and knew that with every month she would be less and less. It was odd how sure of him she was when she was not going to have a baby, of what an easy confidence in his love, and how he seemed to slip away from her when she was. Already, though she had only just begun, he was miles away from the living mood in which he folded her in his arms and called her his little sheep.

Herr Dremmel, who was supping, and was not in possession of the context, recommended thinking. He added after a pause that only a woman would have suggested a distinction.

Ingeborg did not make the obvious reply, but said she thought if she might talk to somebody, to Robert for instance, and with her hand in his, rather *tight* in his while she talked, so that she might feel safe, feel not quite so loose and unheld together in an enormous awful world —

Herr Dremmel looked at his watch and said perhaps he would have time to hold her hand next week.

A few days later she said, equally without supplying him with the context, 'It's blessing disguising itself, that's what it is.'

Herr Dremmel, who again was supping, said nothing, preferring to wait.

'Blessing only pretending to be cruelty. Not really cruelty at all.'

Herr Dremmel still preferred to wait.

'I thought at first it was cruelty,' she said, 'but now I think perhaps – perhaps it's blessing.'

'What did you think was cruelty, Ingeborg?' asked Herr Dremmel, who disliked the repetition of such a word.

'Having this next baby so quickly – without time to forget.'

Her eyes grew bright.

'Cruelty, Ingeborg?'

Herr Dremmel said one did not, when one was a pastor's wife, call Providence names.

'That's what I'm saying,' she said. 'I thought at first it was cruel, but now I see it's really ever so much better not to waste time between one's children, and then be well for the rest of one's days. It – it will make the contrast afterwards, when one has done with pain, so splendid.'

She looked at him and pressed her hands together. Vivid recollections lit her eyes. 'But I'd give up these splendid contrasts very *willingly*,' she whispered, her face gone suddenly terror-stricken.

Herr Dremmel said that family life had always been praised not only for its beauty but for its necessity as the foundation of the State.

'You told me,' said Ingeborg, who had a trick which good men sometimes found irritating of remembering everything they had ever said, 'the foundation of the State was manure.'

Herr Dremmel said so it was. And so was family life. He would not, he informed her, quibble over terms. What he wished to make clear was that there could not be family life without a family to have it in.

'And don't you call you and me and Robertlet a family?' she asked.

'One child?' said Herr Dremmel. 'You would limit the family to one child? That is a highly unchristian line of conduct.'

'But the Christian lines of conduct seem to *hurt* so,' murmured

Ingeborg. 'Oh, I know there have to be brothers and sisters,' she added quickly before he could speak, 'and it *is* best to get it over and have done with it. It's only when I'm – it's only sometimes that I think Robertlet would have been enough family till – till I'd had time to forget—'

Again the light of terror came into her eyes. She knew it was there. She looked down at her plate to hide it.

Twice after that she came back from her thinking down by the lake and attempted to talk to him about questions of life and death. Herr Dremmel was bored by questions of life and death unless they were his own ones. He met them, however, patiently. She arrived panting, for it was uphill back to the house, desperately needing her vision rubbed a little clearer against his so that she might reach out to reassurance and courage, and he took on an air of patience almost before she had begun. In the presence of that premature resignation she faltered off into silence. Also what she had wanted to say got tangled into the silliest sentences, – she heard them being silly as they came out. No wonder he looked resigned. She could have wept with chagrin at her inarticulateness, her want of real education, her incapacity for getting her thoughts torn away from their confusion and safely landed into speech. And there stood Robert, waiting, with that air of patience . . .

But how odd it was, the difference between his talk before she was going to have a baby and his silence – surely resigned silence – when she was! She wished she knew more about husbands. She wished that during the years at home instead of writing all those diocesan letters she had ripely reflected on the Conjugalities.

As the days went by her need of somebody to talk to, her dread of being alone with her imagination and its flashes, became altogether intolerable. She went at last, driven by panic, to the village mothers, asking anxious questions about how they had felt, how they had managed, going round on days when she was better to the cottages where families were longest. But nothing came of this; the attitude everywhere was a dull acceptance, a shrug of the shoulder, a tiredness.

Then she sought out the postman's wife, who looked particularly motherly and bright, and found that she was childless.

Then she met the forester one day in the woods, and was so far gone in need that she almost began to ask him her anxious questions, for he looked more motherly even than the postman's wife.

Then she thought of Baroness Glambeck, who before Robertlet's birth had been helpful in practical ways – would she not be helpful now in these spiritual stresses ? – and she walked over there with difficulty one afternoon in November through the deep wet sand, approaching her as one naked soul delivered by its urgencies from the web of reticence and convention approaches another. But nothing could be less naked that day than the Baroness's soul. It was dressed even to gloves and a bonnet. It had no urgencies ; and Hildebrand von Glambeck was there, the only son in the family of six, the member of it who had married most money, and his mother was proudly pouring out coffee for him in festal silk.

It was entirely contrary to custom for one's pastor's wife to walk in without having first inquired whether her visit would be acceptable ; and when the Baroness perceived the sandy and disordered figure coming towards her down the long room she was not only annoyed but dismayed. She had not seen this dearest of her children for six months, and it was the first opportunity she had had since his arrival the evening before of being alone with him, for he had brought a friend with him from Berlin, and not till after luncheon had the friend, who painted, been satisfactorily disposed of out of doors in the park, where he announced his intention of staying as long as the sun stayed on a certain beech-tree. She wanted to ask her boy questions. She had sent the Baron out riding round his farms so as to be able to ask questions. She wanted to know about his life in Berlin, to her so remote and so full of drawbacks that yet glittered, a high, dangerous, less truly aristocratic life than this of lofty stagnation in God's provinces, but shone upon after all by the presence of her Emperor and King. In her heart she believed that the Almighty had also some years ago, probably about the time of her marriage when she too retired into them, withdrawn into the provinces, and there particularly presided over those best of the Fatherland's nobles who stayed with a pure persistency in the places where they happened to have been born. On His departure for the country, the Baroness decided, He had handed over Berlin and Potsdam to the care of the First of His children, her Emperor and King ; and so it was that the provinces were higher and more truly aristocratic than Berlin and Potsdam, and so it was that Berlin and Potsdam nevertheless ran them very close.

And now, just as she had so cleverly contrived this hour with Hildebrand for getting at all those intimate details of his life that a mother loves but does not care to talk about before her husband, this hour for hearing about his children, his meals, his money, his dear wife's success in society and appearances, thanks to her having married into the nobility, at Court, his own health, his indigestion – that ancient tormentor of his peace, *armer Junge* – and whether he had seen or heard anything of poor Emmi, his eldest sister, who had miserably married six thousand marks a year and lived impossibly at Spandau and could not be got to admit she did not like it, – just as she was going to be satisfied on all these points came that eccentric and pushing Frau Pastor and spoilt it all. Also Hildebrand was in the very middle of one of those sad stories of scandal that one wishes one had not to listen to but naturally wants to hear the end of.

So great was the Baroness's disappointment that she found it impossible to stop herself from affecting inability to recognise the Frau Pastor till she was actually touching the coffee table. 'Ah,' she then said, not getting up but slowly putting out her hand to take the hand that was being offered, and staring as though she were trying to remember where and when she had seen her before, 'ah – Frau Pastor? This is indeed an honour.'

'Present, me, mamma,' said Hildebrand, who had got on to his feet the instant Ingeborg appeared in the doorway.

The ceremony performed he sank again into his chair and did nothing more at all, being waited on by his mother and leaving it to her to see that the visitor was given cream and sugar and cake, until the moment arrived when Ingeborg, made abundantly and elaborately aware that she was interrupting, prepared crestfallen to go away again. Then once more he started up, alert and with his heels together.

'Well, and what did her husband do?' asked the Baroness, turning again to Hildebrand as soon as Ingeborg had been got quiet on a chair with coffee, determined to hear the end of the story.

My dear mother,' said Hildebrand, shrugging his shoulders up to his ears, 'what could he do?'

'He shot her?'

'Of course.'

'Naturally,' said the Baroness, nodding approval. 'Was she killed?'

'No. Badly wounded. But it was enough. His honour was avenged.'

'And she will not,' said the Baroness grimly, 'begin these tricks again.'

Ingeborg roused herself with an effort to say something. She was extraordinarily disappointed and unnerved by not finding the Baroness alone. 'Why did he shoot her?' she asked. It seemed to her in her tiredness so very energetic of him to have shot her.

The Baroness turned a cold eye on her. 'Because, Frau Pastor,' she said, 'she was his sinning wife.'

'Oh,' said Ingeborg; and added an inquiry, in a nervous desire to make for a brief space agreeable small talk before going away again, whether in Germany they always shot each other when they sinned.

'Not each other,' said the Baroness severely. 'At least, not if it is a husband and his wife. He alone shoots.'

'Oh,' said Ingeborg, considering this.

She was sitting inertly on her chair, holding her cup of coffee slanting, too much dejected to drink it.

'And then does that make her love him again?' she asked, in her small tired voice.

The Baroness did not answer.

'Only blood,' said Hildebrand, 'can wipe out a husband's dishonour.'

'How *nasty*!' said Ingeborg dejectedly.

Life seemed all blood. She drooped over her cup, thinking of the cruelty with which things were apparently packed. The Baroness and Hildebrand, after a pregnant silence, turned from her and began to talk of somebody they called poor Emmi. Ingeborg sat alone with her cup, wondering how she could get away before she began to cry. Dreadful how easily she cried now. She must buy some more handkerchiefs. They seemed lately to be always at the wash.

She roused herself again. She really must say something. As her way was when confused and unnerved, she caught at the first thing she found tumbling about in her mind. 'Why was Emmi poor?' she asked in her small tired voice.

There was another pregnant silence.

To shorten it Ingeborg asked whether Emmi was the wife who had been shot — 'The sinning one,' she explained as nobody answered.

The silence became awful.

She looked up, startled by it. From the expression on their faces and the general feel of things she thought that perhaps they wouldn't mind if she went home now.

She got up, dropping the spoon out of her saucer. 'I – think I must be going,' she said. 'It's a long way home.'

'It seems hardly worth while to have come,' said the Baroness with extraordinary chill.

To which Ingeborg, absorbed in the failure of her effort to find help and comfort, answered droopingly 'No.'

Outside the sun had just dropped behind the forest line, and she would have to walk fast if she wanted to be home before dark. The mist was already rising over the meadows beyond the trees of the garden and beginning to mix with the rose and lilac of the sky. The sandy avenue she had come along on that hot July day when first she discovered Glambeck lay at her feet in the still beauty of the last of its dresses for the year, very delicate, very transparent already, the leaves of the beeches almost all on the ground, making of the road a ribbon of light. A November smell of dampness and peat smoke from cottage chimneys filled the air. There was a brooding peace over the world, as though in every house, in every family, brotherly love must needs in such gentleness continue.

She went carefully down the steps, for her body was already growing cumbersome, and along the golden way of the avenue. She tried not to cry, not to smudge the beautiful evening with her own disappointments. How foolish she had been to suppose that because she wanted to talk Baroness Glambeck would want to listen ! Moods did not coincide so conveniently. She walked along, diligently stopping any stray tear with her handkerchief before it could disgrace her by coming out on to her cheeks. Presently Baroness Glambeck might passionately want to listen – it was quite conceivable – and she herself would not in the least want to talk. How foolish it all was ! One had to stand on one's own feet. It was no good going about calling out for help. It was less than no good crying. Some day, if she continued intrepidly in this career of maternity which seemed to be marked out for her, she too would be happily pouring out coffee for a grown-up and successful man-child, all her impatiences and pangs long since forgotten. You clearly couldn't have a grown-up man-child to love and be proud of if you hadn't begun him in time. He had at some period or other to be begun. And he had to be begun in time, else one might easily be too old for acute appreciation. She went as quickly as she could down the avenue, thinking on large valiant lines and underneath her thinking feeling altogether forsaken. It must be nice, a warm thing to live where one's friends and relatives were within reach, where one could, for instance, when one felt extra lonely go and have tea with one's mother . . .

A man carrying what seemed to be a great deal of something indefinite was coming down the avenue towards her. She looked at him vaguely, absorbed in her thoughts. It was not the Baron, and except for him she knew nobody. She was within a yard or two of him when a quantity of sheets of paper, long slender brushes, odd articles she did not recognise, suddenly seemed to burst out from his person and scatter themselves over the beech-leaves on the ground.

'Oh damn,' said the man, making efforts to catch them.

Ingeborg, always eager to help, began clumsily to pick up those nearest her. He had a camp stool on one arm, and what appeared to be a mackintosh, and was altogether greatly hampered.

'Look here, don't do that,' he exclaimed, struggling with these things which also apparently were slipping from him.

'Oh, but how lovely !' said Ingeborg, holding one of the sheets of paper she had picked up at arm's length and staring with her red eyes at a beech-tree on it, a celestial beech-tree surely, aflame with so great a glory of light that it could not possibly be earthly but only the sort of tree they have in heaven. Close, it was just splashes of colour ; you had to hold it away from you to see it at all. She blew away some grains of sand that were on it and then held it once more as far from her as her arm would go. 'Oh, but how lovely !' she said again. 'Look – doesn't it *shine* ?'

'Of course it shines. That was what it was doing,' he said, coming and looking at the sketch over her shoulder a minute, his hands full of the things he had collected from the ground. 'They said they'd send a servant for all this, and they didn't. I hate carrying things.'

'I'll carry some,' said Ingeborg.

'Nonsense. And you're not going there.'

'I've been. But I'd go back as far as the steps if you like.'

'Nonsense. I'll leave them at the foot of this tree. He'll see them all right.'

'Not this – you mustn't leave this,' she said, still gazing at the sketch.

'No. I'll take that. And I'm coming with you a little way, because I can't conceive where you can be going to at this time of the day that isn't to the Glambecks' and I'm curious. Also because it's so funny of you to be English.'

'I think it's much funnier of you,' said Ingeborg, picking up a pencil out of a rut in the sand and adding it to the pile he was making against the trunk of the nearest tree. 'And I'm only going home.'

'Home?'

He undid the pile and began again. He had got it wrong. The camp-stool of course must be the foundation, then the smaller fly-away things, then, neatly folded and tucking them all in, the mackintosh. She must be an English governess or superior nurse on a neighbouring estate since she talked of home. If so he did not want to go with her; nothing he could think of seemed to him quite so tiresome as an English governess or superior nurse.

He finished tucking in the mackintosh and turned round and took the sketch from her. He was, she perceived, a long, thin-necked man with a short red beard. She was, he perceived, somebody in a badly fitting tweed coat and skirt, a person with a used sort of nose and weak eyes.

'Now then,' he said, 'I'll go with you anyhow to the end of the avenue. Where is home?'

'Kökensee,' said Ingeborg, trotting to keep up with him. 'It's the next village. I'm the pastor's wife.'

Ingram – for it was that celebrated artist, then, at thirty-five, already known all over Europe as more especially and letting alone his small exquisite things a surprising, indeed a disturbingly surprising painter of portraits – glanced down at her and stepped out more vigorously. 'That's an amusing thing to be,' he said. 'And quite new.'

'It isn't very new. I've been it eighteen months. Why do you think it's amusing?'

'It's different from anything else. Nobody was ever a pastor's wife in – what did you call it? – before.'

'Kökensee.'

'Kökensee. Kökensee. I like that. You're unique to live in Kökensee. Nobody else has achieved that.'

'It wasn't very difficult. I just stayed passive and was brought.'

'And they didn't mind?'

'Who didn't?'

'Your people. Your father and mother. Or are you Melchisedec and never had any?'

'Why should they mind?'

'Coming so far. It's rather the end of the world. You're right up against the edge of Russia.'

'I wanted to.'

'Of course. I didn't suppose you were dragged across Europe by your hair to Kökensee. I'll come all the way with you. I want to see Kökensee.'

'Don't walk so fast, then,' said Ingeborg, panting. 'I *can't* walk like that.'

He looked at her as he went slower. 'Is that the effect of Kökensee?' he said. 'Why can't you walk like that? You're only a girl.'

'I'm not a girl at all. I'm a wife, I'm a mother. I'm everything really now except a mother-in-law and a grandmother. That's all there's still left to be. I think they're rather dull things, both of them.'

'You won't think so when you've got there.'

'That's the dreadfullest part of it.'

'It's a kindly trick Time plays on us. Are you a real pastor's wife who goes about her parish being an example?'

'I haven't yet. But I'm going to.'

'What – not begun in eighteen months? But what do you do then all day long?'

'First I cook, and then I – don't cook.'

They were out in the open, on the bit of road that passed between meadows. Ingram stopped and looked at something over to the left with sudden absorbed attention. She followed his eyes, but did not see much, – a wisp of mist along the grass, the top twigs of a willow emerging from it, and above it the faint sky. He said nothing, and presently went on walking faster than ever.

'*Please* go a little slower,' begged Ingeborg, her heart thumping with effort.

'I think, you know,' said Ingram, suiting himself to her, 'you should be able to walk better than that.'

'Yes,' said Ingeborg.

'I suppose that's the danger of places like Kökensee – one lets oneself get slack.'

'Yes,' said Ingeborg.

'You mustn't, you know. Imagine losing one's lines. Just think of the horrible indefinite lines of a fat woman.'

'Yes,' said Ingeborg. 'Do you paint much?' she asked, unable to endure this turn of the conversation.

He looked at her and laughed. 'A good deal,' he said. Then he added, 'I'm Ingram.'

'Is that your name? Mine's Dremmel.'

'*Edward* Ingram,' he said, looking at her. It was inconceivable she should not know.

'*Ingeborg* Dremmel,' she said, as though it were a game.

He was silent a moment. Then he stopped with a jerk. 'I don't think I'll come any further,' he said. 'The Glambecks will be wondering what has become of me. Glambeck brought me down for a couple of nights, and I can't be not there all the time.'

'But you wanted to see Kökensee—'

'Doesn't anybody ever read in Kökensee?'

'Read?'

'Papers? Books? Reviews? Criticisms? What the world's doing in all the million places that aren't Kökensee? Who everybody is? What's being thought and created?'

He had an oddly nettled look.

'Robert takes in the Norddeutscheallgemeinezeitung, and I've been reading Kipling—'

'Kipling! Well, good-bye.'

'But isn't Kipling – why, till I married I had only the Litany.'

'What on earth for?'

'That and Psalms and things. I felt very *empty* on the Litany.'

'I can imagine it. I'd lose no more time then in furnishing my emptiness. Good-bye.'

'Oh, don't go – wait a moment. It's such ages since I've—. Furnishing it how? What ought I—?'

'Read, read, read – everything you can lay your hands on.'

'But there *isn't* anything to lay hands on.'

'My dear lady, haven't you post-cards? Write to London and order the reviews to be sent out to you. Get some notion of people and ideas. Good-bye.'

'Oh – but won't you really come and look at Kökensee?'

'It's a dark place. I'm afraid what I'd see there would be nothing.'

'There'll be more light to-morrow—'

'I'm going south again to-morrow with Glambeck. I only came for a day. I was curious about provincial German interiors. Good-bye.'

'Oh, but do—'

'My advice is very sound, you know. One can't shut one's eyes and just sleep while the procession of men and women who are making the world goes past one, unless' – his eyes glanced over the want of trimness of her figure, the untidy way her loose coat was fastened – 'unless one doesn't mind running to seed.'

'But I *do* mind,' cried Ingeborg. 'It's the last thing I want to run to—'

'Then don't. Good-bye.'

He took off his hat and was already several steps away from her by the time it was on his head again. Then he turned round and called out to the dejected little figure standing where he had left it in the sandy road with the grey curtain of mist blurring it: 'It really is *everybody's* duty to know at least something of what's being done in the world.'

And he jerked away into the dusk towards Glambeck.

She stood a long while looking at the place where the gloom had blotted him out. Wonderful to have met somebody who really talked to one, who actually told one what to do. She went home making impulsive resolutions, suddenly brave again, her chin in the air. Ill or not ill she was not going to be beaten, she was not going to wait another day before beginning to fill her stupid mind. It was monstrous she should be so ignorant, so uneducated. What was she made of, then, what poor cheap stuff, that she could think of nothing better than to cry because she did not feel as well as she used to? Weren't there heaps of things to do even when one was ill? Had she not herself heard of sick people whose minds triumphed so entirely over their prostrate flesh that from really quite perpetual beds they shed brightness on whole parishes?

She wrote that night to Mudie demanding catalogues of him almost with fierceness, and ordered as a beginning, the *Spectator* and *Hibbert Journal*, both of which at Redchester had been mentioned in her presence by prebendaries. When they arrived she read them laboriously from cover to cover, and then ordered all the monthly reviews they advertised. She subscribed at once to the *Times* and to a weekly paper called the *Clarion* because it was alluded to in one of the reviews; she showered post cards on Mudie, for whatever books she read about she immediately bought, deciding that that was as good a way of starting as any other; and she had not been reading papers a week before she came across Edward Ingram's name.

A great light dawned on her. '*Oh*, – ' she said with a little catch of the breath, turning hot; and became aware that she had just been having the most recognisably interesting encounter of her life.

CHAPTER 22

In seven years Ingeborg had six children. She completely realised during that period the Psalmist's ideal of a reward for a good man and was altogether the fruitful vine about the walls of his house. She was uninterruptedly fruitful. She rambled richly. She saw herself, at first with an astonished chagrin and afterwards with resignation, swarming up to the eaves of her little home, pauseless, gapless, luxuriantly threatening to choke the very chimneys. At the beginning she deplored this uninterrupted abundance, for she could not but see that beneath it the family roof grew a little rotten, and sometimes, though she made feeble efforts to keep it out, a rather dismal rain of discomfort soaked in and dimmed the brightness of things. Good servants would not come to such a teeming household. The children that were there suffered because of the children that were soon going to be there. It was a pity, she thought, that when one produced a new child one could not simultaneously produce a new mother for it, so that it should be as well looked after as one's first child had been. She could mend their stockings, because that could be done lying on a sofa, but she was never sure about anything else that concerned them. And there were so many things, such endless vital things to be seen to if babies were to flourish. And when the first ones grew bigger and she might have begun those intimate expeditions and communions with them she used to plan, she found that too was impossible, for she was so deeply engaged in providing them with more brothers and sisters that she was unable to move.

The days between her first and second child were the best. She was still strong enough to tub Robertlet every night and prepare his food, and keep a watchful eye on him most of the time; also, he was only one, and easy to deal with. And he was so exact and punctual in his ways that he seemed like a clock you wound up at regular intervals and knew would then go on by itself; and his clothes, naturally, were all new and needed little mending; and she still had Ilse, who did not marry till a year later; and she had persuaded herself, for one must needs persuade oneself of something, that after this next baby there would be a pause.

This persuasion, and the few admonishments Edward Ingram had thrown at her that afternoon, helped her extraordinarily. So easily could she be stirred to courage and enthusiasm that she was able to forget most of her fears and discomforts in the new business of training her mind to triumph over her body, and she got through a surprising quantity of mixed reading that winter and spring; and when at last in the following May her hour had come, she marched off almost recklessly with her two plaits already hanging down her back and her head held high and her eyes wide and shining to the fatal bedroom where Death she supposed, but refused to care, sat waiting to see if he could not get her this time, so filled was she with the spirit she had been cultivating for six months of proud determination not to be beaten.

She was however, beaten.

It was the absence of pauses that beat her. She came to be, as the German phrase put it, in a continual condition of being blest. She came to be also continually more bloodless. Gradually sinking away more and more from energy as one child after the other sapped her up, she left off reading, dropping the more difficult things first. The *Hibbert Journal* went almost at once. Soon the *Times* was looked at languidly and not opened. The *National Review* gave her an earache. Presently she was too far gone even for the *Spectator*. The *Clarion* lasted longest, but a growing distaste for its tone caused it finally to be abandoned. For she was becoming definitely religious; she was ceasing to criticise or to ask Why? She would sit for hours contemplating the beauty of acquiescences. It gave her a boneless satisfaction. The more anæmic she grew the easier religion seemed to be. It was much the least difficult thing to be passive, to yield, not to think, not to decide, never to want explanations. And everybody praised her. How nice that was! Baroness Glambeck approved, Frau Dosch approved loudly. The elder Frau Dremmel came out each year twice and silently approved of a mother whose offspring was so strikingly like herself; while as for Kökensee, it regarded her with the respect due to a person becoming proverbial. It is true Robert seemed to love her rather less than more, in spite of her obviously deserving to be loved more than ever now that she was at one with him about Providence; yet it was hardly fair to say that either, for nobody could be kinder than he was when he was not busy. He was busy from morning to night. How nice that was, she thought, her hands folded; she had always thought it nice to be busy.

Of her six children Robertlet flourished, and so did the sister who came after him. The next two died, one doing it boldly of mumps, a thing that had never been achieved before and greatly interested the doctor, who predicted a memorable future for him if he had been going to have one, and the other, more explicably, by falling out of the punt when his very existence depended on his keeping in it. Then they took to being born dead; two of them in succession did this; and it was after the second had done it that Ingeborg reached her lowest ebb of vitality and could hardly be got to say a sentence that did not include heaven.

When she had been up and dressed two months and still lay about on sofas being religious, Herr Dremmel, who was patient but slowly becoming conscious that there was an atmosphere of *chapelle ardente* about his parlour on his coming into it with the innocent briskness of a good man to his supper, thought perhaps the Meuk doctor, who by now was a familiar feature in his life, had better come over and advise; and so it was that Ingeborg went to Zoppot, that bracing and beautiful seaside resort near Danzig, leaving her home for the first time since her marriage, going indeed with as much unwillingness as so will-less a person could possess, but sent off regardless of her moist opposition by the doctor, who would not even allow her to take Robertlet and Ditti with her.

She went in the care of the nurse who had helped her after Robertlet's birth, and she was to stay there all June and all July, and all August and September as well if necessary.

'But what will they do without me?' she kept on feebly saying. 'And my duties – how can I leave everything?'

Tears poured down her face at her departure. She gave keepsakes to both the servants. She sent for the sexton, with whom she had latterly grown friendly, and tried to speak but could not. She folded the impassive Robertlet and Ditti to her heart so many times that they were stirred to something almost approaching activity and resistance.

'Your prayers — you won't forget what Mummy taught you?' she wept, as though she were taking leave of them for ever.

'Dear Robert,' she sobbed, clinging to him with her cheek against his on the platform at Meuk where he saw her off, 'do forgive me if I've been a bad wife to you. I *have* tried. You won't forget — will you — ever — that I *did* try?'

The nurse gave her a spoonful of Brand's Meat Jelly. The journey was a journey of jelly combating grief. All the way each relapse into woe was instantly interrupted by jelly; and it was not till the evening, when they reached the little pension on the sands which was to be their home for two months, and Ingeborg going to the open window gave a quick cry as the full freshness and saltness and heaving glancing beauty burst upon her, that the nurse threw the rest of the tin away and put her trust altogether in the sea.

Herr Dremmel returned to his wifeless home in a meditative frame of mind. As he jolted along in the same carriage, only grown more shaky, in which he had brought his bride back seven years before, he indulged, first, in a brief wonder at the ups and downs of women; from this he passed to a consideration of the superior reliability of chemicals; from this, again, he proceeded to reflect that, nevertheless, a man's life should be decorated at the edges, and that the most satisfactory decoration was a wife and family. Ingeborg, in spite of her ups and downs, had been a good wife to him, and he did not regret having attached her to his edges, but then he also had done his part and been a good husband to her. Few marriages, he thought, could have been so harmonious and successful as theirs. He loved her as an honest man should love his wife, — at judicious intervals. Always he had affection for her, and liked being with her when she was feeling well. Her money — every wife should have a little — had helped him much, indeed had made most of the successes that had rewarded his labours possible, and she had given him a child a year, which was, he was aware, the maximum output and rendered him civically satisfactory. That these children should, four of them, not have succeeded in staying alive, and that the two who had should bear so striking a resemblance to his mother, a person he knew for unintelligent, were misfortunes, but one did not dwell on misfortunes; one turned one's back on them and went away and worked. The central fact of life, its core of splendour, he said to himself as, arrived at home, he hung up his hat in the passage and prepared

to plunge with renewed appetite into his laboratory, was work;
but, he added as he passed the open door of the sitting-room and
was reminded by its untidiness of domesticities, since one had to
withdraw occasionally from the heat of that great middle light
and refresh oneself in something cooler, one needed a place of
relaxation where the interest was more attenuated, a ring of
relative tepidity round the bright centre of one's life, and this ring
was excellently supplied by the object commonly called the family
circle. The harder he worked, the more hotly he pursued knowledge, the more urgent was a man's need for intervals of tepidity.
One sought out one's little wife and rested one's brain; one took
one's son on one's knee; one pulled, perhaps, the plait of one's
daughter.

Life for Herr Dremmel was both great and simple. During the
seven years of his marriage it had become continually more so.
There were times he could remember previous to that event when
he had lost sight of this truth in a confused hankering, periods
during which he had hankered persistently, moments that astonished him afterwards to call to mind when, the lilacs being out in
the garden and the young corn of the fields asprout in the warm
spring sun, his laboratory, that place of hopes and visions, had
incredibly appeared to him to be mere bones. Marriage had
banished these distortions of perception, and he had lived seven
years in the full magnificent consciousness of the greatness and
simplicity of life. He was armoured by his singleness of purpose.
He never came out of his armour and was petty. Not once, while
Ingeborg in a distant corner of the house was fearing that she had
hurt him, or offended him, or had made him think she did not
love him, had he been hurt or offended or thinking anything of
the sort. He was absorbed in great things, great interests, great
values. There was no room in his thoughts for meditations on
minor concerns. The days were not wide enough for the bigness
they had to hold, and it never would have occurred to him to
devote any portion of their already limited space to inquiring if he
had been hurt. His interested eyes, carefully examining and
comparing and criticising phenomena, had no time for introspec-
tion. As the years passed and successes followed upon his patience,
his absorption and subjugation by his work became increasingly
profound; for a man has but a handful of years, and cannot
during that brief span live too inquisitively. Herr Dremmel was
wringing more out of Nature, who only asks to be forced to tell,

each year. He was accumulating experiences and knowledge of an interest and value so great that everything else was trivial beside them. The passing day was forgotten in the interest of the day that was to come. The future was what his brain was perpetually concerned with, and an eye ranging with growing keenness over a growingly splendid and detailed vision cannot observe, it would be an interruption, a waste to observe, the fluctuations in the moods of, for instance, a family or a parish.

Wives, children, and parishes are adornments, obligations, and means of livelihood. They are what a man has as well, but only as well. Herr Dremmel during these years had trained his parish to be unobtrusive in return for his own unobtrusiveness, and in spite of occasional restiveness on the part of Baron Glambeck, who continued from time to time, on the ground that the parish was becoming heathen and displaying the smug contentment charac- teristic of that condition, to endeavour to persuade the authorities to remove him somewhere else, was more firmly established than ever in the heart of a flock that only wanted to be left alone; and as for his wife and children, he regarded them benevolently as the necessary foundation of his existence, the airy cellars that kept the fabric above sweet and dry. Like cellars, one had to have them, and one was glad when they were good, but one did not live in them. As a wise man who wished to do fine work before being overtaken by the incapacitations of death, he had contrived his life so that it should contain enough love to make him able to forget love. It is not, he had come to know very well since his marriage, by doing without but by having that one can clear one's mind of wanting; and it is only the cleared mind that can achieve anything at all in the great work of helping the world to move more quickly on its journey towards the light.

For some weeks after Ingeborg's departure he was immensely unaware of her absence. It was June, that crowded month for him who has experimental fields; and small discomforts at home, such as ill-served unpunctual meals and rooms growing steadily less dusted, at no time attracted his notice. He would come out of his laboratory after a good morning's work in much the same spirit with which the bridegroom issuing from his chamber, a person details cannot touch, is filled, and would eat contentedly any food he found lying about and be off to his fields almost before Robertlet and Ditti had done struggling with their bibs and saying their preliminary grace.

The children, however, took no base advantage of this being left to themselves. Robertlet did not turn on Ditti and seize her dinner because she was a girl; Ditti did not conceal more than her share of pudding in her pocket for comfort during the empty afternoon hours. They sat in silence working through the meal, using their knives to eat with instead of their forks, for knives rather than forks were in their blood, and unmoved by the way in which bits they had carefully stalked round and round their plates ended by tumbling over the edge on to the tablecloth. They were patient children, and when that happened they made no comment, but dropping their knives also on the tablecloth picked up the bits in their fingers and ate them. At the end Ditti said the closing grace as her mother had taught her, Robertlet having officiated at the opening one, and they both stood behind their chairs with their eyes shut while she expressed gratitude in German to the dear Saviour who had had the friendliness to be their guest on that occasion, and having reached the Amen, in which Robertlet joined, they did not fall upon each other and fight, as other unshepherded children filled with meat and pudding might have done, but left the room in a sober file and went to the kitchen and requested the servant Rosa, who was the one who would have been their nurse if they had had one, to accompany them to their bedroom and see that they cleaned their teeth.

They spent the afternoons in not being naughty.

Herr Dremmel, accordingly, because of this health and sobriety in his children and his own indifference to his comfort, had no domestic worries such as engulf other men whose wives are away to disturb him, and it was not till July was drawing to a close and a long drought forced leisure upon him that Ingeborg's image began to obtrude itself through the chinks of his work.

At first he thought of her as a mother, as somebody heavy, continually recovering from or preparing for illness; but presently he began to think of her as a wife, as his wife, as his proper complement and relaxation from all this toil shut up in a dull laboratory. She seemed to grow brighter and lighter thought of like that, and by the time he received a letter asking if she might stay away another fortnight to complete what was being a thorough cure she was so brightly in his mind that he felt extremely disappointed.

He wrote giving the permission she asked, and made the discovery that his house looked empty and that a fortnight was long. He paced the garden in the hot evenings, smoking beneath the lime-trees where he and she at the beginning used so gaily to breakfast, and forgot how slow of movement and mind she had been for several years, how little he had really seen of her, how more and more his attitude towards her had been one of patience; and when he went in to his supper, which he suddenly did not like and criticised, what he found himself looking for was not the figure he had been used to find lying silent on the sofa, but the quick, light, flitting thing that laughed and pulled his ears, the Ingeborg of the beginning, his little sheep.

On the day she came home, although it was the very height of harvesting and the first samples of the year's grain lay on his table waiting to be examined, he gave up the afternoon to driving in to Meuk to meet her, and waited on the platform with an impatient expectancy he had not felt for years.

'It is not good for man to live alone,' were his first words as he embraced her largely in the door of the railway carriage, while the porter, in a fever to get out the hand luggage and run and attend to other passengers, had to wait till he had done. 'Little sheep, how could you stay away so long from the old shepherd?'

She was looking very well, he thought – sunburnt and with many new freckles, rounder, quite young, a sweet little wife for a long solitary husband to have coming home to him.

He lifted her proudly into the carriage and drove through Meuk with his arm round her, waving the other one at the doctor who rattled past them in his own high shaky vehicle and shouting, 'Cured!'

The doctor, however, seemed surprised at seeing Ingeborg, and did not smile back but looked inscrutably at them both.

She asked about the welfare of the children, and whether their ears had been properly washed.

'Ears?' exclaimed Herr Dremmel. 'And what, pray, have the ears of others to do with a reunited wedded couple?'

She hoped, a little hurriedly, that Rosa and the cook had been good to him.

'Rosa and the cook?' he cried. 'What talk is this of Rosa and the cook? If you are not silent with your domesticities I will kiss you here and now in the middle of the open high-road.'

She said she had never really thanked him for letting her go to Zoppot and be there so long.

'Too long, little one,' he interrupted, drawing her closer. 'Almost had I forgotten what a dear little wife I possess.'

'But I'm going to make up for it all now,' she said, 'and work harder than I've ever done in my life.'

'At making the good Robert happy,' he said, pinching her ear.

'And doing things for the children. Dreadful to think of them all this time without me. Were they good?'

'Good as fishes.'

'Robert – fishes?'

'They are well, little one, and happy. That is enough about the children. Tell me rather about you, how you filled up your days.'

'I walked, I sailed, I bathed, I lay in the sun, and I made resolutions.'

'Excellent. I shall await the result with interest.'

'I hope you'll like them. I know they'll be very good for the children.'

She had so earnest a face that he pulled it round by the chin and peered at it. Seen close she was always prettiest, full of delicacy and charm of soft fair skin, and after examining her a moment with a pleased smile he stooped down and did, after all, kiss her.

She flushed and resisted.

'What?' he said, amused. 'The little wife growing virginal again?'

'You've made my hat crooked,' she said, putting up her hands to straighten it. 'Robert, how are the fields?'

'I will not talk about the fields. I will talk about you.'

'Oh, Robert. You know,' she added nervously, 'I'm not *really* well yet. I've still got to go on taking tiresome things – that tonic, you know. The doctor there said I'm still anæmic—'

'We will feed her on portions of the strongest ox.'

'So you mustn't mind if I – if I—'

'I mind nothing if only I once more have my little wife at home,' said Herr Dremmel; and when he helped her down on to the parsonage steps, where stood Robertlet and Ditti in a stiff and proper row waiting motionless till their mother should have got near enough for them to present her with the nosegays they were holding, he kissed her again, and again pinched her ear, and praised God aloud that his widowerhood was over.

They had tea, a meal that had long before been substituted for the heavier refreshment of coffee, in a parlour filled with flowers by Rosa and the cook, the very cake, baked for the occasion, being strewn with them. Herr Dremmel lounged on the sofa behind the table looking placidly content, with one arm round his wife, while Robertlet and Ditti awed by the splendours of the decorations for their mother's home-coming and their own best clothes and spotless bibs, sat opposite, being more completely good than ever. From their side of the table they stared unflinchingly at the two people on the sofa, – at their comfortably reclining, pleased-looking father, whom they knew so differently as a being always hurriedly going somewhere else, at their mother sitting up very straight, with her veil pushed up over her nose, pouring out tea and smiling at them and keeping on giving them more jam and more milk and more cake even after, aware from their sensations that overflowing could not be far off, they had informed her by anxious repetitions of the word *satt*, which she did not seem to hear, that they were already in a dangerous condition. And they wondered dimly why, when she poured out the tea, her hand shook and made it spill.

'I will now,' said Herr Dremmel when the meal was finished, getting up and brushing crumbs out of the many folds that were characteristic of his clothes, 'retire for a space into my laboratory.'

He looked at Ingeborg and smiled. 'Picture it,' he said. 'The only solace I have now had for two months and a half has been in the bony arms of my laboratory. I grow weary of them. It is well to have one's little wife home again. A man, to do his work, needs his life complete, equipped in each of its directions. His laboratory seems bony to him if he has not also a wife; his wife would seem not bony enough if he had not also a laboratory. Bony and boneless, bony and boneless – it is the swing of the pendulum of the wise man's life.' And he bent over her and lifted her face up again by putting his finger under her chin. 'Is it not so, little one?' he asked, smiling.

'I – suppose so,' said Ingeborg.

'Suppose so!'

He laughed, and pulled an escaping tendril of her hair, and went away in great contentment and immersed himself very happily in the saucers of new grain waiting to be weighed and counted.

It was a fine August afternoon, and his windows were open, for there was no wind to blow his papers about, and he was pleased when he presently became aware out of the corner of an eye withdrawn an instant from its work that his wife had come out on to the path below and was walking up and down it in the way she used to before the acuter period of the sofa and the interest in life beyond the grave had set in.

He liked to see her there. There was a grass bank sloping up from the path to beneath his windows, and by standing on tip-toe on the top of this and stretching up an arm as far as it would go one was just able to tap against the glass. He remembered how she used to do this when first they were married, on very fine days, to try to lure him out from his duties into dalliance with her among the lilacs. It amused him to find himself almost inclined to hope she would do it now, for it was long since there had been dalliance and he felt this was an occasion, this restoration to normality, on which some slight trifling in a garden would not be inappropriate.

But Ingeborg, though she loitered there nearly half an hour, did not even look up. She wandered up and down in the cool shade the house threw across the path in the afternoon, her hat off, apparently merely enjoying the beauty of a summer day bending towards its evening, and presently he forgot her in the vivid interest of what he was doing; so that it was with the surprised expression of some one who has forgotten and is trying to recall that he looked at her when, after a knock at the door which he had not heard, he saw her come in and stand at the corner of his table waiting till he had done counting – a process he conducted aloud – to the end of the row of grains he was engaged upon.

His thoughts were still chiefly with them as he looked up at her when he had done and had written down the result, but there was room in them also for a slight wonder that she should be there. She had not penetrated into his laboratory for years. She had been tamed, after a period of recurring insurrections, into respect for its sanctity. But he did not mind being interrupted on this occasion; on the contrary, as soon as he had fully returned to consciousness he was pleased. There was a large warmth pervading Herr Dremmel that afternoon which made him inclined not to mind anything. 'Well, little one ?' he said.

Immediately she began to deliver what sounded like a speech. He gazed at her in astonishment. She appeared to be in a condition of extreme excitement; she was addressing him rapidly in a trembling voice; she was much flushed, and was holding on to the edge of the table. It was so sudden and so headlong that it was like nothing so much as the gushing forth of the long corked-up contents of an over-full bottle, and he gazed at her in an astonishment that did not for some time permit him to gather the drift of what she was saying.

When he did she had already got to the word Ruins.

'Ruins?' repeated Herr Dremmel.

'Ruins, ruins. It *must* stop – it *can't* go on. Oh, I saw it so clearly the last part of the time in Zoppot. I suppose it was the sea wind blew me clear. Our existence, Robert, our decently happy existence in a decently happy home with properly cared-for children—'

'But,' interrupted Herr Dremmel, raising his hand, – 'one moment – what is it that must stop?'

'Oh, don't you see all that will be in ruins about us – but in *ruins*, Robert – all our happy life – if I go on in this – in this wild career of – of unbridled motherhood?'

Herr Dremmel stared. 'Unbridled—?' he began; then he repeated, so deep was his astonishment, 'Wild career of – Ingeborg, did you say unbridled motherhood?'

'Yes,' said Ingeborg, pressing her hands together, evidently extraordinarily agitated. 'I learned that by heart at Zoppot, on purpose to say to you. I knew if I didn't directly I got into this room I'd forget everything I meant to say. I know it sounds ridiculous, the way I say it—'

'Unbridled motherhood?' repeated Herr Dremmel. 'But – are you not a pastor's wife?'

'Oh yes, yes, – I know, I know. I know there's Duty and Providence, but there's me too – there is me too. And, Robert, won't you see? We shall be happy again if I'm well, we shall be two real people instead of just one person and a bit of one – you and a battered thing on a sofa—'

'Ingeborg, you call a wife and a mother engaged in carrying out her obligations a battered thing on a sofa?'

'Yes,' said Ingeborg, hurrying on to the principal sentence of those she had prepared at Zoppot and learned by heart, desperately clutching at it before Robert's questions had undermined her courage and befogged the issues. 'Yes, and I've come to the conclusion after ripe meditation – after ripe – yes – the production of the – of the – yes, of the already extinct—' (dead seemed an unkind word, almost rude) 'is wasteful, and that – and that— Oh, Robert,' she cried, flinging out her hands and letting go all the rest of the things she had learned to say, 'don't you think this persistent parenthood might end now?'

He stared at her in utter amazement.

'It – it *disagrees* with me,' she said, tears in her voice and in her anxious, appealing eyes.

'Am I to under—'

'Anyhow *I* can't go on,' she cried, twisting her fingers about in an agony. 'There's so little of me to go on *with*. I'm getting stupider every day. I've got no brains left. I've got no anything. Why, I can hardly get together enough courage to tell you this. Oh, Robert,' she appealed, 'it isn't as though it made you *really* happier – you don't really *particularly* notice the children when they're there – it isn't as though it made anybody *really* happier – and – and – I'm dreadfully sorry, but I've done.'

And she dropped on to the floor beside him and put her cheek against his sleeve and tried to make up by kissing it and clinging to it for her subversion of that strange tremendous combination of Duty and Providence that so bestrode her life. 'If only you wouldn't *mind*—' she kept on saying.

But Herr Dremmel, for the first time since he had known her, was deeply offended, deeply hurt. She had pierced his armour at the one vulnerable spot. His manhood was outraged; his kindness, his patience, his affection were forgotten and spurned. He looked down at the head against his arm with a face in which wounded pride, wrath, shockedness at so great a defiance of duty, and the amazed aggrievement of him whose gifts and blessings are not wanted, struggled together. Then, as she still went on clinging and incoherently suggesting that he should not mind, he rose up, took her by the hand, helped her to her feet, and led her to the door; and there, after facing her a moment in silence with it opened in his hand while she stood blinking up at him with appealing eyes, he said dreadfully: 'Evidently you do not and never have loved me.'

CHAPTER 23

Ingeborg crept away down the passage with the sound in her ears of the key being turned in the lock behind her.

She was crushed. That Robert should think she had never loved him, that he should not even let her tell him how much she had and did! She stared out of the little window at the foot of the stairs at the untidy vegetables in the garden. This was the quality of life, — Brussels sprouts, and a door being locked behind one. It was all grey and difficult and tragic. She had hurt Robert, offended him. He was in there thinking she didn't love him. What he had said was peculiarly shattering coming from a mouth that had been always kind. Yet what was there to do but this? The alternative, it seemed, was somebody's dying; and if the children did live there would be the death of the spirit, the decay of all lovely things in the home, the darkening of all light; there would be neglect, apathy, an utter running to seed. But she felt guilty and conscience-stricken. She was no longer sure she was right. Perhaps it was indeed her duty to go on, perhaps she was indeed being wicked and cruel. The clearness of vision that had been hers at Zoppot was blurred; she was confused, infinitely distressed. Yet through the distress and confusion there kept on jabbing something like a little spear of light, and always it pointed in this one direction . . .

She stood leaning against the wall by the open window, a miserable mixture of doubt and conviction, remorse and determination. All her life she had been servile, — servile with the sudden rare tremendous insurrections that upheave certain natures brought up in servility, swift tempests more devastating than the steady fighting of systematic rebels. Her insurrections were epoch-making. When they occurred the destiny of an entire family was changed. Fathers and husbands were not prepared for anything but continued acquiescence in one so constantly acquiescent. As far as she was concerned they felt they might sleep peacefully in their beds. Then this obedient thing, this pliable uncontradicting thing would return, for instance, from an illicit trip abroad, betrothed to an unknown foreigner, and somehow in spite of violent opposition marry him; or, as in this second volcanic upheaval, with no preliminaries whatever refuse point blank – the final effect on Herr Dremmel's mind of her incoherence was a point blankness – to live with her husband as his wife.

Behind the locked door his anger was as great as her distressed confusion outside it. She was to be his wife but not his wife. Under his roof. A perpetual irritation. She had decreed, this woman who had nothing to decree, that there were to be no more Dremmels. The indignation of the thwarted ancestor was heavy upon him. Her moral obliquity shocked him, her disregard for the give and take necessary if a civilised community is to continue efficient. How was he going to work with that constant reminder about his house of his past placidities? Already it had begun, the annoyance, the hindering, for here he was sitting in front of his samples making mistakes in weighing, adding up wrong, forced by humiliatingly different results each time to count the grains over and over again.

Driven by the stress of the situation to unfairness, he remembered with a kind of bitter affection those widows who had darkened his past so soothingly before his marriage, the emotional peace their bony dustiness, their bonneted dinginess had secured him. They had been, he perceived, like a dark blind shading his eyes from the tormenting glare of too much domesticity. The most infuriated of that black and blessed band had been better than this threatening excess of relationship. Not one had ever come between him and his steady reaching forward. Not one had even once caused him to count his grains twice over. A man who wishes to work, he told himself, must clear his life of women; of all women, that is – for there are certain elementary actions connected with saucepans and bedmaking that only women will do – except widows. A wife who is not a wife and who yet persists in looking as if she were one, can be nothing but a goad and a burden for an honest man. Either she should look like some one used up and finished or she should continue to discharge her honourable functions until such time as she developed the physical unattractiveness that placed her definitely on the list of women one respects. That Ingeborg should choose the moment when she seemed younger and rounder than ever to revolt against Duty and Providence appeared to him in his first wrath deliberately malicious. He was amazed. He could not believe he was being called out of his important and serious work, beckoned out of it just when it was going so well, in order to be hurt, in order to be made acquainted with pain, and by her of all people in the world whom he used to call – surely he had been kind? – his little sheep. To be hit by one's sheep! To be hit violently by it so that the blows actually shook one at the very moment of greatest affection for it, of rejoicing over its return, of plunging one's hands most confidently into the comfort of its wool!

Herr Dremmel was amazed.

He stayed in his laboratory in this condition till supper; then, during the meal, he carefully read a book which he propped up in front of him against the loaf, while Ingeborg, ministering to him with the eager deftness of the conscience-stricken, watched for a sign of forgiveness out of the corners of red eyes.

He stayed after supper in his laboratory till past midnight, still being amazed, reduced indeed at last to walking up and down that calm temple of untiring attempts to nail down ultimate causes, considering how best he could bring his wife to reason.

The business of bringing a woman to reason had always seemed to him quite the most extravagant way of wasting good time. To have to discuss, argue, explain, threaten, adjure, only in order to get back to the point from which nobody ought ever to have started, was the silliest of all silly necessities. Again he fumed at the thought of an untractable, undutiful wife about him, and recognised the acute need to be clear of feminine childishness, egotism, unforeseeable resiliences, if a man would work. In his stirred state it appeared altogether monstrous that the whole world should be blotted out, the great wide world of magnificent opportunity and spacious interest, even for a day, even for an hour, by the power to make him uncomfortable, by the power to make him concentrate his brains on an irrelevant situation, of one small woman.

He went to their room about half-past twelve determined to have no more of the nonsense. He would bring her then and there by the shortest possible route to reason. He would have it out even to the extent of severity and have done with it. He was master, and if she forced him to emphasize the fact he would.

Carrying the lamp he went to their room with the firm footsteps of one who has ceased to be going to stand things.

But the room was empty. It was as chillily empty of wifely traces as it had been since the beginning of June.

'This is paltry,' thought Herr Dremmel, feeling the offence was now so great as to have become ridiculous; and determined to discover into what fastness she had withdrawn and fetch her out of it, he went lamp in hand doggedly through the house looking for her, beginning with the thorough patience of one accustomed to research in the kitchen, where shy cockroaches peeped at him round the legs of tables, examining the parlour, stuffy with the exhaustion of an ended day, penetrating into a room in which Rosa and the cook reared themselves up in their beds to regard him with horror unspeakable, and at last stumbling up the narrow staircase to where Robertlet and Ditti slept the sleep of the unvaryingly just.

Here, in a third small bed of the truckle type, lay his defaulting wife, her face to the wall, her body composed into an excess of motionlessness.

'Ingeborg!' he called, holding the lamp high over his head.

But she did not stir.

'Ingeborg!' he called again.

But never did woman sleep so soundly.

He walked across to the bed and bent over, searching her face by the light of the lamp. Most of it was buried in the pillow, but the one eye visible was tightly shut, more immensely asleep than any eye he had ever seen.

The indifference that could sleep while her outraged husband was looking for her revolted him. Without making any further attempt to wake her he turned on his heel, and slamming the door behind him went downstairs again.

'That is thieves at last,' remarked Ditti, who had been expecting them for years, brought out of her dreams – good dreams – by the noise of the door.

'Yes,' said Robertlet, also roused from dreams that did him credit.

'We must now get under the clothes,' said Ditti, who had settled long ago what would be the right thing to do.

'Yes,' said Robertlet.

'You needn't,' said Ingeborg out of the darkness – they both started, they had forgotten she was there – 'it was only Papa.'

But the thought of Papa coming up to their room and banging the door in the middle of the night filled them in its strangeness with an even greater uneasiness; they would have preferred thieves; and after some preliminary lying quiet and being good they one after the other withdrew as silently as possible beneath the comfort of the clothes, where they waited in neat patience for the next thing Papa might do until, stifled but uncomplaining, they once more fell asleep.

There followed some days of strain in the Kökensee parsonage.

Herr Dremmel retired into an extremity of silence, made no allusion to these regrettable incidents, became at meals a mere figure behind a newspaper, and at other times was not there at all.

He had decided that he would not waste his energies in anger. At the earliest opportunity he would drive in to Meuk, call on the doctor, and after explaining the effect of Zoppot, a place which was to have cured her, on his wife, request him now to prescribe a cure for the cure. It was Ingeborg's business to come to her husband and ask for forgiveness, and he would give her these few days in which to do it. If she did not he would know, after consultation with the doctor, what course to take, – whether of severity, or whether, setting aside his manhood, it was not rather an occasion on which one ought to coax. He was, after all, too humane to resort without medical sanction to scenes. Perhaps what she needed was only a corrective to Zoppot. There was such a thing as excess of salubriousness.

Having made up his mind, he found himself calmer, able to work again in the knowledge that in a few days he would be clear, with the aid of the doctor, as to what should be done; and Ingeborg had nothing to complain of except that he would not speak. Several times she tried to reopen the so hastily closed subject, but got no further in the face of his monumental silence than 'But, Robert—'

She took the children for outings in the forest, and while they did not chatter merrily together and did not play at games she thought over all the ways that were really tactful of luring him to reasonable discussion. She knew she had made a lamentable first appearance in the *rôle* of a retiring mother, but how difficult it was when you felt overwhelmingly to talk objectively. And then there were tears. A woman cried, and what a handicap that was. Before the first semicolon in any vital discourse with one's husband was reached one was dissolved in tears, thought Ingeborg, ashamed and resentful; and Robert grew so calm and patient, so disconcertingly calm and patient when faced by crying; he sat there like some large god, untouched by human distress, waiting for the return of reason. It is true he cried too sometimes, but only about odd things like Christmas Eves and sons if they were sufficiently new born, – things that came under the category surely of cheerful, at most of cheerfully touching; but he never cried about these great important issues, these questions on which all one's happiness hung. Life would run more easily, she thought, if husbands and wives had the same taste in tears.

Four days after her return home she asked him to forgive her.

It was at the end of supper, and he had just removed his book from the supporting loaf and was getting up to go when she ran across to him with the quickness of despair and laid hold of him by both his sleeves and said, 'Forgive me.'

He looked down at her with a gleam in his eye; he would not have to go to Meuk after all.

'Do,' she begged. 'Robert. Do. You know I love you. I'm so miserable to have hurt you. Do let's be friends. Won't we?'

'Friends?' echoed Herr Dremmel, drawing back. 'Is that all you have to say to me?'

'Oh, do be friends. I can't bear this.'

'Ingeborg,' he said with the severity of disappointment, pulling his sleeves out of her hands and going to the door, 'have you then not yet discovered that a true husband and wife can never be friends?'

'Oh, but how dreadful!' said Ingeborg, dropping her hands by her side and staring after him as he went out.

Towards the end of the week, when her unassisted meditations continued to produce no suggestions of any use for removing the stain that undoubtedly rested on her, she thought she would go into Meuk and seek the counsel of the doctor. He had always been good to her, kind and understanding. She would go to him more in the spirit of one who goes to a priest than to a doctor, and inquire of him earnestly what she should do to be saved.

She found the position at home unendurable. If the doctor told her that it was her duty to go on having children, and that it was mere chance the two last had been born dead, she would resume her career. It was a miserable career – a terrible, maimed thing – but less miserable than doubt as to whether one were not being wicked and Robert was being utterly right. Not for nothing was she the daughter of a bishop, and had enjoyed for twenty-two years the privileges of a Christian home. Also she well knew that the public opinion of Kökensee and Glambeck would be against her in this matter of rebellion, and she felt too weak to stand up alone against these big things. She had never been able to hold out long against prolonged disapproval; nor had she ever been able to endure that people round her should not be happy. By the end of the week she was so wretched and so full of doubts that she decided to put her trust in Meuk and abide by the decision of its doctor; and so it happened that she set out on the five-mile walk to it on the same day on which Herr Dremmel drove there.

He had driven off in the middle of the morning with sandwiches for himself and the coachman in the direction of the experiment ground, telling her he would not be in till the evening, so she seized the favourable opportunity and, also armed with sandwiches, started soon after twelve o'clock for Meuk. The doctor's consulting hour was, she knew, from two to three, and if she was there punctually at two she could talk to him, have her fate decided, and be home again by four.

She walked along the edge of the harvested rye-fields eating her sandwiches as she went, and refusing to think for this brief hour and a half of the difficulties of life. Her mind was weary of them. She would put them away from her for this one walk. It was the brightest of August middays. The world seemed filled with every element of happiness. Some people, probably friends of the Glambecks, were shooting partridges over the stubble. The lupin fields were in their full glory, and their peculiar orange scent met her all along the way. There was a mile of sandy track to be waded through, and then came four good miles of hard white high-road between reddening mountain ashes to Meuk. Walking in that fresh warmth, so bright with colour, so sweet with scents, she could not but begin gradually to glow, and by the time she arrived at the doctor's house however wan her spirits might be the rest of her was so rosy that the servant who opened the door tried to head her off from the waiting-room to the other end of the passage, persuaded that what she had come for could not be the doctor, but an animated call on the doctor's wife. She entered the waiting-room, a dingy place, with much the effect of a shaft of light piercing through a fog; and there, sitting at the table, turning over the fingered and aged piles of illustrated weeklies, she found Herr Dremmel.

For a moment they stared at each other.

There was no one else there. Through folding doors could be heard the murmur of a patient consulting in the next room. Meuk was not usually a sick place, and nine times out of ten the doctor read his newspaper undisturbed from two to three; this was the tenth time, and though it had only just struck two a patient was with him already.

Herr Dremmel and Ingeborg stared at each other for a moment without speaking. Then he said, suddenly angered by the realisation that she had come into Meuk without asking him if she might, 'You did not tell me you were coming here.'

'No,' said Ingeborg.

'Why have you come?'

She sat down as inconspicuously as she could on the edge of a chair in a corner and clung to her umbrella. It was the awkwardest thing meeting Robert there.

'I – I just thought I would,' she murmured.

'You do not look ill. You were not ill this morning.'

'It's – psychological,' murmured Ingeborg unnerved, and laying hold of the first word that darted into her undisciplined brain.

'Psycho— ?'

'Are *you* ill, Robert?' she asked, suddenly anxious. 'Why have *you* come?'

'My dear wife, that is my affair,' said Herr Dremmel, who was particularly annoyed and puzzled by her presence.

'Oh,' murmured Ingeborg. She had never yet heard herself called his dear wife, and felt the immensity of her relegation to her proper place.

He fluttered the pages of the *Fliegende Blätter*; she held on tighter to what seemed to be her only friend, her umbrella.

'Did you walk?' he asked presently, letting off the question at her like a gun.

'Yes – oh yes,' said Ingeborg, with hasty meekness.

What had she come for? thought Herr Dremmel, fluttering the pages faster. Ridiculous to pretend she needed a doctor. She looked, sitting there with her unusual pink cheeks, like a flourishing sixteen – at most eighteen.

What had he come for? thought Ingeborg, wishing life would not deal so upsettingly in coincidences, and keeping her eyes carefully on the carpet. Then a swift fear jumped at her heart, – suppose he were ill? Suppose he had begun to have one of those large, determined, obscure diseases that seem to mow down men and make the world so much a place of widows? She had observed that for one widower in Kökensee and the surrounding district there were ten widows. The women appeared to ail through life, constantly being smitten down by one thing after the other, but at least they stayed alive; while the men, who went year by year out robustly to work, died after a single smiting. 'Perhaps it's want of practice in being smitten,' she thought; and looked anxiously under her eyelashes at Robert, struggling with a desire to go over and implore him to tell her what was the matter. In another moment she would have gone, driven across by her impulses, if the folding doors had not been thrown open and the doctor appeared bowing.

'*Darf ich bitten*?' said the doctor to Herr Dremmel, not perceiving Ingeborg, who was shuttered out of sight by the one half of the door he had opened. 'Ah – it is the Herr Pastor,' he added less officially on recognising him, and advanced holding out his hand. 'I hope, my friend, there is nothing wrong with you?'

Herr Dremmel did not answer, but seizing his hat made a movement of a forestalling character towards the consulting room; and the doctor turning to follow him beheld Ingeborg in her corner behind the door.

'Ah – the Frau Pastor,' he said, bowing again and again advancing with an extended hand. 'Which,' he added, looking from one to the other, 'is the patient?'

But Herr Dremmel's back, disappearing with determination into the next room, suggested an acute need of assistance not visible in his wife's retiring attitude.

'You'll tell me the *truth* about him, won't you?' she whispered anxiously. 'You won't hide things from me?'

The doctor looked grave. 'Is it so serious?' he asked; and hurried after Herr Dremmel and shut the door.

Ingeborg sat and waited for what seemed a long time. She heard much murmuring, and often both voices murmured together, which puzzled her. Sometimes, indeed, they ceased to be murmurs and rose to a point at which they became distinct – 'You forget I am a Christian pastor,' she heard Robert say – but they dropped again, though never into a pause, never into those moments of silence during which Robert might be guessed to be putting out his tongue or having suspect portions of his person prodded. She sat there worried and anxious, all her own affairs forgotten in this fear of something amiss with him; and when at last the door opened again and both men came out she got up eagerly and said, 'Well ?'

Herr Dremmel was looking very solemn; more entirely solemn than she had ever seen him; almost as though he had already attained to that crown of a man's career, that final touch of all, that last gift to the world, a widow and orphans. The doctor's face was a careful blank.

'Well ?' said Ingeborg again, greatly alarmed.

'Does the Frau Pastor also wish to consult me ?' asked the doctor.

'Yes. I did. But it doesn't really matter now. Robert—'

Herr Dremmel was putting on his hat very firmly and going towards the outer door without saying good-bye to the doctor. 'I will wait for you outside and drive you home, Ingeborg,' he said, not looking round.

She stared after him. 'Is he very ill ?' she asked, turning to the doctor.

'No.'

'No ?'

'No,' said the doctor, with a stress on it.

'But—'

'And you look very well, too. Pray keep so. It is not necessary, judging from your appearance, to consult me further. I will conduct you to your carriage.'

'But—' said Ingeborg, who found herself being offered an arm and led ceremoniously after Robert.

'Take your tonic, be much in the sun, and alter nothing in your present mode of life,' said the doctor.

'But Robert—'

'The Herr Pastor enjoys excellent health, and will throw himself with more zeal than ever into his work.'

'Then why—'

'And the Frau Pastor will do her duty.'

'Yes.'

She stopped and faced him. 'Yes,' she said, 'I'm going to, but – what is my duty ?'

'My dear Frau Pastor, there is only one left. You have discharged all the others. Your one duty is to keep well in body and mind, provide your two children with a capable mother and your husband with a companion possessed of the intelligent amiability that springs from good health.'

'But Robert— ?'

'He has been consulting me about you. I will not allow you to turn him, who deserves so well of fate, into that unhappy object a widower.'

'Oh ? So really— ?'

He opened the front door. 'Yes,' he said, 'really.'

And he handed her up into the seat next to Herr Dremmel and waved them off on their homeward journey with friendly gestures.

And Ingeborg, now aware that the real cause of Robert's preternatural gloom was the dread of losing her, not the dread of leaving her, was deeply touched and full of a desire to express her appreciation. She slid her hand through his arm and spent the time between Meuk and Kökensee earnestly endeavouring to reassure him. He was not, after all, she eagerly explained, going to be a widower.

He bore her comforting in silence.

CHAPTER 24

Being a wise man, Herr Dremmel lost no time in fidgeting or lamenting over the inevitable, but having heard the doctor's summing up, which was expressed in the one firm word repeated over and over again like a series of blows, *ausgeschlossen*, he ruled Ingeborg out of his thoughts as a wife and proceeded to train himself to contemplate her as a sister.

After a short period of solemnity, for he was not sure whether the training would not be tormenting and grievously interfere with his work, he became serene again, for to his satisfaction he found it easy. The annoyance of having supposed his wife to be undutiful, the pain of having believed her to be deliberately hurting him, was removed. He was faced by a simple fact that had nothing to do with personalities. It was unfortunate that he should have married someone who was so very, he could not help thinking, easily killed, but on the other hand he was less dependent on domestic joys than most members of that peculiarly dependent profession the Church, for he had his brains. He was surprised how easy, once he recognised its inevitability, the readjustment of the relationship was, how easily and comfortably he forgot. She seemed to drop off him like a leaf off a tree in autumn, a light thing whose detachment from the great remaining strength, the reaching down and reaching up, was not felt. His mind became fitted with wife-tight compartments. He ceased, he who had feared these things might come to be an obsession, so much as to see that she was pretty, that she was soft, that she was sweet. Just as when first he met her he had been pleased and interested to find he could fall in love so now he was pleased and interested to find, when it was a matter of reason and necessity, he could fall out again. He was, it seemed, master of himself. Passions were his servants, and came only as it were when he rang the bell. All one had to do then was not to ring the bell. With satisfaction he observed that in a crisis of the emotions (he supposed one might fairly call it that) the training he had bestowed on his reason, the attention he had given it from his youth up, was bearing fruit not only abundant but ripe. Ingeborg was transformed in his eyes with gratifying rapidity into a sister, – a gentle maiden sister who on the demise of his wife had taken over the housekeeping; and when in the evenings he bade her a kind good-night he found himself doing it quite naturally on her forehead. He did not tell her she had become a sister; he merely rearranged his life on these new lines; and he did, as the doctor had predicted, throw himself into his work with more zeal than ever, and very soon was once again being pervaded by the blessed calms, the serenities, the unequalled harmonies that are the portion of him who diligently does what he is interested in.

But Ingeborg, who had neglected her reason in her youth and whose mind consequently was strictly undisciplined, spent the first few weeks of being a sister in a condition of what can only be described as fluffing about. She took hold of an end of life here that seemed to be sticking out and tugged it, and of an end of life there that seemed to be sticking out and tugged it, and looked at them inquiringly and let them go again. She did not quite know, so rich in liberty had she suddenly become, where to begin. There were so many ends to life, and she was so free to choose that she blinked a little. Here were her days, swept out and empty for her at last. Here she was able to say magnificently, 'Next month I'll do this or that,' sure of her months, sure of their being arrangeable things, flexible to her will, not each just a great black leaden weight holding her pinned down more and more heavily to a sofa. And not only could she say confidently what she would do next month, but also, and this small thing like many other small things of the sort seemed curiously new and delightful, she could say confidently what she would wear. All those dreary tea-gowns in which she had trailed through the seven years of her marriage, dark garments whose sole sad function was to hide, were given to Ilse, her first servant, who had married poverty and who frugally turned them into trousers of assorted shapes for her husband, embittering him permanently; and from long-forgotten cupboards she got out small neat frocks again, portions of her unworn tremendous trousseau, short things, washable and tidy, and was refreshed into respect for herself as a decent human being by the mere putting of them on.

Her days at first held any number of these new sensations or rather recognitions of sensations that used in her girlhood to be a matter of course, but now were seen to be extraordinarily precious. She spilt over like a brimming chalice of gratefulness for the great common things of life, – sleep, hunger, power to move about, freedom from fear, freedom from pain. Her returning health ran through her veins like some exquisite delicate wine. She was now thirty, and had never felt so young. Wonderful to wake up in the morning to another day of being well. Wonderful being allowed to be alive in a world so utterly beautiful, so full of opportunity. She had all the thankfulness, the tender giving of herself up confidently to joy of the convalescent. She was happy just to sit on fine mornings on the doorstep in the sun drinking things in. Robertlet and Ditti had never been so much kissed; Rosa and the cook had never been asked so often after their ailing mothers; Kökensee had never been so near having a series of entertainments arranged for it. The very cat was stroked with a fresh sense of fellowship, the very watchdog, at one time suspected of surliness, was loved anew; and when she passed through the yard she did not fail to pause and gaze with a sunny determined kindness at the pig.

But though she passionately wanted to make everybody and everything happy in return for Robert's goodness to her, in return for the kind way she thought he was accepting her decision and not once after that first outbreak reproaching her, she had been anchored too long to one definite behaviour not to feel a little unsteady when first let loose. She hovered uncertainly round the edges of life, fingering them, trying to feel the point where she could best catch hold and climb into its fulness again.

It was oddly difficult.

Was it that she had been out of things for so many years? Had she then become a specialist? As the weeks passed and the first sheer delight in just being well was blunted by repetition, she began to be puzzled. Everything began to puzzle her, – herself, Robert, the children, the servants. Robert puzzled her extremely. Whenever before she had been happy, a cheerful singing thing, he had loved her. She knew he had. She had only to be in a gay mood, in the mood that recklessly didn't mind whether he liked it or not but sat on his knee and insisted on his listening while she talked, half in earnest and half amused, about the bigger, vaguer, windier aspects of life, for him to come up out of the depths of his meditations and laugh and pet her. Now nothing fetched him up. He was quite unresponsive. He seemed beyond her reach, in some strange retreat where she could not get at him. She had never felt so far away from him. He was not angry evidently; he was quite kind. She could not guess that this steady unenthusiastic kindness was the natural expression of a fraternal regard.

'But he does *love* me,' she said to herself, altogether unaware of the smallness of the place in the world occupied by negative persons like sisters – 'he does *love* me.'

She said it several times a day, hugging it to herself as the weeks went on in much the same way that a coachman, growing cold on his box, hugs his chest, not having anything else to hug, at intervals to keep his circulation going; and particularly she said it on her way up to the attic after the administration of the good-night kiss.

In spite of this assurance, she found herself presently beginning to hesitate before she spoke to him or touched him, wondering whether he would like it. She tried to shake off these increasing timidities, and once or twice intrepidly stroked his hair: but his head, bent over his dinner or his book, seemed unconscious that she was doing it, and she felt unable to go on.

'But he does *love* me,' she said to herself.

It was not long before she perceived definitely that she had ceased to amuse him, and the moment she discovered this she ceased to be amusing: her gaiety went out like a light.

'But he does *love* me,' she still said to herself.

He called her Ingeborg regularly, never wife or little one, and it soon came to be unthinkable that she should ever have been his treasure, snail, or sheep. He did it however quite kindly, with no trace of the rebuke it used invariably to contain.

'But he does *love* me,' she still said to herself.

Puzzled, she racked her brain to think of ways to please him, and tried to make his house as comfortably perfect for him as possible, performing every duty she could find or invent with a thoroughness that by eleven o'clock in the morning had exhausted the supply. Herr Dremmel, however, was not accessible by ways of order and good food; he had never noticed their absence, and he did not now notice their presence. She saw after a while herself that his sum of happiness was not in the least increased by them.

How could she make him happy, then? What could she do to make his life the brightest serene thing?

It was a shock to her, an immense and shattering surprise, the day she realised that all this time he was, in fact, being happy. She walked in the garden long that day, staring hard at this new perception, pondering, astonished.

'But he does *I*—' she began; and stopped.

Did he? What was the good of saying he did if he didn't? Was everything with him, and perhaps with other husbands – she knew so little about husbands – bound up with parenthood? Was it true, what he said to her the day she begged him to be friends, that a husband and wife could never be friends? She felt so entirely able to love Robert, to love him tenderly and deeply, without perpetually being somebody's mother. Perhaps wives could be friends and husbands couldn't. She wished she knew more about these things. She felt she did not rightly understand; and suspected, walking up and down the damp October garden, that being a bishop's daughter was an inefficient preparation for being anybody's wife. It kept one's mind muffled. You were brought up not to look. If you wanted to see you had to be furtive and peep at life over the edge, as it were, of your Prayer-book, which made you feel wicked and didn't give you any sort of a view. All bishop's daughters, she said to herself walking fast, for her thoughts became tumultuous on this subject, ought to be maiden ladies; or, if they couldn't manage that as St Paul would say, they should at least only marry more bishops. Not curates, not vicars, not mysterious elusivenesses like German pastors, but bishops. People they were used to. People they understood. Continuations. Second volumes. Sequels. Aprons. Curates might have convulsive moments that would worry souls blanched white by the keeping out of the light, souls like celery, no whiter than anybody else's if left properly to themselves, but blanched by a continual banking up round them of episcopal mould; and even a vicar might conceivably sometimes be headlong; while as for a German pastor . . . She flung out her hands.

Well, Robert was not headlong. No one could accuse him of anything but the most steady sequence in his steps. But he was, she thought, not having the clue to Herr Dremmel's conduct, incomprehensible. With the simple faith of women, that faith that holds out against so many enlightenments and whose artless mainspring is vanity, she had believed quite firmly that every sweet and admiring assurance he had ever given her would go on changelessly and indefinitely holding good, she had believed she knew and understood him better than he did himself, and that at any time she wanted to she had only to reach out her hand to be able to help herself to more of his love. This faith in herself and in her power, if she really wished, to charm him, she called having faith in him. It took six weeks of steadily continued mild indifference on Herr Dremmel's part, of placid imperviousness to all approaches of an affectionate nature, of the most obvious keen relish in his work, keener than he had yet shown, to reveal the truth at last to her; and greatly was she astonished. He was happy, and he was happy without her. 'And that,' said Ingeborg, unable to resist the conclusion pressed upon her, 'isn't love.'

She stopped a moment beneath the gently dripping trees and took off her knitted cap and shook it dry, for she had inadvertently brushed against an overhanging branch on which last summer's leaves still wetly clung.

She pulled out her handkerchief and rubbed her cap thoughtfully. It had been raining all the morning, and now late in the afternoon the garden was a quiet grey place of fallen leaves and gathering dusk and occasional small shakings of wet off the trees when a silent bird perched on the sodden branches. Some drops fell on her bare head while she was drying her cap. She put up her hand mechanically and rubbed them off. She stood wiping her cap long after it was dry, absorbed in thought.

'I don't know what it is,' she said presently, half aloud, 'but I do know what it isn't.'

She put on her cap again, pulling it over her ears with both hands and much care, and staring while she did it at a slug in the path in front of her.

'And what it isn't,' she said after another interval, shaking her head and screwing up her face into an expression of profoundest negation, 'is love.'

'*Well*,' she added, deeply astonished.

Then, with a flash of insight, 'It's because he works.'

Then, with a quick desire to cover up the wound to her vanity, 'If he didn't get lost in his work he'd *remember* he loves me – it's only that he *forgets*.'

Then, with a white flare of candour, 'He's a bigger thing than I am.'

Then, with the old eagerness to help, 'So it's my business to see that he can be big in happy peace.'

Then, remembrance smiting her with its flat, cold hand. 'But he *is* happy.'

Then, 'So where do I come in?'

Then, with a great, frank acceptance of the truth. 'I don't come in.'

Then, swept by swift, indignant honesty, 'Why should I *want* to come in? What is all this coming in? Oh' – she stamped her foot – 'the simple fact, the naked fact when I've pulled all the silly clothes off is that I only want him to be happy if it's I who make him happy, and I'm nothing but a – I'm just a—' She twisted round on her heels, her arms flung out, in search of the exact raw word – 'I'm nothing but just a common tyrant.'

At tea-time her condition can best, though yet imperfectly, be described as chastened.

CHAPTER 25

Nevertheless, though she tried to face it squarely and help herself by indignation at her own selfish vanity, she felt a great emptiness round her, a great chill.

It was impossible to get used all at once to this new knowledge, so astonishing after seven years of conviction that one was loved and so astonishing when one remembered that as recently as August – one could positively count the days – just coming home again after an absence had drawn forth from Robert any number of manifestations of it. It had the suddenness and completeness of the switching off of light. A second before, one was illuminated; another second, and one was groping in the dark. For she did grope. She was groping for reasons. It seemed for a long time so incredible that her entire importance and interest as a human being should depend on whether she was or was not what he called a true wife that she preferred to go on groping rather than take hold of this as an explanation.

She had been so sure of Robert. She had been so familiar with him and unafraid. When she thought of her days at home, of her abject fear of her father, of her insignificance, she felt that Robert's love and admiration had lifted her up from being a creeping thing to being a creature with quite bright brave wings. He had come suddenly into her life and told her she was a *süsses Kleines*: and behold she became a *süsses Kleines*. And now he didn't think her even that any more; he had dropped her again, and she was already falling back into the old state of timidity towards the man in the house.

She turned to the children and the housekeeping and to a search for something she could do in the parish, so that at least while she was making efforts to clear her confusion about Robert she might not be wasting time. If she was no use to him she might be of use to the less independent. She was entirely humble at this moment, and would have thanked a dog if it had been so kind as to allow her to persuade it to wag its tail. It had always been her hope throughout each of her illnesses that presently when that one was over she would get up and begin to do good, and now here she was, finally up, with two children who had not yet had much mother, two servants whose lives might perhaps be made more interesting, a whole field outside her gates for practise in deeds of mercy, and enormous tracts of time on her hands. All she had to do was to begin.

But it was rather like an over-delayed resurrection. Things had filled up. Everybody seemed used to being left alone, and such a thing as district-visiting, so familiar to a person bred in Redchester, was unknown in East Prussia. The wife of a country pastor had as many duties in her own house as one woman could perform in a day, and nobody expected to see her going about into other houses consoling and alleviating. Also, the peasants thought, why should one be consoled and alleviated? The social difference between the peasant and the pastor was so small and rested so often only on education that it would have appeared equally natural, if the thing could from any point of view have been made natural, for the wife of the peasant to go and console and alleviate the parsonage. Who wanted sympathy in Kökensee? Certainly not the men, and the women were too busy with family cares, those many crushing cares that yet kept them interested and alive, to have time for consolations. And those with most cares, most children who died, most internal complaints, most gloom and weariness, achieved just because of these things almost as much distinction and popularity in the village as those with most money. Ingeborg herself was popular so long as her children were drowned out of punts, or died of mumps, or were stillborn; but now that nothing happened to her and she went about, after having had six of them, still straight and slender, Kökensee regarded her coldly and with distrust. Doing nothing for anybody on a sofa in an untidy black tea-gown she had been respected. Trim and anxious to be of use she was disapproved of.

When she went round to try to interest the women in the getting up of little gatherings that were to brighten the parish once a fortnight during the winter months, they shook their heads over their wash-tubs and told each other after she had gone that it was because she kept two servants. *Hausfraus* who did not to do their own work, they said, shaking their heads with many *ja, ja's,* were sure to get into mischief. All they asked of the pastor's wife was that she should attend to her own business and let them attend to theirs. They did not walk into her living-room; why should she walk into theirs? They did not want to brighten her winter; why should she want to brighten theirs? She should take example from her husband, they said, who never visited anybody. But a Frau who kept two servants and who after six children still wore skirts shorter than a Confirmation candidate's – *ja, ja, das kommt davon.*

And things had filled up at home. Rosa and the cook had been used so long to managing alone, and were so completely obsessed by the idea that the Frau Pastor was half dead and that her one real function was to lie down, that they regarded her suddenly frequent appearances in the kitchen with the uneasiness and discomfort with which they would have regarded the appearances of a ghost. No more than if she had been a ghost did they know what to do with her. She did not seem real, separated from her bedroom and her beef-tea. They could not work with her. She would make them jump when, on looking up, they saw her in their midst, having come in unheard with her strange lightness of movement. Their nerves were shaken when they discovered her on her knees in odd corners of the house doing things with dusters. To see her prodding potatoes over the fire, and weighing meat, and approaching onions familiarly made them creep.

It was like some dreadful miracle.

It was like, said Rosa, whispering, being obliged to cook dinners and make beds with the help of – side by side with—

'With what then?' cried the cook, pretending courage but catching fear from Rosa's face.

'*Mit einem Lazarus,*' whispered Rosa, behind her hand.

The cook shrieked.

They did not however give notice, being good girls and prepared to bear much, till they saw their names in red ink in one of the squares ruled on a sheet of paper the Frau Pastor pinned up on the sitting-room wall above her writing-table.

For a day or two they were filled with nameless horror because the ink was red. Then, when they discovered what the numbers against the square, 3–4, meant, the horror was swept away in indignation, for it was the hour in the afternoon in which they usually mended or knitted and gossiped together, and it appeared that the Frau Pastor intended to come and sit with them during this hour and read aloud.

'Nice books are so – so nice,' said Ingeborg, explaining her idea. 'Don't you think you'll like nice books ?'

She faltered a little, because of the expression on their faces.

'There is the pig,' said the cook desperately.

'The pig ?'

'It has to be fed between three and four.'

'Oh, but we're not going to mind things like *pigs*,' said Ingeborg with a slightly laboured brightness.

The next day they gave notice.

But the plan pinned up in the parlour had nothing, except during this one hour, to do with Rosa and the cook; it had been drawn up solely on behalf of Robertlet and Ditti.

Ingeborg had pored over it for days, making careful squares with a ruler and doing all the principal words in red ink, her hair touzled by the stresses of thinking out and her cheeks flushed. The winter was upon them, and already rain and gales made being out of doors impossible except for one daily courageous trudge after dinner with the children in waterproofs and goloshes, and she thought that with a little arranging she might shorten and brighten the long months to the spring. The children were so passive. They seemed hardly conscious, she thought, of the world round them. Wouldn't they enjoy themselves more if they could be taught to look at things ? Their resemblance to the elder Frau Dremmel was remarkable, it is true, but of course only superficial. Why they were apathetic was because they had had so little mother in their lives. She had only been able to teach them their prayers and their grace, and beyond that had had to leave them to God. Now, however, she could take over her charge again, and teach them things that would make them lissom, quick, interested and gay.

What would make Robertlet and Ditti lissom, quick, interested and gay ? She pored profoundly over this question, and was steeped in red ink and with the end of her pen bitten off and the floor white with torn-up plans before she had answered it.

At the end of the winter she thought she could not have answered it right. There was something wrong with education. The children had been immensely patient. They had borne immensely with their mother. Yet by the end of a whole winter's application of the plan they knew only how cats and dogs were spelt, and the sole wonder that they felt after six months' parental effort to stir them to that important preliminary to knowledge was a dim surprise that such familiar beasts should need spelling.

It was very unfortunate, but they could not be got, for instance, to like the heavenly bodies. Useless for their mother to press them upon their notice on clear evenings when all the sky was a-blink. From first to last they saw nothing in the sunsets that lit the white winter world into a vast cave of colour except a sign that it must be tea-time. Not once could they be induced to shudder at the thought, on great starry nights, of infinite space. They were unmoved by the information that they were being hurled at an incredible speed through it; and they didn't mind the moon being all those miles away. In the dancing class it was Ingeborg who danced. In the gymnastic class it was she who grew lissom. The *English and German Chatting*, owing to an absence in Robertlet and Ditti of any of the ingredients of chat, was a monologue; and for the course on *Introductions to Insects Collected in the House* it was Ingeborg who caught the flies.

They were, however, very good. Nothing to which they were subjected altered that. When their mother in spite of discouragements went on bravely, so did they. When out of doors she snowballed them they stood patiently till she had done. She showed them how to make a snow man, and they did not complain. She gave them little sledges at Christmas, and explained the emotions to be extracted from these objects by sliding on them swiftly down slopes, and they bore her no ill-will when, having slid, they fell off, but quietly preferred the level garden paths and drew each other in turn on one sledge up and down them, while their mother on the other sledge did the sorts of things they had come to expect from mothers, and kept on disappearing over the brink of the slope to the frozen lake head first and face downwards.

'It's very *difficult*,' thought Ingeborg sometimes, as the winter dragged on.

There she was, heavy with facts about flies and stars and distances extracted in the evenings during her preparation hours from the *Encyclopædia Britannica* which had been procured from London for the purpose – the parsonage groaned beneath it – and longing to unload them, and she was not able to because the two vessels which ought to have received them were fitted so impenetrably with lids.

They seemed to grow, if anything, more lidded. Quieter and

quieter. The hour at the end of the day, marked on the plan Lap, an hour she had thought might easily become beautiful, something her children would remember years hence, which was to have been all white intimacy, with kisses and talks about angels and the best and quickest ways of getting to heaven, while Robertlet sat in the lap on Mondays, Wednesdays and Fridays, and Ditti sat in it on Tuesdays, Thursdays and Saturdays (there being scarcity in laps), was from the beginning an hour of semi-somnolence for the children, of staring sleepily into the glow of the stove, resting while they waited for what their mother would do or say next.

Ingeborg was inclined to be disheartened at this hour. It was the last one of the children's day, and the day had been long. There was the firelight, the mother's lap and knee, the mother herself ready to kiss and be confided in and more than ready to confide in her turn those discoveries she had made in the regions of science, and nothing happened. Robertlet and Ditti either stared fixedly at the glow from the open stove door or at Ingeborg herself; but whichever they stared at they did it in silence.

'What are you thinking of?' she would ask them sometimes, disturbing their dreamless dreams, their happy freedom from thought. And then together they would answer, 'Nothing.'

'No, but tell me really – you can't *really* think of nothing. It's impossible. Nothing is—' she floundered – 'is always *something*—'

But the next time she asked the same question they answered with one voice just as before, 'Nothing.'

Then it occurred to her that perhaps they were having too much mother. This also happened in the hour called Lap.

'A mother,' she reflected, both her arms round her children according to plan, 'must often be rather a nuisance.'

She looked down with a new sympathy at Ditti's head reposing, also according to plan, on her shoulder.

'Especially if she's a devoted mother.'

She laid her cheek on the black smooth hair, parted and pigtailed and as unlike Robert's fair furry stuff or her own as it was like the elder Frau Dremmel's.

'A devoted mother,' continued Ingeborg to herself, her eyes on the glowing heart of the stove and her cheek on Ditti's head, 'is one who gives up all her time to trying to make her children different.'

'*I'm* a devoted mother,' she added, after a pause in which she had faced her conscience.

'How dreadful!' she thought.

She began to kiss Ditti's head very softly.

'How too dreadful to be in the power of somebody different; of somebody quick if you're not quick, or dull if you're not dull, and anyhow so old, so very old compared to you, and have to be made like her! How would I like being in my mother-in-law's power, with years and years for her to work at forcing me to be what she'd think I ought to be? And what she'd think I ought to be would be herself, what she tries to be. Of course. You can't think outside yourself.'

She drew the children tighter. 'You *poor* little things!' she exclaimed aloud, suddenly overcome by the vision of what it must be like to have to put up with a person so fundamentally alien through a whole winter; and she kissed them one after the other, holding their faces close to hers with her hands against their cheeks in a passion of apology.

Even to that exclamation, a quite new one in a quite new voice, they said nothing, but waited patiently for what would no doubt happen next.

CHAPTER 26

What happened next was that they went to school.

Just as Ingeborg was beginning to ask herself rather shy questions — for she was very full of respects — about the value of education and the claims of free development, the State stepped in and swept Robertlet and Ditti away from her into its competent keeping. In an instant, so it seemed to her afterwards when in the empty house she had nothing to do but put away their traces, she was bereft.

'You never told me *this* is what happens to mothers,' she said to Herr Dremmel the day the brief order from the Chief Inspector of Schools arrived.

Herr Dremmel, who was annoyed that he should have forgotten his parental and civic duties, and still more annoyed, it being April and his fields needing as much attention as a new-born infant, or a young woman one wishes, impelled by amorous motives, to marry, that there should be parental and civic duties to forget, was short with her.

'Every German of six has to be educated,' he said.

'But they *are* being educated,' said Ingeborg, her mind weighted with all she herself had learned.

He waved her aside.

'But, Robert — my children — surely there's some way of educating them besides sending them away from me?'

He continued to wave her aside.

There was no doubt about it: the children had to go, and they went.

Of the alternatives, their being taught at home by a person with Government certificates, or attending the village school, Herr Dremmel would not hear. He was having differences of a personal nature with the village schoolmaster, who refused with a steadi-

ness that annoyed Herr Dremmel to recognise that he was a
Schafskopf, while Herr Dremmel held, and patiently explained,
that a person who is born a *Schafskopf* should be simple and
frank about it, and not persist in behaving as if he were not one;
and as for a teacher in the house, that was altogether impossible
because there was no room.

'There's the laboratory,' said Ingeborg recklessly, to whom
anything seemed better than letting her children go.

'The lab— ?'

'Only to sleep in,' she eagerly explained – 'just sleep in, you
know. The teacher needn't be there at all in the daytime, for
instance.'

'Ingeborg—' began Herr Dremmel; then he thought better of
it, and merely held out his cup for more tea. Women were really
much to be pitied. Their entire inability to reach even an elementary conception of values . . .

The children went to school in Meuk. They lodged with their
grandmother, and were to come home on those vague Sundays
when the weather was good and Herr Dremmel did not require
the horses. Ingeborg could not believe in such a complete sweep
out of her life. She loved Robertlet and Ditti with an extreme and
odd tenderness. There was self-reproach in it, and a passionate
desire to protect. It was the love sometimes found in those who
have to do all the loving by themselves. It was an acute and
quivering thing. After her experiences in the winter she had doubts
whether education at present was what they wanted. It was not
school they wanted, she thought, but to run wild. She knew it
would have been perhaps difficult to get them to run in this
manner, but thought if she had had them a little longer and had
thoroughly revised her plan, purging it of science and filling them
up instead with different forms of wildness, she might eventually
have induced them to. There could have been a carefully graduated
course in wildness, she thought, beginning quietly with weeding
paths, and going on by steps of ever-increasing abandonment to
tree-climbing, bird-nesting, and midnight raids on apples . . .

And while she wandered about the deserted garden and was
desolate, Robertlet and Ditti, safe in their grandmother's house,
were having the most beautiful dumplings every day for dinner
that seemed to fit into each part of them as warmly and neatly as
though they were bits of their own bodies come back, after having
been artificially separated, to fill them with a delicious hot

contentment, and their grandmother was saying to them at regular intervals with a raised forefinger, 'My children, never forget that you are Germans.'

There was nothing left for Ingeborg but, as she told Herr Dremmel the first Sunday Robertlet and Ditti had been coming home and then for some obscure reason did not come, thrusting the information tactlessly at tea-time between his attention and his book, her own inside.

'After all,' she said, as usual quite suddenly, breaking a valuable silence, 'there's still me.'

Herr Dremmel said nothing, for it was one of those statements of fact that luckily do not require an answer.

'Nobody,' said Ingeborg, throwing her head back a little, 'can take that away.'

Herr Dremmel said nothing to that either, chiefly because he did not want to. He had no time nor desire to guess at meanings which were, no doubt, after all not there.

'Whatever happens,' she said, 'I've still got my own inside.'

'Ingeborg,' said Herr Dremmel, 'I will not ask you what you mean in case you should tell me.'

There was a drought going on, and Herr Dremmel, who justly prided himself on his sweetness of temper, was not as patient as usual; so Ingeborg, silenced, went into the garden where the drought was making the world glow and shimmer, and reflected that on the object she called her inside alone now depended her happiness.

It was useless to depend on others; it was useless to depend, as she had done in her ridiculous vanity, on others depending on her. After all, each year had a May in it and the birds sang. She would send away the extra servant and do the work herself, as she used to at first. She would begin again to develop her intelligence, and write that evening to London for the *Spectator*. Something, she remembered, had warmed and quickened her all those years ago after her meeting with Ingram, – was it the *Spectator?* She would make plans. She would draw up plans in red ink. There were a thousand things she might study. There were languages.

She walked up and down the garden. If she let herself be beaten back this time into neglect of herself and indifference she would be done for. There was no one to save her. She would lapse and lapse; and not into fatnesses and peace like other women in Germany lopped of their children and of a class above the class

that stood at that instrument of salvation its own washtub, not
into afternoon slumbers and benevolences of a woolly nature that
kept one's hands knitting while one's brains went to sleep till
presently one was dead, but into something fretful and nipped,
with a little shrivelled, skinny, steadily dwindling mind.

Her eyes grew very wide at this dreadful picture. Now was the
moment, she thought, turning away from it quickly, now that
there had come this pause in her life, to go over to England for a
visit and see her relations and talk and come back refreshed to a
new chapter of existence in Kökensee. She had not been out of
Kökensee, except to Zoppot, since her marriage, and her throat
tightened at the thought of England. But the Bishop had never
forgiven her marriage; and her having had six children had also,
it seemed from her mother's letters when there used to be letters,
made an unfavourable impression on him. It had, in fact, upset
him. He had considered such conduct too distinctively German to
be passed over; and when she added to the error in taste of having
had them the further error or rather negligence – it must have
been criminal, thought the Bishop – of not being able to keep
them alive, the Palace, after having four times with an increasing
severity condoled, withdrew into a disapproval so profound that
it could only express itself adequately by silence.

And a stay with Judith was out of the question. One had for a
stay with Judith to have clothes, and she had no clothes; at least,
none newer than eight years old – her immense unworn trousseau
dogged her through the years – for Judith gave many parties at
the Master's Lodge, brilliant gatherings, her mother called them
in her rare letters, where London, come down on purpose and
expressed in Prime and other ministers as well as in the fine flower
of the aristocracy and a few selected fragrances from the world of
literature and art – once her mother wrote that Ingram, the great
painter, had been at the last party, and was so much enslaved by
Judith's loveliness that he had asked as a favour to be allowed to
paint her – sat at Judith's feet.

No; England was not for her. Her place was in Kökensee, and
her business now was to do what her governesses used to call
improve her mind. Perhaps if she improved it enough Robert
would talk to her again sometimes, and this time not on the Little
Treasure basis but on the solid one of intellectual companionship.
Might she not end by being a real helpmeet to him? Somebody

who would gradually learn to be quiet and analytical and artful with grains ?

She went indoors and wrote then and there to London, renewing the long-ended subscriptions to the *Times*, *Spectator*, *Clarion*, *Hibbert Journal* and the rest. She asked for a catalogue of the newest publications that were not novels, – her determination was too serious just then for novels, – ordered Herbert Spencer's First Principles, for she felt she would like to have some principles, especially first ones, and said she would be glad of any little hint the newsagent could give her as to what he thought a married Lady ought to know; and she spent the rest of the evening and the two following days laying the foundations of intellectual companionship by getting up the article *Manure* in the *Encyclopædia Britannica* and paraphrasing it into conversational observations that sounded to her so clever when she tried them on Herr Dremmel three days later at tea-time that she was astonished herself.

She was still more astonished when Herr Dremmel, having listened, remarked that her facts were wrong.

'But they can't *possibly*—' she began; then broke off, feeling the awkwardness of a position in which one was unable to argue without at once revealing the *Encyclopædia*.

CHAPTER 27

This was in May. By the end of the following May Ingeborg had read so much that she felt quite uncomfortable.

It had been a fine confused reading, in which Ruskin jostled Mr Roger Fry and Shelley lingered, as it were, in the lap of Mr Masefield. The newsagent, who must have lived chiefly a great many years before, steadily sent her mid, early, and pre-Victorian literature; and she, ordering on her own account books advertised in the weekly papers, found herself as a result one day in the placid arms of the Lake Poets and the next being disciplined by Mr Marinetti, one day ambling unconcernedly with Lamb and the next caught in the exquisite intricacies of Mr Henry James. She read books of travel, she learned poetry by heart, she grew skilful at combining her studies with her cooking; and propping up Keats on the dresser could run to him for a fresh line in the very middle of the pudding almost without the pudding minding. And since she loved to hear the beautiful words she learned aloud, and the kitchen was full of a pleasant buzzing, a murmurous sound of sonnets as well as flies, to which the servant got used in time.

But though she set about this new life with solemnity – for was she not a lopped and lonely woman whose husband had left off loving her and whose children had been taken away? – cheerfulness kept on creeping in. The chief obstacle to any sort of continued gloom was that there was a morning to every day. Also she had enthusiasms, those most uplifting and outlifting from oneself of spiritual attitudes, and developed a pretty talent for tingling. She would tingle on the least provocation, with joy over a poem, with admiration over the description of a picture, and thrilled and quivered with response to tales of Beauty, – of the beauty of the cathedrals in France, miracles of coloured glass held together delicately by stone, blown together, she could only think

from the descriptions, in their exquisite fragility by the breath of
God rather than built up slowly by men's hands; of the beauty of
places, the lagoons round Venice at sunrise, the desert towards
evening; of the beauty of love, faithful, splendid, equal love; of
all the beauty men made with their hands, little spuddy things
running over dead stuff, blocks of stone, bits of glass and canvas,
fashioning and fashioning till at last there was the vision, pulled
out of a brain and caught for ever into the glory of line and
colour. She longed to talk about the wonderful and stirring and
vivid things life outside Kökensee seemed to flash with. What must
it be like to people who knew and had seen? What could it be like
to see for oneself, to travel, to go to France and its cathedrals, to
go to Italy in the spring-time when the jewels of the world could
be looked at in a setting of clear skies and generous flowers? Or
in autumn, when Kökensee was grey and tortured with rainstorms,
to go away there into serenity, to where the sun burned the
chestnuts golden all day long and the air smelt of ripened grapes?

And she had only seen the Rigi.

Well, that was something; and it seemed somehow appropriate
for a pastor's wife. She turned again to her books. What she had
was very good; and she had found an old woman in the village
who did not mind being comforted, so that added to everything
else was now the joy of gratitude.

It seemed, indeed, that she was to have a run of joys that spring,
for besides these came suddenly yet another, the joy so long
dreamed of having some one to talk to. And such a some one,
thought Ingeborg, entirely dazzled by her good fortune, – for it
was Ingram.

She was paddling the punt as usual down the lake one afternoon, a pile of books at her feet, when, passing the end of the arm
of reeds that stretched out round her hidden bay, she perceived
that her little beach was not empty; and pausing astonished with
her paddle arrested in the air to look, she recognised in the middle
of a confusion of objects strewn round him that no doubt had to
do with painting, sitting with his elbows on his drawn-up knees
and his chin in his hand, Ingram.

He was doing nothing: just staring. She came from behind the
arm of reeds, half drifting along noiselessly out towards the middle
of the lake, straight across his line of sight.

For an instant he stared motionless, while she, holding her
paddle out of the water, stared equally motionless at him. Then

he seized his sketching book and began furiously to draw. She was out in the sun and had no hat on. Her hair was the strangest colour against the background of water and sky, more like a larch in autumn than anything he could think of. She seemed the vividest thing, suddenly cleaving the pallors and uncertainties of reeds and water and flecked northern sky.

'Don't move,' he shouted in what he supposed was German, sketching violently.

'So it's you?' she called back in English, and her voice sang.

'Yes, it's me all right,' he said, his pencil flying.

He did not recognize her. He had seen too many people in seven years to keep the foggy figure of that distant November evening in his mind.

'I'm coming in,' she called, digging her paddle into the water.

'Sit still,' he shouted.

'But I want to talk.'

'Sit *still*.'

She sat still, watching him, unable to believe her good fortune. If he were only here again for a single day and she could only talk to him for a single hour, what a refreshment, what a delight! To talk in English; to talk to some one who had painted Judith; to talk to some one so wonderful; to talk at *all*! She was as little shy as a person stranded on a desert island would be of anybody, kings included, who should appear after years on the solitary beach.

'Well?' she called, after sitting patiently for what she felt must be half an hour but which was five minutes.

He did not answer, absorbed in what he was doing.

She waited for what seemed another half-hour, and then turned the punt in the direction of the shore.

I'm coming in,' she called; and as he did not answer she paddled towards the bay.

He stared at her, his head a little on one side, as she came close. 'What are you going to do?' he asked, seeing she was manœuvring the punt into the corner under the oak tree.

'Land,' said Ingeborg.

He got up and caught hold of the chain fastened to the punt's nose and dragged it up the beach.

'How do you do?' she said, jumping out and holding out her hand. 'Mr Ingram,' she aded, looking up at him, her face quite solemn with pleasure.

'Well now, but who on earth are you ?' he asked, shaking her hand and staring. Her clothes, now that she was standing up, were the oddest things, recalling back numbers of Punch. 'You're not staying at the Glambecks', and except for the Glambecks' there isn't anywhere to stay.'

'But I told you I was the pastor's wife.'

'You did ?'

'Last time. Well, and I still am.'

'But when was last time ?'

'Don't you remember ? You were staying with the Glambecks then too.'

'But I haven't stayed with the Glambecks for an eternity. At least ten years.'

'Seven,' said Ingeborg. 'Seven and a half. It was in November.'

'But you must have been in pinafores.'

'And you walked down the avenue with me. Don't you remember ?'

'No,' said Ingram, staring at her.

'And you scolded me because I couldn't walk as fast as you did. Don't you remember ?'

'No,' said Ingram.

'And you said I'd run to seed if I wasn't careful. Don't you remember ?'

'No,' said Ingram.

'And I had on my grey coat and skirt. Don't you remember ?'

'No, no, no,' said Ingram, smiting his forehead, 'and I don't believe a word of it. You're just making it up. Look here,' he said, clearing away his things to make room for her, 'sit down and let us talk. Are you real ?'

'Yes, and I live in Kökensee, just round the corner behind the reeds. But I told you that before,' said Ingeborg.

'You do live ?' he said, pushing his things aside. 'You're not just a flame-headed little dream that will presently disappear again ?'

'My name's Dremmel. Frau Dremmel. But I told you that before too.'

'The things a man forgets !' he exclaimed, spreading a silk handkerchief over the coarse grass. 'There. Sit on that.'

'You're laughing at me,' she said, sitting down, 'and I don't mind a bit. I'm much too glad to see you.'

'If I laugh it's with pleasure,' he said, staring at the effect of her against the pale green of the reeds, – where had he seen just that

before, that Scandinavian colouring, that burning sort of brightness in the hair ? 'It's so amusing of you to be Frau anything.'

She smiled at him with the frankness of a pleased boy.

'You're very *nice*, you know,' he said, smiling back.

'You didn't think so last time. You called me your dear lady,
and asked me if I never read.'

'Well, and didn't you ?' he said, sitting down too, but a little
way off so that he could get her effect better.

'Yes, do sit down. Then I shan't be so dreadfully afraid you're
going.'

'Why, but I've only just found you.'

'But last time you disappeared almost at once into the fog, and
you'd only just found me then,' she said, her hands clasped round
her knees, her face the face of the entirely happy.

'After all I seem to have made some progress in seven years,' he
said. 'I apparently couldn't see then.'

'No, it was me. I was very invisible—'

'Invisible ?'

'Oh, moth-eaten, dilapidated, dun-coloured. And I'd been
crying.'

'You ? Look here, nobody with your kind of colouring should
ever cry. It's a sin. It would be most distressing, seriously, if you
were ever less white than you are at this moment.'

'See how nice it is not to be a painter,' said Ingeborg. 'I don't
mind a bit if you're white or not so long as it's you.'

'But why should you like it to be me ?' asked Ingram, to whom
flattery, used as he was to it, was very pleasant, and feeling the
comfort of the cat who is being gently tickled behind the ear.

'Because,' said Ingeborg earnestly, 'you're somebody
wonderful.'

'Oh, but you'll make me purr,' he said.

'And I see your name in the papers at least once a week,' she
said.

'Oh the glory !'

'And Berlin's got two of your pictures. Bought for the nation.'

'Yes, it has. And haggled till it got them a dead bargain.'

'And you've painted my sister.'

'What ?' he said quickly, staring at her again. 'Why of course.
That's it. That's who you remind me of. The amazing Judith.'

'Are you such friends ?' she asked, surprised.

'Oh well then, the wife of the Master of Ananias. Let us give

her her honours. She's the most entirely beautiful woman I've
seen. But—'

'But what?'

'Oh well. I did a very good portrait of her. The old boy didn't
like it.'

'What old boy?'

'The Master. He tried to stop my showing it. And so did the
other old boy.'

'What other old boy?'

'The Bishop.'

'But if it was so good?'

'It was. It was exact. It was the living woman. It was a portrait
of sheer, exquisite flesh.'

'Well then,' said Ingeborg.

'Oh, but you know bishops—' He shrugged his shoulders.
'Italy's got it now. It's at Venice. The State bought it. You must
go and see it next time you're there.'

'I will,' she laughed, 'the very next time.' And her laugh was the
laugh of joyful amusement itself.

Ingram was now forty-three or four, and leaner than ever. His
high shoulders were narrow, his thin neck came a long way out of
his collar at the back and was partly hidden in front by his short
red beard. His hair, darker than his beard, was plastered down
neatly. He had very light, piercing eyes, and a nose that Ingeborg
liked. She liked everything. She liked his tweed clothes, and his big
thin hands, – the wonderful hands that did the wonderful pictures,
– and his long thin nimble legs. She liked the way he fidgeted, and
the quickness of his movements. And she glowed with pride to
think she was sitting with a man who was mentioned in the papers
at least once a week and whose pictures were bought by States,
and she glowed with happiness because he did not this time seem
anxious to go back to the Glambecks at once; but most of all she
glowed with the heavenliness, the absolute heavenliness, of being
talked to.

'And you're her sister,' he said, staring at her. 'Now that really
is astonishing.'

'But everybody can't be beautiful.'

'A sister of hers here, tucked away in this desert. It *is* a desert
you know. I've come to it because I wanted a desert, – one does
sometimes after too much of the opposite. But I go away again,

and you live in it. What have you been doing all these years, since I was here last?'

'Oh, I've – been busy.'

'But not here? Not all the time here?'

'Yes, all of it.'

'What, not away at all?'

'I went to Zoppot once.'

'Zoppot? Where's Zoppot? I never heard of Zoppot. I don't believe Zoppot's any good. Do you mean to say you've not been to a town, to a place where people say things and hear things and rub themselves alive against each other, since last I was here?'

'Well, but pastors' wives don't rub.'

'But it's incredible. It's like death. Why didn't you?'

'Because I couldn't.'

'As though it weren't possible to tear oneself free at least every now and then.'

'You wait till you're a pastor's wife.'

'But how do you manage to be so alive? For you shine, you know. When I think of all the things *I've* done since I was here last—' He broke off, and looked away from her across the lake. 'Oh well. Sickening things, really, most of them,' he finished.

'Wonderful pictures,' said Ingeborg, leaning forward and flushing with her enthusiasm. 'That's what you've done.'

'Yes. One paints and paints. But in between – it's those in betweens the work-fits that hash one up. What do *you* do in between?'

'In between what?'

'Whatever it is you do in the morning and whatever it is you do in the evening.'

'I enjoy myself.'

'Yes. Yes. That's what *I'd* like to do.'

'But don't you?'

'I can't.'

'What – *you* can't?' she said. 'But you live in beauty. You make it. You pour it over the world—'

She stopped abruptly, hit by a sudden thought. 'I beg your pardon,' she said. 'I don't know anything really. Perhaps – you're in mourning?'

He looked at her. 'No,' he said, 'I'm not in mourning.'

'Or perhaps – no, you're not ill. And you can't be poor. Well then, why in the world don't you enjoy yourself?'

'Aren't you ever bored?' he answered.

'The days aren't long enough.'

He looked round at the empty landscape and shuddered.

'Here. In Kökensee,' he said. 'It's spring now. But what about the wet days, the howling days? What about unmanageable months like February? Why' – he turned to her – 'you must be a perfect little seething vessel of independent happiness, bubbling over with just your own contentments.'

'I never was called a seething vessel before,' said Ingeborg, hugging her knees, her eyes dancing. 'What an impression for a respectable woman to produce!'

'What a gift to possess, you mean. The greatest of all. To carry one's happiness about with one.'

'But that's exactly what *you* do. Aren't you spilling joy at every step? Splashing it into all the galleries of the world? Leaving beauty behind you wherever you've been?'

He twisted himself round to lie at full length and look up at her. 'What delightful things you say!' he said. 'I wish I could think you mean them.'

'Mean them?' she exclaimed, flushing again. 'Do you suppose I'd waste the precious minutes saying things I don't mean? I haven't talked to any one really for years, – not to any one who answered back. And now it's *you*. Why, it's too wonderful. As though I'd waste a second of it.'

'You're the queerest, most surprising thing to find here on the edge of the world,' he said, gazing up at her. 'And there's the sun just got at your hair through the trees. Are you always full of molten enthusiasms for people?'

'Only for you.'

'But what am I to say to these repeated pattings?' he cried.

'You got into my imagination that day I met you and you've been in it ever since. I was in the stupidest state of dull giving in. You pulled me out.'

He stared at her, his chin on his hand. 'Imagine me pulling anybody out of anything,' he said. 'Generally I pull them in.'

'It's true I've had relapses,' she said. 'Five relapses.'

'Five?'

She nodded. 'Five since then. But here I am, seething as you call it, and it's you who started me, and I believe I shall go on now doing it uninterruptedly for ever.'

Ingram put out his hand with a quick movement, as though he

were going to touch the edge of her dress. 'Teach me how to seethe,' he said.

'That's rather like asking a worm to give lessons in twinkling to a star.'

'Wonderful,' he said softly, after a little pause, 'to lie here having sweet things said to one. Why didn't I find you before? I've been being bored at the Glambeck's for a whole frightful week.'

'Oh, have you been there a week already?' she asked anxiously. 'Then you'll go away soon?'

'I was going to-morrow.'

'That's like last time. You were just going when I met you.'

'But now I'm going to stay. I'm going to stay and paint you.'

She jumped. '*Oh –*' she exclaimed, awe-struck. '*Oh—*'

'Paint you, and paint you, and paint you,' said Ingram, 'and see if I can catch some of your happiness for myself. Get at your secret. Find out where it all comes from.'

'But it comes from *you* – at this moment it's all you—'

'It doesn't. It's inside you. And I want to get as much of it as I can. I'm dusty and hot and sick of everything. I'll come and stay near you and paint you, and you shall make me clean and cool again.'

'The stuff you talk!' she said, leaning forward, her face full of laughter. 'As though I could do anything for *you*. You're really making fun of me the whole time. But I don't care. I don't care about anything so long as you won't go away.'

'You needn't be afraid I'm going away. I'm going to have a bath of remoteness and peace. I'll chuck the Glambecks and get a room in your village. I'll come every day and paint you. You're like a little golden leaf, a beach leaf in autumn blown suddenly from God knows where across my path.'

'Now it's you making *me* purr,' she said.

'You're like everything that's clear and bright and cool and fresh.'

'Oh,' murmured Ingeborg, radiant, 'and I haven't even got a tail to wag!'

'Already, after only ten minutes of you, I feel as if I were eating cold, fresh, very crisp lettuce.'

'That's not nearly so nice. I don't think I like being lettuce.'

'I don't care. You are. And I'm going to paint you. I'm going to paint your soul. Tell me some addresses for lodgings,' he said, snatching up a sheet of paper and a pencil.

'There aren't any.'

'Then I must stay at your vicarage.'

'You'll have to sleep with Robert, then.'

'What? Who is Robert?'

'My husband.'

'Oh. Yes. But how absurd that sounds!'

'What does?'

'Your having a husband.'

'I don't see how you can help having a husband if you're a wife.'

'No. It's inevitable. But it's — quaint. That you should be anybody's wife, let alone a pastor's. Here in Kökensee.'

She got up impulsively. 'Come and see him,' she said. 'You wouldn't last time. Come now. Let me make tea for you. Let me have the pride of making tea for you.'

'But not this minute?' he begged, as she stood over him holding out her hand to pull him up.

'Yes, yes. He's in now. He'll be out in his fields later. He'll be frightfully pleased. We'll tell him about the picture. Oh, but you did *mean* it, didn't you?' she added, suddenly anxious.

He got up reluctantly and grumbling. 'I don't want to see Robert. Why should I see Robert? I don't believe I'm going to like Robert,' he muttered, looking down at her from what seemed an immense height. 'Of course I mean it about the picture,' he added in a different voice, quick and interested. 'It'll be a companion portrait to your sister's.'

He laughed. 'That would really be very amusing,' he said, stooping down and neatly putting his scattered things together.

Ingeborg flushed. 'But — that's rather cruel fun, isn't it, that you're making of me now?' she murmured.

'What?' he asked, straightening himself to look at her.

The light had gone out of her face.

'What? Why — didn't I tell you my picture of you is to be the portrait of a spirit?'

He pounced on things and gathered them up in his arms.

'Come along,' he said impatiently, 'and be intelligent. Let me beg you to be intelligent. Come along. I suppose I'm to go in the punt. What's in it? Books by the dozen. What's this? Eucken? Keats? Pragmatism? Oh Lord.'

'Why oh Lord?' she asked, getting in and picking up the paddle while he gave the punt a vigorous shove off and jumped on to it as it went. She was radiant again. She was tingling with pride and joy. He really meant it about the picture. He hadn't made fun of her. On the contrary . . . 'Why oh Lord?' she asked. 'You said that, or something like it, last time because I *didn't* read.'

'Well, now I say it because you do,' he said, crouching at the opposite end watching her movements as she paddled.

'But that doesn't seem to have much consistency, does it,' she said.

'Hang consistency. I don't want you addled. And you'll get addled if you topple all these different stuffs into your little head together.'

'But I'd rather be addled than empty.'

'Nonsense. If I could I'd stop your doing anything that may alter you a hairsbreadth from what you are at this monent.'

To that she remarked, suspending her paddle in mid air, her face as sparkling as the shining drops that flashed from it, that she really was greatly enjoying herself; and they both laughed.

Ingram waited in the parlour, where he stood taking in with attentive eyes the details of that neglected, almost snubbed little room, while Ingeborg went to the laboratory, so happy and proud that she forgot she was breaking rules, to fetch, as she said, Robert.

Robert however, would not be fetched. He looked up at her with a great reproach on her entrance, for as invariably happened on the rare occasions when the tremendousness of what she had to say seemed to her to justify interrupting, he thought he had just arrived within reach, after an infinite patient stalking, of the coy elusive heart of a problem.

'Mr Ingram's here,' she said breathlessly.

He gazed at her over his spectacles.

'In the parlour,' said Ingeborg. 'He's come to tea. Isn't that wonderful? He's going to paint—'

'Who is here, Ingeborg?'

'Mr Ingram. Edward Ingram. Come and talk to him while I get tea.'

She had even forgotten to shut the door in her excitement, and a puff of wind from the open window picked up Herr Dremmel's papers and blew them into confusion.

He endeavoured to catch them, and requested her in a tone of controlled irritation to shut the door.

'Oh, how dreadful of me !' she said hastily doing it but with gaiety.

'I do not know,' then said Herr Dremmel, mastering his annoyance, 'Mr Ingram.'

'But, Robert, it's *the* Mr Ingram. Edward Ingram. The greatest artist there is now. The great portrait painter. Berlin has—'

'Is he a connection of your family's, Ingeborg ?'

'No, but he painted Ju—'

'Then it is not necessary for me to interrupt my afternoon on his behalf.'

And Herr Dremmel bent his head over his papers again.

'But, Robert, he's *great* – he's *very* great—'

Herr Dremmel, with a wetted thumb, diligently rearranged his pages.

'But – why, I told him you'd love to see him. What am I to say to him if you don't come ?'

Herr Dremmel, his eye caught by a sentence he had written, was reading with a deep enormous appetite.

'Tea,' said Ingeborg desperately. 'There's tea. You always *do* come to tea. It'll be ready in a minute—'

He looked up at her, gathering her into his consciousness. 'Tea ?' he said.

But even as he said it his thoughts fell off to his problem, and without removing his eyes from hers he began carefully to consider a new aspect of it that in that instant had occurred to him.

There was nothing for it but to go away. So she went.

CHAPTER 28

Ingram's visit to the Glambecks had in any case been coming to an end the next day, when he was to have gone to Königsberg on his way to the Caucasus, a place he hoped might trick him by its novelty for at least a time out of boredom, and the Baron and Baroness were greatly surprised when he told them he was not going to the Caucasus but to Kökensee instead.

With one voice they exclaimed, 'Kökensee?'

'To paint the pastor's wife's hair,' said Ingram.

The Baron and Baroness were silent. The explanation seemed to them beyond comment. Its disreputableness robbed them of speech. Herr Ingram, of course, an artist of renown – if he had not been of very great renown they could not have seen their way to admitting him on terms of equality into their circle – might paint whoever's hair he pleased; but was there not some ecclesiastical law forbidding that the hair of one's pastor's wife should be painted? To have one's hair painted when one was a pastor's wife was hardly more respectable than having it dyed. People of family were painted in order to hand down their portrait to succeeding generations, but you had to have generations, you had to have scions, you had to have a noble stock for the scions to spring from, and the painting was entered into soberly, discreetly, advisedly, in the fear of God, for the delectation of children, not lightly or wantonly, not for effect, not, as Herr Ingram had added of Frau Pastor's hair, because any portion of one's person was strangely beautiful. Strangely beautiful? They looked at each other; and the Baroness raised her large and undulating white hands from her black lap for a moment and let them drop on to it again, and the Baron slowly nodded his entire agreement.

Ingram had found a room in the village inn at Kökensee, a place so sordid, so entirely impossible as the next habitation after theirs for one who had been their guest, that the Baron and Baroness were concerned for what their servants must think when they heard him direct their coachman in the presence of their butler and footman, as he clambered nimbly into the dogcart, to take him to it. And the Baroness went and wrote at once to her son Hildebrand in Berlin, who had introduced Ingram to Glambeck, and told him she did not intend permitting Herr Ingram to visit her again. '*To please you,*' she wrote, '*I did it. But how true it is that these artists can never rise beyond being artists! I have finished with outsiders, however clever. Give me gentlemen.*'

She did not mention, she found she could not mention, the hair; and to the Baron that evening she expressed the hope that at least the picture would only be in watercolour. Watercolour, she felt, seemed somehow nearer the Commandments than oils.

It was impossible to paint a serious picture of Ingeborg in the dark little parlour of the parsonage, and as there was no other room at all that they could use Ingram began a series of sketches of her out of doors, in the garden, in the punt, anywhere and everywhere.

'I must get some idea of you,' he said, perceiving that a reason for his coming every day had to be provided. 'Later on I'll do the real picture. In a proper studio.'

'I wonder how I'll get to a proper studio?' smiled Ingeborg.

'I've got a very good one in Venice. You must sit to me there.'

'As though it were round the corner! But these are very wonderful,' she said, taking up the sketches. 'I wish I were really like that.'

'It's exactly you as you were at the moment.'

'Nonsense,' she said; but she glowed.

She knew it was not true, but she loved to believe he somehow, by some miracle, saw her so. The sketches were exquisite; little impressions of happy moments caught into immortality by a master. Hardly ever did he do more than her head and throat, and sometimes the delicate descent to her shoulder. The day she saw his idea of the back of her neck she flushed with pleasure, it was such a beautiful thing.

'That's not me,' she murmured.

'Isn't it? I don't believe anybody has ever explained to you what you're like.'

'There wasn't any need to. I can see for myself.'

'Apparently that's just what you can't do. It was high time I came.'

'Oh, but wasn't it,' she agreed earnestly.

He thought her frankness, her unadorned way of saying what she felt, as refreshing and as surprising as being splashed with clear cold shining mountain water. He had never met anything feminine that was quite so near absolute simplicity. He might call her the most extravagantly flattering things, and she appreciated them and savoured them with a kind of objective delight that interested him at first extraordinarily. Then it began to annoy him.

'You're as unselfconscious,' he told her one afternoon a little crossly, when he had been ransacking heaven and earth and most of the poets for images to compare her with, and she had sat immensely pleased and interested and urging him at intervals to go on, 'as a choir-boy.'

'But what a nice, clean, soaped sort of thing to be like!' she said. 'And so much more alive than lettuces.'

'I wonder if you *are* alive?' he said, staring at her; and she looked at him with her head on one side and told him that if she were not a bishop's daughter and a pastor's wife and a child of many prayers and trained from infancy to keep carefully within the limits of the allowable in female speech she would reply to that, 'You bet.'

'But that's only if I were vulgar that I'd say that,' she explained. 'Gentility is the sole barrier, I expect really, between me and excess.'

'You and excess! You little funny, cold-watery, early-morning thing. One would as soon connect the dawn and the fields before sunrise and small birds and the greenest of green young leaves with excess.'

He was more near being quite happy during this first week than he could remember to have been since that period of pinafore in which the world is all mother and daisies. He was enjoying the interest of complete contrast, the freshness that lies about beginnings. From this remoteness, this queer intimate German setting, he looked at his usual life as at something entirely foolish, hurried, noisy and tiresome. All those women – good heavens, all those women – who collected and coagulated about his path, what terrible things they seemed from here! Women he had painted, who rose up and reproached him because his idea of them and their idea were different; women he had fallen in love with, or tried to persuade himself he had fallen in love with, or tried to hope he would presently be able to persuade himself he had fallen in love with; women who had fallen in love with him, and fluffed and flapped about him, monsters of soft enveloping suffocation; women he had wronged – absurd word; women who had claims on him – claims on him! on him who belonged only to art and the universe. And there was his wife – good heavens, yes, his wife . . .

From these distresses and irksomenesses, from a shouting world, from the crowds and popularity that pushed between him and the one thing that mattered, his work, from the horrors of home life, the horrors of society and vain repetitions of genialities, from all the people who talked about Thought, and Art, and the Mind of the World, from jealousies, affections, praises, passions, excitement, boredom, he felt very safe at Kökensee. To be over there in the middle of the distracting emptiness of London was like having the sour dust of a neglected market-place blown into one's face. To be over here in Kökensee was to feel like a single goldfish in a bowl of clear water. Ingeborg was the clear water. Kökensee was the bowl. For a week he swam with delight in this new element; for a week he felt so good and innocent, exercising himself in its cool translucency, that almost did he seem a gold fish in a bib. Then Ingeborg began to annoy him; and she annoyed him for the precise reason that had till then charmed him, her curious resemblance to a boy,

This frank affection, this unconcealed delight in his society, this ever-ready excessive admiration, were arresting at first and amusing and delicious after the sham freshness, the tricks, the sham daring things of the women he had known. They were like a bath at the end of a hot night; like a country platform at the end of a stuffy railway journey. But you cannot sit in a bath all day, or stay permanently on a platform. You do want to go on. You do want things to develop.

Ingram was nettled by Ingeborg's apparent inability to develop. It was all very well, it was charming to be like a boy for a little while, but to persist in it was tiresome. Nothing he could say, nothing he could apply to her in the way of warm and varied epithet, brought the faintest trace of selfconsciousness into her eyes. What can be done, he thought, with a woman who will not be selfconscious? She received his speeches with enthusiasm, she hailed them with delight and laughter, and, what was particularly disconcerting, she answered back. Answered back with equal warmth and with equal variety, – sometimes, he suspected, annoyed at being outdone in epithet, with even more. To judge from her talk she almost made love to him. He would have supposed it was quite making love if he had not known, if he had not been so acutely aware that it was not. With a face of radiance and a voice of joy she would say suddenly that God had been very good to her; and when he asked in what way, would answer earnestly, 'In sending you here.' And then she would add in that peculiar sweet voice – she certainly had, though Ingram, a peculiar sweet voice, a little husky, again a little like a choir-boy's, but a choir-boy with a slight sore throat – 'I've missed you dreadfully all these years. I've been lonely for you.'

And the honesty of her; the honest sincerity of her eyes when she said these things. No choir-boy older than ten could look at one with quite such a straight simplicity.

Every day punctually at two o'clock, by which time the daily convulsion of dinner and its washing up was over at the parsonage, he walked across from his inn, while Kökensee's mouths behind curtains and round doors guttered with excited commentary, telling himself as he gazed down the peaceful street that this was the emptiest, gossip-freest place in the world, to the Dremmel gate; and dodging the various rich puddles of the yard, passed round the corner of the house along the lilac path beneath the laboratory windows to where, at the end of the lime-tree avenue, Ingeborg sat waiting. Then he would sketch her, or pretend to sketch her according as the mood was on him, and they would talk.

By the second day he knew all about her life since her marriage, her six children – they amazed and appalled him – her pursuit, started by him, of culture, her housekeeping, her pride in Robert's cleverness, her solitude, her thirst for some one to talk to. Persons like Ilse and Rosa, Frau Dremmel, Robertlet and Ditti, became extraordinarily real to him. He made little drawings of them while she talked up the edge of his paper. And he also knew, by the second day, all about her life in Redchester, its filial ardours, its duties, its difficulties when it came to disentangling itself from the Bishop; and his paper sprawled up its other edge with tiny bishops and unattached, expressive aprons. The one thing she concealed

from him of the larger happenings of her life was Lucerne, but
even that he knew after a week.

'So you can do things,' he said, looking at her with a new
interest. 'You can do real live things.'

'Oh yes. If I'm properly goaded.'

'I wonder what you mean by properly goaded?'

'Well, I was goaded then. Goaded by being kept in one place
uninterruptedly for years.'

'That's what is happening to you now.'

'Oh, but this is different. And I've been to Zoppot.'

'Zoppot!'

'Besides, *you're* here.'

'But I won't be here for ever.'

'Oh, but you'll be somewhere in the same world.'

'As though that were any good.'

'Of course it is. I shall read about you in the papers.'

'Nonsense,' he said crossly. 'The papers.'

'And I shall curl up in your memory.'

'As if I were dead. You sometimes really are beyond words
ridiculous.'

'I expect it's because I've had so little education,' she said
meekly.

At tea-time almost every day Herr Dremmel joined them in the
garden, and the conversation became stately. The sketches were
produced, and he made polite comments. He discussed art with
Ingram, and Ingram discussed fertilizers with him, and as neither
knew anything about the other's speciality they discussed by force
of intelligence. Ingeborg poured out the tea and listened full of
pride in them both. She thought how much they must be liking
and admiring each other. Robert's sound sense, his quaint and
often majestic English, his obviously notable scientific attainments
must, she felt sure, deeply impress Ingram. And of course to see
and speak to the great Ingram every day could not but give
immense gratification to Robert, now that he had become aware
of who he was. She sat between the two men in her old-fashioned
voluminous white frock, looking from one to the other with eager
pride while they talked. She did not say anything herself out of
respect for such a combination of brains, but she was all ears. She
drank the words in. It was more mind-widening she felt even than
the *Clarion*.

Ingram hated tea-time at the parsonage. Every day it was more of an effort to meet Herr Dremmel's ceremoniousness appropriately, and his scientific thirst for facts about art bored Ingram intolerably. He detested the large soft creases of his clothes and the way they buttoned and bulged between the buttonings. He disliked him for having sleeves and trousers that were too long. He shuddered at the thought of the six children. He did not want to hear about superphosphates, and resented having regularly every afternoon to pretend he did; and he did want, and this became a growing wish and a growing awkwardness, to make love to Herr Dremmel's wife.

Herr Dremmel's large unconsciousness of such a possibility annoyed him particularly, his obliviousness to the attractiveness of Ingeborg. He would certainly deserve, thought Ingram, anything he got. It was scandalous not to take more care of a little thing like that. Every day at tea-time he was enraged by this want of care in Herr Dremmel, and every day before and after tea he was engrossed, if abortive efforts to philander can be called so, in not taking care of her himself.

'You see,' said Ingeborg when he commented on the immense personal absences and withdrawals of Herr Dremmel, 'Robert is very *great*. He's wonderful. The things he does with just grains! And of course if one is going to achieve anything one has to give up every minute to it. Why, even when he loved me he usen't to—'

'Even when he loved you?' interrupted Ingram. 'What, doesn't he now?'

'Oh yes, yes,' she said quickly, flushing. 'I meant – of course he does. And besides, one always loves one's wife.'

'No, one doesn't.'

'Yes, one does.'

They left it at that.

At the end of his second week in Kökensee Ingram found himself increasing the number of his adjectives and images and comparisons, growing almost eagerly poetical, for the force of proximity and want of any one else to talk to or to think about was beginning to work, and it was becoming the one thing that seemed to him to matter to get selfconsciousness into her frank eyes, something besides or instead of that glow of admiring friendliness. He was now very much attracted, and almost equally exasperated. She was, after all, a woman; and it was absurd, it was incredible, that he, Ingram, with all these opportunities should not be able to shake her out of her first position of just wonder at him as an artist and a celebrity.

She was so warm and friendly and close in one sense, and so nowhere at all in another; so responsive, so quick, so ready to pile the sweetest honey of flattery and admiration on him and so blank to the fact that – well, that there they were, he and she. And then she had a sense of fun that interrupted, a sense most admirable in a woman at any other time, but not when she is being made love to. Also she was very irrelevant; he could not fix her; she tumbled about mentally, and that hindered progress too. Not that he cared a straw for her mentality except in so far as its quality was a hindrance; it was that other part of her, her queer little soul that interested him, her happiness and zest of life, and, of course, the graces and harmonies of her lines and colouring.

'You know, I suppose,' he said to her one evening as they walked slowly back along the path through the ryefield, and the cool scents of the ended summer's day rose in their faces as they walked, 'that I'd give a hundred days of life in London or Paris for an hour of this atmosphere, this cleanness that there is about you.

'I don't think a hundred's much. I'd give them *all* to be with you. Here. Now. In the rye-field. Isn't it wonderful this evening – isn't it beautiful? Did you smell that?' She stopped and raised her nose selectingly. 'Just that instant? That's convolvulus.'

'You have such faith in my gods,' he went on, when he could get her away from the convolvulus, 'such a bravery of belief, such a dear bravery of belief.'

'Well, but of course,' she said, turning shining eyes on to him. 'Who wouldn't believe in your gods? Art, love of beauty—'

'But it isn't only art. My gods are all sweet things and all fine things,' said Ingram, convinced at the moment that he had never done anything but worship gods of that particular flavour, so thoroughly was he being purged by the hyssop of life in Kökensee.

'Oh,' said Ingeborg with an awed enthusiasm, 'how wonderful it is that you should be exactly what you are! But it's *clever* of you,' she added with a little movement of her hands, smiling up at him, 'to be so *exactly* what you are.'

'And do you know what exactly you are? You're the open window in the prison-house of my life.'

She held her breath a moment. 'How very beautiful!' she then said. 'How *very* beautiful! And how kind you are to think of me like that! But why is it a prison-house? You of all people—'

'It isn't living, you see. It's existence in caricature over there. It's like dining perpetually with Madame Tussaud's waxworks, or anything else totally unreal and incredible.'

'But I don't understand how a great artist—'

'And you're like an open window, like the sky, like sweet air, like freedom, like secret light—'

'Oh,' she murmured, deprecating but enchanted.

'When I'm with you I feel an intolerable disgust for all the chatter and flatulence of that other life.'

'And when I'm with you,' she said, 'I feel as if I were stuffed with – oh, with stars.'

He was silent a moment. Then, determined not to be outdone, he said:

'When I'm with you I begin to feel like a star myself.'

'As though you weren't always one.'

'No. It's only you. Till I found you I was just an angry ball of mud.'

'But—'

'A thirsty man in a stuffy room.'

'But—'

'An emptiness, a wailing blank, an eviscerated thing.'

'A what?' asked Ingeborg, who had not heard that word before.

'And you,' he went on, 'are the cool water that quenches me, the scent of roses come into the room, liquid light to my clay.'

She drew a deep breath. 'It's wonderful, wonderful,' she said. 'And it sounds so real somehow – really almost as though you meant it. Oh, I don't mind you making fun of me a bit if only you'll go on saying lovely things like that.'

'Fun of you? Have you no idea, then, positively no idea, how sweet you are?'

He bent down and looked into her face. 'With little kisses in each of your eyes,' he said, scrutinizing them.

CHAPTER 29

In Redchester nobody talked of kisses. They were things not mentioned. They were things allowable only under strictly defined conditions – if you did not want to kiss, for instance, and the other person did not like it – and confined in their application to the related. Like pews in a parish church, they were reserved for families. Aunts might kiss; freely. Especially if they were bearded, – Ingeborg had an aunt with a beard. Mothers might kiss; she had seen her calm mother kiss a new-born baby with a sort of devouring, a cannibalism. Bishops might kiss, within a certain restricted area. As for husbands they did kiss, and nothing stopped them till the day when they suddenly didn't. But no one, aunts, mothers, bishops or husbands regarded the practice as a suitable basis for conversation.

How refreshing therefore, and how altogether delightful it was that Ingram should be so natural, and how she loved to know that, though of course he was pretending about the little kisses in her eyes, he thought it worth while to pretend! With glee and pride and amusement she wondered what Redchester would say if it could hear the great man it too honoured being so simple and at the same time so very kind. For the first time she did not answer back; she was silent, thinking amused and pleasant thoughts. And Ingram walking beside her with his hands in his pockets and a gayness about his heels felt triumphant, for he had, he thought got through to her selfconsciousness, he had got her quiet at last.

Not that he did not enjoy the incense she burned before him, the unabashed expression of her admiration, but a man wants room for his lovemaking, and once he is embarked on that pleasant exercise he does not want the words taken out of his mouth. Ingeborg was always taking the words out of his mouth and then flinging them back at him again with, as it were, a flower

stuck behind their ear. He had known that if once he could pierce
through to her selfconsciousness she would leave off doing this,
she would become aware that he was a man and she was a
woman. She would become passive. She would let go of persisting
that he was a demi-god and she a sort of humble pew-opener or
its equivalent in his temple. Now apparently he had pierced
through, and her silence as she walked beside him with her eyes
on the ground was more sweet to him than anything she had ever
said.

Before, however, they had reached the gap in the lilac hedge
that formed the simple entrance on that side to the Dremmel
garden there she was beginning again.

'In Redchester—' she began.

'Oh,' he interrupted, 'are you going to give me a description of
the town and its environs so as to keep me from giving you a
description of yourself?'

'No,' she laughed. 'You know I could listen to you for ever.'

The same frankness; the same shining look. Ingram wanted to
kick.

'I was thinking,' she went on, 'how nobody in Redchester ever
talked about kisses. Even little ones.'

'So you are shocked?'

'No. What a word! I'm full of wonder at the miracle of you –
you – being so kind to me – *me*. Saying such beautiful things,
thinking such beautiful things.'

This trick of gratitude was really maddening.

'Tell me about Redchester,' he said shortly. 'Don't they kiss
each other there?'

'Oh yes. But they don't have them in their eyes.'

He shuddered.

'And people don't mention them, unless it's aunts. And then not
like that. No aunt could ever possibly be of the pregnant parts
needful for the invention of a phrase like that. And if she were I
don't suppose I'd want to listen.'

'You do at least then want to listen.'

'Want to? Aren't I listening always to every word you say with
both my ears? What a mercy,' she added with thankfulness, 'what
a real mercy, what an escape, that you're *not* an aunt!'

'You can't call it exactly a hairsbreadth escape,' he said moodily.
'I don't feel even the rough beginnings of an aunt anywhere about
me.'

He walked with her through the darkness of the lime-tree avenue, refusing to stay to supper. Why could he not then and there in that solitary dark place catch her in his arms and force her to wake up, to leave off being a choir-boy, a pew-opener? Or shake her. One or the other. At that moment he did not much care which. But he could not. He told himself that why he could not was because she would be so limitlessly surprised, and that for all her surprise he would be no nearer, not an inch nearer to whatever it was in her he was now so eager to reach. She might even – indeed he felt certain she would – thank him profusely for such a further mark of esteem, for being, as she would say, so very kind.

'Are you tired?' she asked, peering up at his face in the scented gloom, for it was the time of the flowering of the lime-trees, on his suddenly stopping and saying good night.

'No.'

'You're feeling quite well?'

'Perfectly.'

'Then,' she said, 'why go away?'

'I'm in slack water. I have no talk. I'd bore you. Good night.'

The next day, having found the morning quite intolerably long, he approached her directly they were alone on the difficult subject of husbands.

'It's no good, Ingeborg,' he said, ' – yes, I'm going to call you Ingeborg – we're fellow-pilgrims you and I along this rocky ridiculousness called life, and we'll soon be dead, and so, my dear, let us be friends for just this little while—'

'Oh but of course, of course—'

'It's no good, you know, barring certain very obvious subjects because of that idiotic prepossession one has for what is known as good taste. The only really living thing is bad taste. All the preliminaries to real union, union of any sort, mind or body, consist in the chucking away of reticences and cautions and proprieties, and each single preliminary is in bad taste. If we're going to be friends we'll have to go in for that. Bad taste. Execrable taste. Now—'

He stopped.

'Well?'

She was looking at him in a kind of alarm. This was the longest speech by far he had made, and she could not imagine what was coming at the end. He was busy as usual flinging her on to paper – the number of his studies of her was by this time something monstrous – and was glancing at her swiftly and professionally at every sentence.

'About husbands. Tell me what you think about husbands.'

'About husbands ? But *they're* not bad taste,' she said.

'Tell me what you think about them.'

'Well, they're people one is very fond of,' she said, with her hands clasped round her knees.

'Oh. You find that.'

'Yes. Don't you ?'

'I never had one.'

'The advantages of being a woman ! They're people one is fond of once and for all. They rescue one from Redchester. They're good and kind. They help one roll up great balls of common memories, and all the memories grow somehow into tender things at last. And they're patient. Even when they've found out how tiresome one is they still go on being patient. And – one loves them.'

'And – they love you.'

She flushed. 'Of course,' she said.

'You're amusing with your of courses and once for alls. Really you know there are no such things. Nothing necessarily follows. I mean, not when you get to human beings.'

Ingeborg fidgeted. Too well did she know the dishonesty of her Of course; too well did she remember the sudden switching off, after Zoppot, of Robert's love. But the rest was strictly true anyhow, she thought. She did love him, – dear Robert. The difference between him and an amazing friend like Ingram was, she explained to herself, that she was interested in Ingram, profoundly interested, and she was not interested in Robert. That, she supposed, was because she loved Robert. Perfect love, she said to herself, watching with careful attention the approach of a hairy and rather awful caterpillar across the path towards her shoes, perfect love cast out a lot of things besides fear. It cast out, for instance, conversation. And interest, which one couldn't very well have without conversation. Interest of course was an altogether second-rate feeling compared to love, and because it was second-rate it was noisier, expressing itself with a copiousness unnecessary when one got to the higher stages of feeling. One loved one's Robert, and one kept quiet. Far the highest thing was to love; but – she drew her feet up quickly under her – how very interesting and it was being interested !

'Well ?' he said, looking at her, 'go on.'

'Well, but I can't go on because I've finished. There isn't any more.'

'It's a soon exhausted subject.'

'That's because it's so simple and so – so dear. You know where you are with husbands.'

'You mean you're not anywhere.'

'Oh,' she said, throwing back her head and facing him courageously, 'how you don't *realise*. And anyhow,' she added, 'if that were true it would be a very placid and restful state to be in.'

'Negation. Death. Do you find it placid and restful with me ?'

'No,' she said quickly.

He put down his brushes and stared at her. 'What a mercy !' he said. 'What a mercy ! I was beginning to be afraid you did.'

By the end of the third week an odd thing had happened. He was no nearer piercing through her outer husk to any emotions she might possess than before, but she, astonishingly, had pierced through his.

The outer husk of Ingram at this time and for some years previously was a desire at all costs to dodge boredom, to get tight hold of anything that promised to excite him, squeeze it with diligence till the last drop of entertainment had been extracted, and then let it go again considerably crumpled. It was the kind of husk that causes divergences of opinion with one's wife. And behind it sat, wrapped in flame, the thing that was with him untouchably first, his work. He did not know how or why, but in that third week Ingeborg got through this husk and became mixed up in a curious inextricable way with the flaming holy thing inside.

High above, immeasurably above, any interest he had ever felt in women was his work. The divers lovemakings with which his past bristled as an ancient churchyard bristles with battered tombstones, had all been conducted as it were on his doorstep. He came out to the lady, the lady destined so soon to be a tombstone, often with passion, sometimes with illusions, and always with immense good-will to believe that here was the real thing at last, but she never came in. She might and did catch cold there for anything he cared, she should never cross the threshold and start interfering, delaying, coming between. In the end she got left out there alone, along with the scraper, feeling chilly.

And here was Ingeborg through the door, and not interfering, not delaying, but positively furthering.

The increasing beauty of his studies of her first made him suspect it. Their beauty began to surprise him, to take him unawares, as though it were a thing outside and apart from his own will. He had found so few things in humanity that seemed beautiful, and his pictures had been pictures of resentments, – impish and wonderful exposures by a master of the littleness at the back of brave shows. For a fortnight now he had sketched and sketched and splashed about with colour just as an excuse for staying on, in the desire to make love to Ingeborg, to refresh himself for a space at this unexpectedly limpid little spring. He had been attracted, irritated, increasingly attracted, greatly exasperated, greatly attracted. He had grown eager, determined, almost anxious at last. But these various emotions had been felt by him strictly on his doorstep. She was merely a substitute, and at that only a temporary substitute, for the Caucasus.

Then in the third week he perceived that she had left off being that. She was no longer just an odd little thing, an attractive, delicious little thing to him, of the colouring he best loved, the fairness, the whiteness, a thing that offered up incense before him with unflagging zeal, a thing full of contentments and generous ready friendship; she still was all that, but she was more. Like Adam when God breathed into his nostrils the breath of life, she had become a living soul, and that of which she was the living soul was his work. Not only her soul but his had begun to get into his studies of her. Each successive study unveiled more of an inner beauty. Each fixed into form and colour qualities in her and qualities in him who apprehended them that he had not known were there. It was as if he watched, while his hand was held and guided sure swift touch by sure swift touch by some one else, some one altogether greater, some splendid master from some splendid other world, who laid hold of him as one lays hold of a learner and showed him these things and said at each fresh stroke, 'Look – this is what she is like, the essence of her, the spirit . . . and see, it is what you are like too, for you recognise it.'

In that third week late one afternoon they went on the lake. Ingeborg paddled slowly along the middle of the quiet water towards the sunset, and Ingram sat at the other end with his back to it and watched her becoming more and more transfigured as the sun got lower.

Very early in their acquaintance he had conveyed to her that she ought always to wear white and that hats were foolish and unnecessary; therefore she did wear white, and sat hatless in the punt. The light blinded her. She could see nothing of him but a dark hunch against a blaze of sky. But when she wanted to turn the punt towards the relief of the shadows along the shore he instantly stopped her, and told her to keep on straight into the eye of the sun.

'But I can't see,' she said.

'But I can. It's for my picture. It's going to be a study of light.'

'Shall you be able to do it from the sketches?'

'No. From you.'

'Why, you said you couldn't anywhere here because there wasn't a proper place.'

'There isn't. I'm going to do it in Venice. In my studio there.'

'But can you from memory?'

'No. From you.'

She laughed. 'How I wish I could!' she said. 'I ache and ache to see things, to go to Italy—'

She sighed. The vision of it was unendurably beautiful.

'Well, you'll have to. Not only because it's monstrous you shouldn't, monstrous and shocking and unbelievable that you should be stuck in Kökensee for years on end and never see or hear or know any of the big things of life, but because you can't spoil my great picture – the greatest I shall ever have done.'

'Robert could never leave his work.'

'I don't want Robert to leave anything. It's you I'm going to paint. And I can't do without you.'

'How very awkward,' she smiled, 'because Robert can't do without me either.'

He plunged his arm into the water with sudden extreme violence, scooped a handful of it high into the air, and dashed it back again.

It had seemed to him obvious throughout his life that when it came to the supremest things not only did one give up everything oneself for them but other people were bound to give up everything too. The world and the centuries were to be enriched – he had a magnificent private faith in his position as a creator – and it was the duty of those persons who were needful to the process to deliver themselves, their souls and bodies, up to him in what he was convinced was an entirely reasonable sacrifice. If any one were necessary to his work, even only indirectly by keeping him content while he did it so that he could produce his best, it was that person's duty to come to his help. A paramount duty; passing the love of home or family. He would do as much, he was convinced, for some one else who should instead of him possess the gift. Here had he been in a state of dissatisfaction and restlessness for years, and his work, though his reputation leapt along, was he very well knew not what it could have been. Boredom had seized him; a great disgust of humanity. There had been harassing private complications; his wife had turned tiresome, refusing to understand. And now he had found this, – this thing, he thought, looking at her in the kind of fury that seized him at the merest approach to any thwarting that touched his work, of light and fire and cleanness, this little hidden precious stone, hidden for him, waiting for him to come and make of her a supreme work of art, and she was putting forward middle-class obstacles, Philistine difficulties, ludicrous trivialities – Robert, in short – to the achievement of it.

'Do you realise,' he said, leaning forward and staring at her with his strange pale eyes, 'what it means to be painted by me?'

'My utter glorification,' she answered, 'my utter pride.'

He waved his hand impatiently. 'It means,' he said, 'and in this case it would supremely mean, another one added to the great possessions of the world.'

'Oh,' said Ingeborg; and then, after a slight holding of her breath, again 'oh.'

She was awe-struck. His voice came out of the black shadow of him at her through clenched teeth, which gave it a strange awe-striking quality. She felt, with the sunset blinding her and that black figure in front of her and the intense clenchedness of the voice issuing from it, in the presence of immensities. She wondered whether it would have been any worse – instantly she corrected the word (it had been the merest slip of her brain) to more glorious – to be sitting in a punt with, simultaneously, Shakespeare, Sophocles, Homer, and the entire Renaissance. Weak a thing though her paddle was she pressed it tightly in her arms.

'It's – a great responsibility,' she said lamely.

'Of course it is,' he said, still in that clenched voice. 'And it has to be met greatly.'

'But what have *I*—'

'Here's this picture – I feel it in me, I tell you I feel it and know it – going to be the crowning work of my life, going to be a thing of living beauty throughout the generations, going to be the

Portrait of a Lady that draws the world to look at it during all the ages after we are dead—'

He broke off. He left off hurling the sentences at her. He began to beg.

'Ingeborg,' he said, 'you've cleaned me up and glorified me like the sunshine during this stay here, without meaning to clean or bothering to clean a bit. You've become the eyes of the universe to me, and if it weren't for you now the whole thing would be an eyeless monster and a mask and a horror. Without you – why, even during the mornings here when I mayn't come to you I'm like a ship laid up in an out-of-the-way port, an aeroplane without an engine, a book with the first and last pages lost. The mornings are like a realistic novel of Gissing's after a fairy tale. The afternoons are like a bright vision in a crystal, like a dream, like one of the drops into fairyland quite common people sometimes take. You're the littlest thing, and you leave the most enormous blank. It's extraordinary the *goneness* of things directly I'm away from you. I did poor work before I found you, poor I mean compared to what I know it might be, and I'll do none at all or mere ruins if I have to work without you now. Work is everything to me, and I'm not going to be able to do it if you're not there. Jeer at me if you like. Jeer at me for a parasite. I've been an empty thing without you all these years. You can't let me go again. You can't let me drop back into the old angers, into the old falling short of the highest. You're the spirit of my inmost. You're my response, my reality, my glorification, my transmuter into a god. And the picture I'm going to do of you will be the Portrait of a Lady who gave him back his Soul.'

CHAPTER 30

She stared at his black outline helplessly. She was overwhelmed. What could a respectable pastor's wife say to such a speech? It had the genuine ring. She did not believe it all, – not, that is, the portions of it which that back part of her mind, the part that leapt about with disconcerting agility of irrelevant questioning when it most oughtn't to, called the decorations, for how could any one like Ingram really think those wonderful things of any one like her? – but she no longer suspected him of making fun. He meant some of it. What was underneath it he meant, she felt. She was scared, and at the same time caught up into rapture. Was it possible that at last she was wanted, at last she could help some one? He wanted her, he, Ingram, of all people in the world; and only a few weeks ago she had been going about Kökensee so completely unwanted that if a dog wagged its tail at her she had been glad.

'It – it's a great responsibility,' she murmured a second time, while her face was transfigured with more than just the sunset.

It was. For there was Robert.

Robert, she felt even at this moment in the uplifted state when everything seems easy and possible, would not understand. Robert had no need of her himself, but he would not let her go for all that to Venice. Robert had altogether not grasped Ingram's importance in the world; he could not, perhaps, be expected to, for he did not like art. Robert, she was deadly certain, would not leave his work for an hour to take her anywhere for any purpose however high; and without him how could she go to Venice? People didn't go to Venice with somebody who wasn't their husband. They might go there with a whole trainful of indifferent persons if they were indifferent. Directly you liked somebody, directly it became wonderful to be taken there, to be shown the way, looked after, prevented from getting lost, you didn't go. It simply, as with kissing, was a matter of liking. Society seemed based on hate. You might kiss the people you didn't want to kiss; you might go to Venice with any amount of strangers because you didn't like strangers. And in a case like this – 'Oh, in a case like this,' she suddenly cried out aloud, flinging the paddle into the punt and twisting her hands together, overcome by the vision of the glories that were going to be missed, 'when it's so important, when it so tremendously matters – to be caught by convention!'

He had got her. The swift conviction flashed through him as he jerked his feet out of the way of the paddle. Got her differently from what he had first aimed at perhaps, still incredibly without sex-consciousness, but she would come to Venice, she would come and sit to him, he was going to do his masterpiece, and the rest was inevitable.

'How do you mean?' he said, his eyes on her.

'To think the great picture's never going to be painted!'

'And why?'

'Because of convention, because of all these mad rules—'

She was twisting her fingers about in the way she did when much stirred.

'It's doomed,' she said, 'doomed.' And she looked at him with eyes full of amazement, of aggrievedness, of, actually, tears.

'Ingeborg—' he began.

'Do you know how I've longed to go just to Italy?' she interrupted with just the same headlong impulsiveness that had swept her into Dent's Travel Bureau years before. 'How I've read about it and thought about it till I'm sick with longing? Why, I've looked out trains. And the things I've read! I know all about its treasures – oh, not only its treasures of art and old histories, but other treasures, light and colour and scent, the things I love now, the things I know now in pale mean little versions. I know all sorts of things. I know there's a great rush of wistaria along the wall as you go up to the Certosa, covering its whole length with bunch upon bunch of flowers—'

'Which Certosa?'

'Pavia, Pavia – and all the open space in front of it is drenched in April with that divinest smell. And I know about the little red monthly roses scrambling in and out of the Campo Santo above Genoa in January – in January! Red roses in January. While here.... And I know about the fireflies in the gardens round

Florence – that's May, early May, while here we still sit up against the stoves. And I know about the chestnut woods, real chestnuts that you eat afterwards, along the steep sides of the lakes, miles and miles of them, with deep green moss underneath, and I know about the queer black grapes that sting your tongue and fill the world with a smell of strawberries in September, and what the Appian way looks like in April when it is all waving flowery grass burning in an immensity of light, and I know the honey-colour of the houses in the old parts of Rome, and that the irises they sell there in the streets are like pale pink coral, – and all one needs to do to see these things for oneself is to catch a train at Meuk. *Any* day one could catch that train at Meuk. Every day it starts and one is never there. And Kökensee would roll back like a curtain, and the world be changed like a garment, like an old stiff clayey garment, like an old shroud, into all *that*. Think of it. What a background, what a background for the painting of the greatest picture in the world !'

She stopped and took up the paddle again. 'I wonder,' she said, with sudden listlessness, 'why I say all this to you ?'

'Because,' said Ingram, in a low voice, 'you're my sister and my mate.'

She dipped the paddle into the water and turned the punt towards home.

'Oh well,' she said, the enthusiasm gone out of her.

The water and the sky and the forests along the banks and the spire of the Kökensee church at the end of the lake looked dark and sad going this way. At first she could see nothing after the blinding light of the other direction, then everything cleared into dun colour and bleakness. 'How one talks,' she said. 'I say things – enthusiastic things, and you say things – beautiful kind things, and it's all no good.'

'Isn't it. Not only do we say them but we're going to do them. You're coming with me to Venice, my dear. Haven't you read in those travel books of yours what the lagoons look like at sunset ?'

She made an impatient movement.

'Ingeborg, let us reason together.'

'I can't reason.'

'Well, listen to me then doing it by myself.'

And he proceeded to do it. All the way down the lake he did it, and up along the path through the rye, and afterwards in the garden pacing up and down in the gathering twilight beneath the lime-trees he did it. 'Wonderful,' he thought in that submerged portion of the back of his mind where imps of criticism sat and scoffed, 'the trouble one takes at the beginning over a woman.'

She let him talk, listening quite in silence, her hands clasped behind her, her eyes observing every incident of the pale summer path, the broken twigs scattered on it, some withered sweet-peas she had worn that afternoon, a column of ants over which she stepped carefully each time. Till the stars came out and the owls appeared he eagerly reasoned. He talked of the folly of conventions, of the ridiculous way people deliberately chain themselves up, padlock themselves to some bogey of a theory of right and wrong, are so deeply in their souls improper that they dare not loose their chain one inch or unlock themselves an instant to go on the simplest of adventures. Such people, he explained, were in their essence profoundly and incurably immoral. They needed the straight waistcoat and padded room of principles. Their only hope lay in chains. 'With them,' he said, 'sane human beings such as you and I have nothing to do.' But what about the others, the free spirits increasing daily in number, the fundamentally fine and clean, who wanted no safeguards and were engaged in demonstrating continually to the world that two friends, man and woman, could very well, say, travel together, be away seeing beautiful things together, with the simplicity of children or of a brother and sister, and return safe after the longest absence with not a memory between them that they need regret?

Why, there were, – he instanced names, well-known ones, of people who, he said, had gone and come back openly, frankly, determined demonstrators for the public good of the natural. And then there were, – he instanced more names, names of people even Ingeborg had heard of; and finding this unexpectedly impressive he went on inventing with a growing recklessness, taking any people well-known enough to have been heard of by Ingeborg and sending them to Venice in twos, in haphazard juxtapositions that presently began to amuse him tremendously. No doubt they had gone, or would go sooner or later, he thought, greatly tickled by the vision of some of his couples. 'There was Lilienkopf – you know, the African millionaire. *He* went to Venice with Lady Missenden.' He flung back his head and laughed. The thought of Lilienkopf and Lady Missenden. . . . 'They too came back without a regret,' he said; and laughed and laughed.

She watched him gravely. She knew neither Lilienkopf nor Lady Missenden, and was not in the mood for laughter.

'Even bishops go,' said Ingram. 'They go for walking tours.'

'But not to Venice?'

'No. To shrines. Why, Cathedral cities are honeycombed with secret pilgrims.'

'But why secret? You said—'

'Well, careful pilgrims. Pilgrims who make careful departures. One has to depart carefully, you know. Not because of oneself but because of offending those who are not imbued with the pilgrim spirit. For instance Robert.'

'Oh – Robert. I *see* his face if I suggested he should let me be a pilgrim.'

'But of course you mustn't suggest.'

'What?' She stood still and looked up at him. 'Just go?'

'Of course. It was what you did when you ran away to Lucerne. If you'd suggested you'd never have got there. And you did that for merest fun. While this—'

He looked at her, and the impishness died out of his face.

'Why this,' he said, after a silence, 'this is the giving back to me of my soul. I need you, my dear. I need you as a dark room needs a lamp, as a cold room needs a fire. My work will be nothing without you – how can it be with no light to see by? It will be empty, dead. It will be like the sky without the star that makes it beautiful, the hay without the flower that scents it, the cloak one is given by God to keep out the cold and wickedness of life slipped off because there was no clasp to hold it tight over one's heart. . . .'

She began to warm again. She had been a little cooled while he laughed by himself over Lady Missenden's unregretted journeyings. To go to Italy; to go to Italy at all; but to go under such conditions, wanted, indispensable to the creation of a great work of art; it was the most amazing cluster of joys surely that had ever been offered to woman.

'How long would I have to be away?' she asked. 'How long is the shortest time one wants for a picture?'

He airily told her a month would be enough, and, on her exclaiming, immediately reduced it to a week.

'But getting there and coming back—'

'Well, say ten days,' he said. 'Surely you could get away for ten days? To do,' he added looking at her, 'some long-delayed shopping in Berlin.'

'But I don't want to shop.'

'Oh, Ingeborg, you're relapsing into your choir-boy condition again. Of course you don't want to shop. Of course you don't want to go to Berlin. But it's what you'll say to Robert.'

'Oh ?' she said. 'But isn't that – wouldn't that be rather—'

'Why can't you be as simple as when you went to Lucerne ? You wanted to go, so you went. And you were leaving your father who tremendously needed you. You were his right hand. Here you're nobody's right hand. I'm not asking you to do anything that would hurt Robert. All you've got to do is to arrange so that he knows nothing beyond Berlin. Surely after these years he can let you go away for ten days ?'

She walked with him in silence down the lilac path as far as the gate into the yard. She was exalted, but her exaltation was shot with doubt. What he said sounded so entirely right, so obviously right. She had no reasoning to put up against it. She longed intolerably to go. She was quite certain it was a high and beatiful thing to go. And yet—

Herr Dremmel's laboratory windows were open, for the evening was heavy and quiet, and they could see him in the lamplight, with disregarded moths fluttering round his head, bent over his work.

'Good night,' Ingram called in at the window with the peculiar cordial voice reserved for husbands ; but Herr Dremmel was too much engrossed to hear.

Towards two o'clock there was a thunderstorm and sheets of rain, and when Ingeborg got up next morning it was to find the summer gone. The house was cold and dark and mournful, and it was raining steadily. Looking out of the front door at the yard that had been so bright and dusty for five weeks she thought she had never seen such a sudden desolation. The rain rained on the ivy with a drawn-out dull dripping. The pig standing solitary in the mud was the wettest pig. The puddles were all over little buttons made of raindrops. Invariably after a thunderstorm the weather broke up for days, sometimes for weeks. What would she and Ingram do now ? She thought ; what in the world would they do now ? Shut up in the dark little parlour, he unable to work, and no walks, and no punting, – why, he'd go, of course, and the wonder-time was at an end.

'A week of this,' said Herr Dremmel, coming out of his

laboratory to stand on the doorstep and rub his hands in satisfaction, 'a week of this will save the situation.'

'Which situation, Robert?' she asked, her mind as confused and dull as the untidy grey sky.

He looked at her.

'Oh yes,' she said hastily, 'of course — the experiment fields. Yes, I suppose this is what they've been wanting all through that heavenly weather.'

'It was a weather,' said Herr Dremmel, 'that had nothing to do with heaven and everything to do with hell. Devils no doubt might grow in it, wax fat and big and heavy-eared, devils used to drought, but certainly not the kindly fruits of the earth.'

And for an instant he gave his mind to reflection on how great might be the barrier created between two people living together by a different taste in weather.

Ingram arrived at two o'clock in a state of extreme irritation. He splashed through the farmyard with the collar of his coat turned up and angrily holding an umbrella. In his wet-weather mood it seemed to him entirely absurd and unworthy to be wading through an East Prussian farmyard mess in pouring rain, beneath an umbrella, in order to sit with a woman. He wanted to be at work. He was obsessed by his picture. He was in the fever to begin that seizes the artist after idleness, the fever to get away, to be off back to the real concern of life, – the fierce fever of creation. He had not yet had to come into the house on his daily visits, and when he got into the passage he was immediately and deeply offended by the smell that met him of what an hour before had been a German dinner. The smell came out, as it were, weighty with welcome. It advanced *en bloc*. It was massive, deep, enveloping. The front door stood open, but nothing but great spaces of time could rid the house in the afternoons of that peculiar and all-pervading smell. He was shocked to think his white and golden one, his little image of living ivory and living gold, must needs on a day like this be swathed about in such fumes, must sit in them and breathe them, and that his communings with her were going to be conducted through a heavy curtain of what seemed to be different varieties of cabbage and all of them malignant.

The narrow gloom of the house, its unpiercedness on that north side by any but the coldest light, its abrupt ending almost at once in the kitchen and servant part, struck him as incredibly, preposterously sordid. What place to put a woman in! What a place,

having put her in it, to neglect her in! The thought of Herr
Dremmel's neglects, those neglects that had made his own stay
possible and pleasant, infuriated him. How dare he? thought
Ingram, angrily wiping his boots.

Herr Dremmel, Kökensee, everything connected with the place
except Ingeborg, seemed in his changed mood ignoble. He forgot
the weeks of sunshine there had been, the large afternoons in the
garden and forest and rye-fields, the floating on great stretches of
calm water, and just hated everything. Kökensee was Godfor-
saken, distant, alien, ugly, dirty, dripping, evil-smelling. Ingeborg
herself when she came running out of the parlour to him into the
concentrated cabbage of the corridor seemed less shining, drabber
than before. And so unfortunately active was his imagination, so
quick to riot, that almost he could fancy for one dreadful instant
as he looked at her that there was cabbage in her very hair.

'Ingeborg,' he said the moment he was in the parlour, 'I cannot
stand this. I can't endure *this* sort of thing, you know.'

He rubbed both his hands through his hair and gnawed at a
finger and fixed his eyes on hers in a kind of angry reproach.

'I was afraid you wouldn't like it,' she said apologetically,
feeling somehow as though the weather were her fault.

'Like it! And I can't idle here any more. You can't expect me to
hang on here any more—'

'Oh, but I never *expected*—' she interrupted hastily, surprised
and distressed that she should have produced any such impression.

'Well, it comes to the same thing, your making difficulties about
coming away, your wanting such a lot of persuading.'

He stopped in his quick pacing of the little room and stared at
her. 'Why, you're giving me *trouble*,' he said, in a voice of high
astonishment.

And as she stood looking at him with her lips fallen apart, her
eyes full of a new and anxious questioning, he began to pace
about again, across and round and up and down the unworthy
little room.

'God,' he said, swiftly pacing, 'how I do hate miss-ishness!'

And indeed it seemed to him wholly, amazingly monstrous that
his great new work should be being held up a day by any scruples
of any sort whatever.

'This grey headache of a sky,' he said, jerking himself for a
moment to the window, 'this mud, this muggy chilliness—'

'But—' she began.

'The days here are lines – just length without breadth or thickness or any substance—'

'But surely – till to-day—'

'I feel in a sort of well in this place, out of sight of faith and kindliness – you shutting them out,' he turned on her, 'you deliberately shutting them out, putting the lid on the glory of light and life, being an extinguisher for the sake of nothing and nobody at all, just for the sake of a phantom of an idea about Robert—'

'But surely—' she said.

'I'm bored and bored here. This morning was a frightful thing. I daren't in this state even make a sketch of you. I'd spoil it. It'll rain for ever. I can't stay in this room. I'd begin to rave—'

'But of course you can't stay in it. Of course you must go.'

'Go! When I can't work without you? When you're so everything to me that during the hours I'm away from you little things you've said and done float in my mind like little shining phosphorescent things in a dark cold sea, and I creep into warm little thoughts of you like some creature that shivers and gets back into its nest? I told you I was a parasite. I told you I depend on you. I told you you make me exist for myself. How can you let me beg? How can you let *me* beg?'

They stood facing each other in the middle of the room, his light eyes blazing down into hers.

'You – you're sure I'd be back in ten days?' she said.

And he had the presence of mind not to catch her to his heart.

CHAPTER 31

From the moment she said she would go Ingram was a changed creature. He became brisk, business-like, cheerful. Not a trace was left of the exasperated wet man who had come round through the rain, and there were no more poetic images. He was reassuringly like a pleased elder brother, a brother all alert contentment. The table was cleared by his swift hands of the litter of her English studies, and the map out of the *Reichskursbuch* spread on it; and with the help of an old Baedeker his sharp eyes had noticed lurking in a corner he expounded to her what she was to do. He wrote down her train from Meuk to Allenstein and her train from Allenstein to Berlin; he told her where she was to stay the night in Berlin, a city he appeared to know intimately; and he made a drawing in pencil of the streets that led to it from the station.

'The dotted line,' he said, explaining his drawing, 'is Ingeborg's little footsteps.'

She was to stay at one of those refuges for timid ladies with connections in the Church which are scattered about Berlin and called *Christliche Hospize*, places where, besides coffee and rolls, there are prayers and a harmonium for breakfast. She was to meet him next day at the Anhalter station, that happy jump-off for the south, and he would leave Kökensee at once, perhaps that evening, and wait for her in Berlin. They would proceed to Venice intermittently, getting out of the train at various points in order to see certain things – there was a walk he wanted to take her across the hills of Lake Maggiore, for instance—

'But I've only got ten days,' she reminded him.

'Oh, you'll see. One can do a lot—' and there was Bergamo he wanted to show her; she would, he assured her, greatly love Bergamo; and certainly they would go to Pavia if only to see if the wistaria were still in flower.

Her eyes danced. The sight of the map and the time-table was enough. She hung over him eagerly, following his pointing finger as it moved over mountains and lakes. She was like a schoolboy watching the planning out of his first trip abroad. There was no room in her for any thoughts but thoughts of glee. The names were music to her – Locarno, Cannobio, Luino, Varese, Bergamo, Brescia, Venice. She lost sight of the higher aspect of the adventure, the picture, her position as indispensable assistant in the production of a great work; her brain was buzzing with just the idea of trains and places and new countries and utter fun. After the years of inaction in Kökensee, just to go in a train to Berlin would have been tremendous enough to set her blood pulsing; and here she was going on and on, further and further, into more and more light, more and more colour and heat and splendour and all new things, till actually at last she would reach it, the heart of the world, and be in Italy.

'Oh,' she murmured, 'but it's too *good* to be true—'

And the Rigi, which up to then had been the high-water mark of her experience, collapsed into a little lump of pale indifferent mould.

When the tea began to bump against the door and she went out to help the servant, Ingram put every sign of intending travel neatly away, and by the time Herr Dremmel joined them there was no hint of anything anywhere in the room but sobriety except in Ingeborg's eyes. They danced and danced. She longed to jump up and fling her arms round Robert's neck and tell him she was off to Italy. She wanted him to share her joy, to know how happy she was. She felt all lit up and bright inside, while Ingram, on the contrary, looked forbiddingly solemn. He presently began to make solemn comments on the change in the weather, and after hearing Herr Dremmel's view and sympathising with his gratification, said that as regarded himself it put an end to his work of preparation for the painting of Frau Dremmel's portrait, and therefore he was leaving the next morning and would take the opportunity, when Herr Dremmel presently retired to his laboratory, of making his farewells.

Herr Dremmel expressed polite regrets. Ingram politely thanked him. Ingeborg felt suddenly less lit up, and her eyes left off dancing. She wanted, for some odd reason, to slip her hand into Robert's. It grew and grew on her, the desire to go and sit very close to Robert. If only he would come too, if only he would for once take a holiday and come and see these beautiful things with her, how happy they would all be! It seemed a forlorn thing to leave him there alone in the rain while she went jaunting off to Italy. Well, but he wouldn't come; he liked rain; and he wouldn't let her go either if she were frankly to ask him to. The example of Lady Missenden or of any of those well-known persons would not, she knew, move him. Nor would anything she could say on the shameful absurdity of supposing evil. Liberal though he was and large as were his scoffings at convention, he was not as liberal and large, she felt sure, as Ingram, and she suspected that the conventions he scoffed at were those which did not touch himself. She could not risk asking. She must go. She must, must go. Yet—

She got up impulsively, and on the pretext of taking his cup from him went to him and put her hand with a little stroking movement on his hair. Herr Dremmel did not observe it, but Ingram did; and after tea and until he left that evening not to see her again till they met at the Anhalter station in Berlin, he was amazingly natural and ordinary and cheery, more exactly like a brother than any brother that had ever been seen or imagined.

'Of course,' he said quite at the last, turning back from the doorstep before finally committing himself to the liquid masses of the dissolved farmyard – 'of course I can *depend* on you?'

She laughed. She stood on the top step with the light of the lamp in the passage behind her, a little torch of resolution and adventure and imagination well let loose.

'I'm going to Italy,' she said, flinging out both her arms as though she would put them round that land of dreams; and so complex is man and so simple in his complexity that Ingram went away in the wet twilight quite sincerely offering thanks to God.

But when it came to the moment of telling Robert about Berlin and shopping, her heart beat very uncomfortably. It was at tea-time the next afternoon. All day she had been trying to do it, but her tongue refused. At breakfast she tried, and at dinner she tried, and in between she went twice to the laboratory door and stood on the mat, and instead of going in went away again on the carefullest toe-tips. And there was Ingram getting to Berlin, got to Berlin, kicking his heels there waiting . . .

At tea-time, after a tempestuous walk in the wet during which, as she splashed through sodden miles of sad-coloured wilderness, she took her gods to witness that the thing should be done that afternoon, she did finally bring it out. She had meant to say with an immense naturalness that she wished to go to Berlin in order to buy boots. She had thought of boots as simple objects, quickly bought and resembling each other; not like hats or dresses which might lead later on to explanations. And she needed boots. She really would buy them. It would, she felt, help her to be natural if what she said so far as it went were true.

But so greatly was she chagrined in her soul that she should have to talk of boots at all instead of telling him, her Robert, her after all *kind* Robert, with delight of Italy and of her discoveries in beautiful new feelings, that when she had gulped and cleared her throat and gulped again and opened her mouth she found herself not talking of boots nor yet of Berlin, but addressing him with something of the indignant irrelevance of a suffragette who because she has been forcibly fed demands the vote.

He had, as his custom was, brought literature with him, and was sitting bent over his cup with the book propped against the hot-water jug. It was called *Eliminierung der Minusvarianten*, and was apparently, as all the books he brought to meals also were apparently, absorbing. The sound of the dripping of the rain on the ivy was unbroken at first except by the sound of Herr Dremmel drinking his tea, and the room was so gloomy under the pall of heavy sky that almost one needed a lamp.

'You see,' said Ingeborg, most of the blood in her body surging up into her face as she suddenly, after ten minutes' silent struggle, leaned across the table and plunged into the inevitable, 'my feeling so uncomfortable about a simple thing like this is really the measure of the subjection of women.'

Herr Dremmel raised his head but not his eyes from his book, expressing thereby both a civilised attentiveness to anything she might wish to say and a continued interest in the sentence he was at. When he had finished it he looked at her over his spectacles, and inquired if she had spoken.

'Why should I not go and come unquestioned?' she asked, flushed with indignation that his prejudices should be forcing her to the low cunning that substituted boots for Italy. '*You* do.'

He examined her impartially. 'What do I do, Ingeborg?' he asked with patience.

'Go away when you want to and come back when you choose. You've been quite far. You went once to a place the other side of Berlin. Oh, I know it's business you go on, but I don't think that makes it any better – on the contrary, it isn't half as good a reason as going because it's beautiful to go, and fine and splendid. And it isn't as though I even had to ask you to give me money for it. I simply roll in that hundred a year you allow me. I haven't spent a quarter on it for years. My cupboard upstairs is stuffed with notes.'

He looked at her, but finding it impossible to discover any meaning in her remarks began to read again.

'Robert—'

With patience he again removed his eyes from his book and looked at her. Beneath the table she was pressing her hands together, twisting them about in her lap.

'Well, Ingeborg?' he said.

'Don't you think it's unworthy, the way women have to ask permission to do things?'

'No,' said Herr Dremmel; but he was thinking of the *Minusvarianten*, and it was mere chance that he did not say Yes.

'When husbands go away they don't ask their wives' permission, and it never would occur to the wives that they ought to. So why should the wives have to ask the husbands'?'

Herr Dremmel gazed at her a moment, and then made a stately, excluding, but entirely kindly movement with his right hand. 'Ingeborg,' he said, 'I am not interested.' And he began to read again.

She poured herself out some more tea, drank it hastily and hot, and said with a great effort, 'It's nonsense about permissions. I – I'm going to Berlin.'

Then she waited with her heart in her mouth and both hands clutching the edge of the table.

But nothing happened. He read on.

'Robert—' she said.

Once more he endeavoured to place his attention at her disposal, dragging it away reluctantly from his book. 'Yes, Ingeborg?' he said.

'Robert – I'm going to Berlin.'

'Are you, Ingeborg?' he inquired with perfect mildness. 'Why?'

'I've got to get things. Shop.'

'And why Berlin, Ingeborg? Is not Meuk nearer?'

'Boots,' she said. 'There aren't any in Meuk. I never *saw* any in Meuk.'

'And in Königsberg? That also is nearer than Berlin.'

'You must have heard,' she said, laying hold, because she was afraid, of the first words that came into her head, 'of Berlin wool. Well, the same thing exactly applies to boots.'

He stared at her as one who feels about for some point of contact with an alien intelligence.

'Naturally if you have to go you must,' he said.

'Yes. For ten days.'

'Ten, Ingeborg? On account of boots?'

She nodded defiantly, her hands beneath the table twisted into knots.

He adjusted his mind to the conception.

'Ten days for boots?'

'Ten, ten,' she said recklessly, prepared to brave any amount of opposition. 'I want to see a few things while I'm about it, – the galleries, for instance. It isn't going to be *all* boots. I haven't stirred from here since our marriage, except to go to Zoppot – it's time I went – it's really *ridiculously* time I went—'

'But,' said Herr Dremmel, with the complete reasonableness of one who is indifferent and has no desire whatever to argue, 'but naturally. Of course, Ingeborg.'

'Then – you don't mind?'

'But why should I mind?'

'You – you're not even surprised?'

'But why should I be surprised?' And once again he reflected on her apparently permanent obtuseness to values.

She gazed at him with the astonishment of a child who has screwed itself up for a beating and finds itself instead being blessed. She felt relief, but a pained relief; an aggrieved, almost angry relief; such as he feels who putting his entire strength into the effort to lift a vessel he fears is too heavy for him finds it light and empty. Her soul, as it were, tumbled over backwards and sprawled.

'How funny!' she murmured. 'How very funny! and here I've been afraid to tell you.'

But once more he had ceased to listen. His eye had been caught by a statement on the page in front of him that interested him acutely, and he read with avidity to the end of the chapter. Then he got up with the book in his hand and went to the door, thinking over what he had read.

She sat looking after him.

'I expect – I think – I suppose I shall start tomorrow,' she said as he opened the door.

'Start?' he repeated absently. 'Why should you start?'

'Oh, Robert – I can't get there if I don't start.'

'Get where, Ingeborg?' he asked, his eyes on hers but his thoughts in unimaginable distances.

'Oh, Robert – but to Berlin, of course.'

'Berlin. Yes. Very well. Berlin.'

And, deeply turning over the new and pregnant possibilities suggested to him by what he had just been reading, he went out.

CHAPTER 32

As though to assure her of what she already knew, that she was on the threshold of the most glorious ten days of her life, the world when she looked out of the window next morning was radiant with sunshine and sparkling with freshness. Far away on the edge of Russia the great rain clouds that had come up to Kökensee from the west and folded it for two days in a stupor of mist were disappearing in one long purple line. The garden glistened and laughed. Sweet fragrances from the responsive earth hurried to meet the sun like eager kisses. If she had needed reassuring, this happy morning warm and scented would have done it; but now that the night was over, a time when those who are going to have doubts do have them, and the dark sodden days when if facts are gong to be blurred they are blurred, she felt no scruples nor any misgivings, – she had simply got to the beginning of the most wonderful holiday of her life.

Everything was easy. Robert went away after an early breakfast to his fields to see the improvement forty-eight hours' soaking must have made, and obviously did not mind her impending departure in the least; one of the horses, till lately lame, was recovered, Karl told her, and able to take her in to Meuk; the servant Klara seemed proud to be left in sole charge; the train left Meuk so conveniently that she would have time to visit Robertlet and Ditti on the way. Singing she packed her smallest trunk; singing she thrust money from the cupboard where it had so long lain useless into her blouse, – one, two, three, ten blue German notes of a hundred marks each – while she wondered, but not much, if it would be enough, and wondered, but equally not much, if it would be too little; singing she pinned on unfamiliar objects such as a hat and veil, and sought out gloves; singing she handed over the keys to Klara; singing she stood on the steps watching Karl harness the horses. All the birds of Kökensee were singing too, and the pig sunning itself in a thick ecstasy of appreciation also sang according to its lights, and it was not its fault, she thought excusingly, if what happened when it sang was that it grunted.

'Life is really the heavenliest thing,' she said to herself, buttoning her gloves, her face sober with excess of joy. 'The *things* it has round its corners! the dear surprises of happiness.' And when the buttons came off she didn't mind, but excused them too on the ground that they were not used to being buttoned and let her gloves happily dangle. She would have excused everything that day. She would have forgiven everybody every sin.

Klara brought her out a packet of sandwiches with her luggage, and a little bunch of rain-washed flowers.

'How kind every one is!' she thought, smiling at Klara, wondering if she would mind very much if she kissed her, her heart one single all-embracing Thank you that reached right round the world. And then suddenly, just as Karl was ready and the carriage was actually at the door and the little trunk being put into it, and her umbrella and sandwiches and flowers, she ran back into the house and scribbled a note to Robert and put it on the table in his laboratory where he would not be able to avoid seeing it when he came in that afternoon.

'I *can't* not tell him,' was the thought that had winged her impulse, 'I *can't* not tell the truth this heavenly, God-given day of joy.'

'*It wasn't true about the boots,*' she wrote, inking her gloves, too frantically hurried to take them off. '*I'm going to Italy with Mr Ingram – to Venice – it's his picture – and of course other things too on the way – if you think it over you won't really mind – I must run or I'll miss the train—*

'*Ingeborg.*'

And she climbed up into the carriage and drove off greatly relieved and strong in her faith, if you gave him time and quiet, in Robert's understanding of a thing so transparently reasonable. She would write again, she said to herself, a real letter from Berlin and put her points of view and Ingram's before her. Of course that was the right thing to do. Of course a highly intelligent man like Robert was bound ultimately to understand.

But her train did not get to Berlin till eleven o'clock that night, and when she reached the *Christliche Hospiz* she found a letter from Ingram telling her she must be at the Anhalter station next morning at nine, and though she meant to get up early and write she spent the time, being very tired, asleep instead, and it was only when the strains of a harmonium penetrated into her room and wandered round her head making slow Lutheran noises that she woke up and realised how nearly she was on the verge of missing the train to Italy.

Breakfastless and prayerless and almost without paying her bill she hurried forth from the *Christliche Hospiz*, her clothes full of an odd smell of napthalin and the meals that had been eaten there before she arrived, the ancient meals of all the yesterdays. From the smell she concluded, cautiously and reluctantly sniffing while she put down both windows of her cab, that what they had to eat in the *Christliche Hospiz* was the chorales of the harmonium expressed in cabbage; and whether it was the cab or whether it was her clothes she did not know, but there inside it with her still was cabbage.

'It's the odour of piety,' she explained hastily to Ingram when he on meeting her at the station looked at her with what she thought a severe inquiry.

'It's that you're within an ace of missing the train,' he said, catching hold of her elbow and hurrying her down the platform to a door that still stood open, with an angry official, glaring dreadfully in spite of his tip, waiting beside it to shut it.

'I'm so very sorry,' she said, panting a little as she dropped into a corner of the carriage opposite him and the train slipped away from the station, 'but I couldn't get here any sooner.'

'Why couldn't you?' he asked, still severely, for he had spent a distressing and turbulent half-hour. 'You only had to get up in time.'

'But I couldn't get up because I was asleep.'

'Nonsense, Ingeborg. You could tell them to call you.'

'Well, but I didn't tell them.'

'And why don't you button your gloves? Here – I'll button them.'

'You can't. There aren't any buttons.'

'What? No buttons.'

'They came off.'

'But why in heaven's name didn't you sew them on again?'

'Do buttons matter? I was in such a tremendous hurry to start.' And she smiled at him a smile of perfect happiness.

'To come to me. To come to me,' he said, his eyes on hers.

'Yes. And Italy.'

'Italy! Well, you very nearly missed me. What would you have done then?'

'Oh, gone to Italy.'

'What, just the same?'

'Well, Italy *is* Italy, isn't it? Look at this sky. Isn't it wonderful to-day, isn't it perfectly glorious? Can the sky in Italy possibly be bluer than this?'

He made an impatient movement. 'Choir-boy,' he said; and added, catching sight of her finger-tips, 'Why is your glove all over ink?'

'Because I wrote to Robert in it.'

'What? You came away without saying anything at all?'

'Oh no. I said all the things about Berlin and shopping, and he didn't mind a bit.'

'There now – didn't I tell you? But what did you write?'

'Oh, just the truth. That I'm going with you to Italy.'

'What? You did?'

'I couldn't bear after all to start like that, in that – that lying sort of way.'

'And you wrote that you were going with me?'

'Yes. And I said—'

'And he'll find the letter when he comes in?'

'Yes. He can't help seeing it. I put it on his laboratory table, right in the middle.'

Ingram leaned forward, his face flushed, laughter and triumph in his eyes, and caught hold of her right hand in its inky glove.

'Adorable inkstains,' he said, looking at them and then looking up at her. 'You little burner of ships.'

And as she opened her mouth in what was evidently going to be a question he hurried her away from it with a string of his phrases.

'You are all the happiness,' he said, with an energy of conviction astonishing at half-past nine in the morning, 'and all the music, and all the colour, and all the fragrance there is in the world.'

'Then you haven't noticed the cabbage?' she said, immensely relieved.

He let go her hand. 'What cabbage?' he asked shortly, for it nettled him to be interrupted when he was spinning images, and it more than nettled him to be interrupted in the middle of an emotion.

But when she began – vividly – to describe the inner condition of the *Christliche Hospiz* he stopped her.

'I don't want to talk of anything ugly to-day,' he said. 'Not to-day of all days in my life.' And he added, leaning forward again and looking into her eyes, 'Ingeborg, do you know what to-day is?'

'Thursday,' said Ingeborg.

The conductor – it was a corridor train, and though they had the compartment to themselves the passage outside was busy with people squeezing past each other and begging each other's pardons – came in to look at their tickets.

'There is a restaurant car on the train,' he said in German, giving information with Prussian care, a disciplinary care for the comfort of his passengers, who were to be made comfortable, to be forced to use the means of grace provided, or the authorities would know the reason why.

'Yes,' said Ingram.

'You do not change,' said the conductor, with Prussian determination that his passengers should not, even if they wanted to and liked it, go astray.

'No,' said Ingram.

'Not until Basel,' said the conductor menacingly, almost as if he wanted to pick a quarrel.

'No,' said Ingram.

'At Basel you change,' said the conductor eyeing him, ready to leap on opposition.

'Yes,' said Ingram.

'You will arrive at Basel at 11.40 to-night,' said the conductor, in tones behind which hung 'Do you hear? You've just go to.'

'Yes,' said Ingram.

'At Basel—'

'Oh, go to *hell*,' said Ingram, suddenly, violently, and in his own tongue.

The conductor immediately put his heels together and saluted. From the extreme want of control of the gentleman's manner he knew him at once for an officer of high rank disguised for travelling purposes in civilian garments, and silently and deferentially withdrew.

'If there's a restaurant car can I have some breakfast?' asked Ingeborg.

'Haven't you had any? You poor little thing. Come along.'

She followed him out into the corridor, he going first to clear people out of the way and turning to give her his hand at the crossings from one coach to the next. The restaurant was in front of the train, and it required perseverance and the opening of many difficult doors to get to it. Each time he turned to help her and gripped hold of her hand as they swayed against the sides and were bumped they looked at each other and laughed. What fun it all was, she thought, and how entirely new and delicious being taken care of as though she were a thing that mattered, a precious thing!

He had had breakfast in Berlin, but he sat watching her with an alert interest that missed not the smallest of her movements, very reminiscent in his attitude and pleasure of a cat watching its own dear mouse, observing it with a whiskered relish, its own dear particular mouse that it has ached for for years before it ever met it, filling itself dismally meanwhile with the wrong mice who disagreed with it, – its mouse that, annexed and safely incorporated, was going to do it so much good and make it twice the cat it was before; and he buttered her roll for her, and poured out her tea, and did all the things a cat would do in such a situation if it were a man, pleased that its mouse should fatten, aware that anything it ate and drank would ultimately, so to speak, remain in the family.

The splendid June morning, the last morning of June, shone golden through the long, continuous windows of the car. The fields of the Mark lay bathed in light. It was early still, but it had already begun to be hot, and haymakers straightening themselves to watch the train go by wiped their faces, and the prudent cows were gathered in the shade of trees, and in the car the ventilator twirled and hummed, and the waiter in his white linen jacket who brought her strawberries, each one of which had been examined and passed as fit and sound by the proper authorities suitably housed in Berlin in buildings erected for the purpose, was a credit to the Prussian State Railway byelaw which decrees, briefly and implacably, that waiters shall be cool.

She pulled out one of the blue German hundred mark notes from her blouse when he brought the bill, and more of them came out with it.

'What on earth is all that for?' Ingram asked.

'To pay with. And you must tell me how much my ticket was to – wasn't it Locarno you said we got out at?'

'You can't go about with money loose like that. Give it to me. I'll take care of it for you.'

She gave it to him, nine blue notes out of her blouse and the change of the tenth out of a little bag she had brought and was finding great difficulty, so much unused was she to little bags, in remembering.

'I hope it's enough,' she said. 'Don't forget I've got to get back again.'

He laughed, tucking the notes away into his pocket-book. 'Enough? It's a fortune. You can go to the end of the world with this,' he said.

'Isn't it all glorious, isn't it all too wonderful to be true?' she said, her face radiant.

'Yes. And the most glorious part of it is that you can't go anywhere now,' he said, putting the pocket-book in his breast pocket and patting it and looking at her and laughing, 'without me.'

'But I don't want to. I'd much *rather* go with you. It's so extraordinarily sweet that you want me to. You know, I never can quite believe it.'

He bent across the table. 'Little glory of my heart,' he murmured.

The waiter came back with the change.

'I wish Robert were here,' said Ingeborg gazing round her out of the windows with immense contentment. 'If only he could have got away I believe he'd have loved it.'

Ingram pushed back his chair with a jerk. 'I don't think he'd have loved it at all,' he said; and going back through the length of the train to their compartment though he helped her at the difficult places it was by putting out his hand behind him for her to clutch; he did not this time turn round and look into her eyes and laugh.

It grew very hot as the day wore on, and extremely dusty. The thunderstorm that had deluged East Prussia had not come that way, and there had been no rain from the look of things for a long while. The dust came in in clouds, and they were obliged to shut the windows, but it still came in through chinks and settled all over them and choked them, and even lay in the delicate details of Ingeborg's nose. He had made her take off her hat and veil, so she had nothing to protect her, and he watched her with a singular annoyance turning gradually drab-coloured. He wanted to lean forward and dust her, he hated to see her whiteness being soiled, it fidgeted him intolerably. He himself stood long train journeys badly; but though it was so hot, so insufferably hot, she was as active and restless as a child, continually jumping up and running out into the dreadful blazing corridor to see what there was to see that side.

They passed Weimar; and she was of an intemperate zeal on the subject of Goethe, putting down the window and craning out to look and quoting *Kennst Du das Land wo die Citrone blüht*, – quoting to him, who loathed quotations even in cool weather. They passed Eisenach; and again she displayed zeal, talking eagerly of Luther and the Wartburg and the inkpot and the devil, – and of St Elizabeth of course: he knew she would get to St Elizabeth. She told him the legends, – told him who knew all legends, told him who had a headache and could only keep alive by going into the lavatory and plunging his head every few minutes into cold water, and she did not in the least mind when she craned out of the window to look at things that she should come back into the carriage again with her hair in every sort of direction and her face not only dusty but with smuts.

At the hottest moment of the day he felt for a lurid instant as if it were not one choir-boy he was with but with the entire choir having its summer treat and being taken by him single-handed for a long dog-day to the Crystal Palace; but that was after luncheon in the restaurant car, a luncheon that seemed to his fevered imagination to consist of bits of live cinder served in sulphur and eaten in a heaving, swaying lake of brimstone. Even the waiter who attended to their table was, in the teeth of regulations, a melted man; and when the inspector passed through, looking about him with the eye of a Prussian eagle to see that all was in order and the standard set by law was being reached of cool waiters and hot food and tepid passengers, he instantly pounced on the manifestly melted waiter who, unable to deny the obvious fact that he was beaded, put his heels together and endeavoured to escape a fine by anxious explanation that he knew he was in a perspiration but that it was a cold one.

They were having tea when they passed Frankfurt, and dinner when they passed Heidelberg. A great full moon was rising behind the castle at Heidelberg, and the Neckar was a streak of light. The

summer day was coming to an end in perfect calm. The quiet
roads leading away into woods and through orchards were starred
on either side with white flowers. In the dusk it was only the white
flowers that still shone, the stitchworts, the clusters of Star of
Bethlehem, the spikes of white helleborine; and all the colours of
the day, the blue of the chickory and delicate lilac of dwarf
mallows, the bright yellow of wood loosestrife and rose-colour of
campions, were already put out for the night.

Ingeborg gazed through the window with the face of a happy
goblin. Her eyes looked brighter than ever out of their surrounding
smuts, and her hair was all ends, little upright ends that stirred in
the draught. The dreadful day, the hours and hours of heat and
choking airlessness, had made no impression on her apparently,
except to turn her from clean to dirty, while Ingram lay back in
his corner a thing hardly human, wanting nothing now in the
world but cold water poured over him and he to lie while it was
poured on a slab of iced marble. But the sun was down at last,
dew was falling and quieting the dust, and the final journey to the
restaurant car had been made, a journey on which it was Ingeborg
who opened the doors and nobody helped anybody at the crossings. He had walked behind her, and had fretfully observed her
dress and how odd it was, like old back numbers of illustrated
papers, the sleeves wrong, the skirt wrong, too much of it in
places, too little in others, but mostly there was too much, for it
was the year when women were skimpy.

'You'll have to get some clothes in Italy,' he said to her at
dinner.

'What for?' she asked, surprised.

'What for? To put on,' he said with a limp acerbity.

But now at last between Strassburg and Bâle, when all glare had
finally departed and the lamp in their compartment was muffled
into grateful gloom by the shade he drew across it, and the
windows were wide open to the great dusky starry night, and a
thousand dewy scents were stirred in the fields as the train passed
through them, he began to feel better.

At his suggestion she had gone out and washed her face, so that
he could look at it again, delicately fair in the dusk, with
satisfaction. And presently because of some curves the rails took
the moon shone in on her while he still sat in shadow, and her
face, turned upwards to the stars with the wonder on it of her
happiness, once more seemed to him the most spiritual thing he

had yet found in a woman, — unconscious spirit, exquisitely independent and aloof. He watched her out of the shadow of his corner for a long time, taking in every curve and line, trying to fix her look of serenity and clear content on his memory, the expression of an inner tranquillity, of happy giving oneself up to the moment that he had not seen before except in children. To watch her like that soothed him gradually quite out of the fever and fret of the day. As his habit was, he forgot his other mood as if he had never had it. Growing cool and comfortable with the growing coolness of the night, his irritations, and impatiences, and desire — it had for several hours in the afternoon been paramount with him — for personal absence from her, were things wiped out of recollection. He forgot, in the quiet of her attitude, that she had ever been restless, and in her expressive and beautiful silence that she had ever quoted, and, watching her whiteness, that she had ever been drab. She was, he thought considering her, his head very comfortable now on the cushions and a most blessed draught deliciously lifting his hair, like the soft breast of a white bird. She was like diamonds, only that she was kind and gentle. She was like spring water on a thirsty day. She was like a very clear, delicate white wine. Yes; but what was it she was most like?

He searched about for it in his mind, his eyes on her face; and presently he found it, and leaned forward out of the shadow to tell her.

'Ingeborg,' he said, and at the moment he entirely meant it, 'you are like the peace of God.'

CHAPTER 33

At Bâle there was hurry and bustle, the half-hour they ought to have had there wasted away by some unaccountable loosening of the bandages of discipline on the German side to four minutes – the conductor when questioned said the engine had gone wrong, and explained, with a shrug that was to help hide his shame in this failure of the infallible, that engines were but human – and again there was an undignified scamper down steps and up steps and along platforms, and they arrived panting, pushed in by porters, only just in time into a compartment studded round with sleeping Swiss.

Ingram left Ingeborg sitting temporarily on the edge of the seat clasping her umbrella and coat and little bag, while he walked through the train in search of more space, refusing to believe such a repulsive thing could happen to him as that he should be obliged to travel to Bellinzona with four sleeping Swiss; but the train seemed to be a popular one, or else a national festival was preparing for some other upheaval that caused people to move about that night in numbers, and all the compartments were full.

He went back to Ingeborg in a condition of resentful gloom. The four Swiss were sleeping in the four corners, and the carriage smelt of crumbs. He opened the window, and there was an immediate simultaneous resurrection of the four Swiss into angry life. Ingram, fluent in French, met them with an equal volubility, standing with his back to the open window protecting it from their assaults, while Ingeborg looked on in alarm; but the conductor when he came pronounced in favour of the four Swiss. Pacified, they instantly fell asleep again; and Ingram, at least not taking care of their legs, strode out into the corridor, where he stood staring through the open window at midnight nature and cursing himself for not having broken the journey at Bâle, while Ingeborg peeped anxiously at his back round her coat and her umbrella.

From Bâle to Lucerne he was as unaware of her as if he had never met her, so very angry was he and so very tired. Then at Lucerne two of the Swiss got out, and turning round he saw her asleep in the compartment, tumbled over a little to one side, still holding her things, and once again she filled his heart. She was utterly asleep, in the most uncomfortable position, dropped away in the middle of how she happened to be sitting like a child does or a puppy ; and he went in and sat down beside her and lifted her head very cautiously and gently on to his arm.

She opened her eyes and looked up at him along his sleeve without moving, in a sort of surprise.

'This is Lucerne,' he whispered, bending down; how soft she was, and how little !

'Is it ? Why, that's where Robert and I—'

But she was asleep again.

She slept till he woke her up before Bellinzona, and so she never knew the moment she had thrilled to think of when they would in the dawn of the summer morning come out on the other side of the St Gothard into what in spite of anything the Swiss might say was Italy ; and still half asleep, mechanically putting on her hat and pausing to rub her eyes while he urged her to be quick, she did not realise where she was. When she did, and looked eagerly at the window, it was to turn to him immediately in consternation.

'*Oh*,' she said.

'Yes,' said Ingram, passing his hand quicky over his hair, a gesture of his when annoyed.

It was raining.

They got out on to what seemed the most melancholy platform in the world, a grey wet junction with a grey level sky low down over it and over all the country round it. The Locarno train was waiting, and they went to it in silence. It was a quarter to six, a difficult time of day. The train, almost empty, jogged slowly through the valley of the Ticino. Down the windows raindrops chased each other. On the road alongside the railway, a road bound also for Locarno and dreary with brown puddles, an occasional high cart crawled drawn by a mule and driven by a huddled human being beneath a vast umbrella. The lake when they came in sight of it was a yawn of mist.

Ingeborg stared out at these things in silence. It was incredible that this should be Italy – again in spite of anything the Swiss might say – while on the other side of the Alps all Germany, including Kökensee, lay shimmering in light and colour. Ingram sat in the farthest corner of the carriage, his hands thrust in his pockets, his hat pulled over his eyes, looking straight in front of him. He was a mass of varied and profound exasperations. Everything exasperated him, even to the long trickle slowly creeping towards him down the floor from Ingeborg's wet umbrella. There was nothing she could have said or done at that moment that would not have rubbed his exasperation into a flame of swift and devastating speech. Luckily she said and did nothing, but sat quite silent with her face turned away towards the blurred window panes. But if she did not speak or do she yet was; and he was acutely conscious, though he never took his eyes off the cushions opposite, of every detail of her in that grey and horrible light, of her crumpled clothes, her drooping smudgedness, her hat grown careless and her hair in wisps. He had wanted to show her Italy, he had extraordinarily wanted to show her Italy in its summer magnificence, and there was – this. As a result what he now extraordinarily wanted was to upbraid her. He did not stop to analyse why.

At the hôtel in Locarno where they went for baths and breakfast – he had planned originally to show her the beautiful walk from there along the side of the lake to Cannobio, but now beyond baths and breakfast he had no plan – a person in shirt sleeves and a green apron who inadequately represented the hall porter, for it was not yet seven and the hall porter was still in bed, unintelligently and unfortunately spoke to Ingeborg of Ingram in his hearing as Monsieur votre père.

This strangely annoyed Ingram. 'It's your short skirt,' he said, with suppressed sulphur. 'You positively must get some clothes. Dressed like that you suggest perambulators.'

'But this is my *best* dress,' she protested. 'It's quite new. I mean, I've never had it on before since it was made.'

And with the easy tactlessness of one who has not yet learned to be afraid, she looked at him and laughed.

'Why,' she said, 'this morning I'm perambulators and only last night, quite late last night, I was the peace of God.'

To this, however, he did not trust himself to reply, but vanished with a kind of pounce into his bathroom.

He came to breakfast clean, but in a mood that could bear

nothing, least of all good temper. Ingeborg was by nature good tempered. She sat there pleased and refreshed – after all, he remembered resentfully, she had had five hours' sleep in the train while he had not had a wink – gaily making the best of things. She pointed out the strength of the coffee and the crispness of the rolls. She asked him if he did not think it a nice hôtel. She did not agree when he alluded to the waiter as blighted. She predicted a break in the weather at eleven, and said that it had always come true what her old nurse used to tell her, that rain at seven meant fine at eleven.

He hated her old nurse.

Until he had had some sleep, a long steady sleep, he would, he knew, be nothing but jarred nerves. When then after breakfast she inquired, with a cheerful air of being ready for anything, what they were going to do next, he briefly announced that he was going to sleep.

'Oh? Shall I have to go too?' she asked, her face falling.

'Of course not.'

'Then,' she said eagerly. 'I'll go out and explore.'

'What in this rain?'

'Oh, I've got goloshes.'

Goloshes! He retreated into his room,

It annoyed him intensely that she should be not only ready but pleased to go out for her first walk in Italy without him. He threw himself angrily on the bed, rang the bell, and bade the person who answered it, the same young man in shirt sleeves and a green apron who had welcomed them, tell Madame that if he were not awake by luncheon time she was not to wait for him, but was to have luncheon at the proper hour just the same.

The young man sought out Ingeborg in her room. She was tugging on her goloshes, one foot on a chair, her face flushed with effort and expectancy.,

'*Monsieur votre père*—' he began.

'*Ce n'est pas mon père,*' said Ingeborg, turning an amused face to him as she tugged.

'Monsieur votre mari—'

'*Quoi?* Certainement pas,' said Ingeborg, who in spite of her prize for French was unacquainted with the refinements of that language. '*Ce n'est pas mon mari,*' she said, energetically repudiating.

'*Ah – Monsieur n'est pas le mari de Madame*,' said the young man trippingly.

'*Certainement pas*,' said Ingeborg. '*Mon mari est à la maison.*'

'*Ah – tiens*,' said the young man.

'*C'est mon ami*,' said Ingeborg.

'*Ah – tiens, tiens*,' said the young man; and he delivered his message with a sudden ease and comfort of manner.

But though the young man's manner grew easy, after his report of this brief dialogue the hôtel's manner grew stiff, for on the slip of paper presented to Ingram to be filled in with his name he had, unaware of the things Ingeborg was saying, described himself and her as Mr and Mrs Dobson, and the hôtel, in which English Church services were held, and which was at that moment, though the season was over, being stayed in by several representative English spinsters, and a clergyman also from England with a wife and grown-up daughters, most respectable nice ladies who all took him out every day twice, once after breakfast and once after tea, for a little walk – the hôtel decided, putting its heads together in the manager's office, that it would, using tact, encourage the Dobsons to depart.

It could do nothing, however, for a moment, for the lady had disappeared with an umbrella into the wet, and the gentleman, it could hear, was sleeping; and this condition of things continued for many hours, the lady not coming into luncheon but remaining in the wet, and the gentleman, it could hear, going on sleeping. Then it became aware that they were both having tea in a distant corner of the slippery windowed wilderness of bamboo chairs and tables described in its prospectus as the Handsome Palmy Lounge, and that they had drawn up a second table to the one their tea was on and piled it with undesirably dripping branches of the yellow broom that grew high up in the hills, and that they were being noticed with suspicion by the hôtel's authentic guests who were used to having their tea in the silent stupor of the really married, because the gentleman, contrary to the observed habits of genuine husbands was talking to the lady instead of reading the Daily Mail.

The hôtel was nothing if not competent. It could handle any sort of situation competently, from runaway couples to that most unpleasant form of guest of all, the kind that came alive and went away dead. Full of tact, it allowed the lady and gentleman to finish their tea undisturbed; then it sent some one sleek to inform them that, most unfortunately, their rooms had been engaged for weeks beforehand for that very night, and therefore—

But before this person could even begin to be competent the gentleman requested him to have a carriage round in half an hour as he intended going on that evening; and thus the parting was accomplished, as all partings should be, urbanely, and the manager was able to display his doorstep suavity and bow and wish them a pleasant journey.

The Dobsons departed in a gay mood, with the branches of yellow broom rhythmically nodding between them over the edge of the waterproof apron that buttoned them in. Ingram had slept soundly for seven hours, and felt altogether renewed. He was taking her to Cannobio, along the road he had hoped to walk with her in sunshine; but Ingeborg, who had climbed hills till her blood raced and glowed, saw peculiar beauties even in the wetness, and would not believe that sun could make things lovelier. Outside Locarno, in that flat and grassy place beyond the town where the beautiful small hills draw back for a little from the lake, and the ox-eyed daisies grow so big, and the roads are strewn white with the blossoms of acacias, it stopped raining and Ingram had the hood put down. The mountains on the other side of the lake were indigo-coloured, with pulled-off tufts of woolly clouds lying along them down near the water. The lake was a steely black. The valley brooded in sullen lushness; and the branches of broom they carried with them in the carriage cut through the sombre background like a golden knife.

'The one doubt I have,' said Ingeborg, breathing in the warm scented air in long breaths, 'is that it's all too good to be true.'

'It isn't,' said Ingram, safely disentangled for a while from the intricate effect on his enthusiasms of fatigue and dirt and headaches, 'it's absolutely good and absolutely true. But only,' he said, turning and looking at her, 'because you're here, you dear close sister of my dreams. Without you it would be nothing but grey empty space in which I would just hang horribly.'

'You wouldn't. You couldn't not be happy in this,' she said, gazing about her.

'If you weren't here I wouldn't see it,' said Ingram, firmly believing it in the face of the fact that nothing ever escaped his acute vision. 'I see all this only through you. You are my eyes. Without you I go blind, I grope about with the light gone out. You don't know what you are to me, you little shining crystal thing, – you don't begin to realise it, my dear, my dear sweet Found-at-Last.'

'And this morning,' said Ingeborg, smiling at him, but only with a passing smile on her way to all the other things she wanted to look at, 'you said I suggested perambulators.'

For a space they drove on in silence, for he deplored her trick of reminding him of past moods. But beyond Ascona, where the mountains come down to the lake and leave only just room enough between them and the water for the road to twist through, he recovered again, consoled by her joy in the beauty of the drive and unable to see her happiness without feeling pleased. After all, what he most loved in her was that she was, so miraculously, a child; a child with gleams of wisdom flickering like a lizard's tongue in her mouth, and who even when she was silly was silly also somehow in gleams, – gleams of silver and sunshine. And always at the back of her, far away, hidden in what he thought of as depths of burning light, was that elusive thing by which he was so passionately attracted, the thing he was going to paint, the thing his own secret self crept to, knowing that here was warmth, here was understanding, her dear, dear little soul.

The evening at Cannobio was unsatisfactory. Ingeborg manifestly enjoyed herself, but it was with an absorption in what she was seeing and an obliviousness to himself that seemed to him both excessive and tiresome. Here was everything to make two people so happily alone whisper, – warmth, dusk, the broad shadow of plane-trees, unruffled water, lights romantically twinkling in corners, the twanging of a distant guitar, laughter and singing and the glint of red wine from the little lit-up tables along the front of the restaurants beneath the arcade at the back of the piazza, and he there, Ingram, after all a person of real importance, Edward Ingram at her feet, only asking to be allowed to explain to her in every variety of phrase how sweet she was. But she was dead to her opportunities. There wasn't another woman in Europe, he told himself angrily, who would not have whispered.

They wandered out of their hôtel after dinner, a square pink Italian albergo facing the lake where the town left off, and free, as indeed Cannobio altogether was, from transitory English with their awful eyes, and they strolled about looking at things. He did not look much, for he knew these Italian sights and sounds by heart and at that moment only wanted to look at her; but the least little thing caught her attention away from him absolutely, to the exclusion of anything he might be saying. Positively she even preferred to listen to the throb of the steamer coming nearer from the other end of the lake than to him; and she interrupted him in the middle of a sentence that intimately concerned herself to stand still in the piazza and ask him what he thought of the smells.

'I don't think about them at all,' he said shortly.

'Oh, but there are such a lot of them,' she exclaimed, sorting them out with her lifted nose. 'There's the smell of roses, and the smell of lake, and the smell of frying, and there's more roses, and then there's garlic, and then there's a quite dim one, and then there's a little puff of something else – I don't know what – sheer Italy, I expect. *I* never smelt so many smells,' she ended, with a gesture of astonishment.

He tried to get her away from them. He led her to a bench beneath a plane-tree. 'Come and sit by me and I will tell you things,' he said, luring her. 'Look, there's the moon got free from the clouds – and do you see how the coloured lights of the steamer that's coming shine right down a ladder of light into the water? And what do you think of the feel of the air, little sister? Isn't it soft and gentle? Doesn't it remind you of all kind and tender things?'

'But much the most wonderful of anything are these smells,' she said, absorbed in them. 'There are at least twelve different ones.'

'Never mind them. I want to talk.'

'But they're so amusing,' she said. 'There are interesting ones, and exciting ones, and beautiful ones, and disquieting ones, and awful ones, and too-perfect-for-anything ones, and they're all chasing each other up and down and round and round us.'

He lit a cigarette. 'There,' he said, 'that will blot the whole lot of them into only one, and you'll talk to me reasonably. Let us talk while we can, my dear. In a little time we shall be dead to all feeling for ever and ever.'

'Yes, we shall be little shreds of rottenness,' she said placidly.

'God, who wastes a sunset every night—' he said, getting up to stamp on the match he had thrown away –

'If they were mine,' she interrupted, 'I'd keep them all in a gallery or a portfolio.'

' – understands, I suppose,' he went on, sitting down again, 'why such dear things as this evening here, this time of being alone together here, should end and be forgotten.'

'As long as I live,' she said with earnestness, 'it will not be forgotten. All my other memories will be like a string of – oh, just beads and nuts and fir-cones, till I get to this one, and then on the string there'll be suddenly a shining jewel.'

'Really ? Really ?' he murmured, stooping to look into her eyes, revived by this speech. 'Little flame in my heart, really ?'

'Oh,' said Ingeborg dreamily, in her husky, soft voice, 'but the wonderfullest thing, the wonderfullest jewel. My first Italian town – Cannobio . . .'

He ceased to be revived. He smoked in silence. The effect on her of Italy was as surprising as it was unexpected. At Kökensee she had been entirely concentrated on him, eagerly listening only to him, drinking in only what he said, worshipping. Here she seemed possessed by a rage for any sights and sounds merely because they were new. There had been moments from the very start in Berlin when he almost felt of secondary interest, and they appeared to be becoming permanent. It was disturbing. It was incredible. It was grotesque. Perhaps it would be as well to take her away from the lakes, from all that part of the country which apparently caught her imagination on its most sensitive side. Perhaps Milan for a while, with pavements and museums . . .

'Please will you give me some of that money ?' she asked across his reflections.

'Which money ?' he said, looking at her.

'My money.'

'What on earth for ?'

'I want to send Robert a picture postcard.'

He threw his cigarette away. 'It would be most improper,' he said, passing his hand rapidly over his hair. 'Highly improper.'

'Improper ?' she echoed, staring at him. 'To send Robert a picture postcard ?'

'Grossly. It simply isn't done.'

'What ? Not send Robert – but he'd like to see where we've got to.'

'For Heaven's sake don't *talk* about Robert,' he exclaimed, getting up quickly ; the idea of the picture postcard profoundly shocked him.

'Not talk about him ?' she repeated, staring at him in astonishment. 'But he's my husband.'

'Exactly. That's what makes him so improper.'

'What? Why, I thought husbands were just the very things that never could be improper.'

'Ingeborg,' he said, walking angrily up and down in front of her, 'are you or are you not being taken care of on this – this holiday by me? Are you or are you not travelling with me?'

'Yes, I know. But I don't see why I shouldn't send Rob—'

'Well, then, if you don't see you must believe. You've just got to believe me when I tell you certain things are impossible.'

'But Robert—'

'Good heavens, don't *talk* of Robert. If I beg you not to, if I tell you it spoils things for me, if I ask you as a favour—' He stopped in front of her. 'My dear, my little mate, my everything that's central and alive among the husks—'

'Of course I won't, then. At least I'll try to remember not to,' she said, looking at him with a smile that had effort in it as well as surprise. 'But I don't see why a picture postcard—'

The steamer they had seen for so long, the last one of the day from Arona to Locarno, was nearing the pier, and the piazza suddenly swarmed with busy groups preparing to go on it or see each other off.

'Let's come away,' said Ingram, impatiently. 'Let's come *away*,' he repeated with a stamp of his foot. 'I hate this crowd.'

She got up and walked beside him towards the hôtel, her eyes on the ground.

'I really can't see why I shouldn't send Robert—' she began.

'Oh, damn Robert!' he exclaimed violently.

She looked at him. 'Damn Robert?' she echoed, immensely surprised. 'But – don't you *like* Robert?'

'No,' said Ingram. 'No,' he said, even louder. 'Not here. Not now. Now don't,' he added in extreme irritation as he saw her mouth opening, 'ask me why, don't ask me to explain. Go to bed, Ingeborg. It's time all children under ten were in bed. And get up early, please, because we're going to start the first thing for – anyhow, for somewhere else.'

CHAPTER 34

Ingram was not only a great painter, he was practised in minor accomplishments, and among them was the art of running away. He had done it several times and had attained fluency. Indeed, so easy had practice made it that it grew to be hardly running so much as walking. He walked away, at last quite leisurely, from an uncommenting wife to a lady whose affection for him was invariably already so great that there was nothing left for it to do but to decline; and when it had declined, assisted and encouraged in various ways by him, the chief cooling factor being his expressed impatience to get to his painting again undisturbed by non-essentials — each lady found it cooling to be called a non-essential — he avoided the part that is sometimes a little difficult, the part in which recriminations are apt to gather like clouds about a sunset, the part that lies round ends, by skilful treatment, by a gradual surrounding of her who was now not so much a lover as a patient with an atmosphere of affection for her home. She came by imperceptible degrees to thirst for her home. She came to thirst, and such was his skill that she thirsted healthily, for her husband or her father or whoever it was she had left, for worries, catastrophes, disgrace, — for anything so long as it was so obliging as not to be love. If poorer in other ways she departed at least richer in philosophy, without a trace of jealousy of what he might do next, not minding what he did if only she did not have to do it too, and he, until such time as he again was lured from paths of austerity and work by the hope that he had found the one predestined mate, enjoyed the condition in which he was altogether happiest, the freedom of spirit that disdains love.

But how different from those comfortable excursions, as straightforward and as uneventful to him in their transitory salubrious warming as bread and milk, was this running away! It was distressingly different. Almost, except that he had no desire to laugh, ridiculously different. The first step, the process of the actual removal from Kökensee to Berlin, from legality to illicitness, had in its smoothness been positively glib ; and he had supposed that, once alone together, lovemaking, which was the very marrow of running away – else why run ? – would follow with a similar glibness. Nothing, however, seemed less inclined to follow. The only things that did follow were two confused exasperating days in which his moods varied with every hour, almost at last with everything she said. The capaciousness of her beliefs and accept-ances amazed him. They were as capacious as her enthusiasms. She believed so firmly what he had told her over there away in Kökensee, where of course a man had to say things in order to get a beginning made, about the friendly frequent journeyings of other people, she had so heartily accepted his assurance that it was absurd and disgraceful in its suggestion of evil-mindedness not to travel frankly anywhere with anybody – 'Are we not the children of light, you and I ?' he had asked her – the things a man says ! he thought ; but they should not be brought up against him in this manner, clad in an invincible armour of acceptance – 'And shall we be hindered in our free comings and goings by the dingy scruples of those heavy others, the groping and afraid children of darkness ?' – that plainly the idea that she was doing anything even remotely wrong had not occurred to her. The basis of her holiday was this belief in frank companionship. She had no difficulty, he observed, himself infinitely fretted by this constant closeness to her, in being just a frank companion. She was so carelessly secure in friendship, so empty of any thought beside, that she could and did say things to him which said by any other woman in the same situation would have instantly led to love-making. But Ingram, who was fastidious, could no more make love to her, violently begin, robustly stand no nonsense, so long as she was steeped in obliviousness, than he could to a child or a chair. There must be some response, some consciousness. Her obtuseness to the real situation was so terribly healthy-minded that it was almost a disease ; the awful candour of soul of bishops' daughters and pastors' wives appalled him.

For three days the weather continued heavy, pressing down on his eyes. He did not sleep. He was all nerves. In the morning, a time he had not yet known her in, for at Kökensee they were together only in the afternoons, she produced the effect on him of some one different and in some subtle annoying way strange. Was it because she flickered more in the mornings? He could not describe it better than that, – she flickered. She always flickered mentally, her thoughts just giving each subject a little lick and then blowing off it to something else, but in the afternoons and evenings the flickering was often beautiful, or at those warmer more indulgent hours it seemed so, and in the morning it was not. A man in the morning wants somebody pinned down for a companion, somebody reasonable and fixed. Nothing but a rather silent reasonableness, and if enunciations are unavoidable brief ones, go well with coffee and with rolls. At breakfast he found he could hardly speak to her so exceedingly then was she on his nerves, – her dreadful healthy restedness when he had been tossing all night, her fearful readiness for the new day when he had not even begun to recover from the old one, her regularity of enthusiasm, her punctual happiness. And every evening he was in love with her.

He was exasperated. This being with her among the hills and lakes of Italy that he had thought of as going to be the sweetest time he had known was sheer exasperation; for even in the evenings when he was in love with her – the condition, indeed, set in at any time from tea onwards, and could on occasion be induced before tea if she happened to say the right things – he was irritably in love, and hardly knew whether it would give him more satisfaction to shake her or to kiss her. And annoying and perplexing as her untroubled conscience was it was yet not so annoying and perplexing as her wild joy in Italy. Who would not be galled by the discovery that he has become a background? Who would have supposed that she who in Kökensee thought him so wonderful, so clearly realised who he was, who walked with him there in the rye-fields and offered him every sort of incense that sweet words could invent, would, let loose in Italy, take the background he had so carefully chosen for his lovemaking and hug it to her heart and be absorbed in it and adore it beyond reason, and that he himself would turn into the background, – incredible as it seemed, into just the background of his own background?

When he took her up into the hills, into solitary places where the chestnut woods went on for miles and no one ever came but charcoal-burners, he was not, as it were, there. When he took her on the lake in a sailing-boat and they hung motionless on the good-will of the wind, he was not there either. When they rested after a hot climb, deep in some high meadow not yet reached by the ascending haymakers, and through the stalks of its bee-haunted flowers, its delicate bending scabious and frail ragged-robins, could see little bits of lake far below and the white villages on the mountains opposite, and the whole world was only asking to be made a frame of for love, where, he inquired of himself, in the picture that was in her mind and irradiating her eyes, was he? He had not imagined, so far behind him were his own discoveries of the new, that any one could be so greedily absorbed. Watching her, while she watched everything except him, he decided he would take her to Milan. He would try something ugly. Milan this heavy hot weather ought to give her back to him if anything would. They would stay in a street where there were tramcars and noises, and they would frequent museums. They would walk much on pavements, and have their food in English Tea Rooms. While the cure was in progress she might be getting herself some decent clothes, for really her clothes were distressing, and when it was accomplished, and she was thoroughly bored with things, and had come back to being aware of him, he would carry her off to Venice and begin work, – work, the best thing in life, the one thing that keeps on yet is never monotonous, the supreme thing always new and joyful. But he was afraid of Venice. Venice was too beautiful. She would not sit quiet there while he painted her; she would want to go out and look. Impossible to take her there until she had learned to blot out everything in the world with his image alone. This blotting out, he perceived, would have to be achieved in Milan, and quickly. He was starving for his work. So acute was his hunger to begin the great picture that right under-neath all his other emotions and wishes and moods was a violent impatience at being kept from it by what his subconsciousness alluded to with resentful incorrectness as a parcel of women.

It was the evening at Luino that he definitely decided on Milan.

They had walked that day along the wooded paths that lead ultimately across to Ponte Tresa, and she had once again, on returning to Luino and seeing a revolving column of picture postcards outside a tobacconist's shop and catching sight of some that showed the place of rocks and falling water in which they had eaten their luncheon, wanted to send one to Robert. She had not said so, but she had hovered round the column looking hungry. Picture postcards seemed to have a dreadful fascination

for her; and as for Ingram, the mere sight of them at this point of
their journey made him see red. He had instantly observed her
hungry hovering, and had flared out into a leaping rebuke in
which there was more of the angry schoolmaster than the lover.
He had felt it himself, and seen, quick as he was to see, a little
look of surprised and questioning fear for a moment in her eyes.

'Well, it's because you're always thinking of Robert,' he flashed
at her in an attempt that caught fire on the way to apologise.

'Not *always*,' she said hesitatingly, with a smile that for the first
time was propitiating; and the accidents of the pavement making
him walk for a few yards in front of her she found herself looking
at his back, his high thin shoulders and the rims of his ears, with
a startled feeling of entire strangeness.

A dim thought rose and disappeared again somewhere in the
back of her mind, a whisper of a thought, hardly breathed and
gone again, – 'I'm *used* to Robert.'

He took her to Milan next day. That loud and sweltering city
was, by its hot dulness, to bore her into awareness of him, to toss
her by sheer elimination of other interests to his breast. Inexorably
he kept her on the steamer and turned a deaf ear to her prayers
that they might land when it stopped at attractive villages on its
journey down the lake. She thought this unreasonable; for why
come at all to these lovely places, come so close that one could
almost touch them, and then whisk away and hardly let one look?
And she could not help feeling, after he had been short with her
about the Borromean islands, at one of which unfortunately the
steamer touched, that it would be both blessed and splendid to
travel round here alone, – free, able to get out at islands if one
wanted to.

'Yes, those are islands,' he said, when first they loomed on her
enraptured gaze. 'Yes, one can land on them, but we're not going
to. Yes, yes, beautiful – but we've got to catch the train.'

She began to turn a slightly perplexed attention to him. Surely
he was different from what he was at Kökensee? And there were
the Borromean islands slipping away, the beautiful islands; there
they were being passed, going out of her life; it was unlikely she
would ever see them again . . .

To Ingram on that leaden afternoon the lake looked like a
coffin, and the islands as dull and shabby as three nails in it; to
Ingeborg they looked like three little miracles of God. Just as he
who for the first time goes abroad would give up Rome if he might

stop at Calais, so did Ingeborg hanker after detailed exploration of new places she was inexorably whisked away from. The Borromean islands were beautiful, but if they had been dull she still would have hankered after them. Beautiful or dull they were different from Kökensee; and when the travelled Ingram put his hopes in Milan he did not realise how great on Ingeborg after her strictly cloistered Kökensee existence was the effect of the merely different. The platform at Arona, the flat fields the train presently lumbered across, the factories and suburbs of Milan, the noisy streets throbbing heavily with heat that grey and lowering afternoon, the shapes of things, of dull things, of tram-cars and cabs and washerwomen, the shop windows, the behaviour and foreign faces of dogs, the behaviour of children, the Italian eyes all turned to her, all staring at her, – they fascinated and absorbed her like the development of a vivid dream. Who were these people? What would they all do next? What were they feeling, thinking, saying? Where were they going, what had they had for breakfast, what were the rooms like they had just come out of, what sorts of things did they keep in their cupboards?

'If one of them would lend me a cupboard,' she exclaimed to Ingram, 'and leave me alone with what it has got inside it, I believe I'd know all Italy by the time I'd done with it. Everything, everything – the desires of its soul and its body, and what it works at and plays at and eats, and what it hopes is going to happen to it after it is dead.'

And he had been supposing, from her silence as she walked beside him, that she was finding Milan dull. Hastily he led her away from the streets into an English Tea Room and made her sit with her back to the window and gave her rusks.

But though her childhood had been spent among these objects, which were esteemed at the Palace because falling just short at the last moment of quite sweetness and quite niceness they discouraged sinful gorging, they had none of their ancient sobering effect on her there in Milan. She ate them and ate them, and remained as brightly detached from them as before. Their dryness choked out none of her lively interest, their reminiscent flavour did not quiet her, not even when combined, as it presently was, with the sound of church bells floating across the roofs. She might have been in Redchester with those Sunday bells ringing and all the rusks. Sitting opposite to her at the marble-topped table in the deserted shop Ingram decided he would give her no meals more amusing than this in Milan. So long as she kept him there she should, except breakfast, have all her meals in that one place: modest meals, meals damping to the spirits and surely in the long run lowering, the most inflaming dish provided by the Tea Room being – it announced it on the wall – poached eggs.

He kept her there as long as he could, long after the tea was cold, and tried, so deeply upset was he becoming by the delays her curious immaturity was causing in the normal development of running away, actually in that place of buns to make love to her. But how difficult it was! He too had eaten rusks. He wanted to tell her he adored her, and it reached her across the teapot in the form of comments on the uncertainties of her behaviour. He wanted to tell her her body was as delicate as flowers and delightful as dawn, and it came out a criticism of the quality – also the quantity – of her enthusiasms. He endeavoured to sing the praise of the inmost core of her, the inexpressible, illuminating, understanding and wholly sweet core, and instead he found himself acidly deprecating her clothes.

Ingeborg sat listening with half an ear and eyes bright with longing to be out in the streets again. She was fidgeting to get away from the shop, and was sorry he should choose just that moment to smoke so great a number of cigarettes. Even the young lady who guarded the cakes appeared to think the visit for one based only on tea and rusks had lasted long enough, and came and cleared away and inquired in English, it being her native tongue, whether she could not, now, get them anything else.

'The curious admixture in you,' said Ingram, starting out with the intention of comparing her to light in the darkness and immediately getting off the rails, 'the curious admixture in you of streaks of childishness and spasmodic maturity. You are at one moment so entirely impulsive and irresponsible, and a moment before you were quite intelligent and reasonable, and a moment afterwards you are splendid in courage and recklessness.'

'When was I splendid in courage and recklessness?' she asked, bringing more attention to bear on him.

'When you left your home to come to me. The start off was splendid. Who could dream it would fizzle out into – well, into this?'

'But has it fizzled out? You're not' – she leaned across the table a little anxiously – 'you're not scolding me?'

'On the contrary, I'm trying to tell you all you are to me.'

'Oh,' said Ingeborg.

'I intend somehow to isolate my consciousness of your streaks—'

'Streaks?'

'As bees wax up a dead invader.'

'Oh – a dead invader?'

'I don't, you see, believe in the damning effect of one specific outbreak, nor of one or two—'

'You're not – you're not *really* scolding me?' she asked, again a little anxiously.

'On the contrary, I'm believing in and clinging to your dear innermost.'

'Oh,' said Ingeborg.

'I believe these streaks and patches and spots your superficial self has may be good in their ultimate effect, may save us, by interrupting, from those too serene spells that dogs'-ear love with usage and carelessness.'

She gazed at him, her mouth a little open. He lit yet another cigarette.

'But it's rather like,' he said, flinging the match away into a corner whither the young lady followed it and with a pursed reproachfulness trod it out, 'it's rather like finding a crock of gold in one's garden and only being able to peep at it sometimes, and having to go away and work very hard for eleven shillings a week.'

She went on gazing at him in silence.

'And not even for eleven shillings,' said Ingram, reflecting on all he had already endured. 'Work very hard for nothing.'

She leant across the table again. 'I never *mean* to be tiresome,' she said.

'Little star,' he said stoutly.

'It's always involuntary, my tiresomeness,' she said, addressing him earnestly. 'Oh, but it's so involuntary – and the dull surfaces I know I have, and the scaly imperfections—'

He knocked the ashes off his cigarette with unnecessary vigour, almost as though they were bits of an annoying relative's body.

'I'm warped, and encrusted, and blundering,' went on Ingeborg, who was always thorough when it came to adjectives.

In his irritable state, to have her abjectly cheapening herself vexed him as much as everything else she had done that day had vexed him. He might, under provocation, point out her weaknesses, but she must not point them out to him. He wanted to worship her, and she persisted in preventing him. Distressing to have a god who refuses to sit quiet on its pedestal, who insists on skipping off it to show you its shortcomings and beg your pardon. How could he make love to her if she talked like this? It would be like trying to make love to a Prayer-book.

'Is it because it is Sunday,' he said, 'that you are impelled to acknowledge and confess your faults? You make me feel as if a verger had passed by and pushed me into a pew.'

'Well, but I *am* warped and encrusted and blundering,' she persisted.

'You are not,' he said irritably. 'Haven't I told you you are my star and my miracle?'

'Yes, but—'

'I tell you,' he said, determined to believe it, 'that you are the very bath of my tired spirit.'

'How kind you are!' she said. 'You're as kind to me as if you were my brother. Sometimes I think you are rather like my brother. I never *had* a brother, but you're very like, I think, the one I would have had if I had had one.' She warmed to the idea. 'I feel as if my brother—' she said, preparing to launch into enthusiasm; but he interrupted her by getting up.

'It seems waste,' he said, reaching for his hat,' 'to talk about your brother, as you've never had him. Shall we go?'

She jumped up at once with the air of one released. He himself could not any longer endure the tea-room or he would have stayed in it. Gloomily he went out with her into the streets again and noted that if anything she seemed more active and eager than before – thoroughly, indeed, rested and refreshed. Gloomily he realised during the next hour or two that she had an eye for buildings, and that they were always the wrong ones. Gloomily he discovered an odd liking in her for anything however bad that was wrought in iron. He could not get her past some of the iron gates of the palaces. He hated bad gates. Without experience she could not compare and did not select, and her interest was all-embracing, indiscriminating as a child's. He took pains to avoid the Piazza del Duomo, but by some accident of a twisting street and a momentary inattentiveness he did find himself at last, after much walking as he had thought away from it, all of a sudden facing it. Urging her on by her elbow he hurried her nervously across it, hoping she would not see the Cathedral; but the

Cathedral being difficult not to see she did see it, and remained, as he had feared she would, rooted.

'Ingeborg,' he exclaimed, 'if you tell me you like that—'

'Oh, let me look, let me look,' she cried, holding his sleeve while he tried to get her away. 'It's so funny – it's so *different*—'

'Ingeborg—' he almost begged; but from its outside to its inside was an inevitable step, and that she should gasp on first getting in seemed also, after she had done it, inevitable.

Ingram found himself sight-seeing; looking at windows; following her down vaults; towed by beadles. He rubbed his hand violently over his hair.

'But this is intolerable,' he cried aloud to himself. 'I shall go mad—'

And he strode after her and caught her arm just as she was disappearing over the brim of the crypt.

'Ingeborg,' he said, his eyes blazing at her in a bright astonishment, 'do you mean to tell me that I shall not reach *you*, that I'm not going to get ever at *you* till I paint you?'

She turned in the gloom and looked up at him.

'Oh, I know I'll get you then,' he went on excitedly, while the interrupted beadle impatiently rattled his keys. 'Nothing can hide you away from me then. I don't paint, you see, by myself—'

She stared up at him.

'And all this you're doing, all this waste of running about – have you then forgotten the picture?'

It was as though he had shaken her suddenly awake. She stared at him in a shock of recollection. Why, of course – the picture. Why – incredible, but she had forgotten it. Actually forgotten it in the wild excitement of travelling; actually she had been wanting to linger at each new place, she who had only ten days altogether, she who had come only after all because of the picture, the great picture, the first really great thing that had touched her life. And here she was with him, its waiting creator, dragging him about who held future beauty in his cunning guided hand among all the mixed stuff left as a burden on the generations by the past, curious about the stuff with an uneducated stupid curiosity, wasting time, ridiculously blocking the way to something great, to the greatest of the achievements of a great artist.

She was sobered. She was overcome by the vivid recognition of her cheap enthusiasm.

'Oh,' she said, staring up at him, wide awake, entirely ashamed, 'how *patient* you've been with me!'

And as he still held her by the arm, his eyes blazing down at her from the top step of the crypt, she could find no way of expressing her shame and contrition except by bending her head and laying her cheek on his hand.

CHAPTER 35

They stood there for what seemed to the beadle at the bottom an intolerable time, the lady, evidently nobody certificated, with her cheek on the gentleman's hand, and he himself, as honest a man as ever wanted to get his tip and be done with it, kept waiting with nothing to do but curse and rattle his keys; and though it was summer the crypt was cold, and so would his feet be soon; and what could the world be coming to when people carried their caressings even into crypts? Becoming maddened by these delays the beadle cursed them both, their present, past and future, roundly and thoroughly and also profanely — for by the accident of his calling he was very perfect in profanity — beneath his breath.

'I'm so sorry, so sorry,' Ingeborg was murmuring, who did nothing by halves, neither penitence, nor humility nor gratitude.

'My worshipped child,' whispered Ingram, immensely moved by this swift change in her, and changed as swiftly himself by the softness of her cheek against his hand.

'Oughtn't we to go to Venice to-night?' she asked, still standing in that oddly touching attitude of apology.

'Not to-night.'

'But how can a picture get painted in just that little time?'

'Ah, but you know I'm good at pictures.'

'But I can't stay a minute longer than Thursday. I have to be back on Saturday at the very latest.'

'You'll see. It will all be quite easy.'

'But to think that I *forgot* the picture!' she said, looking up at him shocked, while the ancient humility in which the Bishop had so carefully trained her descended on her once more, only four-fold this time, like a garment grown voluminous since last it was put on.

They had for some reason been talking in murmurs, and the

embittered beadle, losing his self-control, began to say things audibly. Strong in the knowledge of tourist ignorance when it came to real language in Italian, he said exactly what he thought; and what he thought was so monstrous, so inappropriate to beadles and to the atomosphere of a crypt, besides being so extremely and personally rude, that it roused Ingram, who knew Italian almost better than the beadle – for his included scholarly bye-ways in vituperation, strange and curious twists beyond the reach of the uneducated – to pour a sudden great burning blast of red-hot contumely down on to his head; and having done this he turned, and holding Ingeborg's hand led her up the steps again, leaving the beadle at the bottom, solitary, shrivelled, and singed.

They thought no more of crypt and beadles. They looked neither to the right nor to the left. Ingram held her by the hand all the way down the Cathedral, and the piazza when they came out on to it with its crowds of vociferating men and bell-ringing tramcars and sellers of souvenirs seemed to Ingeborg nothing now but a noisy irrelevance. Whole strips of postcards were thrust unnoticed into her face. The purpose of her journey was the picture. Marvellous that she should have lost sight of it and of the wonder and pride of being needed for it, – needed at last for anything, she who so profoundly had longed to be needed, but needed for this, as a collaborator actually; even though passive and humble, in the creation of something splendid.

He put her into a cab and drove with her away from the fuss and din. She was exquisite again to him, adorable altogether. The memory of the fret and hot irritation of the day was wiped out as though it had never been by that other memory of her sweet apology on the steps of the crypt. He told the driver, for it was towards evening, to take them to those gardens described by the guide-book as probably the finest public park in Italy; and presently, as they walked together in the remoter parts, the dusk dropped down like a curtain between them and the Sunday night crowd collecting round the fountains. Tall trees, and clumps of box, and rose-bushes shut out everything except mystery; and she in that quiet place of trickling water and dim flowers began again to talk to him as she had talked at Kökensee, softly, deliciously, about nothing except himself. It was like the shadow of a great rock in a thirsty land; it was infinite refreshment and relief.

She talked about the picture, with reverence, adoringly. She told him how in the rush of new impressions she had been forgetting everything that really mattered, not only that greatest of them all, but the other things she had to thank him for besides, – Italy, her unexpected holiday, due so entirely to him. She said, her husky voice softer than ever with gratitude, 'You have been giving me happiness and happiness. You've heaped happiness on me with both your hands.' She said, searching only for words that should be sweet enough, 'Do you know I could cry to think of it all – of all you've been to me since you came to Kökensee. When I'm back there again, this time with you will be like a hidden precious stone, and when I'm stupid and thinking that life is dull I'll get it out and look at it, and it will flash colour and light at me.'

'When you talk like that,' said Ingram, greatly stirred, 'it is as though a little soul had come back into a deserted and forgotten body.'

'Is it?' she murmured, so glad that she could please him, perfectly melted into the one desire to make up.

'When you talk like that,' he said, 'life becomes a thing so happy that it shines golden inside. You have the soul I have always sought, the thing that comes through me like light through a stained-glass window, so that I am lit, so that my heart is all sweet fire.'

'And you,' said Ingeborg, picking up his image as she so often irritatingly did, only now it did not irritate him, and flinging it back with a fresh adornment, 'the thought of you, the memory of you when I've gone back to my everyday life, will be like a perfect rose-window in a grey wall.'

'As though we could be separated again. As though being in love with somebody miles away isn't just intolerable ache. Oh, my dear, why do you look at me?' he asked with a large simplicity of manner that made her ashamed of her surprise; 'because I talk of being in love? Why shouldn't two people simply love each other and say so? And if I love you it isn't with the greedy possessive love I've had for women before, but as though the feeling one has for the light on crystals or for clear shining after rain, the feeling of beauty in deep and delicate things, has become personified and exalted.'

She made a little deprecating gesture. He was almost too kind to her; too kind. But nobody could reasonably object to being loved like crystals and clearness after rain. Robert couldn't possibly mind that.

She cast about for things to say back, shining things to match his, but he found them all first; it was impossible to keep up with him.

'You're delicate and fine, like translucent gold,' he said. 'And you are brave, and various, and alive. And you are full of sweet little fancies, little swirls of mood, kind eager things. Never in my life is there the remotest chance that I shall meet so good and deep a happiness as you again, and I put my heart once and for all between your dear cool little hands.'

She felt bent beneath this generosity, she who had been so tiresome; and not only tiresome, but she who had had doubts, unworthy ones she now saw, round about breakfast time, for instance, piercing through her silly delight in Italy, as to whether she were giving even any satisfaction.

'I perceive,' he went on, 'I've never really loved before. I've played with dolls, and expressed myself to dummies – like a boy with a ball he *must* play with, and failing a playfellow he bumps it against a wall and catches it again. But you play back, my living dear heart—'

More and more was she invaded by a happy surprise. The *things* she had been doing without knowing it! All the right ones, apparently, the whole time – playing back, coming up to his expectations; and moments such as those at the Borromean Islands, and when there were picture postcards, and just recently in the tea-room, had not in the least been what she supposed. She had not understood. She glowed to think she had not understood.

'I've been so wearied and distressed with life,' he went on, talking in a low, moved voice. 'It has seemed at last such an old hairy thing of jealousies and shame and disillusionments, and work falling short of its best, and endless coming and going of people, and me for ever left with a blunted edge. And now you come, you, and are like a great sweet wind blowing across it, and like clear skies, and a moon rising before sunset. It is as though you had taken up a brush and painted out the old ugly tangles and made a new picture of me in luminous clear water-colour.'

Her surprise grew and grew, and her gladness that she had been mistaken.

'Those streaks,' she thought. 'He didn't really *mean* what he said about those streaks—'

'Somehow, though quite intelligent all along,' continued Ingram, 'I've been shallow and hard in my feelings about everything. Now I feel love like a deep soft river flowing through my heart. I love every one because I love you. I can set out to make people happy, I can do and say fine and generous things because of the love of you shining in my heart—'

'That beadle,' she thought, 'he didn't really *mean* what he said to that beadle—'

'You're what I've been looking for in women all my life,' he went on. 'You're the dream come true. I've only tried to love before. And now you've come, and made me love, which we all dream of doing, and given me love, which we all dream of getting—'

Her pleasure became tingled with a faint uneasiness, for she wouldn't have thought, left to herself, that she had been giving him love. Pastor's wives didn't give love except to their pastors. Friendship, yes; she had given him warm friendship, and an abject admiration of his gifts, and pride and gratefulness – oh, such pride and gratefulness – that he should like being with her and saying lovely things to her; but love? She had supposed love was reserved for lovers. Well, if he liked to call it love . . . one must not be missish . . . it was very kind of him . . . It was, also, more and more wonderful to her that she had been doing and being and giving all these things without knowing it. Her suddenly discovered accomplishments staggered her. 'Is it possible,' she thought with amazement, 'that I'm *clever*?'

And as if he had heard the word lovers in her mind he said it.

'Other lovers,' he said, 'are engaged perpetually in sycophantic adaptations—'

'In what?'

She thought he had been going to say engaged to be married, for though she had known even at Redchester, in spite of the care taken to shut such knowledge out, that the world included wicked persons who loved without engagements or marriages, sometimes indeed even without having been properly introduced, persons who were afterwards punished by the correctly plighted by not being asked to tea, they were, the Bishop informed an anxious inquirer once when he had supposed her out of the room, in God's infinite mercy numerically negligible.

But Ingram did not heed her. 'Except us,' he went on.

'Us?' she echoed. Well, if one took the word in its widest sense . . .

'We fit,' he said. 'We fit, and reflect each other. I in your heart, you in my heart, like two mirrors that hang opposite one another for ever.'

A doubt as to the expediency of so much talk of hearts and love crept into her mind, but she quieted it by remembering how much worse the Song of Solomon was – 'And yet so respectable really,' she said, continuing her thought aloud, 'and all only about the Church.'

'What is so respectable? Come and sit on that seat by the bush covered with roses,' he said. 'Look – in this faint light they are as white and delicate as you.'

'The Song of Solomon. It – just happened to come into my head. Things do,' she added, beginning to lay hold of the first words that occurred to her, no longer at her ease.

She sat down on the edge of the seat where he put her.

'It's stone,' she said nervously, looking up at him, for he had taken a step back and was considering her, his head on one side. 'Do you think it's good for us?'

'You beautiful little thing,' he murmured, considering her. 'You exquisite little lover.'

Her hands gripped the edge of the seat more tightly. A sudden very definite longing for Robert seized her.

'Oh, but—' she began, and faltered.

She tried again. 'It's so *kind* of you, but – you know – but I don't think—'

'What don't you think, my dear, my discoverer, my creator, my restorer—'

'Oh, I know there was Solomon,' she faltered, holding on to the seat, 'saying things too and they meant something else, but – but isn't this different? Different because – well, I suppose through my not being the Church? I'm very *sorry*,' she added apologetically, 'that I'm not the Church – because then I suppose nothing would really matter?'

'You mean you don't want me to call you lover?'

'Well, I am *married*,' she said, in the voice of one who apologised for drawing his attention to it. 'There *is* no getting away from that.'

'But we have got away from it,' said Ingram, sitting down beside her and loosening the hand nearest him from its tight hold on the seat and kissing it, while she watched him in an uneasiness and dismay that now were extreme. 'That's exactly what we have done. Oh,' he went on, kissing her hand with what seemed to her a quite extraordinary emotion, 'you brave, beautiful little thing, you must know – you can't not know – how completely and gloriously you have burned your ships !'

'Ships ?' she echoed.

She stared at him a moment, then added with a catch in her breath :

'Which – ships ?'

'Ingeborg, Ingeborg, my fastness, my safety, my darling, my reality, my courage—' said Ingram, kissing her hand between each word.

'Yes,' she said, brushing that aside, 'but which ships ?'

'My strength, my helper, friend, sister, lover, unmerited mate—'

'Yes, but won't you leave off a minute ? It – it would be *convenient* if you'd leave off a minute and tell me which ships ?'

He did leave off, to look into her eyes in the dusk, eyes fixed on him in a concentration of questioning that left his epithets on one side as so much irrelevant lumber.

'Little worshipful thing,' he said, still gripping her hand, 'did you really think you could go back ? Did you really think you could ?'

'Go back where ?'

'To that unworthy rubbish heap, Kökensee ?'

She stared at him. Their faces, close together, were white in the dusk, and their eyes looking into each other's were like glowing dark patches.

'Why should I not think so ?' she said.

'Because, you little artist in recklessness, you've burned your ships.'

She made an impatient movement, and he tightened his hold on her hand.

'Please,' she said, 'do you mind *telling* me about the ships.'

'One of them was this.'

'Was what ?'

'Coming to Italy with me.'

'You said heaps of people—'

'Oh yes, I know – a man has to say things. And the other was writing that letter to Robert. If you'd left it at boots and Berlin !'

He laughed triumphantly and kissed her hand again.

'But that wouldn't have helped either really,' he went on,

'because directly the ten days were up and you hadn't come back he'd have known—'

'Hadn't come back?'

'Oh, Ingeborg – little love, little Parsifal among women, dear divine ignorance and obtuseness – I adore you for believing the picture could be done in a week!'

'But you *said*—'

'Oh yes, yes, I know – a man has to say things at the beginning—'

'What beginning?'

'Of this – of love, happiness, all the wonders of joy we're going to have—'

'Please do you mind not talking about those other things for a minute? Why do you tell me I can't go back, I can't go home?'

'They wouldn't have you. Isn't it ridiculous – isn't it glorious?'

'What, not have me *home*? They wouldn't *have* me? Who wouldn't? There isn't a they. I've only got Robert—'

'He wouldn't. After that letter he couldn't. And Kökensee wouldn't and couldn't. And Glambeck wouldn't and couldn't. And Germany, if you like, wouldn't and couldn't. The whole world gives you to me. You're my mate now for ever.'

She watched him kissing her hand as though it did not belong to her. She was adjusting a new thought that was pushing its way like a frozen spear into her mind, trying to let it in, seeing she could not keep it out, among all those happy thoughts so warmly there already about Ingram and her holiday and the kindness and beauty of life without its too cruelly killing too many of them too quickly. 'Do you mean—' she began; then she stopped, because what was the use of asking him what he meant? Quite suddenly she knew.

An immense slow coldness, an icy fog, seemed to settle down on her and blot out happiness. All the dear accustomed things of life, the small warm things of quietness and security, the everyday things one nestled up to and knew, were sliding away from her. 'So that,' she heard herself saying in a funny clear voice, 'there's only God?'

'How, only God?' he asked, looking up at her.

'Only God left who wouldn't call it adultery?'

The word in her mouth shocked him.

CHAPTER 36

She sat quite still after that while he talked. After that one deplorable bald word she said no more at all; and Ingram's passionate explanations and asseverations only every now and then caught her ear. She was going home. That was all she knew and could think of. Back to Robert. Away from Ingram. Somehow. At once. Robert would turn her out – Ingram was saying so, she heard that. Robert might kill her – Ingram was saying so, she heard that too; he didn't say kill, he called it ill-using, but whatever it was who cared? She would at least, she thought with a new grimness, be killed legitimately. She was going back to Robert, going to tell him she was sorry. Anyhow that. Then he could do what he chose. But how to get to him? Oh, how to get to him? Her thoughts whirled. Ingram wouldn't let her go, but she was going. Ingram had her money, but she was going. That very night. Her thoughts, whirling and whizzing, went breathless here in dark, terrifying places. And while she was flying along on them like a leaf on a hurricane blast, Ingram, was still kissing her hand, still pouring out phrases as he had been doing ever since – surely ever since Time began? She stared at him, remembering him in a kind of wonder. She caught a word here and there: pellucid, he was saying something was, translucent. She felt no resentment. She had deserved all she had got. Not Ingram and what he had told her or not told her mattered, but Robert. How to reach Robert, how to get near enough to him to say, 'See – I've come back. Draggled and muddied. Everybody believes it. You'll believe it, though I tell you it's not true. And if you believe it or not it's your ruin. You'll have to leave this place, and all your work and hopes. Now kill me.'

'A man,' she heard Ingram going on, still passionately explain-

ing what was so completely plain, 'must pretend things at the
beginning to get his dear woman—'

'Of course, of course,' nodded her thoughts in hurried agreement, rushing past him to the swift turning over of ways of
reaching Robert, — who cared about dear women ? — how to hide
from Ingram that she was going, how to keep him from suspecting
her, from watching her every instant ...

A vision of herself in the restaurant-car handing him over the
money she had, chaining herself of her own accord to him, rose
for a moment – danced mockingly, it was so ludicrously important
an action and at the same time so small and natural – before her
eyes. The chances of life ! The way small simplicities worked out
great devastations. She threw back her head in a brief, astonished
laugh.

Instantly Ingram kissed her throat.

'I – I—' she gasped, getting up quickly.

'It – has been so hot all day,' she said with a little look of
apologising, remembering to gather her terror and misery tightly
round her like a cloak, so that it should not touch him, so that he
should not by so much as a flutter of it feel that it was there ; for
then he would watch her, and she – she gripped her hands together
– would be lost, lost . . .

'I think I'm – tired – ,' she said.

He became immediately all reasonableness, the kindly reasonableness of one who has cleared away much confusion and can
now afford to wait.

He got up too, agreeing about the heat of the day, and
reminding her also of its length, of the journeys by land and water
it had contained, and of the inadequate meal of rusks that had
been their sole support for nearly six hours. No wonder she was
tired. He was tenderness and concern itself. 'Poor little *dear* thing,'
he whispered, drawing her hand through his arm and holding it
there clasped in his other hand as he led her away towards the
entrance and went with her out into the streets again, making her
walk slowly lest she should be more tired, restraining her when
she tried to hurry ; and seeing a cheerful restaurant with crowded
tables on the pavement in front of it, suggested they should stop
at it and have supper.

But Ingeborg said in a low voice, kept carefully controlled, that
she was afraid she would go to sleep over supper she was so tired ;
might she have some milk at the hôtel and go to bed ?

His tenderness for her as he conceded the milk was nurse-like.

But he, she murmured, he must have supper — would he not send her back in a cab and stay here and have some?

No, he would certainly not trust a thing so precious to some careless cabman; he would take her back to the hôtel, and then perhaps have food.

But the hôtel, she murmured, was so stuffy — did he think he would like food there?

Well, perhaps when she was safely in it he would come out again to one of these pavement places.

She seemed more pliantly feminine as she went with quiet steps through the streets on his arm than he had yet known her. It was as though she had wonderfully been converted from boyhood to womanhood, smitten suddenly with womanhood there in those gardens, and every muscle of her mind and will had relaxed into a sweet fatigue of abandonment. He adored her like that, so gentle, giving no trouble, accepting the situation and his comfortings and his pattings of the hand on his arm and all his further explanations and asseverations with a grown-up dear reasonableness he had not yet seen in her. In return he took infinite care of her, protective and possessive, whenever they came to a crowd or a puddle. And he stroked her hand, and looked into her face, demanding and receiving an answering obedient smile. And he wanted her and asked her to lean heavily on his arm so that she should not be so tired. In a word, he was fond.

They were staying at an hôtel near the station, just off the station square down a side street, a place frequented only by middle-class Italians and commercial travellers, noisy with passing tramcars and of little promise in the matter of food. Ingram had taken rooms there that afternoon when the determination was strong upon him that Ingeborg, in Milan, should not be comfortable. Now he was sorry; for the happy turn things had taken, the immense stride he had made in the direction of Venice by opening her eyes to the facts of the situation, made this excess of martyrdom unnecessary. But there they were, the rooms, engaged and unpacked in, on the first floor almost on a level with the ceaseless passing tops of the bumping tramcars, and it was too late that night to change.

He felt, however, very apologetic now as he went with her up the dingy stairs to the door of her room in case some too cheery

commercial traveller should meet her on the way and dare to look
at her.

'It's an unworthy place for my little shining mate,' he said, 'but
Venice will make up for it all. You'll love my rooms there – the
spaciousness of them, and the sunset on the lagoons from the
windows. To-morrow we'll go—'

He searched her face as she stood in the crude top light of the
corridor. Naturally she was tired after such a day, but he observed
a further dimness about her, a kind of opaqueness, like that of a
lamp whose light has been put out, and it afflicted him. The light
would be lit again, he knew, and burn more brightly than ever,
but it afflicted him that even for a moment it should go out; and
swiftly glancing up and down the passage he took both her hands
in his and kissed them.

'Little dear one,' he said, 'little sister – you do forgive me?'

'Oh, but of course, of course,' said Ingeborg quickly, with all
her heart; and she felt for a moment the acute desolation of life,
the inevitable hurtings, the eternal impossibility, whatever steps
one took, of not treading to death something that, too, was living
and beautiful, – this thing or that thing, one or the other.

Her eyes as she looked at him were suddenly veiled with tears.
Her thoughts stopped swirling round ways of escape. And very
vivid was the perception that her escape, if she did succeed in it,
was going to be from something she would never find again, from
a light and a warmth, however fitful, and a greatness . . . If he had
been her brother she would have put her arms round him and
kissed him. If she had been his mother she would have solemnly
blessed him. As it was there was nothing to be done but the
bleak banality of turning away into her room and shutting the
door.

She heard his footstpes going down the passage. She went to the
window, and saw him going down the street. There was not an
instant to lose – she must find out a train now, while he was away,
have that at least ready in her mind for the moment when she
somehow had got the money. First that; then think out how to
get the money.

She stole into the passage again, – stole, for she felt a breathless
fear that in spite of his being so manifestly gone he yet would hear
her somehow if she made a noise and come back – stole along it
and down the stairs into the entrance hall where hung enormously
a giant time-table, conspicuous and convenient in an hôtel that

supplied no *concierge* to answer questions, and whose *clientèle* was particularly restless.

Nobody was in the hall. It was not an hour of arrival or departure; and the man in the green apron she had seen there before, who at odd moments became that which in better hôtels is uninterruptedly a *concierge*, was nowhere to be seen either. She had to get on a chair, the trains to Berlin were so high up on the great sheet, and tremblingly she kept an eye on the street door, through whose glass panels she could see people passing up and down the street, and they in their turn could and did see her. Yes, – there was a night train at 1.30. It came from Rome. Travellers might arrive by it. The hôtel door would be open. Her thoughts flew. It got to Berlin at six something of the morning after the next morning . . .

Suddenly the glass door opened, and she jumped so violently that she nearly fell off her chair, and she fled upstairs, panic-stricken, without even looking to see if it were Ingram.

Safe in her room she was horrified at herself for such a panic. How was she going to do everything there was to be done if she were like that? She stood in the middle of the floor twisting her hands. If in her life she had needed complete self-control and clear thinking and calm acting she knew it was now. But how to keep calm and clear when her body was shaking with fear? She felt, standing there struggling with herself, so entirely forlorn, so entirely cut off from warmth and love, so horribly with nothing she could look back to and believe in and nothing she could look forward to and hope in, that just to speak to somebody, just to speak to a stranger who because he was a stranger would have no prejudices against her, would simply recognise a familiar distress – for surely the other human beings in the hôtel must all at some time have been unhappy? – seemed a thing of comfort beyond expressing. Her longing was intolerable to get close for a moment to another human soul, to ask of it how it had fared when it too went down into the sea without ships, leaving its ships all burned behind it, and yet its business had inexorably been in deep waters. 'Oh, haven't you been unhappy too?' she wanted to ask of it; 'haven't you sometimes been very unhappy? Dear fellow-soul – please – tell me – haven't you sometimes felt *bitter* cold?'

But there was no one; there was no brotherhood in the world,, except at the rare obvious moments of common catastrophes and deaths.

She began to walk up and down the room. Half-past one that night was the hour of her escape, and somehow between now and then she must get the money. Perhaps by some chance he had left it in his room? Forgotten in a moment of carelessness in the pocket of the coat he had changed when they arrived that afternoon? It was not likely, for he was, she had noticed, of an extreme neatness and care about all such things. He never forgot. He never mislaid. Still, – there was the chance.

She opened the door again, this time in deadly fear, for perhaps he would be coming back, not choosing after all to stay out there having supper.

There was no one in the passage. His room, she knew, was further down; she had seen him going into it, four doors down on the same side as hers. She went out and stood a moment listening, then began to walk along towards it with an air of unconcern as though rightfully going down the corridor till she came to his door; then with her heart in her mouth she bolted in.

The lights from the street and the houses opposite shone in through the unshuttered window, and she could see into every corner of the shabby hôtel bedroom, a reproduction of the one she was in herself, trailed over dingily by traces of hundreds of commercial travellers and smelling memorially, as hers did too, of their smoke and their pomades. She was hot and cold with fear; guilty as a thief. His coat hung behind the door. She ran her trembling fingers over it. Not a thing in any of his pockets. Nowhere anything that she could see. His unpacking had been done with orderliness itself. Of couse he would not forget his pocket-book. With a gasp that was almost relief she slipped out of the room, shut the door quickly behind her, and assuming what she tried to hope was an unconcerned swagger, a sort of 'I'm-as-good-as-you-are' air for the impressing of any one she might meet, walked down the passage again.

Just as she reached her door Ingram appeared, hurrying up the stairs two steps at a time.

She clutched hold of the handle of her door, suddenly unable to stand.

'I – I—' she began.

But he did not seem surprised to see her there; he was intent on something else.

'Just think,' he said, coming quickly towards her. 'I left my pocket-book in my room, full of notes. The whole afternoon lying in the drawer of the table. I wonder—'

He hurried past her almost at a run.

She got into her room somehow, feeling Heaven had forsaken her.

After a minute or two she heard him coming along again. He stopped at her door and called to her softly –

'It's all right. It was still there. Wasn't it lucky?'

'Very,' said Ingeborg; but so faintly that he did not hear.

'Good night, my little one,' she heard him say. 'Now I'm going out to get that supper.'

'Good night,' said Ingeborg, again so faintly that he heard nothing; and after a pause of listening he went away.

She tumbled down on to the bed. She felt sick. It was a quarter-past-ten. She had three hours to wait. She knew what she was going to do, try to do. At one o'clock she would take off her shoes and go down the passage and see if his door was locked. He would be asleep. He must, oh he must be asleep, – she twisted about in the terror that smote her at the thought that he might perhaps not be asleep . . .

'God *does* love me?' she said to herself. 'I *am* His child? Haven't I sinned and repented? Haven't I done all the things? He's bound to help me, to save me. It *is* the wicked He saves – I *am* wicked—'

Her heart stood still at the fearful thought that perhaps she had not yet been after all wicked enough, not wicked enough to be saved.

People belonging to the other rooms began to come back to bed. Somebody in the next room sang while he was undressing, a gay Italian song, and presently he smoked, and the smoke came in under the door between her room and his.

She lay in the dark, or rather in the lights and shadows of the uncurtained room, and every two or three minutes a tramcar passed and shut out other sounds. Ingram must have come in long ago. When it was midnight she got up and arranged her shoes and hat just inside the door so that she could seize them as she came back, supposing she had been successful, and rush on straight downstairs and out and to the station. All other thoughts were now lost in the intentness with which she was concentrated on what she had to do exactly next. She would not let herself look aside at the abyss yawning if she were not successful. She gripped hold of the thing she had to do, the getting of the money, and fixed her whole self on that alone.

She lay down on the bed again, her hands clenched as though in them she held her determination. Once her thoughts did slip off to Robert, to the extreme desolation of what was waiting for her there, and tears came through her tightly shut eyelids.

'It's what you've deserved,' she whispered, struggling to stop them. 'Yes, but *he* hasn't deserved it — Robert hasn't deserved it — you've ruined *him*—' she was forced to go on.

She shook off the unnerving thoughts. By her watch it was a quarter to one.

She stood up and began to listen.

The tramcars passed now only every ten minutes. In between their passing the hôtel was quiet. She would wait for the approach of the next one — in the stillness she could hear it coming a long way off — then she would run down the passage in her stockinged feet to Ingram's door and open it just as the noise was loudest.

An icy hand seemed holding her heart, so icy that it burned. She had not known she had so many pulses in her body. They shook her and shook her; great heavy, hammering things. She crept to her door and opened it a chink. There was a dim light in the passage. She heard the distant rumbling of a tramcar. Now — she must run.

But she could not. She stood and shook. There it was, coming nearer, and not another for ten minutes. She began to sob and say prayers. The tramcar struck its bell sharply, it had reached the corner of the piazza, it would be passing in another minute. She wrenched the door open and ran like a flying shadow down the passage and just as the car was at its loudest turned the handle of Ingram's door.

It was not locked. She stood inside. The tramcar rumbled away into the distance. Ingram — she nearly wept for relief — was breathing deeply, was asleep.

'But how funny,' she thought, after one terrified glance at him as he lay in the bar of light the street lamp cast on the bed, thinking with a top layer of attention while underneath she was enirely concentrated on the pocket-book, 'how funny to go to bed in one's beard ! . . .'

She stole over to the table and peered about frantically among the things scattered on it, saw nothing, began with breathless care to try to open its drawer noiselessly, listening all the while for the least pause in the breathing on the bed, and all the while with the foolish detached layer of thoughts running in her head like some senseless tune –

'*Funny* to go to bed in a beard – *funny* to sleep in a thing like that – *funny* not to take it off at night and hang it up outside the door with one's clothes and have it properly brushed—'

The drawer creaked as it opened. The regular breathing paused. She stood motionless, hit rigid with terror. Then the breathing began again; and, after all, there was nothing in the drawer.

She looked round the room in despair. On the little table by his pillow lay his watch and handkerchief. Nothing else. But in the table was a small drawer. She must look in that too; she must go over and look in that; but how to open it so close to his head without waking him? She crept across to it, stopping at each step. Holding her breath she waited and listened before daring to take another. The drawer was not quite shut, and the slight noise of pulling its chink a little wider did not interrupt Ingram's breathing. She put in her hand and drew out the pocket-book, drew out some notes – Italian notes, the first she found, a handful of them – pushed the pocket-book into the drawer again, and was in the act of turning to run when she was rooted to the floor.

Ingram was looking at her.

His eyes were open, and he was looking at her. Sleepily, hardly awake, like one trying to focus a thought. She stood fascinated with horror, staring at him, not able to move, her hand behind her back clutching the money. Then he put out his arm and caught her dress.

'Ingeborg?' he said in a sleepy wonder, still half in the deep dreams he had come up out of, 'You? My little angel love – you? You've come?'

'Yes – yes,' she stammered, trying to pull her dress away, wild with fear, flinging herself as usual in extremity on to the first words that came into her head – 'Yes, yes, but I must go back to my room a minute – just one minute – please let me go – just one minute – I – I've forgotten my toothbrush—'

And Ingram, steeped in the heaviness of the first real sleep he had had for nights and only half awake, murmured, with the happy, foolish reasonableness of that condition –

'Don't be long, then, sweetest little mate,' and let her go.

CHAPTER 37

Two days later the porter at the Meuk station beheld Frau Paster Dremmel trying to open the door of a third-class compartment in the early afternoon train from Allenstein, and going to her assistance, there being no other passenger to distract him, was surprised to find she had no luggage. Yet only the week before with his own hands he had put in a trunk for her and labelled it Berlin. With the interest of a lonely man whose time is his own, he inquired whether she had lost it, and was surprised to find she did not answer. He then told her, or rather called her, for she was moving away, that the pastoral carriage had not yet come for her, and was surprised again, for again she did not answer. He stood watching her, wondering what was wrong. He was too much accustomed to dilapidations and dirt in himself to see them in others, so that these outer signs of exhaustion and prolonged travelling escaped him. Puzzled, he shook his head as she disappeared through the station door; then he remembered that the poor lady was an *Engländerin*, and was able to turn away calmed, with the satisfaction of him who has found the right label and stuck it on.

Meuk, as she passed through it, shook its head over her too, consoling itself when she returned no greetings, did not even seem to see greetings, with the same explanation and shrug, – *Engländerin*. Robertlet and Ditti, walking along neatly to afternoon school, and suddenly aware of the approach down the street towards them of a disordered parent who not only did not stop but apparently did not see them, murmured to each other, being by now well instructed by their grandmother, the same explanation – *Engländerin*. Frau Dremmel, leaning on her window-sill to watch her charges safely round the corner, and lingering a moment in the mellow summer air, explained her daughter-in-law, who went by without a glance, walking conspicuously in the middle of the road, with no parcel in her hand to legitimise her being out and not so much as an umbrella to give her a countenance, just with empty ungloved hands hanging down, and a scandalous scarcity of hairpins and her clothes all twisted, in the same brief manner, *Engländerin.* Baroness Glambeck, driving towards the town along the shade-flecked high-road, bent on one of those errands of mercy that are forced at intervals upon the great, with a basket of the properties, principally home-made jam and mittens, at her feet, endeavoured though vainly to mitigate the shock she received on being cut by her own pastor's wife, and a pastor's wife producing curiously the effect of somehow being in tatters, by using the same word to the female dependent who accompanied her on these occasions because somebody had to carry the jam – *Engländerin.* The very birds in the branches, being German birds, were no doubt singing it; the dogs, as they met her, scented misfortune and barked furiously, instantly detecting the alien, angered by her batteredness, discovering nothing in her clothes however diligently they sniffed that an honest German dog could care about; and when on a lonely stretch of the road she came to a tramp, instead of begging he offered her a drink.

The lane turning off to Kökensee was so lovely that afternoon in the bright bravery of early summer, and so glanced and shone and darted with busy birds and insects and the glory of young leaves in the sun, that the dingy human figure faltering along it seemed an indecency. In that vigorous world what place was there for blind fatigue? In that world of triumph what place for a failure? It was the sort of day that used to make Ingeborg's heart lift up; now she saw nothing, felt nothing, except that the sand was deep.

She began to cry presently because the sand was deep. It seemed to give way on purpose beneath her feet, try on purpose to make her stumble and not get home. The line of roofs up against the afternoon sky did not appear to come any nearer, and yet she kept on trying to get home. The tears fell down her face as she laboured along. She was afraid she wouldn't get home in time before she had to leave off walking because she couldn't walk any further. It seemed to her a dreadful thing that she who could walk so well should not be able to walk now and get home. And this white sand – how fine it was, how it slid away on each side of one's feet wherever one put them! And it got into one's shoes, and one couldn't stop and empty them for fear if one sat down one wouldn't be able to get up again, and then one wouldn't get home. Slower and more slowly she laboured along. By the time she reached the steep part just before the village she was crawling like a hurt insect. She had forgotten to eat on the journey, and in Milan there had only been the rusks.

The street was asleep, empty that fine afternoon, the inhabitants away at work in the fields, and only the pig and the geese were visible in the parsonage yard. Luckily the gate in the wire-netting fence that shut off the house and garden was not latched, for she could not have opened it, but would have stood there holding on to it and foolishly sobbing till some one came and helped. The least obstacle now would be a thing that in no way could be got over. The front door was shut, and sooner than go up the steps and try to get it open, she went round the path to the side of the house where the lilacs grew and Robert's window was. That way she could reach the kitchen, whose door stood always open and was level with the garden. Robert would be out in his fields. She would go into his laboratory and wait for him. Nobody but Robert *knew* yet. She had come back before the end of her leave. His shame was not yet public property. If he just beat her, she thought, in a disinterested weak way, and there was an end of it, wouldn't that do? Then no one need ever know, and he could stay on in Kökensee and go on with his work, and she wouldn't have ruined him. It was the thought of having ruined Robert that clove her heart in two. To have ruined him, when all her ambition and all her hope had been to make him so happy . . .

Well did she know that a pastor whose wife had broken the seventh commandment would be driven out, would be impossibly scandalous in any parish. And her not having broken it was quite beside the point; it didn't matter what you didn't do so long as you looked as though you had done it. And if Robert killed her it wouldn't help him either; he would have done the only decent thing, as the Baroness and her son Hildebrand had said that time long ago, and avenged his honour in the proper German way, but there were drawbacks to avenging one's honour, – one was, illogically, punished for doing it, and even though it were mild punishment, any punishment ended a pastor's career.

She crept round the corner of the house. She was so tired that if she had to wait for him long in his laboratory she felt sure she wouldn't be able to keep awake. Well, if he came in and killed her while she was asleep it would be for her the pleasantest thing; she was so very tired that it would be nice, she thought vaguely, to wake up afterwards and find oneself comfortably dead. But Robert was not in his fields. From the path beneath his window she could see his head, as she had seen it hundreds of times, bending over his desk.

At the sight she stopped, and her heart seemed to shrink into quite a little, scarcely beating thing. There he was, her dishonoured husband, the being who in her life had been kindest to her, had loved her most, still working, still going on doggedly among the ruins she had created, up to the last moment when public opinion, brutal and stupid, making her the chief thing when she so utterly was not, while it thrust her and her wishes and intimate knowledge aside as not mattering when, as in the question of more children, or no more children, they so utterly did, would on her sole account, on the sole account of what seemed to her at that moment the most profoundly naturally unimportant thing in life, a woman who had been silly, put a stop to his fine work and refuse to give the world a chance to profit by his brains.

Well, she couldn't think about that now. She couldn't hold on to any of her thoughts for more than an instant. She only knew that the moment had come for facing him, and that she was very tired. She really was extraordinarily tired. Her mind was just as dim and reluctant to move as her body. Whatever Robert was going to do to her she would cling to him with her arms round his neck while he did it. She was so tired that she thought if he didn't mind her just putting her arms round his neck she would very likely go to sleep while he beat her. But poor Robert, she thought, – how hot it was going to make him to have to be violent, to have to beat! It was not at all good beating weather ... And it was almost a pity to waste punishment on somebody too tired to be able properly to appreciate it, to take it, as it were, properly in.

She moved along down the path towards the back door. When one came to think of it it was a strange thing to be going into Robert to be hurt. Well, but she had deserved it; she perfectly understood about his honour and its needs. Oh yes, she perfectly understood that. A man has to – what had she just been going to think? What does a man have to? Oh well. If only what he did to her could blot out every consequence of what she had done to him, be a full, perfect, and sufficient – no, that was profane; tiresome how one thought in the phrases of the Prayer-book and

how difficult it was if one had had much to do with prayer-books
not to be profane. As it was, her punishment wouldn't do anybody
any good that she could see. Funny, the punishment idea. Of what
use was it really? The consequences of the things one did were
surely enough in their devastating effect; why increase devasta-
tion? And forgiveness didn't seem to be of much use either. It
blotted out the past, she had heard people in pulpits say, but it
didn't blot out the future, that daily living among consequences
which she perceived was going to be so dreadful.

Well, she couldn't think now. And here was the kitchen door;
and here – yes, wasn't that Klara, staring at her open-mouthed,
arrested in the middle of emptying a bucket? Why did she stare at
her? Did she then *know*?

'*Allmächtiger Gott,*' exclaimed Klara, dropping the bucket.

Yes, evidently Klara knew, she thought, dragging her dusty feet
across the kitchen into the passage, and *allmächtiger Gott* was
what one said in Germany when one's disgraced mistress came
back, instead of *guten Tag*. Well, it didn't matter. The dark little
passage; one almost had to grope one's way along it when the
front door was shut. And it had not been aired apparently since
she went away, and it was heavy and choked with kitchen smell.
She supposed it must be this thickness of atmosphere that made
her, on Robert's doormat with her hand on the latch, feel suddenly
so very like fainting. And it really was dark; surely it didn't only
seem dark because she suddenly couldn't see? Alarmed, she
remembered how she had fainted after her conscience-stricken
journey back from Lucerne. Was she then to go through life
making at intervals conscience-stricken journeys back, and fainting at the critical moment at their end?

In terror lest she should do it now if she waited a moment
longer, and so twist things round in that dishonourable womanly
way which commits the wrong and then bringing in the appeal of
bodily weakness secures the comforting, secures, almost, the
apology, she seized all her courage, swept its fragments together
into a firm clutching, and opened the door.

Herr Dremmel was at his table, writing. He did not look up.

'Robert,' she said faintly, her back against the door, her hands
behind her spread out and clinging to it, 'here I am.'

Herr Dremmel continued writing. He was, to all appearances,
absorbed; and his forehead, that hot afternoon, was covered with
the drops of concentration.

'Robert,' she said at last again, in a voice that shook however hard she tried to keep it steady, 'here I am.'

Herr Dremmel finished his sentence. Then he raised his head and looked at her.

Staring back at him in misery and fear, and yet beside the fear with a dreadful courage, she recognised the look. It was the look he had when he was collecting his attention, bringing it up from distant deep places to the surface, to herself. How strange that he should at this moment have to collect it, that it did not instantly spring at her, that she and the havoc she had brought into his life should not be soaked into every part of his consciousness !

'What did you say, Ingeborg ?' he said, looking at her with that so recognisable look.

For all her study of him she felt she did not yet know Robert.

'I only said,' she stammered, that I — that here — that here I *was*.'

He looked at her for a further space of silence. Then it flashed upon her that he was, dreadfully, pretending. He was acting. He was going to torment her before punishing her. He was going to be slowly cruel.

Herr Dremmel, as though he were gathering himself together — gathering himself, she thought watching him and growing cold at his uncanniness, for a horrible spring — inquired of her if she had walked.

'Yes,' said Ingeborg, even more faintly, her eyes full of watchful fear.

He continued to look at her, but his hand while he did so felt about on the table for the pen he had laid down.

She recognised this look too, — amazing, horrible, how he could act — it was the one he had when, talking to somebody, a new illumination of the subject he was writing about came into his mind.

She felt sure now that the worst was going to happen to her ; but first there was to be torture, a long playing about. These revealed depths of cunning cruelty in him, of talent for cleverest acting, froze her blood. Where was Robert, the man of large simplicities she believed she had known ? It was a strange man, then, she had been living with ? He had never, through all the years, been the one she thought she had married.

'Please—' she said, holding out both hands, 'Robert — don't. Won't you — won't you be natural ?'

He still looked at her in silence. Then he said with a sudden air of remembering, 'Did you get your boots, Ingeborg?'

This was dreadful. That he should even talk about the boots! Throw in her face that paltry preliminary lying.

'You *know* I didn't,' she said, tears of shame for him that he could be so cruel coming into her eyes.

Again Herr Dremmel looked at her as though collecting, as though endeavouring to remember and to find.

'I know?' he repeated, after a pause of reflective gazing during which Ingeborg had flushed vividly and gone white again, so much shocked was she at the glimpse she was getting into inhumanity. It was devilish, she thought. But Robert devilish? Her universe seemed tumbling about her ears.

'I think,' she said, lifting her head with the pride he ought to have felt and so evidently, so lamentably, didn't, 'one should give one's punishment like a man.'

There was another pause, during which Herr Dremmel, with his eyes on hers, appeared to ruminate.

Then he said, 'Did you have a pleasant time?'

This was fiendish. Even when acting, thought Ingeborg, there were depths of baseness the decent refused to portray.

'I think,' she said in a trembling voice, 'if you wouldn't mind leaving off pretending – oh,' she broke off, pressing her hands together, 'what's the good, Robert? What's the *good*? Don't let us waste time. Don't make it worse, more hideous – you got my letter – you know all about it—'

'Your letter?' said Herr Dremmel.

She begged him, she entreated him to leave off pretending. 'Don't, don't keep on like this,' she besought – 'it's such a dreadful way of doing it – it's so unworthy—'

'Ingeborg,' said Herr Dremmel, 'will you not cultive calm? You have journeyed and you have walked, but you have done neither sufficiently to justify intemperateness. Perhaps, if you must be intemperate, you will have the goodness to go and be so in your own room. Then we shall neither of us disturb the other.'

'No,' said Ingeborg, wringing her hands, 'no. I won't go. I won't go into any other room till you've finished with me.'

'But,' said Herr Dremmel, 'I have finished with you. And I wish,' he added, pulling out his watch, 'to have tea. I am driving to my fields at five o'clock.'

'Oh, Robert,' she begged, inexpressibly shocked, he meant to go on tormenting her then indefinitely ? — 'please, please do whatever you're going to do to me and get it over. Here I am ony *waiting* to be punished—'

'Punished ?' repeated Herr Dremmel.

'Why,' cried Ingeborg, her eyes bright with grief and shame for this steady persistence in baseness, 'why I don't think you're *fit* to punish me ! You're not *fit* to punish a decent woman. You're contemptible.'

Herr Dremmel stared. 'This,' he then said, 'is abuse. At least,' he added, 'it bears a close resemblance to that which in a reasonable human being would be abuse. However, Ingeborg, speech in you does not, as I have often observed, accurately represent meaning. I should rather say,' he amended, 'a meaning.'

She moved across to the table to him, her eyes shining. He held his pen ready to go on writing so soon as she should be good enough to leave off interrupting.

'Robert,' she said, leaning with both hands on the table, her voice shaking, 'I — I never thought I'd have to be *ashamed* of you. I could bear anything but having to be *ashamed* of you—'

'Perhaps, then, Ingeborg,' said Herr Dremmel, 'you will have the goodness to go and be ashamed of me in your own room. Then we shall neither of us disturb the other.'

'You are being so horrible that you're twisting things all wrong, and putting me in the position of having to forgive *you* when it's *you* who've got to forgive *me*—'

'Pray, then, Ingeborg, go and forgive me in your own room. Then we shall neither of us—'

'You're being cruel — oh, but it's unbelievable — you, my husband — you're playing with me like a cat with a miserable mouse, a miserable, sorry mouse, something helpless that can't do anything back and wouldn't if it could — and see how you make me talk, when it's you who ought to be talking ! Do, do, Robert, begin to talk — begin to say things, do things, get it over. You've had my letter, you know perfectly what I did—'

'I have had no letter, Ingeborg.'

'How dreadful of you to say that !' she cried, her face full of horror at him. 'When you know you have and you know I know you have — that letter I left for you — on this table—'

'I have seen no letter on this table.'

'But I *put* it here — I put it *here*—'

She lifted her hand to point out passionately the very spot to him; and underneath her hand was the letter.

Her heart gave one great bump and seemed to stop beating. The letter was where she had put it and was unopened.

She looked up at Herr Dremmel. She turned red; she turned white; she tasted the very extremity of shame. 'I – beg your pardon,' she whispered.

Herr Dremmel wore a slight air of apology. 'One omits, occasionally, to notice,' he said.

'Yes,' breathed Ingeborg.

She stood quite still, her eyes on his face.

He pulled out his watch. 'Perhaps now, Ingeborg,' he said, 'you will be so good as to see about tea. I am driving to my fields—'

'Yes,' breathed Ingeborg.

He bent over his work and began writing again.

She put out her hand and slowly took up the letter. Tradition, copious imbibing of the precepts of bishops, were impelling her towards that action frequently fatal to the permanent peace of families, the making of a clean breast.

'Do you – do you – do you want to—' she began tremblingly, half holding out the letter.

Then her voice failed; and her principles failed; and the precepts of a lifetime failed; and she put it in her pocket.

'It's – stale,' she whispered, explaining.

But Herr Dremmel went on writing. He had forgotten the letter.

She turned away and went slowly towards the door.

In the middle of the room she hesitated, and looked back. 'I – I'd *like* to kiss you,' she faltered.

But Herr Dremmel went on writing. He had forgotten Ingeborg.